4/14

| LOCKSTEP |

| LOCKSTEP |

Karl Schroeder

A TOM DOHERTY ASSOCIATES BOOK

NEW YORK

LOCKSTEP

Copyright © 2014 by Karl Schroeder

A Tor Book
Published by Tom Doherty Associates, LLC
175 Fifth Avenue
New York, NY 10010

www.tor-forge.com

Tor® is a registered trademark of Tom Doherty Associates, LLC.

Library of Congress Cataloging-in-Publication Data

Schroeder, Karl, 1962–
   Lockstep / Karl Schroeder. — 1st ed.
     p. cm.
  "A Tom Doherty Associates Book."
  ISBN 978-0-7653-3726-9 (hardcover)
  ISBN 978-1-4668-3336-4 (e-book)
 1. Imaginary places—Fiction.   I. Title.

  PR9199.3.S269L63 2014
  813'.54—dc23
                 2013025526

Tor books may be purchased for educational, business, or promotional use. For information on bulk purchases, please contact Macmillan Corporate and Premium Sales Department at 1-800-221-7945, extension 5442, or write specialmarkets@macmillan.com.

First Edition: March 2014

Printed in the United States of America

0 9 8 7 6 5 4 3 2 1

| LOCKSTEP |

Prologue: Barsoom

TWO BRIGHT MOONS CHASED each other across a butterscotch sky. Down on the plain, something big was galloping, its feet touching down only once a second. It was too far away to make out what it was, but the broad-shouldered man on the balcony could see each puff of dust it left and the long line of them leading away.

Whatever it was, it was drawing that line at an angle to a much bigger mark—an ancient canal, dry now for thousands of years, that swept in from one horizon, passed this lonely peak with its crumbled towers and collapsed stairs, and exited the scene over the opposite horizon. Dunes were trying to erase the canal, but they'd never succeed.

The gray-haired man smoothed his hand along the stone banister. It had amused him to leave its ancient worn stone intact when he renovated this palace. He'd done the same with the rest of the mountain peak—balcony, tower, and dome had all been preserved where they could be. The result was a jarring mix of sharp new edges and worn, almost natural curves, but he liked that.

His moment of contentment was interrupted by approaching footsteps. It was easy to tell by their nervous, clipped gait that it was his most trusted adviser, Memorum. Normally Memorum simply said what was on his mind, but this time he stopped and didn't even clear his throat.

"What?" He turned to shoot a bemused look at the man. "Did somebody die?"

Memorum didn't answer, and for a moment the gray-haired man wondered if somebody had. He stepped away from the rail. "Is she—"

"*They found him.*"

"Ah." He turned back to the view, reaching deliberately for the stone to steady himself. "Ah. Really." It took him awhile to work up the courage for the next question.

"Alive?"

"Yes, sir, as best we can tell."

He shook his head in wonder. "We built 'em good in the old days."

"It's been forty years."

"I think we can agree it's been longer than that." He ran his hands along the balustrade again.

There was a long silence, then Memorum said, "What do we do now?"

"What do we *do*? You know what to do, Memorum. He can't be allowed back."

"But—sir!"

"You heard me. Send him on if he's still wintering over, or kill him if he's not. Either way . . . he can't be allowed back."

"Sir, it's not my place, but he's still—"

"It's been forty years, Memorum. He's nothing to me."

"And what is he to *her*?"

He glared at his servant. "That's none of your business!"

"But she's waited so long—"

"She can continue to wait."

He walked away, across flagstones so old they were worn from the generations of feet that had crisscrossed them.

"She made her choice to wait for him rather than stay with us. Let her wait till the end of time, for all I care."

Memorum left, and after the servant's footsteps had faded, the gray-haired man staggered to sit on an ancient stone seat that looked out over the plain. With no one to see him do it, he hugged himself and bent forward, gasping.

He knew he would always remember this: the quality of the brass-lit sky, the puffs of dust from that running beast on the plain, how the red stone of the balcony rail had felt under his fingers just before he heard the news.

And he knew he would always remember, and always wish he could forget, how he felt about himself right now.

| One |

TOBY WYATT McGONIGAL AWOKE to biting cold and utter silence. When he opened his eyes he saw nothing, only a perfect black.

"Hello?" His voice was a rough croak, its sound so surprising to him that he coughed. He tried to put his hand to his mouth, but it moved only a few centimeters before striking some flat surface.

A lid, covering him where he lay.

A momentary panic took him, but as he banged his knees, hands, and forehead against the cold curved substance, he realized something else.

He was weightless.

With that realization, all his muscles relaxed; he let all the air out of his lungs in a whoosh, then laughed. Of course he was weightless. He wasn't on Earth, buried alive in some coffin. He was in space. He was on his way to do something, for the family, for his brother, and if he was awake now that meant he'd reached his destination. Hibernation time was over.

That single moment of panic had worn him out, but hibernation was like that; he remembered the weakness from last time. It should pass in a few hours.

Gradually his fluttering pulse slowed, and when he felt more in control he groped until he found his glasses, which he'd stowed at his side when he'd gotten into his little ship's cicada bed, weeks—or was it months, now?—ago.

He slid on the augmented reality glasses, wincing at the icy cold against his temples.

"Ship, give me a status report," he said. Nothing happened. "A little light, at least?"

Maybe the glasses' batteries had drained. Considering how long he'd been out, that was likely. It was stupid that he hadn't thought of that, though; he relied on them as his interface to everything— ship, communications, and the all-important gameworld, Consensus, where he spent most of his time.

Who knew what Peter had gotten up to in Consensus while he was asleep? His brother would have had time to invent whole new civilizations, colonize new systems—who knew what? Knowing what had happened in the game while he was asleep was nearly as important to Toby as making sure he'd arrived at Rockette on time.

Everything was still black; the ship hadn't replied. "Glasses, load Consensus," Toby said. Maybe there was a communications problem; since Consensus was local to the glasses, it at least should boot up if they were online at all.

Weak flickers of light appeared at infinity, then resolved into words: POWER CRITICALLY LOW. Toby had never seen that message before, but it was obvious what it meant.

"Consensus . . . load me some personalities. Sol? Miranda? Can you hear me?"

There was no answer from any of them, and suddenly panic had him shaking the cicada bed's exit handles. An alarm buzzed and finally there was light outside of the glasses; more glowing letters had appeared in the translucent material: VACUUM DETECTED. "Crap!" Something was wrong, the ship's systems had failed, he was stuck here with no way out—

"*Toby.*" It was Miranda's voice, coming through his glasses' earpiece. "There's an emergency suit under your mattress. Put it on and the bed will open."

He felt around until he had the suit's glove in his hand. He gave it a squeeze and the thing climbed over his body, its pieces snapping into place with reassuring precision.

When the helmet had built itself over his face, it signaled the bed, and with a sucking sound the canopy opened. Toby drifted off its surface and into a place he should know but which, as he looked around, had become frighteningly strange.

His headlamp showed him to be in a round room about thirteen meters in diameter. The place was full of jumbled shapes. Most were turning slowly in midair in zero gravity; all were covered with white, fuzzy hoarfrost.

The suit seemed to have power, so he ordered it to recharge his glasses. Then he said, "Miranda? Can you embody?"

"Yes," she said, then a moment later, Sol added, "On my way, boss."

Two headlamps snapped on off to his left, and moments later two space-suited figures were bumping their way through the debris, the cones of light flicking off now this, now that odd shape. The jumbled stuff was mostly butlers and grippies—bigger and smaller robots that could conspire with your glasses to pretend to be other people or walls or trees or furniture in a virtual world like Consensus. The little grippies could change their shape and texture and pretend to be anything you might pick up. Combined with the glasses' visual and auditory illusions, they'd made this cramped little ship tolerable for Toby on the flight out. At least until he'd gone into hibernation.

"Ship?" he asked again; there was still no response. "What happened?" he asked the other two.

"We've lost main power," said Sol Norton, his voice coming clearly through Toby's glasses. "But I don't know why, and I don't know how long ago."

"What does that mean? Did we miss Rockette?"

There was a long pause. "I'm not jumping to any conclusions," said Sol curtly.

Rockette was the dormant comet their little ship had been headed to. It had just been discovered, and Dad suspected it might be in a very long orbit around the dwarf planet Sedna, which would make it a moon. In order to keep their family's claim on Sedna, all the little world's moons had to be claimed by a McGonigal. Because Dad was on his way to Earth to formalize the claim, Toby had been sent to rendezvous with Rockette. His job was to claim it and then turn around and return to Sedna.

It was a pretty big responsibility; he was only seventeen. He was getting used to doing stuff like this, though. Helping run his parents' colony on Sedna was all-consuming, just as taking care of his traumatized brother, Peter, had been in the year leading up to their leaving Earth.

"We're going down to the bot room," continued Sol. "See what else we can get under manual control."

"Thanks." Toby wasn't surprised that all the other ship's systems might have failed but that his cicada bed had worked just fine. The hibernation beds—technology his parents had bought and perfected—were amazingly reliable. They were what had made it possible for the family to homestead here, with a couple dozen close friends and volunteers, far beyond the orbit of Pluto.

"Well, we can use some of this stuff," said Miranda as she and Sol cast their helmet lamps into the bot room. She sounded optimistic and calm, as always. That was why he'd thought of her when he'd called on his Consensus allies; Miranda, like Sol, was always able to encourage Toby when things became difficult.

Toby bounced over to perch next to them at the hatch. "Why were we woken up? And what's all this weird frost all over everything?"

"It's air, Toby," Miranda said. "Frozen air. Sol, do you see that?"

"Yeah." Sol flipped through the hatch and kicked off through a constellation of motionless robots. These were mostly maintenance and repair bots that were supposed to be able to fix anything that went wrong with the ship. All were dark and lifeless.

He leaned close to the wall to look at the frost. The little forest of white spikes was perfectly clear for a second, then it began to shimmer. The little light on his helmet was enough to evaporate it.

Toby had seen that before, back on Sedna. It meant the temperature in here was not far above absolute zero.

"Hey, wait up!" He clumsily batted aside the dead bots, following the guide of the others' lights. He found them at the back of the bot room, which was the aft-most living chamber in the ship. There was an airlock here, and lots of stowage and tools. And . . .

A hole in the back wall.

It was about a meter across, with odd blocky edges, and outside it he could see stars and the black silhouette of the ship's engine spine.

"The bots tried to patch it," said Miranda, pointing to the squared edges of the hole, "but it was too big. Anyway, all the air would have gone out in the first few seconds."

Sol was cursing under his breath. "But what made it?" He jumped back the way they'd come and after a minute shouted, "Found another!"

It turned out there was a coin-sized hole, clogged with frozen air, through the wall between the main chamber and the bot room. And when they went to the front of that room they found a tiny, pinhead-sized hole there, too.

"I'm sorry, I don't understand," said Toby. Miranda was moving kind of slowly; he hoped her suit wasn't running out of power. "What happened?"

"We hit a pebble," said Sol. "More of a sand grain, actually, from the size of that first hole. We're going so fast that it hit us hard as a bomb. See that first hole? By the time it came through, it was exploding, but it went through us so quickly that the explosion was only this big"—he spread two fingers just a bit—"by the time it hit the back wall there, and only *this* big"—he spread his arms to the width of the hole in the back of the bot room—"when it left us. That's okay—we can patch up Life Support. The big question is whether it hit the drive unit."

"Oh . . ." And that was all Toby could say, as it began to finally sink in just how much trouble they were in. For the next few minutes all he could do was follow the other two back and forth as they tried to revive parts—any parts—of the ship's systems. It turned out their suits really were getting low on power, like Toby's. If it ran out, he'd lose both of them.

Funny, though, that the first coherent thought Toby had over the next while was, *Peter, I'm sorry I left.*

How long now had his brother had been clinging to Toby like a life raft? So long that his emotional dependence had come to define both of them. Having Toby leave him for a few months had devastated Peter. The separation was supposed to help Peter rebuild his own coping abilities. Mom and Evayne would help, and Consensus was part of the plan, of course.

Toby had stayed awake as long as he could. During the weeks of the engine burn, Toby hadn't once switched off his virtual views to look at the real ship that surrounded him. Peter had demanded that he stay awake, stay in Consensus and keep their versions of the gameworld synced.

So as he traveled he'd tangled anxious Peter up with the discovery of fantastic alien planets, and despicable enemies, cunning plots and rousing battles in a universe more colorful than the real one they lived on. Their shared world kept Peter focused and able to cope. What Toby hadn't counted on was how the communications lag with the game servers kept growing. After twenty days, his version of Consensus was totally out of sync with Peter's back on Sedna. And the math couldn't be second-guessed: the tug's life support was nearly half used up. It was time to enter cold sleep.

"Guys, we need to get communications up!"

"We know that, Toby."

If the tug's engines had died, if they'd missed Rockette . . . they could keep on speeding on their course for another ten billion years and never encounter another grain of sand the size of the one they'd hit, much less another planet or a friendly spaceship ready to rescue them.

Toby suddenly had an overwhelming need to do something— anything. Sol and Miranda kept talking about power couplings and radioisotope generators as Toby knocked his way through the dead machines in the bot room. Their calm focus wasn't reassuring anymore; after all, there was nothing really at stake for *them*. He reached the hole in the rear bulkhead and paused to inspect its edges. They were smooth, but he knew he should check for any razor-sharp edges. It wouldn't do to cut his suit open.

He poked his head outside, and there were the stars—brighter and more overwhelmingly numerous than he'd ever seen on Earth. He'd seen them like this on the surface of Sedna, and they always seemed unreal, a fantasy painter's version of the sky. But no, this was the reality of where he was.

Toby had looked up the distances once—just once. Light that could zip around Earth seven times in one second would take eleven hours to go from there to Sedna. After reading that, he'd stopped trying to picture the scale of their isolation. Yet the knowledge always hung there like a weight in the back of his mind.

He aimed his fading headlamp down the long open-work girder that joined the ship's passenger unit to the drive section. He hadn't spent much time inspecting the ship during the flight out, but still knew what things back there should look like.

"Hey, guys."

"Just a minute, Toby."

"No, really. You should see this."

There were a bunch of bot-shaped silhouettes clustered around the engines. And they were *moving*.

"I think some bots are repairing the engines!"

"*What?*" In seconds, Sol was pushing past him, shining a blinding light out that erased the stars. "I should have been in the loop! Why can't I get a signal out of them? Out of the way!"

Toby spotted a handhold on the outside hull; impulsively, he grabbed it and flipped himself out through the hole. Sol's helmet appeared and he shone his own lamp at the bots. He cheered.

"Go, little guys!" Miranda's helmet appeared next to his; for a while they chattered about rerouting power and recharging stuff. The lamplight turned the slowly working bots into dazzling white shapes, throwing everything else into blackness. Toby watched them for a while, then thought of the stars again. He turned away.

Reflected light outlined the ship's curves in ghostly gray. You could still see stars beyond that, of course. He continued turning, following the twisting banner of the Milky Way as it wove toward the ship's bow . . .

. . . And disappeared into a giant arc of blackness that took up a good third of the sky.

"What the—?" He looked around for a better vantage point. Belatedly he remembered that these emergency suits had coils of cable at their waists; he hooked one end of his to the first handhold and then launched himself around the tiny horizon of the ship. Now he could see the length of the bot room and past the living section beyond it to the tug's bow. He should be seeing the cluster of telescopes and other instruments there, as silhouettes against the stars. There were no stars. Instead, a vast circle of perfect black loomed up ahead, with the ship aimed at its center like a dart.

He'd seen the radar profile of Rockette. It was a lumpy potato shape. This perfect circle . . . you only got that crisp perfection in things that were really, really big. Things like planets.

"Guys? Guys! We're . . . I think we're back at Sedna!"

THERE'D ALWAYS BEEN THE chance that their little colony of one hundred people would end up frozen and dead. Maybe Pluto was as far as humans would ever get from Earth; maybe the stars really were too far away. Nobody had ever come up with a magical means of going faster than light, after all. Only governments and a few trillionaires could afford to send probes to Alpha Centauri or the other nearby stars, and even then they took decades to reach their destinations.

But it was still possible—barely—to stake your own claim on an entire planet. Out past the edge of the solar system, thousands of orphan worlds drifted. The known ones had strange names like Quaoar, Eris, Haumea, and Makemake. All were impossibly cold and distant, but if you could be the first person to step onto one, you could own it.

Toby's parents owned Sedna.

Back home on Earth, if you weren't already one of the trillion-aires, you'd never be more than a servant to them. So his parents had scraped together several generations' worth of inheritances and come to homestead in a vast region of space so empty that you could hide a thousand solar systems in it with room to spare. Out here, the nearest boulder-size object was probably farther away than Jupiter was from the sun. Toby had once heard that the Eski-mos had fifty words for snow. Out here, you needed at least fifty for *empty*.

The calm tones of Miranda's voice were reassuring. She and Sol were excitedly reviewing the work the repair bots had done back at the engines. Maybe they could tease some power out of it—get working laser comms going, maybe some heat and light. Unfreeze the air in the cabin.

While they did that, Toby perched on the nose of the ship and stared down at the planet. It was a big black nothing, of course, but he'd watched Sedna recede through the ship's telescope when they'd first left, and he knew one thing should be visible in that vast round cutout in the star field.

There should be a single tiny, forlorn pinprick of light down there, near the equator. Home.

"Let's fire it up. Toby, you coming in? We'll get a better view through the light amplifiers."

"Sure." Sol and Miranda were getting more optimistic by the minute, but Toby's heart was sinking as he flipped back through the hole in the hull and went forward to the inflatable airlock Sol had glued around the main compartment hatch. Toby decided not to mention the absence of the little star that should be down there.

He stayed silent as the other two tested then started the power diverters. Lights flickered on throughout the long cylindrical cabin, starkly gleaming off the frozen sides of the butlers and grippies. Sol and Miranda cheered.

"Now to get some communications going," said Sol.

"Oh, heat and air first, please," pleaded Miranda. "Toby needs to get out of that suit!"

Heating the crew quarters took a long time, as the interstellar cold had to be driven out of everything in the place. Heaters roared, the hoarfrost melted, and eventually the temperature edged up above minus fifty. Sol took off his helmet and gave a virtual sniff. "Like breathing fire," he said. "But it'll get better. And now that the primary CPU's online . . ." He moved to a metal keypad and touched a few buttons.

All around Toby the butlers and grippies were stirring, but Sol quickly shut them down, too. "We don't need more of them going than we've already got."

"Now to see where we are." Sol connected the telescope feed to Toby's glasses; the tug's walls faded and the pale curve of the planet appeared.

The ship's telescope could amplify the thin trickle of starlight touching this world and make out color and detail thousands of kilometers below. For a minute or so, Toby, Sol, and Miranda all stared in silence at what it showed. Then Sol said, "Well . . ."

Toby shook his head; it was just what he'd feared. "That's not Sedna."

It was a crimson world. The screen showed mountains, canyons, and vast flat plains that might be frozen oceans. All were painted in shades of rust and scarlet, as if a vast drop of blood had been hung here in deep space, scattered perhaps by some wounded god a billion years ago.

In this way the planet was exactly like Sedna, or Eris, or any of the millions of comets that peppered interstellar space. All had this bloodred hue. Somebody had explained to Toby that over aeons of time, the slow trickle of cosmic radiation cooked the surfaces of these worlds, producing complex organic molecules— tholins, they called them—that were deep red.

In every other respect, this place was unlike Sedna. Sedna was tiny, its gravity barely able to keep it round. It was absolutely featureless, like a billiard ball. This planet had mountains.

"It's as big as Earth!" Sol was reading the other instruments. "If we can get the engines running . . . find out where we are . . ."

Toby had been examining the mysterious orb. Now he pointed at the image. "What're those?"

"What?" Sol seemed eager for the distraction.

"Those . . . pits? Circles?"

There were more than a dozen on the visible hemisphere: circular white formations, each two hundred or more kilometers across, surrounded by curls and lines of white like splash marks. "Meteor craters," said Miranda dismissively. "Sol, what did the GPS say?"

"No . . ." Toby put two fingers on the screen and zoomed in. "Look there—at the center . . ."

Aeons ago, before the planet was ejected from the star system of its birth, this might have been an ocean shoreline. On one side of the circular white area, the surface was perfectly flat; on the other, hills and rugged canyons meandered into what looked like continental interior. It looked weirdly like someone had thrown a giant white paint bomb across the landscape—yet at its center . . .

Black lines, perfectly straight, crisscrossing each other. Dark rectangles and perfect circles, some tiny, some hundreds of meters across.

A city.

Toby zoomed out and then in on another of the white patches. It also radiated out from a mesh of black lines and dots. He guessed that the others would, too.

"Cities." Sol grinned tightly at Miranda. "Saved, who would have believed it? Just gotta . . . get the comms working . . ."

But she was frowning. "Where are the lights?"

That was true—there were no windows glowing down there, no greenhouse dome lights to keep the eternal darkness of interstellar night at bay. Toby ventured, "Maybe they're underground? A subsurface ocean? Can we look at this in infrared?"

Sol grunted and made some adjustments. The image flickered into false color—bright blues, whites, and mauve. "The colors show differences in temperature to a tenth of a degree or so," he said. The city structures were barely distinguishable from the frozen landscape surrounding them. And the ambient temperature was about the same as Sedna's: a balmy three degrees above absolute zero. Cold enough to turn water ice hard as granite, freeze air, and make any life or mechanical motion impossible.

"Dead," Toby mumbled.

Sol breezily waved a hand. "It's the find of the century, Toby! We just gotta find out where we are and phone home . . ." He was flipping through diagnostic windows, trying different things, but Toby could see exactly what those windows were saying.

"Sol . . . Sol, stop! *The engines are dead!*"

He glanced back. "Yeah, but—"

"They're *dead*. The bots kept them alive just long enough to put us in orbit here. They're not coming back. And . . . we're nowhere near home, are we?"

Sol shrugged and started to say something, but Toby had finally had enough.

"*Stop!*"

Both of his companions turned to stare at Toby.

"Drop the personalities," he said. "Just tell me what's going on!"

In a more level voice, Miranda said, "Even if we got a message off to Sedna—and we doubt we have the power—this world is uncharted. It must be so far away from Sedna, they could never mount a rescue mission. The ship's clocks have been affected so we can't tell you how long it's been . . ."

"We've got enough power to cycle the hibernation system one more time," Sol added, his voice equally calm. "We can set it to go into deep dive. A controlled freeze, so we don't have to leave it to chance about when the power fails totally."

It was true, then. He was dead. He had been ever since that meteor had hit the ship. This time—a brief waking above a planet that was also dead—was just a last spasm of the ship's systems.

Even if he'd had engines, this little ship wasn't designed to land on big worlds. The nearest craft that could do that were back at Sedna. This was a comet runner, incapable of landing near one of those frozen cities. He was stuck in orbit.

There were only two choices now: stay alive as long as possible, eking out a few last days and hours as the lights dimmed and interstellar cold wormed its way through the walls, finally to freeze to death as the ship's power failed; or voluntarily enter the cicada bed, surely never to awake again, and end it all now.

He looked from Sol to Miranda. Their faces were blank, no longer full of that optimistic energy they'd had a few moments ago. Of course it was gone, he didn't need that from them anymore. In fact, he no longer needed them, either.

"You're no good to me anymore," he said. "Switch off." They nodded, and their faces disappeared from the open ovals of the two space suits. Those faces had been projections in his augmented reality glasses anyway. What was left in the suits were the intertwined grippies and butlers that had moved their arms and legs to make it seem like there were people in them. Sol and Miranda— companion personalities that were really just game characters from Consensus—were gone.

Now there was complete silence, and the solitude came crushing in on Toby. Fine. He wanted to be true to who he was, and where he was, if these were his last hours. No more simulated friends to share the moment with; no more softening the reality of it.

He grabbed his suit's helmet. "Get the bed ready," he told the ship. "I'm gonna take one last look around."

With no audience to witness it, he felt no urge to cry. But there was no way the last thing he'd see would be just a picture on a screen. He climbed out onto the ship's hull and looked down at the mysterious planet with his own eyes. There was nothing to see, of course, just a black cutout interrupting the stars. The stars, though . . . they really were beautiful.

He turned around, staring, and then around again. If this were the online world of Consensus, something would appear to save them all—a rescue ship, an alien artifact—and it would appear right . . . about . . .

Now.

He held his breath and waited. The moment dragged on.

"Toby?" It was the ship, speaking for the first and last time in its own flat voice. "Your bed is ready."

He opened his mouth, closed it, then said, "All right. I'm coming."

| Two |

WARMTH AND SOFT BLANKETS cocooned him. Toby wanted to burrow deeper into them to escape the light, and he did. For a while he lay in timeless bliss, unthinking. Then . . .

Then he shouted and flung the blankets aside, and sat up. He stared around, unable to believe what he was seeing.

He was in a big four-poster bed in a . . . well, not exactly a sumptuous bedroom, but a decent one, with tall windows that let in the amber-red light of sunset or sunrise. A soft breeze, somewhat chilly for a virtual world, teased the sinuous drapes.

For a moment he wondered. This couldn't be real, but why then that chill in the air, the cracks in the plaster by the window? He touched his face, but he wasn't wearing glasses. You could implant the visual and auditory interfaces, of course, but the metal and electronics had different thermal characteristics from flesh: they and hibernation technology didn't mix well.

But this *had* to be a simulation—somewhere in the Consensus Empire he'd built with Peter. If he were in reality back on Sedna, he'd be waking in some drafty plastic cell somewhere. Not to open windows and what looked like a truly gorgeous sunset.

He examined the room again. All the styles seemed familiar, reminiscent of the subdued Art Nouveau and Space Modern mix he and Peter had favored for the Consensus Empire. The patterns on the drapes weren't entirely alien, either . . . but maybe he was just imagining things.

There was a dressing bot at the foot of the bed, waiting patiently for him to wake up. It wasn't holding out clothes, at least not with its front arms. Instead, it was offering him a pair of leg exoskeletons, the sort of mechanical assist you gave to people who weren't used to the higher gravity of places like Earth.

The bots in the online worlds never did that sort of thing, because nobody ever pretended that their world had gravity different from Earth normal.

Toby threw his legs over the side of the bed and knew that this was no simulation. His feet crashed to the floor of their own accord, nearly taking the rest of him with them. He had to brace himself against the cushions as an invisible force tried to suck him down. Gravity—*real* gravity.

Numbly, he let the bot clamp the unfamiliar braces around his calves and thighs. It offered a second piece for his back, but though the exos were thin and graceful, designed to be invisible under clothing, Toby waved it away. The bot offered a shirt and trousers, and he put them on—and damn it, they were in the Consensus Empire style, too, though with odd differences here and there. More details, different materials.

He stood up and the exo made the motion as easy as if his body had been virtual. The only problem with that idea was that he could still feel gravity pulling on his insides, which it never did in a simulation.

Toby walked to the open window and looked out on a grand avenue choked with vehicles and moving people. Tall towers soared into the sky, and there were real trees on the nearby rooftops and more down by the street. For a moment he forgot everything else, consumed with the intricate beauty of their leafy canopies.

It was a beauty that shimmered under the light of a strange sky. There was a sunsetlike quality to the light, but there was no sun; instead, the radiance came from a kind of red curling aurora that filled the whole sky. Lines of yellow and pale green flickered and fluttered up and down this astonishing firmament. He was able to open the window farther and crane his neck outside. There was a chill in the air, but he ignored that and gawked upward.

"Ah! So you're awake."

Toby banged his head on the lintel and winced. The voice was a man's, deep but thin somehow, so he went from being startled to puzzled when he turned and saw a slender woman standing in the room's only doorway.

"H-hello—" He'd been about to say more but his hands went to his throat. "What—?" His own voice was absurdly deep, a bull-frog rumble.

The lady laughed, her voice a chop of drumbeats. She was older, though still pretty, and dressed in a flame-red gown. She radiated the confidence of wealth. It was the wealth of people like her that had squeezed Toby's family relentlessly toward poverty. It was people like her who'd made his parents try to colonize Sedna. That was what Dad always said, anyway.

"The air gets them every time," she rumbled. "The natural atmosphere on this planet is a neon and argon mix. We add some oxygen and warm it up, and we can breathe it. But it plays your vocal chords differently than nitrogen."

Toby bowed cautiously. This place was so obviously real, yet so similar to the gameworlds where he spent so much time that he found himself wondering how he would approach a moment like this if this really were a game.

"Thank you for rescuing me," he said, and his own voice was a deep cello. "My name is Toby McGonigal."

Her eyes went wide and she took a step backward, but Toby barely noticed. He'd realized what he'd just said, and what he had not yet thought about. He felt instantly guilty. "My family," he blurted. "I need to contact them."

She tried to speak, oddly discomposed; then her eyelids lowered, and she turned slightly away. "I'm sorry," she said. "That . . . that won't be possible. They died . . . many years ago."

Even the exos couldn't keep Toby's knees from giving out, though they did steer his collapse so he landed in a chair.

He'd exchanged his last e-mails with Peter and Evayne only a day ago, or so it seemed to him. How could they be gone? "How long . . . ?"

"The time stamps on your cicada bed said twenty years since you last went into cold sleep," she said. "But before that, Toby— can I call you that?—you'd deep-dived for so long that your ship's radiation shielding had drained off. You were being slow-cooked by cosmic rays."

The superconducting magnets should have been able to keep their magnetic fields alive for . . . well, practically forever. Suddenly he didn't want to know how long it had been. "Where are we? What is this world?"

She'd come to stand over him and looked startled at his sudden question.

"You're on Lowdown," she said. Her voice made the name into an impossibly deep chord, like the two bottom notes on a pipe organ. "We found your ship in orbit two weeks ago. We've been repairing and regenerating your body ever since. The doctors said you'd be fine to be awakened today."

What she said made no sense. "Our ship in orbit . . . We arrived here two weeks ago? So the engines were working after all!"

But she shook her head. "Your engines had been dead for a long, long time. You'd been in orbit, as I said, for twenty years."

Toby stood up and moved to the window. "But that's impossible. The world we found was dead, a frozen chunk. I mean it had cities, but they were . . ." No, it couldn't be . . . He turned to look at her. She nodded.

"Deep-dived," she said. "We were wintering over, just like you. But for us, it wasn't an emergency."

"Then that's not sunlight?" He nodded at the orange sky.

She laughed. "So far as we know, it's the biggest neon lamp in the universe. We discharge electricity through the air itself and it glows. Quite handy, really."

"But what are you *doing* out here? We were the first to settle this far out. Everybody told us we were crazy, that nobody could survive out here, but . . ." He waved at the obvious disproof of that idea, at the well-designed streets, the tall buildings, and the solid architecture of the room they were in. It was all proof that these people had been here a long, long time.

"You're right," the woman said, and now she sat on the edge of the bed, her expression very serious. "You and your family *were* the first to settle interstellar space. But Toby . . . that was fourteen thousand years ago."

For a long moment there was just faint street noise murmuring up through the open window. The drapes drifted a bit in the cold breeze, but neither the woman nor Toby moved.

Then he was running.

He slammed out of the room before she could shout her surprise. This put him in a long corridor with orange daylight at one end. He ran to the light, passing bots carrying laundry and brooms. He found stairs, began clattering down them, trusting the exos to keep his legs from giving out. She was somewhere behind him, calling his name at first, then cursing, then calling to somebody else.

Down two flights and then he was in a high-ceilinged chamber with big open arches on one side. The building's inner courtyard lay that way. He ran into it, passed six men of various ages who were sitting in wicker chairs around low tables that had drinks on them. The serving bots didn't move as he ran by, but the men boiled out of their chairs, gabbling in shock.

"Ammond!" It was the lady, puffing into the courtyard.

"Damn it, Persea, you couldn't handle a simple task like waking the kid up?"

"He just bolted! I—"

"Forget it. I'll deal with him."

Toby's back was seizing up. Even with the help of the exoskeleton, his muscles simply couldn't handle this gravity. He found himself swerving, staggering, but he kept on going until he found another corridor and at its end another walled courtyard. A gate here seemed to lead to the street. He ran for it but was so deconditioned from weeks in zero gravity that he fell. He was puffing and nearly fainting. All he could see was spots while the world spun, and he felt like puking. His whole body was soaked in sweat.

Suddenly, he was aware of eyes watching him—from his own level near the ground. He blinked. They blinked back from only a couple of paces away.

The head was catlike, its body more an otter's, though the tail, again, was cat. It was perhaps a little bigger than a house cat, but would have been easy to carry. The creature was crouched in the shadow of one of the entranceway pillars, its head cocked as it seemed to be thinking about what to do with Toby.

Two boots appeared behind it, and it looked up. So did Toby.

It was a girl, roughly his own age, dressed in a long open-hooded coat and black leggings. A cap of dark hair framed even blacker eyes. A larger version of the creature that crouched in front of Toby was sitting on her shoulder.

"Quick! They're coming." She reached down and the cat-otter swarmed up her arm, clambered around the one there, and disappeared into a half-visible backpack over her shoulder.

She looked Toby in the eye and shook her head. "You never saw me," she said. "I'm not here."

Then she ran to another entrance that led into the main building, but not, apparently, into the same corridors as he'd just come out of. Before he could shout after her, she was gone.

Toby was so busy staring after her that he didn't hear footsteps approaching behind him. Suddenly a large hand landed on his shoulder, clapped it gently.

"Aw, McGonigal," rumbled a voice of subterranean depth. "There was never gonna be an easy way to tell you."

Toby stood up shakily, waving away help from the man who had followed him out of the building. He was middle-aged, with crow's-feet at the corners of his striking gray eyes, a long face, and a bent nose that looked like somebody might have broken it a long time ago.

His hand rose from Toby's shoulder, was held out now to shake. "I'm Ammond Gon Alon," he said.

"Welcome to your future, son."

IT WAS ALL TOO much, and Toby found himself being led back to his bed, where he proceeded to sleep for nearly a day. He finally dragged himself to the marble-tiled bathroom and allowed a couple of bots to cycle him through a shower and provide new clothes. Then he staggered downstairs to find a vast meal waiting in a tall room with arched stained-glass windows along one wall. The man who'd introduced himself as Ammond was waiting there, as was the woman.

She held out her hand for him to shake. "Persea Eden," she said. "We never finished our introductions yesterday."

She had the cosmetic perfection you expected from rich Earthlings, but she was more likely Martian because she was very tall and slender.

Toby could ask about that, but he had other questions first. He also had questions he didn't want to ask; just thinking about them made him feel sick.

"Did you rescue me?" he asked Ammond.

The older man nodded. "Well, strictly speaking, one of our orbital bots did. Your ship was spotted as we were coming out of dormancy; the telescopes do a census of orbiting and landed ships while the cities are waking up. The bots assumed you were just a visitor from some backwater planet, but Persea's systems are always on the lookout for . . . unusual patterns." He cocked an eyebrow at her. "Would that be a good way to put it?" She nodded. "Your ship looked different. There was a red light on our board when we woke up, so I sent a salvage tug to investigate. The rest you know."

Toby had sat down in front at the long table, which was piled with food he hadn't seen since he'd left Earth. You couldn't get blueberries on Sedna, or mangoes. There were flapjacks, bacon, croissants, and was that maple syrup? His mouth watered just looking at it all.

He began voraciously piling a plate with stuff. After a couple of minutes he noticed the silence and looked up. Ammond and Persea were watching him, identical expressions of bemusement on their faces.

"Sorry," he said. "It's just I haven't eaten in fourteen thousand years."

Just saying this made his stomach knot with grief, but they laughed, which was what he wanted. After stuffing a whole pancake into his mouth (and yes, it really was maple syrup in that little white pitcher) he remembered them again and said, "So you own tugs? What do you do, traffic control?"

This was meant as another joke—in the two years they'd been at Sedna, no one and nothing had come into orbit around the little world. The very idea that you'd need traffic control around an orphan world in between the stars was absurd. But Ammond nodded.

"It's one of my businesses. Lowdown is booming, there's a ridiculous amount of immigration these days. You probably noticed how new this city is."

"Were there other ships in orbit?" He remembered the emptiness, the stars, and a vast circular cutout that was the planet. Nothing had ever seemed so empty, except maybe Sedna in their first days there.

"Uh, over two thousand, I think." Ammond grinned. "Pretty crowded for a little world like ours."

"But . . . there was no radio chatter. And all your cities were . . ."

"Wintering over. So were the ships. You had the bad luck to arrive while everybody was dormant."

"But why were you all hibernating? That's just . . . weird."

Ammond exchanged a glance with Persea. "It's true, then. You've never heard of the locksteps."

He said the word as though it meant something important. Toby shook his head.

Ammond blew out a breath and ran a hand through his hair. "I don't even know where to start," he said.

Persea frowned in thought. "Let's start with this city," she said.

TOBY ATE A HUGE amount of everything, then promptly fell asleep on a couch under a stained-glass window. When he awoke the light was just the same, but he sensed some hours had passed. A bot had noticed he was stirring and went to fetch his rescuers.

"Want to go for a ride?" asked Ammond.

The house was at least four floors tall and wrapped around a big central courtyard. It came as no surprise that it had an inside garage with five vehicles in it. Ammond and Persea picked a big lozenge-shaped ground-effect car, and Ammond sat in the front with a bot driver while Toby and Persea took up the back. In moments they slid out into an orange-lit street full of other cars and bots and bicycles and dashing pedestrians.

The city went on for kilometers. There might be a million people here, most living in glass-walled condominium towers. Presiding over it all was that bizarre orange sky—a giant neon lamp, Persea had claimed.

"It all looks ordinary enough, right?" Ammond said as he let the bot steer them through the dense traffic. "I mean, you might think the whole planet was like this. But it isn't."

Toby remembered what he'd seen from orbit. "There're only a few cities, and there're these big splash marks around them . . ."

"Yes! You saw that, good. It'll make it all easier." They'd come to a roadway and were zipping along at a hundred or more kilometers per hour. In a couple of minutes the towers were behind them, and ahead was an empty snowscape where vast dunes of white marched away into deepening darkness. Some of the dunes were carved by deep runnels and canyons of trickling water, and tortured spires and pillars of ice jutted up here and there like sentinel towers. Blustery gray clouds scudded low over the scene.

Toby looked back, and now he could see how the orange banners of light that lit the city curved up and over its buildings to make a flickering dome. Their light reflected off the clouds that tumbled around the horizon, but past that everything was dark. Midnight dark.

"We can't heat the whole planet," Ammond explained. "First of all, that would take a ridiculous amount of power. We're nowhere near the Laser Wastes here. Second, if we heated the whole place above freezing, the mountains would melt. The continents would dissolve . . . They're all made out of ice, aren't they? So we light up our cities when we're done wintering over, and heat up the air, but even that makes these giant storms—"

There were no roads out here. The car was skating over wind-whipped snowbanks, its fans sending up billows of white. Overhead the clouds were even lower, some twirling in tornadolike gyres. Driving snow was quickly reducing visibility to a few meters.

"It wasn't snowing in the city!"

"Oh, *this* stuff wouldn't make it that far," said Ammond. "It's mostly carbon dioxide, with some nitrogen slush. Things cool down pretty quickly once you leave the city limits."

The structures they'd seen from orbit had been surrounded by these big target-shaped splash marks. Now Toby knew why: they were the eyes of local storms while their citizens were awake. He barked a laugh. Persea turned to see where he was looking.

"Impressive, isn't it? I almost couldn't believe those storms myself, when I first moved here," she said.

The storm was abating. Toby looked back and up, at a sky-topping mountain of cloud lit with lightning flashes and traces of a hellish orange glow.

"You said you'd been asleep for twenty years. How long do you stay awake?" Toby asked her.

"Actually, we sleep for thirty years. You drifted into Lowdown's orbit ten years into our 'winter.' We sleep for thirty years, and then we're awake for a month. That's known as a *turn*."

He stared at her. "A *month*? That's . . . that's ridiculous!"

"What's important is the ratio," explained Ammond. "The ratio between dormancy and living time in a turn. You could use any sort of ratio—five to one, two to one, a hundred to one. We use 360-to-one."

"But why? Does it take that long to recover from these storms?"

"No, though that's a good guess. It's not just Lowdown that uses the 360-to-one ratio. There's over *seventy thousand* other planets do the same."

"Almost all of them," added Persea, "nomad worlds like this one, drifting in interstellar space between the solar system and Alpha Centauri."

Toby had taken a crash course in astronomy before they left for Sedna, and it was only then that he'd learned that interstellar space wasn't completely empty. There were a hundred thousand nomad planets for every star in the galaxy. Most were frozen like Sedna and Lowdown, but some—the really big ones—cradled the heat from their birth for billions of years. These could sustain volcanoes and oceans under thick blankets of atmosphere. Sunless worlds, impossibly lonely, but life might actually exist on these ancient nomads.

But . . . all of these worlds switching themselves off and on like lights? And all on the same weird schedule. "Why? It's crazy," he said. "Why would you possibly want to do that? Go into cold sleep after a month, then sleep for years . . ."

The clouds were clearing, revealing the vast spangling of stars above a black landscape. There were the familiar constellations, proof that they were no more than a few light-years from Earth. Less, if Ammond was telling the truth.

"Two reasons," said Ammond. "You can stop here," he told the driver. They were now perched at the top of a hill overlooking a plain where floodlights showed busy graders and excavators chomping at the landscape. In the distance were more lit buildings, maybe factories.

"If we tried to live like this all the time we'd use up these little worlds in no time," said Ammond. "That's reason one. We live like arctic flowers, with a short growing season and long winter. It works for them, it'll work for us. But secondly . . ."

Persea put a hand on his arm. Toby's head was drooping with sudden exhaustion—and from the reminder of how far through time he'd fallen and how much was now lost to him.

"Maybe . . . we'll talk about that another time," said Ammond.

They drove back to the city in silence.

THE CITY TURNED OFF its orange canopy to create a local night. As it came back on to create a new morning, Toby lay in the sumptuous bed he'd been provided. In a half-waking reverie, he found the amber light reminding him of sunsets on Earth, and he ached with longing to see one again.

As his mind drifted, though, it was one particular sunset that memory summoned. He'd been younger by a few years, and full of nervous energy. On this evening he was in the family's rooftop garden, staring out beyond the manicured lawns and well-trimmed trees, the perfect shingled angles of the neighbors' roofs. A tall wrought-iron fence surrounded this little enclave of civility, and on the other side of it, people were rioting.

He'd seen his father's car pull up a few minutes before, so he knew Dad was safe. The skittering crowds and the clouds of tear gas were unnerving, though. What if they got in? That was impossible, Mom had insisted. But Toby was not so sure.

Indifferent to the chaos in the streets below, the sky was a magnificent ocean of light, fading from mauve behind Toby to shades of lime green and canary yellow near where the sun had just disappeared. The radiance gave everything a half-real aura, just as distance reduced the shouting and screams of the mob to a grumbling murmur.

He heard a louder sound behind him and turned to see his father stepping out of the glass doors of the dormer room. "Toby! Come away from there."

"I want to see, Dad."

"It's not safe."

"Mom said it was."

Father came to stand next to Toby. He pointed, and Toby could see little sparks of red peppering the air above the fence. He'd assumed these were firecrackers somebody was setting off. "Those are bullets being exploded by the community laser defense. People are shooting at us, Tobe. If just one gets through . . ."

Alarmed, Toby had followed his father back to the center of the garden, out of sight of the riot. Only then had he noticed that his dad's eyes were red and that his mouth had a bitter downturn to it. Toby had never seen him like this.

His father made him sit next to him on a bench under a cherry tree. He hunched forward, clasping his hands nervously between his knees. "I . . . I saw Terry Idris as the car was coming through the gate. You remember Terry? He used to come to dinner a lot. Tall, black hair . . . ?" Toby shook his head.

"Terry's a good friend." Dad's voice cracked on that last word. "And he's out there throwing stones at the fence—at our fence. He saw me, I know he did. I . . . I would have picked him up, brought him . . . it's dangerous out there, but . . ."

Toby stared at his father in wonder. "What? Why didn't you?"

"We can't be seen to be sympathizing with the rioters." His father hung his head. "We'd lose our membership, have to move out into the city . . ." Toby understood that this would be a bad thing to do. "It's not right, Toby. Terry's my friend. They . . . they were all my friends."

Toby wasn't sure who *they* were, but he sensed that this was far too important a moment to interrupt.

"Listen, Toby, we can't ever talk about this. The house, the car— they can overhear us anywhere." This was a different *they* now, and Toby knew his dad was talking about their business partners, the political authorities, and everybody else who served the dwindling circle of the trillionaires. You were either in that circle, or outside, with the starving mobs. Toby did understand that.

His father turned to him. "We can't talk about it from this day on, but I want you to know something, Toby. You must understand that I'm not going to stand for it. I'm going to do something to help change things, and it could get rough for us for a while. You may not understand everything that's happening. Just remember, whatever happens, that it's happening to help them." He nodded in the direction of the muffled shouting. "Because they don't deserve what's being done to them."

Toby couldn't remember the rest of that evening. He knew they'd spoken no more about it after they went inside. It wasn't that the house was bugged, exactly. It was that the bots and screens and devices it was crammed with had their own tiny minds, and those minds had been designed to be archconservative, suspicious snoops. The TV, the air-conditioning system, the duster bots—they were all tattletales, loyal not to the people who owned them but to the people who'd built and sold them.

Since he remembered no more, Toby's thoughts drifted away, and he fell asleep again—until suddenly he saw his sister and mother standing in front of him. This was a memory, too, but one from a different time than the first. Here, Evayne was surrounded by a little retinue of walking dolls, their artificial minds set to trauma mode so that they cooed and comforted her as she went about her day. Mother had no such help, and she twisted her hands together as she said over and over, "He'll come back to us. I know he will."

Toby sat up with a shout and was back on Lowdown. And though the amber morning was silent and the skies serene, he was shaking.

THE DAYS INCHED BY. Toby would rise shortly after the sky was turned on and eat a gigantic breakfast before starting his exercises. After a couple of weeks he'd been able to lose the exoskeletons, but real gravity was still tough on him. He walked a little more every day.

He wasn't allowed on the streets. When he asked Persea why, she shrugged and said, "We do a pretty good job of keeping ahead of disease these days, but there's still ten thousand years' worth of new and evolved bugs out there. We need to immunize you by stages before you start even going close to other people. That's partly why it took us so long to wake you up—we had to clear our own systems first."

The vaccines were in the food, apparently. When Persea explained all this to Toby, he almost told her about his encounter with the girl in the outer courtyard; but if she or the animal had given him something, it was probably too late now anyway. He stayed silent, but the idea of countless new diseases lurking in wait for his unsuspecting immune system kept him slightly on edge.

He couldn't go out, but he could walk the rooftops and galleries that stretched between the buildings of Ammond's estate. From there, he could see people in the streets below and almost hear the murmur of their conversations. He kept hoping that he would see the girl again. He hoped she'd been a legitimate visitor to the estate, but her words to him—"I'm not here"—suggested she might have been an intruder. Whichever she was, either she hadn't come back or wasn't allowed to see him in his current state of quarantine.

A clue to why she might have been here lay in one of the estate's central courtyards. There, a series of cages held many little catlike creatures like the one that had confronted him that first day. Persea and Ammond didn't keep them in the main house, but apparently they bred them.

The city outside was full of chattering, lively people, and when Toby knelt on the edge of the rooftop he could hear their voices. They spoke a bewildering variety of languages. They dressed just as diversely. That uneasy familiarity still lay at the heart of all the fashions he saw and in the architecture of the coral-colored towers. Toby couldn't figure it out but soon got used to it.

He probably should have investigated. He should have asked questions. But, on the third day of his waking, Persea gave Toby the personal effects he'd brought with him in the tug. Amid all that were his glasses, and he snatched them up and put them on.

Persea and Ammond didn't wear glasses, but he'd seen them issue silent orders to the household bots. They must have implants—

not uncommon on Earth in Toby's day but incompatible with the freeze-thaw cycles of hibernation. Toby hadn't thought about that too much, since there was so much else to absorb about this world. As soon as he put on his own glasses he summoned the backups of Sol and Miranda stored in them, and he wept when they came to wrap their arms around him, because he couldn't feel their touch.

"You stupid boy, you should be asking questions," Miranda chided him a few days later, when she found out how little he knew. Toby hadn't been spending much time with her; when he wasn't walking the rooftops or exercising or eating, he retreated into the Consensus Empire. Peter had uploaded several months' worth of moves before the accident that had knocked out the tug's engines and brain. This was all new to Toby. He could pretend for hours at a time that Peter was still alive, and that his brother could still surprise him.

"Where's the television, the movies?" Miranda had pressed. "What about music? I haven't heard any since you put your glasses on. How does this world work? You have to find out, Toby."

He did start asking, at first just to get Miranda off his back. The household bots were dumb as stumps and wouldn't answer his questions. And the few humans other than Persea and Ammond whom he met mostly shrugged their shoulders when he asked them anything complicated.

So he knew he was skating along the surface of some more complex situation, seeing the streets, the people, and skies full of air traffic but understanding none of it. When he wasn't being overwhelmed by the sights and sounds of Lowdown he still couldn't focus on the mystery of his current life. His thoughts always drifted back to his lost home, and when that would happen he would pick up his glasses and revisit it—or what little of it he actually had. Most of the glasses' memory was taken up by the Consensus Empire.

Two weeks after his awakening, he heard Ammond and Persea arguing. They were going at it pretty loudly, because they were audible several rooms away; but he couldn't make out what they were saying. A little while later Ammond came to him, appearing cheerful and unconcerned—but maybe a little *too* cheerful. "Well, Toby," he said, "are you ready to do some traveling?"

Toby was wrestling with some butler bots, which twisted and turned in ways guaranteed to give his muscles the best workout. He frowned at Ammond from a nearly upside-down position. "The south polar observatory?" Persea had talked about that; it was one of the places these two owned.

But Ammond shook his head. "Little Auriga. It's a planet about half a light-year from here. We've got some friends there we'd like you to meet, and . . . well, let's face it—it's a beautiful world. I think you'll like it."

Toby gestured for the bots to let him go. "But even the fastest ship would take years to get there. Unless you're antimatter powered, you're looking at decades . . ."

Ammond shrugged. "A little over twelve years, but don't worry. We'll be home in a month."

Freed of the bots and standing on his own, Toby still staggered. "*What?*"

Ammond laughed at the look on his face. "No, of course we're not going to go faster than light! That's impossible, right?

"But think about it, Toby. Little Auriga is a half light-year away. Even in the fastest possible ship any round-trip we took would mean being away from home for a year. But what if you could click a pause button when you leave—a pause button for your whole world? And when you get back from your round-trip, you unpause it and it's like you were never away?

"That's the main reason why our whole world winters over. All the Lockstep worlds pause and unpause on a schedule. We call the schedule a *frequency*, and each wake-sleep cycle is called a *turn*. That makes this is the only place in the universe where we can go to sleep on board a spaceship, wake up at another world a half light-year away, spend a month there, then come home to find only a month's passed at home. There are tens of thousands of worlds open to us, and we could visit any of them and come home to find this one unchanged."

Toby shook his head. "That's the weirdest thing I've ever heard." What was especially weird about it, though, was that it made perfect sense. He had gone into cold sleep to avoid the tedium of the five-month trip to Rockette. What if everybody back home had gone into hibernation at the same time? It would have felt like a pretty short trip. But anybody visiting Sedna in the middle of the whole thing would have found a cold, dead world . . .

He looked over; Ammond was grinning at him.

"What do you say, Toby?" He laughed again. "Would you like to see the universe?"

TOBY OPENED HIS EYES with a start. Were they there already? It seemed like just a few seconds ago that he'd shut his eyes in his little wedge-shaped cabin aboard the Lockstep ship *Vance II*.

Suddenly something eclipsed his view of the far wall—a vast pale oval. He blinked at it, and it swam into focus.

A girl about his own age was eye to eye with him, her face just on the other side of the cicada bed's plastic cover.

She rapped on the material and he jerked. "Can you hear me?" Her words were the first he'd heard in weeks that didn't sound like a giant was speaking them; they must have swapped out the argon in the ship's air. She sounded like a girl.

He nodded. She looked around, the flicking movement of her head making her hair swirl around her in zero gravity. Then she gripped both sides of the bed and stared in at him with unsettling intensity.

"We've only got a couple of seconds before the alarms'll go off," she said. "Listen to me! You can't trust those people who found you. They are not your friends. Do. You. Understand?"

Dumbly, he shook his head. She cursed in frustration.

"You've got to get away from them! The first chance you get. Now, I—look, I gotta go. Before the bots spot me."

Her face swept off and away, leaving only the blank wall.

"Wait, who—" He reached for the bed's release switch, but she'd done something to it. His strength was failing, he felt again the spiral of overwhelming sleepiness that signaled the beginning of hibernation. He had time for just one last startled thought:

She was the girl who'd spoken to him in Ammond's courtyard that first day.

| Three |

TOBY LOOKED AT HIS feet and tried to convince himself that the last time he'd worn these shoes was thirty years ago. He'd gone to bed on Lowdown and when he woke the gravity was different. They were on another world. Despite having been in hibernation before, he couldn't wrap his head around it. It all seemed too easy.

After breakfast in what looked like a windowless airport lounge, he and his new friends had walked a few short corridors and come to a glass-walled elevator. Along with Ammond and Persea and the usual crowd of household bots, he was now descending in this. Their plunge into the depths seemed endless, but he knew this is what you had to do on the coldest worlds: dig deep.

"I don't feel any different," he said to Persea. "I mean, I feel like I just slept an ordinary night. Cold sleep—when we did it before, waking up was like getting over a dose of the flu."

Persea nodded. "What's the flu? —Never mind. We've had a little time to perfect cold sleep. But . . . I don't know, should we tell him?" Free of Lowdown's strange air, her voice was a soft soprano. Toby was having trouble getting used to that, too.

Ammond shrugged. There was light below; they were coming to some destination, and he was leaning down to try to see it. "He'll find out eventually."

Persea sighed. "One of the ways we improved on the old cold

sleep was to implant half the hibernation system in our bodies. When we went to wake you up, we found out you didn't have those. That's . . . kind of shocking to anybody from a lockstep world. So before we revived you we, well, we put them in."

"You what?"

She looked down, apparently embarrassed. "It's perfectly normal. And you didn't feel a thing, did you? Anyway, it's just a mix of artificial organs and nanotech—we call them blue blood cells—oh, and all your cells have a kind of artificial mitochondria in them, too, that can shut down your cellular machinery nearly instantly and start it up again at an external signal. All this stuff works with the cicada beds to make the whole process easier on us. That's why you feel so normal even though we've been asleep for thirty years."

"Ah, right." The cicada beds on the ship had certainly been very different from the pods his parents had designed. Those looked ominously like covered operating tables. The one last night had been a simple bed really, with a hard plastic canopy.

Somebody had spoken to him through that canopy. He'd tried to remember what that had been about, but the memory was elusive.

Thinking about implanted organs, he couldn't help patting his chest and sides. Where had they stuck those things? He didn't have any scars.

"Yeah, but . . ." He forgot what he was going to ask, because just below them the stone walls around the elevator swept back, becoming a ceiling that receded above them. Persea was watching with a half smile when Toby turned his attention downward; he couldn't help the grin of delight that came over him. "It *works*! Ammond, Persea, this is what we wanted to do on Sedna!"

He'd glimpsed the surface of Little Auriga through a small window at the docks. Deep crimson plains under a star-spattered sky: it could have been Sedna, and he'd idly wondered whether the similarities were more than skin-deep. Apparently, they were.

The Sedna colonists had known there was an ocean somewhere

under the frozen surface of the little world. If they could get there, they'd figure out some way to terraform it—that was the plan. Here on Little Auriga, they'd made that plan a reality.

The elevator was descending from the roof of a cavern floored by black water. As they descended, he could see that the space wasn't a single cavern but more of an uneasy interface between ice and water—an undulating realm of air pockets that rose above the waves and bellies of pale white that plunged deep beneath it. It was a kind of frozen maze whose ceiling varied from impossibly high to just skimming the waves. Brilliant lamps shone deep into the blue-green walls and slanting ceilings. Directly below, the lamps revealed a city.

Persea was nodding. "Auriga's a true water world. This ocean's not just a thin layer under the ice. It goes all the way down."

"Of course it stops being water at some point," Ammond said with a laugh. "Down at the bottom, it'll crush diamond. So don't fall in."

The peekaboo interplay of walls and slopes, deeper cavern spaces and green cavities, was unlike anything he'd ever seen before. This was not what he'd imagined the ocean under Sedna would look like, and Toby desperately wanted to be able to share what he was seeing with his parents, with Evayne or Peter.

He glanced up at his benefactors while they chatted together and pointed out sights in the rising city. They weren't laborers, these two. They had the easy confidence of executives, and Ammond had said he owned orbital tugs and other worker bots. Also, they weren't married—at least, they didn't act like it. They never touched.

They were being awfully good to him, and he still didn't know why. He remembered them arguing, and the sudden decision to travel.

And then there was that other thing Persea had said to him this morning. Toby couldn't believe it at first; he'd laughed, then stared at her when he realized she was serious.

"I'm supposed to be using an alias, now?"

"Yes," she'd said, "but just if you talk to strangers. You're Garren Morton, remember that. I'll explain later."

She'd tried to be casual about it, but he could see she was nervous. "And just for now. Okay?"

He should have been alert for signs that something was wrong, but he'd been so sunk in his own misery since waking, he couldn't summon the energy. That had been foolish.

"Are you guys married?" he blurted.

They stared at him, then both laughed. "We're business partners," said Persea. "Didn't we tell you that?"

"So what are we doing here? —I mean, not that it isn't amazing."

"More business, I'm afraid," said Ammond with a sigh. "Maybe we could have conducted it by dispatch, but you're a good excuse to come out here in person. I've always liked Auriga."

But what kind *of excuse am I?* He bit his lip and looked down at the glass-and-steel towers. That wasn't the right question, but he wasn't exactly sure what the right question was. He'd have to figure that out, and soon.

THEY CHECKED INTO AN expensive-looking hotel. The hotel, and the city around it, was just like Earth or Mars, with broad vehicle-choked streets, crowds of pedestrians, and bright light from the sky. You had to look up and squint to notice that there were multiple suns up there—powerful lamps, actually—and that the "sky" behind them was a ceiling of ice.

Standing at the window of their suite, Toby shook his head and said, "Why would a world like this shut itself down for thirty years at a time? I mean, it's obviously rich."

Ammond had changed into an old-fashioned business suit and was adjusting his tie in front of the mirror. "If this city were awake all the time, the other worlds in the lockstep wouldn't be next door anymore, would they? They'd be ten, twenty, thirty years away, instead of just overnight. How do I look?" he asked Persea.

"Fine." She hadn't had to change, but always dressed well.

Toby thought about Ammond's logic, but he couldn't wrap his head around it. "When will you be back?" he asked instead of pursuing the matter. This sort of day, at least, was something he was used to, from the many business meetings his parents had attended in the run-up to their settling Sedna.

To his surprise Ammond said, "Oh, no, you're coming, too. We need you for this one," and Persea said, "You don't have to dress up. Just be yourself." For some reason this last comment struck Ammond as funny, and he kept bursting into laughter as they left the room and went downstairs to hail a botcab.

The cab took them along the waterfront. The city was built into the lower slopes of the cavern wall. Where the floor should be there was a flat plain of black water, turned emerald green here and there by subsurface lights. There were many boats out there, and seeing them added to Toby's homesickness. He longed for Earth as much as he longed for his family.

Way out there, something dark emerged from the water, just a roll of black against the glittering waves. Then a white spout of vapor shot into the air. "Ho!" he shouted. "Did you see that?"

Persea nodded. "Whales."

Whales? With a sudden ache in his heart Toby remembered all the life of Earth he'd left behind: robins and crows, squirrels and horses, circling hawks and darting fish. "How can there be whales?"

"Well, they do go into hibernation with the rest of the place," said Ammond in a reasonable tone. "Takes thirty years for enough plankton and krill to accumulate for a month's meal for 'em, or so I hear. Always wondered what a whale cicada bed looked like, though . . ."

Toby had no idea if he was kidding, but just then the cab pulled in at a long green-glass building that extended like a dock out over the water. "Come on, then." Ammond and Persea hopped out, and Toby followed. The air was cold and fresh.

Household bots let them through the glass doors into a wide foyer. With its pebble garden in the corner, individually spotlit paintings, and low leather couches, the place was either an architect's office or a mansion; Toby couldn't tell, though he knew he could never be comfortable living in such a sterile setting.

Three men approached and shook Ammond's and Persea's hands with much enthusiasm and backslapping. They were like Ammond: older, graying, and obviously used to getting their own way. One turned to Toby and stuck out his hand. "Naim M'boto."

Toby glanced at Ammond as he returned the crushing handshake. Ammond smiled and said, "We're among friends. You can tell him your real name."

"Toby Wyatt McGonigal," said Toby.

"Yes . . ." The man squinted at him. "Yes . . . well, we'll see about that." He turned to Ammond. "Any sign of trackers?"

Ammond shook his head. "We're clean, I swear. Though, even so, we should hurry things along . . ."

"Right." M'boto led the group down a flight of stairs. The glass walls on this level looked into hazy green water; the mirrored undersides of waves danced overhead. Fish darted about just out of reach; their exuberance captivated Toby and for a moment he forgot everything else.

"Toby? Over here." Persea was gesturing from the middle of the main room, which was as wide as the building and so looked into the water on two sides. This was a lounge or living room, with stone flooring, hidden lights, and just a single round white shag carpet in the middle. Four black couches were arranged around this, and clearly the space in the middle usually had low glass tables in it, but these had been pulled aside into a jumble near one wall. Between the couches was—

"Hey, that's a twentier!" Toby ran up to it.

Twentiers were mining bots, very tough, capable of independent action, and cheap. They were called twentiers because they were the twentieth version of something or other. This one looked kind of like a waist-high metal crab, its hard back scuffed and scratched to the point where you could barely make out the original yellow and black chevrons painted there. At its back end, under the carapace, there was an oval sample container, which was as tough as the rest of the bot.

"You know what this is?" said M'boto.

"Sure, we use –I mean, used . . . lots of these back on Sedna." He knelt down and checked the stamped serial numbers on the crab's side. "Actually, this looks like it *is* one of ours."

"These bots were locked to their owners' biocryptography," said M'boto. He was telling this to Ammond and Persea. Persea was chewing a fingernail, her eyes darting about as she listened. "DNA alone wouldn't unlock one," M'boto continued. "You needed a combination of that and voice, gait analysis, retinal scans, finger-prints, and so on, before it would accept you."

"Just like the differential encryption," said Ammond.

"This is the basis of Cicada Corp's power," said M'boto. "And this is an original twentier. We found it ourselves, fifteen years ago." He stepped up beside Toby. "Mr. McGonigal, you might be able to help us. We've been able to recharge this unit, but we can't get it to recognize our commands. I've tried, and so have Perdi and Rustoka, here." He indicated the other two men. "It just ignores us. Could you give it a go?"

Puzzled, Toby shrugged. "All right." He knelt in front of the bot, looking for its biometrics plates. There was one on either side of its blocklike head. He put his hands on the plates and looked into the deep black of its lenses. "Wake up, bot."

Nothing happened.

Then the twentier shook, just as Toby was pulling his hands back. It swayed from side to side, thrusting several legs out and curling them back in again. It raised itself its full half meter in height and said, "Ready," in a perfectly ordinary twentier voice.

Toby stood up. "There you go," he said, dusting his hands as he turned to his hosts.

They stood absolutely frozen, wide-eyed, and gaping at the bot in . . . was it fear? "What the—"

Ammond was the first to recover his poise. He stepped forward and clapped Toby on the shoulder. "Well done, son," he said in a low tone.

"I . . . I can't believe it," said Perdi. Rustoka just kept pulling at his collar, as if it was suddenly too tight.

Toby crossed his arms and glared at them all. "All right," he said in annoyance. "What's this all about?"

M'boto came unfrozen. He glanced at Ammond. "He doesn't know?"

Ammond shook his head. "But now's as good a time as any."

"Well." M'boto turned to Toby. Son, I think you should—"

"I'll do it," interrupted Ammond. He took Toby's arm and tugged him in the direction of the black couches. Suddenly nervous, Toby sat, and Ammond lowered himself opposite. The others stood in a tight knot, watching silently.

"You didn't wake me up and take care of me out of the goodness of your hearts, did you?" said Toby.

Ammond bobbed his head back and forth, neither admitting nor denying it. "We would have rescued anybody in your position. We're not monsters. But you, Toby, have a particular value nobody else could have." He nodded at the twentier, which had thumped back on its metal haunches and was scraping its carapace with a side leg. "Nobody else in the universe could have legitimately unlocked that bot. Only a McGonigal. You were right, Toby—it's one of yours."

He shook his head. "But that would make it—"

"Fourteen thousand years old. Sure—but it's been frozen in the ice, at nearly absolute zero, for that whole time. Preserved, just as you were. If it's from Sedna, as these men said—and if it's yours—then you really are a McGonigal."

Toby shook his head. "So what?"

"So what?" burst out M'boto. "Why, that makes you—"

"—The rightful owner of *Sedna*." Ammond glared at M'boto, who opened his mouth, seemed to think better of it, and closed it again.

Maybe it should have taken a moment for this to sink in, but really, Toby understood instantly. It was this exact sort of thing that had made his parents decide to flee the solar system to begin with.

"All the worlds are owned," he said. "Is that it?" Nobody answered.

"The trillionaires," he went on. "They owned everything on Earth, on Mars. They owned the moon, Mercury, Europa, and Titan. Either you owned a world, or you worked for those who did. It's like that here, isn't it?"

"Not as bad," Persea said hurriedly. "There's a lot more freedom in 360. But still . . . Toby, you have to realize. You own a world."

"Your parents' title to Sedna is still legal," Ammond explained. "The way the lockstep worlds skip forward through time, laws have to be recognized for thousands of years of realtime. Since you're the direct heir of the family that claimed the planet, Sedna is legally yours."

Toby sat back, crossing his arms. "And I suppose there's a lot there, now?" Somehow, all he felt right now was disappointment.

Ammond was nodding eagerly. "Cities, mines, launch facilities, bot factories, a whole ring of captured comets . . . it's the oldest of the lockstep worlds. Toby, you're one of the richest people in the lockstep."

For a while he just sat there, seething. They all watched him nervously. Then: "When were you planning on telling me?"

Persea came and sat down next to him. "Well, *you* tell *me* this," she said gently. "When would have been the proper time?"

She had him there, he had to admit. Still. He half turned away from her. "What's the catch? Why do we need them?" He looked at M'boto and his friends.

Ammond seemed relieved that Toby hadn't fainted or stormed off. "Two reasons," he said eagerly. "First of all, there's going to be resistance when you announce yourself. A lot of resistance. I mean, after all, there're layers of history on Sedna now; it's got its own

hereditary ruling families, and feuds and disputes and land settle-
ment claims going back . . . well, all the way. You may have legal
title to the planet, Toby, but you're going to need powerful allies to
make it stick.

"Secondly . . . well, you're not legally of age yet. Biologically, I
mean, which is how we have to judge it. That means you've got
two choices at this point: become a ward of the state or . . . let
someone adopt you."

Toby stared at him. Then he laughed. "And that someone would
just happen to be you?"

Ammond looked away. "I can't say I didn't think about the
possibility," he mumbled, "but it's your choice, ultimately."

"So that's why you've been so nice to me. Because I'm your
ticket to the trillionaires' club!" He jumped to his feet.

Ammond jumped up, too. "Now, Toby, don't be like that—"

M'boto made a motion with his chin, and Perdi and Rustoka
fanned out as if they meant to block Toby's exit. At some point the
domestic bots had followed them downstairs, and one stood right
in front of the stairway.

Toby assessed the situation. Then he snapped, "Twentier! Heel!"

The mining bot clattered over to crouch at his side. Chips flew
from the tile floor with every step it took. It was more than a match
for anything in this house and M'boto had to know it. "Come on,"
Toby said to it. "We're leaving."

"Oh, sit *down*!" It was Persea, but she wasn't talking to Toby.
She stood between him and the others, and was glaring at them.
"You, you stupid . . . boys!"

Toby hesitated. "This young man knows nothing about us,"
she went on. "Nothing! Why should he trust any of us? And if he
really is the Owner, then we're going to need that trust if he's to
help us. Sit down!"

The men sat. Toby had been watching, and now he said, "Help
you do what?"

Persea put a hand to her brow. She wasn't looking at Toby but
out the glass wall at the blue infinity there. "It's . . . political. A

matter of injustice and rights that need to be wronged. You probably won't care. But it's important to us." Now she did look at him. "I know you think Ammond and I are well-off. We are, I suppose, but we're the only ones in our families who can say that. Same's true for M'boto and these others. But our families—our communities—are suffering, and they'll keep suffering unless we find a way to free them.

"When Ammond and I found you, and realized who you might be . . . well, the temptation was just too much. Maybe, we thought, we could appeal to your better nature . . . but you have the right to do whatever you want. It's just . . . like Ammond said, it won't be easy to regain your birthright."

Toby glared at her. "Who says I want it?"

She came to stand in front of him, though she was wary of the twentier. "Toby, the one thing you have to get through your head is that certain people will never believe that you don't want it. As long as you're alive, you'll be a threat to them. That's why we've been sheltering you, not letting you say too much to people on the street . . . Just the knowledge that you exist is going to cause ripples through the whole lockstep."

Toby sat down heavily on the lowest step of the stairway. "You've got a deal for me, huh."

She glanced back at the men. "We've got some possibilities we can explore together, once you understand your situation a bit better. But clearly we've done too much today. Why don't we head back to the hotel and sort out how we all feel?"

Toby put his hand on the mining bot. "I'm taking this."

M'boto threw up his hands with an angry laugh. "You can't take that to a hotel! What, are you going to hide it in your luggage?"

Toby glared at him. "I'm not leaving it."

Ammond and M'boto held a quick whispering discussion, then M'boto turned back, nodding. "Well, why don't you stay here, then? For tonight, anyway. Maybe we do need to work on this 'trust' thing, like Persea said."

Toby thought about it. With the twentier as his guard, he had little to fear from these men. And he was determined not to let it out of his sight. "Okay," he said reluctantly.

Persea clapped her hands together, beaming. "It's a start," she said. "That's all we can ask."

HE'D PULLED AN ARMCHAIR in front of the glass wall of the underwater bedroom they'd given him. Toby had hoped that watching the fish would soothe him into sleep; he hadn't even tried the bed. Sleep wouldn't come, though, and much as he was trying to keep his sense of wonder about the silvery visions that slid by just a meter away, their darting movements were becoming more annoying than lulling.

Ammond and M'boto had done a lot more talking after Toby agreed to stay the night. There was stuff about the politics of the empire—a tyrant was mentioned, and more stuff about worlds cut off and other worlds forced to live on different frequencies, whatever that meant. Toby hadn't been able to keep it straight, though he knew it was important.

Now his mind refused to settle. He thought about Sedna; about Earth; about his family. What was he now, king of Sedna? That was weird, and ultimately meaningless. He just wanted to go home.

He reached around and patted the scuffed yellow dome of the twentier. "You're all I've got, boy."

It angled its lenses up at him. For a second Toby thought he was going to burst into tears.

He hopped up and paced, windmilling his arms. Every time he got near the room's one door, he glanced at it and frowned. Finally he reached out and pulled it open.

Two of M'boto's household bots stood just outside. "Is there anything you require, sir?" one asked.

"No, no, that's fine." So he really was a prisoner. Toby made to close the door but then noticed something.

The house was a long rectangle, and this room was at its offshore end. From here he had a good view down a hallway to the stairs and the lounge beyond it.

Ammond, Persea, M'boto, and six or seven other people were sitting there, discussing something. Hands were waving, heads were shaking and nodding. It looked important.

Now seriously uneasy, Toby listened carefully but couldn't make out what anybody was saying. Carefully, he closed the door and went to sit on the bed.

"I think we're in trouble," he said to the twentier.

Again, it just looked at him. He looked back, wondering now what it was really capable of. It wasn't a fighting machine. In fact, it probably had multiple layers of programming to keep it from harming anybody. Not three laws, but twenty or thirty. And no real weaponry, just its digging arms.

He knelt to examine it more closely. According to M'boto, it had been locked in a block of frozen nitrogen for fourteen thousand years. Time pretty much stopped at such temperatures. He ran his fingers along its carapace, and they stopped at a narrow, almost invisible seam at its back end.

If you didn't know this was here, you'd probably never notice it. "Hey, twentier," he said softly, "could you open your CPU maintenance hatch for me?"

There was a clank, and the container's lid popped up. "Huh." He reached inside and felt something squarish and hard. What he brought out was a flat data block, about two hand spans long. Gingerly, he pulled it out and turned it over, looking for a label. It looked like standard backup drive, not at all surprising to find one of these things. But it could contain a record of all that the twentier had seen and done since the block was installed.

Something bumped against the glass wall.

Toby nearly dropped the block. Somehow he'd jumped from the floor to the bed without thinking. He blinked at the dark mirror of the wall. It was night now and the few fish he'd seen in the past minutes had only been dimly lit by the lamps in the room.

"Twentier, can you shine a light out there?"

He'd forgotten that the twentier's "light" was an incredibly powerful spotlight, which instantly dazzled Toby and created a hazy cone through the water outside. A couple of minnows swam through it, but there was nothing else.

That bump must have been his imagination. "Turn it off," he said. Then he thought of something.

"Hey, have you got acoustic sensors?"

The twentier laboriously turned its crab body back to face him. "Janus Industries Squatbot Model Twenties are equipped with the latest in acoustic depth-finding and materials-sensing technologies," it said. "This technology allows us to do sonar exploration of solid rock and ice faces to a depth of—"

"Fine, fine. Can you amplify the sounds coming from the far end of the house?" He jabbed a thumb at the door.

"Yes, sir." The twentier waddled up to the door and placed two of its metal arms against it. Suddenly voices filled the room.

"Why should we trust you?" He didn't recognize the voice. It was a woman's, dry and sarcastic. She reminded Toby of a teacher he'd once had. "You work for the Chairman."

"We did," Ammond replied. "So of course we told him the instant we found out who we'd recovered. In hindsight I should have known what that would mean to him. The Chairman himself ordered us to kill the boy."

Toby sucked in a shocked breath. *Kill?* Somebody had ordered Ammond to kill him?

"It would be . . . such a waste." That was Persea's voice. "But we didn't have the resources for the obvious alternative. That's why we're here."

More was said, but Toby couldn't take it in. Ammond and Persea had been working for somebody else—somebody who wanted Toby dead. They'd refused and, what? Run away? So they weren't traveling when they'd come here; they were *fleeing*?

One of the voices penetrated his fog of shock. ". . . So it comes down to a choice: Ammond's idea of a fait accompli, where we head straight to Destrier to wake the mother, or Catai's proposal to build a force from the edges."

"It'll never work! The Chairman'll slap us down faster than we can swap the worlds out."

"Yes, but under my proposed system—"

"—introduces one more layer of complexity—"

"What about the boy?"

That was M'boto's voice. Toby felt a prickling along the nape of his neck, and he suddenly had to sit down. He put an arm around the twentier's carapace for reassurance.

"We're just putting off the other decision," M'boto went on. "You most of all, Ammond. I can see you've grown attached to him. Is this going to be an issue?"

"No no." Ammond's denial came out in a rush. "I'll accept the will of the majority."

"He's a problem," said M'boto. "Rustoka and Perdi can attest to how defiant and suspicious he is. If he's like this when he only has part of the truth, what's he going to be like when he hears all of it?"

"It's not like we can hide it from him," somebody else said.

"I still say he can be brought around," objected Ammond.

"Yes, but can it be done in time? That's the whole point here. We don't have the time now the Chairman knows you have him. And Persea said it herself: how are we ever going to trust him?"

"If he's your legal heir, sir—"

"But that'll happen anyway. No, I say we put the neuroshackle on him now and be done with it."

"I don't think—" Ammond began, but M'boto cut him off. "We can't have any uncertainties at this stage. We need to be absolutely sure he'll comply. No more discussion, let's put it to a vote."

Toby stood up and backed away. What was a neuroshackle? He'd heard stories about Mars, where slaves' loyalty was guaranteed by brain surgery. Was this—?

"In favor?" There was a chorus of *ayes*. "Against?" Ammond, and somebody else, said *nay*.

"Jax, get the psych bot. If we get it out of the way right now we can move on to other matters."

Toby found that his back was against the cold glass wall. He'd been swearing, backing away. But there was nowhere left to go, and he heard footsteps now, approaching the door . . .

Bump.

He shouted and whirled. Something was out there, in the black water. He grabbed one of the oval table lamps next to the bed and held it close to the glass.

Two huge golden eyes reflected the light. They were looking straight at him. The eyes were set in a catlike face, and behind it a lithe, twisting body whose fur was swirling in the currents. It swam back, then darted forward again, bumping against the glass as if it were trying to break through.

He'd seen this creature before, in a courtyard in Lowdown. That time, it hadn't been alone . . .

He heard the door behind him sighing open; he was out of time.

"Twentier! I need to get through this wall!"

"Yes, sir."

There was a shout, calls for help, and feet running up behind him, but Toby had braced his feet against the armchair and pressed his hands against the glossy wall. So when the twentier smashed through the transparent plexi and ice water poured in around him and swept away the men and bots who'd been about to seize him, Toby was able to jump straight into the oncoming surge.

As the twentier tumbled into the bottomless abyss below the city, the cold exploded into Toby from all sides. He choked and it came into his lungs as well.

| Four |

HANDS OR PAWS OR grippies had hold of him. They hauled him over a rough wall and Toby sprawled, retching, among nets and floats and dead fish.

Blurred silhouettes surrounded him—people and some smaller shapes with tall pointed ears, which were aiming those ears at him like antennae. Past this jumble of motion and noisy voices, he could see a dimly lit night sky that seemed to be paved with icebergs.

He took a couple of whooping breaths and knew he wasn't going to drown, but he was shuddering from the cold. Then, suddenly, like a switch being thrown, the cold vanished. In its place, he felt a pleasant warmth spreading out from the core of his body.

"Aw, crap," somebody said. "His implants have kicked in. They're putting him into stasis."

Speckles and lozenges of light were floating in his vision now, and he was finding it hard to chase his last thought. Despite himself, he found himself nodding, his eyes drifting closed.

A deep vibration had joined the warmth; it seemed to be coming from all around him. The sound was like the purr of a cat, only deeper and more powerful. He lay in its grip for what seemed like forever and then heard an answering vibration—a second purr. Only this one was coming from *inside* him.

Cold rushed back into him, and suddenly he was lying on the deck of a boat, shuddering again and coughing. "Nice work, um, we really should name you," somebody said.

As his eyes refocused, Toby followed the sound of the voice and discovered that he was sitting across from the black-haired girl whom he'd seen once in Ammond's courtyard and once outside his cicada bed. She was seated, feet planted wide apart, on a crate under the ship's wheel, her face lit by the green starboard light. Even if he hadn't recognized her face, she wore the same long-tailed coat he'd seen her in the first time. This time he noticed a distinctive locket that glimmered at her throat: a miniature tree inside an oval shape. She reached up absently to touch it with one hand as she rubbed the water off the catlike creature's back.

"Somebody bring him a blanket," she added, as if Toby's chattering and shivering were an afterthought.

He was handed a coarse gray square of cloth that he wrapped around himself. Only then did he realize that there were three other people on the boat besides himself. The vessel itself was small; if you lay down you could practically stretch across its width, and a few paces would take you stem to stern. It was crowded.

A man with skin black as the Sedna sky knelt in front of Toby. "You okay?" His accent was thick but musical and pleasant. Toby couldn't place it.

"Y-yeah. Thanks for—" Well, he wasn't sure what for. He gestured weakly at the water. "Well, you know."

The man laughed. "Sure." He stuck out a beefy hand. "I'm Shylif." He wore a long capelike hooded coat, similar to the girl's, with more layers of black clothing half visible beneath it. "That's Corva." He indicated the girl, who was now working at something with her back to them. "And this is Jaysir." Over at the other rail, a thin-faced young man with uneven stubble on his chin grunted and let go his death grip on the gunwale just long enough to wave. He was swaddled in some sort of bright yellow survival suit and seemed to be trying to fight every pitch and roll of the boat, his body rigid with the effort.

"Toby."

Shylif laughed again. "You really are, are you? Well, it doesn't matter right now. You're going to go back into hibernation if we don't get you properly warmed up." He stood and looked ahead but didn't put his hand on the wheel. The boat seemed to be steering itself.

"They've spotted us." It was the girl—Corva—who was also standing now, looking back the way they'd come. Toby heard faint sirens coming from the receding glitter of city lights.

"Uh, guys? Less talk, more motion," Jaysir said through gritted teeth. "They're gonna be on us any second now. Sheez, you just had to poke the hypermafia in the eye, didn't you?"

The boat, at least, seemed to be paying attention, as it suddenly accelerated through the choppy waves.

Toby looked at the three of them; they made an unlikely rescue squad. "What were you doing out here anyway?"

Jaysir barked an angry laugh. "Talk to Shylif, it was his idea. 'Outflank them' or something, right, Shy?" He shook his head mockingly.

The creature that had tapped on his window appeared at Toby's feet. "And then *this* one . . ." Jaysir rolled his eyes. "Dove out of the boat and we spent ten minutes looking for him. Then what happens? He surfaces with you in tow!"

Little amber eyes met Toby's. He reached out cautiously, and when it let him, he smoothed his hand between its ears. "Thanks . . . What's his name?"

"Doesn't have one," said Jaysir. "Not yet."

There were two more of the creatures in the boat. They wouldn't have taken up much room except that they kept squirming around each other and the humans, running from side to side and looking all around with excited curiosity. "These guys, though," added Jaysir. "Meet Rex and Shadoweye."

Rex had paused to dramatically peer into the darkness off the bow of the boat. That prompted Toby to look out as well. Ahead was . . . nothing. Misty blackness. "Where are we going?"

"Just somewhere to lay low for a while," said the girl. "Unless you want to go back?" He shook his head violently. She *hmmphed.*

"Well, this is great and all, Corva," said Jaysir, "so when were you going to tell us you'd given this guy"—he nodded at the wet creature—"a depth charge?"

"I didn't," said the girl.

"Well, how did he blow that underwater window, then?"

"I did it," croaked Toby.

"What?"

"I broke the window. They were coming for me, to do something . . . to neuroshackle me."

Shylif muttered something and shook his head; Jaysir swore. Corva threw her shoulders back and stared the other two down. "Lucky we were here, then, wasn't it?" she said. Jaysir shrugged and looked down.

"Jay, you should check him for trackers," Shylif said. Jaysir jerked as if someone had given him an electrical shock and forgot about his death grip on the gunwale as he rummaged through a backpack at the stern of the boat. He brought out a long green rod that he waved around Toby.

"Yep, he's hot. There's a whole bunch of them, but nothing I haven't seen before. Just give me one minute, and I'll disable them." He made some adjustments on the rod and waved it more slowly at various points around Toby's torso. "Now, you may feel some little explosions in there . . ."

"He's joking," Shylif said hastily. In any case Toby felt nothing, and after a short time Jaysir grunted in satisfaction and returned his device to the pack. He said, "Nobody's gonna track him now, except, oh, wait, we're out in the *open water,* anybody who looks can just *see* us!"

"Patience, Jay," muttered Shylif. The boat continued to pound through the waves.

There was silence for a while as they followed a circuitous route around down-drooping sections of ice ceiling, some of which touched the water. In places the ceiling rose, too, to become lost in misty darkness above. There were other boats in the water and lights below the surface.

Toby put a hand on his chest. "What did you mean earlier about me going into stasis? And what was that? The purring sound, me falling asleep like that . . . ?"

Jaysir stared at him and laughed, shaking his head. Shylif said, "Give him a break, Jay, some of us didn't grow up with hibernation implants in us."

"Is that what—?"

"They're artificial organs that help you go in and out of hibernation. They hadn't been invented yet . . . where you come from."

Toby shook his head, though Persea had told him about them. He supposed he hadn't actually believed they were real.

He was still freezing, and spray kept sheeting up behind him, sometimes sprinkling across his head and neck. The thought of the bottomless ocean below them was making him queasy, too. But he sat up straighter when Shylif said, "The purring . . . well, that was this little guy." He patted the animal that was sitting at Toby's feet. It accepted the rough mashing of its ears without complaint. "He kept you from going under."

Toby had no idea what to ask about that, so he moved on. "Why were you out here at all? And why'd you follow me from Lowdown?" He looked at Corva as he said this.

Corva shrugged. "We found out who you were, and we knew a little about the people who'd picked you up. It didn't seem like a . . . healthy place for you to come back to us."

Hypermafia, Jaysir had called them. Toby had to laugh at Corva's understatement. But: "How did you find out about me? Nobody else in seventy thousand worlds did, apparently." He tried to keep bitterness out of his voice. "And why should you care?"

Corva and Shylif exchanged glances. Toby was getting really tired of that kind of glance. Corva said, "As to why we care, it's a shame you even have to ask. This one"—she patted the creature with the golden eyes—"had spotted you inside and said you were scared. I don't know how you broke the window, but we saw you in the water, and . . . well, you're important, and that means you're valuable."

"Ah," said Toby. "Some honesty at last."

"Well, I don't know what those other people had planned, but *we* have no intention of keeping you against your will," she said.

"Speak for yourself," said Jaysir. "I think a little ransom might go a long way right about now."

Shylif rolled his eyes but said, "It's no mystery how we found you in the first place. We're stowaways, after all."

When Toby just stared at him, mystified, Corva said, "That means we wake up before everybody else, and we usually go into hibernation after everybody else has gone to sleep. So we were awake on the transport ship that had brought us to Lowdown when your people started filling the airwaves with chatter. We spotted them reeling in your little ship, and when the city's net booted up later that week we matched up what we'd seen to the historical records. I was visiting the place they'd taken you for . . . my own reasons . . . and just as I was leaving you came running out of the building like an army was on your tail. I guessed who you must be, and I knew you'd be confused and all, but what was I to do? Take you and run? They'd have chased us down."

The boat had been bobbing through dark, ill-defined spaces for a while now. Ahead were city lights but sparser than those in the metropolis they'd left behind. Shylif steered the boat in the direction of a run-down dock at the edge of an indistinct jumble of lights.

"Wait," Toby said, "you hibernate illegally? On *ships*."

It was Jaysir this time who gave a crooked grin and spread his arms, saying, "Welcome to the vagabond life! We don't work—but then, neither do most people. We travel, but so does everybody else. The difference is we don't let the government track us."

"And we don't let them tell us when we can go into hibernation and when we have to come out of it," said Shylif.

"In other words, we're free—or as free as you can be in a lock-step," finished Corva.

"And what do you want from me?"

"There're only two things anybody's gonna want from you," she said. "To help them continue the oppression and exploitation of seventy thousand worlds—or set those worlds free."

They pulled up to the dock, which was built of water-worn plastics and carbon fiber. Toby had yet to see wood on this world. Jaysir tied up the boat and proceeded to strip off the garish survival gear. Underneath it he wore the orange leggings of a counterpressure suit and a thermal muscle shirt whose battery pack hung loosely from his belt. He was as scrawny as his face had suggested.

The ice ceiling dipped nearly to water level in this region, and sometimes past it. These squashed spaces were jammed with a great bewildering clutter of buildings—some above the surface, some glowing below it—joined by catwalks, pontoon roads, and tunnels melted through the turquoise ice.

"We're camping out up here," said Shylif, nodding to the complicated mess. "You're welcome to join us for a meal . . . or you could always go back to the people who brought you here."

"What if I went to the police?"

"That would either be the safest move for you, or the most dangerous," said Corva as she clambered out of the tilting boat. "You may know which, but we sure don't."

Back on Earth, the police had officially served the public, but in reality, they'd worked for the trillionaires. Toby looked back at the boat, which he wasn't sure would take orders from him, then at the cold blank water, then at the icebound buildings, where bright spotlights harshly lit the tunnels.

"Look, we're not after selling you," said Corva. "You can walk away right now. Go on." She made a shooing motion, aiming Toby in the direction of a pontoon road that wandered away over fog-capped water.

"You know I can't go back."

"Then come with us or walk away—but make a decision!" She spun on her heel, the tails of her coat belling out, and stalked off. Her friends followed her, two of the catlike animals dancing around their feet. The third one sat and stared up at Toby, unblinking, until he said, "Oh, all right!" He set off after the others.

Up ahead was a cavern with four towering factory façades built into its icy sides. The space between them was utter bedlam—driverless freight carriers shot out of tunnels and slammed through the space at a hundred kilometers per hour, smaller vehicles rumbled through in four directions without stopping, and bots sauntered among them all. There were half a dozen narrow misses every second, but no collisions—and Corva and her friends walked right down the center of the road and into it all. Flinching and jumping at the humming, careering traffic, Toby tried to keep up.

He trusted machine vision and reflexes, but he hadn't been in a place like this before, either on Earth or Sedna. Toby breathed a huge sigh of relief when they reached the far side and Corva clattered down a flight of metal steps into a structure that was half embedded in ice, the other half plunging into the cold depths below.

"Anyway," said Shylif as if there'd been no break in the conversation, "sell a McGonigal? That would be suicidal."

"Much better to have one on our side," said Jaysir.

It wasn't significantly quieter inside the building. Dim lights sketched a hostile tangle of rumbling machines, zigzagging catwalks and scrambling bots. This was where the real work of the city happened, clearly—but it was bots doing it. There wasn't another human in sight.

Corva suddenly turned to Shylif and said, "Told you we'd be back in time for your shift." He sighed and nodded.

Luckily they didn't move into that intimidating maze of machinery but headed down another flight of stairs. Toby expected a windowless room, but when they came out of the stairwell it was into a long glass-walled gallery that looked out into the deep ocean. The factory noise from above had become a muffled background drone. Sleeping rolls were laid out on the floor here, as well as a couple of little camp stoves. Some of the sleeping rolls had big backpacks next to them.

Shylif went to a jumble of bright machinery near the glass. He snapped something onto his wrist, and a suit began to build itself onto his body—not a space suit, however. Through the glass behind him Toby could make out blue ocean under an undulating ceiling of ice, its higher points inhabited by juddering silvery bubbles of air. This pale blue-green surface was lit by bright lamps that stretched far into the indigo distance; below them, all was black.

"You're going out in that?" Toby asked.

"Right," said Shylif, glancing behind himself. "It's not nearly as interesting as it looks. I'll see you all later." With that he let the diving suit's helmet cover his head and then walked to a set of heavy doors at the end of the gallery.

"Stamina," said Jaysir. "Ah, to be young again!"

"He's twice your age," Corva pointed out.

Toby watched as the doors closed and, a minute later, a burst of bubbles and froth spewed into the water somewhere off to the right. Shylif's silvery form shot into the dark water and disappeared.

"Everybody, this is Clark," Corva was saying.

Toby finally noticed the other people in the gallery. Jaysir had joined several other young men at the camp stoves, where an elderly man and two middle-aged women also sat. They greeted Corva's team in a friendly way, but all eyes were on Toby. He grinned weakly and tried to look harmless.

"That's cool," he said, aiming a thumb at the dark water.

Clark? When he realized that Corva had meant him, he nearly corrected her, not because he didn't know what she was doing but because he couldn't picture himself as somebody named Clark. Apparently these five could, though, as they accepted the name with nods. "I'm Dorvas." "Nix." "Elden," said the older man. "Sofial." "Salome."

"We were just about to eat," said William. "Care to join us?"

"S-sure," said Toby. Jaysir shot him a warning look and Corva shook her head. "Maybe later." Jaysir proceeded to spin out an elaborate and loud story about some adventure or other they'd been on all day—one that didn't include boats—and all eyes turned to him.

Corva headed to a corner under a window and plunked herself onto one of the rolls. Rex leaped off her shoulder and went to greet several others of his kind that had emerged from somewhere.

Corva's kit consisted of a sleeping roll, backpack, and a rather nice-looking exoskeleton that was currently rolled into a ball next to the blanket. She wore the same olive-green tunic and black leggings she'd had on the first time he saw her on Lowdown. Still, she didn't have the air of true poverty about her that Toby had seen back on Earth.

"Until you prove to me that you can blend in, you don't talk to people, *Clark*," she said.

He crossed his arms indignantly. "The name is Garren Morton, if you must know," he said. How could she not think he could handle himself in a situation like this? He'd done things like it before, in Consensus and the many other simulations he and his brother and sister had spent so much time in. Being streetwise in strange situations was necessary in those games, and Toby felt he was pretty good at it.

"Yeah?" She raised a dark eyebrow. "Is that a *new* name, or one you were given by the very people who're looking for you now?" He blushed, realizing his mistake. She continued, "You just asked where Shylif was going. You should already know."

Now, that, she surely had no right to say. "Why?"

She sighed. "Because it's basic. Look, in this lockstep, most work is done by bots—and most of that's done while we're all hibernating. They gather resources while the worlds are frozen over, they build stuff and stockpile it. But . . . well, here's a little quiz question for you: who can own bots?"

"Robots? What do you mean, *who*?"

"There, you see?" She threw up her hands. "Only individual, living human beings can legally own multipurpose robots, and the owners must not be in hibernation for a whole turn. Corporations can't own general-purpose bots, they can only own single-purpose machines like the production-line stuff upstairs, or vehicles and such. So that means that all the bots working upstairs are owned by individual people—mostly the people in the city back there." She jabbed a thumb at the far wall.

"So the corporations pay the *bots* to work for them, not humans like they did in ancient times. Right?" Reluctantly, he nodded. "Then the bots hand over their wages to their owners. That's how most people live. But stowaways like us . . . well, some of us don't want to be found. We can't send out registered bots to work for us. Shylif's like that. If he's going to make any money at all, he has to do it outside the normal economy. So he subcontracts to the factory bots."

Toby was trying to keep up. "He . . . *works* for them?"

"He carries stuff, does light maintenance work, things like that. For the bots, yes. That way they don't have to work, which minimizes wear and tear on them. They pay him less than the factory's paying them, but at least it's something. And so, he can buy the things he needs."

She leaned forward. "You need to know this stuff or you're going to stick out like a sore tooth."

"Don't you mean sore thumb?"

She ignored the comment. "Look, you're the ultimate hyper-rich kid, Toby. And more, you're . . ." She seemed to think better of saying what that *more* was. "I don't know how you feel about it all, but it makes me pretty uncomfortable, and I had a little warning about what you were. If more people find out . . . I don't know what will happen. So be careful."

Toby hugged himself, staring down and at the gray walls and at the cavorting furred things. "I want to know," he said. "But nobody's told me anything that makes any sense."

"Well. You know who you are, right?" He nodded. "So does everybody else. Every single human being on all seventy thousand of our lockstep worlds, and all the other locksteps and probably most of the fast worlds, has heard of Toby McGonigal and his family. You're one of the most famous people in history."

"But . . ." He shook his head. "That makes no sense. No sense at all."

Corva pressed her fists against her temples and yawned extravagantly. "Well, it should. If you really do know who you are."

"And who are you? You haven't even told me your name."

"My name's Corva Keishion," she said. "My Universal Number's 14-Tourmaline. Have you got a URN?"

He shook his head, eyeing her with uneasy confusion. She sighed in annoyance, but he didn't care anymore. He just couldn't keep up—and now he was yawning, too, and shivering again.

"You're still wet," Corva observed. She went to rummage in the heap where Shylif had gotten his diving suit and came back with a hollow metal tube. "Try this." She thumbed the outside of the tube and it immediately began blasting hot air at Toby. "Ow!" *Very* hot air.

"I'll stand back. This baby's industrial, it's not meant for hair." She walked back a couple of paces and began waving the tube at Toby like a wand, head to foot. Warmth washed over him. Corva kept yawning extravagantly, and once she was finished with the heater she simply walked over to her bedroll and, without another word to Toby, lay down on it and fell asleep. Her furry companion came over to curl up under her arms. The unnamed one, who seemed to have adopted Toby, came over to sit at his feet.

Jaysir was watching, and after a few more words to the others seated around the stove, he joined Toby as well. "Quite the force of nature, isn't she?" he said, nodding at Corva.

Toby snorted in agreement. He definitely wanted to know more about Corva, but she'd told him he was too ignorant of this future he'd found himself in. He'd have to fix that problem.

"Jaysir," he said, "can I ask you something? "What's a neuroshackle?"

"NAH, I WON'T TELL her story," Jaysir said a little while later. "If Corva wants you to know it, she can tell you herself." They were sitting in a quiet corner, with two of the furry creatures Jaysir had said were denners.

Jaysir might not want to tell Corva's story for her, but he was entirely happy to tell his own, and Shylif's. He'd readily explained what a neuroshackle was, and it was every bit as horrible as Toby had suspected: a means of turning a person into a puppet, willing to do anything for his master, even murder or suicide. Ammond and Persea had been willing, even eager, to make Toby into a slave. He didn't know Jaysir, Corva, and Shylif, but he already felt safer here than he had since awaking on Lowdown.

"This is Shylif's guy, Shadoweye," Jaysir had said to introduce his gold-and-white companion. The other one, which was notably smaller and completely black except for his golden eyes, was still sticking close to Toby, and Jaysir smiled. "You might have to name this guy yourself."

"Who does he belong to?"

"Corva got him for her brother, but . . ." Jaysir shrugged, "that might not work out. We'll have to see."

"What about you? Don't you have a denner? You're a stowaway, too, right?"

"Oh, I use *that*." Jaysir pointed to another corner where a mass of tangled, glittering equipment lay on the concrete under the watchful eye of a hulking cargo bot. "Built it myself. Way more trustworthy than some weird animal, if you ask me. And it's legal—I got a license for it!—'cause I'm not building them for commercial use." Toby couldn't imagine a comfortable way to incorporate oneself into that heap of metal and piping but decided not to say anything.

"Shylif's an outsider, too," said Jaysir now. "And it's a hell of a tale.

"He grew up on Nessus, one of the Alpha Centauri worlds. It's a fast world, terraformed thousands of years ago—but there are lockstep fortresses there."

"Fortresses?"

"Yeah, on fast worlds like Earth or Nessus, lockstep communities need special protection from the elements and vandals and stuff. Shylif's village had grown up around a fortress, which is pretty common. Every thirty years, the fortress's gates would open, and the lockstep people would pour out for a month of celebration and fraternizing with the townspeople. Jubilee, they call it, when two worlds are awake at the same time. Locksteps Jubilee, too, like when 360 and 72 sync up, every two turns for us, every ten for them. Anyway, the last Jubilee had happened about twelve years before Shylif was born. That's the funny thing—you grow up with stories and evidence of these mysterious people from the fortress, and you hope to meet them just once in your whole life. Just as he was becoming a man, Shylif met them.

"Thing is, he was deeply in love. Childhood sweetheart kind of thing, and she loved him, too. When the fortress opened, they both went to meet the people who lived in it. There were the usual parties and tours and stuff. What Shylif didn't know was that there was a man visiting the fortress from somewhere else in the lockstep who had taken a fancy to his girl.

"On the last day of the month, the town held their traditional big send-off for the locksteppers. Shylif lost track of Ouline, his girl. Next morning he asked around, but nobody'd seen her. Gradually it dawned on him: she was still inside the fortress.

"There was nothing to be done. The place was impregnable, and it wasn't going to open again for another three decades."

"That's . . . awful," said Toby. The words felt foolish, not even remotely able to express the despair Shylif must have felt. "What did he do?"

Jaysir looked down, then met Toby's eyes. "He waited."

"He waited for her for thirty years, and when the fortress opened its gates the next time, he was standing there, still waiting.

"Ouline emerged, and she hadn't aged a day. But Shylif had, and so had everybody else she'd known. Her parents were dead, her brothers were grandfathers already. She told Shylif that she'd been lured by a man named Coley, who'd seduced her on the last night of the Jubilee and abandoned her to sleep in one of the rooms of the fortress. He'd deliberately stranded her.

"For Ouline, only a single night had passed—in the blink of an eye she'd lost her whole world, her parents, friends. Even the trees and buildings were different. She couldn't handle what had happened. She . . . she killed herself."

"Aw, no."

Jaysir nodded. "And Shylif, who'd waited thirty years for her, had nothing left. Nothing but revenge. He went hunting Coley, but Coley fled the fortress. Shylif followed and ended up wintering over in another lockstep city. Just like her, in one night"—he snapped his fingers—"he left behind everybody he'd ever known. He's been after Coley ever since. Corva and I met him because he thinks the little monster's gone to ground on Thisbe, her homeworld."

Toby sat back, trying to imagine what Shylif's life had been like. Not like a life lived on Earth in his time. More like something out of ancient history. "And what about you?" he asked.

"I'm a maker." He waited for Toby to react and seemed disappointed at the blank expression he got. "You know? Makers? People who are their own industrial economy?" He nodded at his complicated-looking bot. "Built entirely by me. It does everything—made my clothes, made the fabric for the clothes, mined the hydrocarbons to make the polyester . . . Between me and it, we don't take any resources from the lockstep. *That's* a maker. Me, though, my thing is collecting procedural computer code. It's incredibly rare, but I have one of the biggest collections in the lockstep!" Suddenly he looked shy. "You probably have no idea what I'm talking about."

"Computer programs. Preneuromorphic computers, the digital type?"

Jaysir slapped the concrete floor in delight. "Yes! You do know!"

"Well, we had a few on Sedna. They're good for databases and . . . stuff." A lot of Consensus had run on those old machines, but anything that had to interact with the real world—like the twentier—was based on artificial neurons. That reminded him of the data block he'd found in the little robot's cargo bin. Should he show that to Jaysir?

"I've built my own code library!" Jaysir rattled on about it, but Toby's eyes were starting to cross. The day's adventures had caught up with him, and after a while he waved a hand and said, "I'm only understanding every fifth word you say. 'Cause I'm tired."

"Ah, sure." Jaysir laughed good-naturedly. "I can put even Shylif to sleep talking about this stuff. Crash for a while, then. You can use my roll. We'll probably need to be on the move soon anyway."

Gratefully, Toby rolled himself onto Jaysir's bedding and, just like Corva, fell instantly asleep.

SOMETHING COLD TOUCHED TOBY'S nose. He started awake, to find the two golden eyes of the little denner centimeters from his own. He grinned at it. "Well, hello. Did I oversleep?"

He remembered everything that had happened over the past days, but somehow, at least for now, that small touch made everything okay. The gallery looked exactly the same when he sat up, but its other inhabitants were gone. Jaysir, Corva, and Shylif were waiting with breakfast: dry rolls and fruit, which Toby devoured voraciously. Nobody spoke while he did this. Shylif showed him where to refresh himself, and then they all sat down cross-legged on the floor and looked at each other.

Finally Toby had to break the silence. "What now?"

"They're looking for you," said Shylif. "It's not a police alert; there's a private query gone around to all the bots and now they'll be keeping an eye out."

"So whoever they are, they don't want the authorities to know about you," added Corva. "Which just goes with our theory that they're dissidents or revolutionaries."

Toby scratched his head. "Oh, I dunno about that. They seemed more interested in money than anything."

"Whatever. The point is, they're after you, and I don't think you want to announce yourself to the police either."

"Why not?"

There was that glance between Shylif and Corva again. "Fine! What do you suggest, then?"

Corva reached behind her, making a *tsk-tsk* sound. Her furry companion popped its head out from behind her hip, then climbed into her lap and began its deep, droning purr.

"I'd suggest you try to make a new friend," said Corva, patting Rex's head. "But it looks like you've already done it." She smiled at the little black denner who was sitting loyally next to Toby. "You'll need a denner. Otherwise, you'll have to find a cicada bed at the end of the month—and you can bet they'll be watching all of those, legal and gray tech."

Toby wasn't going to say no to the little guy by his foot, but— "Jaysir said you bought this one for your brother."

She shot a sharp look at the self-styled maker. "What did you tell him?"

Jaysir shrugged. "What he says. You bought it for Halen."

Corva's own denner walked over, and Toby leaned down to stroke his head. "Can he—Rex, right?" he asked Corva, "can he really do everything a cicada bed does? Keep you alive through deep-dive hibernation? Even frozen solid?"

She reached down, too, and put her hands on either side of the furry face and rubbed. Ears and whiskers tilted back and forth, but the purring never slowed.

She nodded. "Yep. And yeah, that's his name. As in, 'Wrecks everything.'"

Wrecks turned his head and gave Toby a slow two-eyed wink.

SOMEBODY HAD SET UP a printer near the airlock, so Jaysir printed some watertight cases for their things, as well as transparent carriers for Wrecks and the other denners. Then they kicked through the parts heap until they found the makings of three diving suits, and Corva, Shylif and Toby let them climb onto their bodies. Jaysir watched, arms crossed. "You're not coming?" Toby asked the maker, who guffawed.

"Trust myself to that bottomless Hell? Forget it, I'm gonna walk. Besides"—he gestured behind him to where the cargo bot was gathering up his complicated hibernation gear—"salt water's not good for my stuff. I'll meet you guys there."

"They won't be watching for him," Shylif added. "It's you we're hiding."

Moments later Toby found himself in an airlock that, for the first time in his life, was not going to turn him over to vacuum on the other side.

"It's funny," he said, feeling the need to talk as water gushed in around his feet. "We were drilling on Sedna when I left. It's got this big subsurface ocean, but it was kilometers down. Dad always said we'd be ocean people someday, but it never happened while I was there."

"It did happen, Toby," Corva said. She sounded sad, and the words made him feel that way, too.

He felt a claustrophobic panic as the water rose over the faceplate of his suit. Before he could react, it was above his head; when he could convince himself that he was still breathing, the panic began to recede and he suddenly thought, *What about the poor denners?* He lifted the carrying case that held his and found two calm eyes gazing back. He had time to notice a little readout on the top that said it had five hours of remaining air; then the airlock's outer door opened.

This was not like being in space. There, Toby felt cradled in a way, by weightlessness and infinity. When he stepped out of this lock he immediately began to sink, and what was below, he knew, was far more hostile than vacuum.

"Clark, turn on your belt thrusters." It was Corva's voice, calm, almost droll.

"How? —Wait. Belt thrusters on!"

"No, silly. The big *switch* on your *belt*."

He got the thrusters going and, when he knew they were keeping him up, finally snuck a look around. This was *not* space. The pearly ice ceiling stretched away to infinity on all sides; bright lamps were stuck in it at intervals, creating a regular pattern of white stars that, in the far distance, blurred together into a deepening blue line. They made the hazy water visible for many meters below, revealing its gorgeous color and the thousands of bizarre and wonderful living things that swam, pulsed, and snaked through it. Some looked like fish, though they had no eyes. They might all be native, or imported, or this whole biosphere might be bioengineered. Toby didn't know and didn't care: what mattered was that they were alive.

The ice was punctured here and there by giant square holes; factory machines and long pipes stuck down into water, and cables drooped into the depths.

"This way," said Shylif as he jetted off to the right. "We could walk, of course, but there're fewer eyes down here. Fewer eyes on things that can talk," he added as a gape-jawed monstrosity thrashed past him.

"Does this ocean go all around the planet?" Toby asked.

Shylif jabbed a thumb at the ice overhead. "Think of that as a continent," he said. "Like any continent, it floats on the planet's mantle, only in this case the continent's made of ice, not rock, and the mantle isn't made of magma, it's water. And that water goes—" he tilted over to look down—"so deep that it might as well be rock, it's compressed so hard. Hot ice, harder than steel, that's the only bottom to this ocean. Anything from up here that fell down there would be unrecognizably squished long before it got to the hot ice layer."

Toby thought of his mining bot and felt a little jab of remorse. It had sacrificed itself for him. He clutched his denner's carrying case more tightly.

In the depths below, gigantic black-on-black shapes moved. Toby hoped they were machines. Luckily Shylif wasn't taking them that way; he angled his jets up at one of the big square openings and for a few minutes they wove in and out of a forest of metal pipes that extended down from it into the limitless abyss. Then the surface appeared above, as opaque as shimmering foil until Toby pierced it. He found himself on the surface among those pipes, which angled up and into the faceless façades of machines that squatted like abstract fishermen around the opening.

"This way." Shylif was heading toward a set of iron steps that descended into the water.

"What do they do here?"

"The ice is almost pure water. So's the ocean. They use electrolysis to slowly pull metals and other elements out of the ocean, but it takes decades to accumulate enough for a month's worth of industrial production. These are the machines that pull it in. But that's not why we're here. We're here 'cause this is where the gray market is."

There were no bots on the metal floor at the top of the steps. Nothing moved at all, in fact, though Toby could hear a thrumming vibration as of giant pumps laboring nearby. The space was well lit and he felt exposed here; still, they paused while Shylif and Corva let their denners out of the capsules they'd traveled here in. Not a drop of water had touched Wrecks's fur, but as he climbed out of the container he shook himself as though he'd just had a dunking and gave something that was midway between a chatter and a meow.

Toby stared at the denner. Growing up he'd always longed for a pet of his own, but he'd never had the courage to ask for one. Taking care of another living creature was an awesome responsibility, one that demanded the greatest of respect and consideration. Was he up to that? He didn't even know how to survive by himself in this strange new world, much less take care of another being, however small.

He thought of Evayne and Peter, and all the ways he'd tried to be a good example to them—not always responsible, maybe, but always an example. He'd been very young when Evayne was born, but he remembered feeling proud and a little scared at his new role in the family. With something like this feeling in him, he followed Corva and Shylif under silver pipes as wide as houses and into a shadowy area of discarded building materials and broken tools.

"Nobody respectable comes down here," Shylif said. "No bots, I mean. It's an exclusion zone left over from the construction; they can no more walk in here than they can deliberately walk into a wall. That makes it a great place for certain kinds of activities."

There were people here, Toby realized—in fact, the zone under the pipes seemed to be a kind of market complete with ramshackle stalls for some vendors and others laying out their wares on blankets. Only a few customers were about, all hooded or helmeted. Toby wondered what might be for sale here that couldn't be bought in the city, but he had no time to browse as Shylif made a straight line through the dimness toward a kind of shack that backed onto a mountain of huge yellow pumps.

Corva rapped on the plastic sheeting that passed for a doorway curtain. "Come," said a raspy voice from inside. They stepped through, and Toby blinked in surprise.

Vaulting tree trunks rose all about, their heights lost in mist and green. Giant ferns slapped against him as he pressed forward. He couldn't hear the pumps anymore, just a cacophony of birdsong, insect chirps, and other animal screeches. And the sound of misty water falling.

"Hey, the ferns are real, treat 'em with respect!"

He blinked and looked around more closely. Under the ferns he spotted sound dampeners, loudspeakers, and a holographic projector. The forest was an illusion, but a good one.

"We want to make sure this denner can sustain my friend here," Corva was saying somewhere nearby.

"Him, huh? Not very promising."

"I also want to buy another one. It's for my brother, he's not with us."

Toby pressed forward, careful not to knock over the ferns' pots, and found Corva and Shylif standing with a very short, barrel-chested man who was dressed in layers of scrap clothing. His heavily muscled limbs were clamped into an exoskeleton frame that he appeared to strain against when he moved. It came to Toby that the exo wasn't there to amplify his strength but to hold it in check.

He gathered the little black denner in his arms, very carefully, and the denner appeared to be enjoying the attention. Toby suppressed the jealous urge to take the creature from him.

The man stepped carefully over to Toby and glared up at him. "You know what you're getting yourself in for?"

"I know how to take care of an . . . a creature, sir. I've done it before."

"Oh, yeah? That would put you decidedly in the minority. What kind of 'creature' have you taken care of before?"

"Cats. When I was a boy." This was untrue, but he felt it would make a plausible lie.

"You're still a boy." The man snorted. "Cats, huh. Well, they're not that different from denners. You probably seen denners, too, right? Lotsa people have 'em, but not like these." He glanced slyly over his shoulder and Toby realized that they were standing beside a large fenced pen. Inside it were a dozen or so of the animals.

He wanted to ask how these ones were different from the usual, but that would show his ignorance and he sensed this would be a bad time to do that. He thought about how to learn what he wanted to know and finally said, "They look like denners."

The short man prodded Toby in the chest with one finger, the force of his thrust nearly knocking Toby over. "And *you* look like a standard human, but yer not. You got synthetic hibernation organs implanted in yer body, like all of us. And these little guys"—he swept an arm to indicate the denners—"have got the counterpart. They was engineered to hibernate outside cicada beds; we've just made an addition. You really prepared to take care of one? This ain't a cat, boy."

"I trust him," said Corva. Toby glanced at her in surprise. She didn't return the look, though—she was too busy staring at the denners in the cage.

"Hrmph." The man flipped over Toby's denner and prodded him here and there. "Yer kit looks healthy and happy enough.

A'right." He motioned for Toby to follow him. "We'll see if you two are compatible."

"Are these really the prices?" Corva was practically wringing her hands as she peered in at the other denners.

"No haggling. Those are the prices.

"Stop ogling yer girl and pay attention," the short man added. Toby blushed and started to stammer an objection, but he waved it away. "Here, take the kit." He unceremoniously dumped the black denner into Toby's arms. "Give him a good scritch."

It took Toby a second to realize what he meant. Then he started stroking the denner above the ears and under the chin. A deep and resonant purr erupted from it, so loud that he almost dropped the creature.

"Huh!" The short man was waving some sort of diagnostic tool at them. "That's a strong tone . . . let me run a couple tests on him." He rummaged around behind a counter for some diagnostic equipment. Meanwhile, Corva had appeared on the other side of the fencing. She had a tragic expression on her face.

"I can't afford one," she said.

Shylif nodded slowly. "I'd like to help you out, but I only have enough for a few days' food."

"Jaysir won't help," she muttered darkly, "he hates denners." She aimed a speculative look at Toby. "You wouldn't happen to have a cash card on you, would you?"

He shook his head. "Sorry. I haven't had to use money yet."

He and the denner put up with some poking and prodding and ticking instruments being waved over them. Finally the little man grunted in surprise. "He's good," he said. "Never would have expected it from such a scrawny little thing . . . but based on these readings, he could even wake me up."

"Then we're good to go?" Suddenly he wondered if the little man could be trusted with the knowledge that they were planning to stow away, and he glanced up at Corva, who laughed.

"Grounce here is legendary among us stowaways," she said.

"He survives on his reputation for discretion. I think we can trust him."

"Who says you can't?" The little man glared at Toby.

A few minutes later, Toby walked out of the shop with his denner on his shoulder—and for the first time, he felt he could really say it *was* his. Or maybe he was its: the little guy was purring ridiculously loudly, and Toby knew he was grinning like an idiot. Corva and Shylif took this in stride. Trying to keep up with the situation, Toby said, "What do we do now? Swim back?"

"Oh, we're not going back," said Corva. "By now somebody'll have told the wrong people about you, and assassins or bots or rentacops'll be descending on the gallery. No, if you're gonna stay out of their hands, we've got to keep going."

"Going? But where?"

She jabbed a finger upward. "Orbit. Find us a transport and deep-dive now, so there're no life signs if they scan it. Disappear from this world entirely. The longer we're awake and running around, the easier it'll be for him to find you."

Toby nodded, then said, "Him? You mean Ammond?"

She gave him that you-idiot look again. "Of course not. His team can't summon the resources here to really suss you out. No, I mean your brother."

"My *what*?"

"You know," said Corva, looking puzzled. "Peter McGonigal. The guy who owns this world, and Lowdown, and all the rest of them? The one they call the Chairman."

| Five |

EVERYTHING BLURRED FOR A second and Toby realized he'd collapsed to his knees. His denner had jumped off his shoulder and was yammering in alarm.

Corva knelt in front of him, a look of alarm on her face. "Toby—what—"He was gasping as though somebody had punched him in the stomach.

"You didn't *know*?" She fell back and, sitting on the ground holding her ankles with her hands, she gazed at him in wonder. "You didn't know that? What did they tell you?"

"That . . . that Ammond and Persea were working for somebody called the Chairman. And that I . . . was the heir to Sedna."

Her laugh was more a bray of disbelief. "Well, that's true. And I guess it's no big surprise about Ammond. So, yes, you're the heir to Sedna. But you're also the heir to everything else. To Lowdown, and Echo, and Destrier and Wallop and the rest of the 360/1 lockstep. All seventy thousand worlds of it. You didn't *know*?"

"P-Peter is alive?"

The look of disbelief on her face shifted; there might have been a hint of sympathy there. "Of course he's alive. Think! It's only been forty years for those who were in the lockstep from the beginning. Peter's alive, and so's your sister, Evayne. Both rich beyond description, powerful enough that sensible people just stay out of their way. But the Chairman—Peter McGonigal—he's . . ." She shook her head. "Bad news, Toby. Bad news."

"Why? What . . ." He clearly remembered Ammond saying, *The Chairman himself ordered us to kill the boy.*

"Chairman," blurted Toby. "Common term, right? There must be loads of chairmen on your seventy thousand worlds." But Corva was shaking her head.

"It's an old term. Ancient. Only ever used to talk about the Chairman of Cicada Corp. Your brother . . . well, your mother, once, but that was before I was born."

"My mother? What about her and Dad—I mean, my parents? Are they alive, too?"

There was a shout from nearby. Jaysir was standing at the edge of the market, his big bot with its clattering, flailing cargo of pipes and cables lurking behind him. Apparently it couldn't cross the invisible line into the market's bot-free zone. "What's goin' on?" Jaysir called.

Shylif stuck out a hand and helped Toby to his feet. Corva was looking everywhere but at Toby as she too stood up and dusted herself off. "Your parents' story is a bit more complicated. Look, we can't tell it here in the middle of the gray market. We've got to keep moving."

Toby felt a crazy laugh rising in him. "Why? Seems to me, I own this." He stamped on the colorless concrete.

"Your brother controls it, but even he doesn't strictly own it." She grabbed his arm, and as his denner swarmed up his body (pricking Toby a dozen times as it used its claws for purchase) she pulled him into a walk. "But come on, we have to get off Auriga before you get caught. I'm happy to talk about this stuff, but not while we have to focus on evading cameras and spy bots."

And she proved true to that threat, as did Shylif and Jaysir. Toby's mind was crowded with questions, but all he got was terse answers while the others led them carefully through the industrial zone. Eventually they found an ore train headed through the human part of the city to the orbital freight elevators. Getting on board it involved watchfulness, careful timing, and a little luck, so when they were finally safe Corva lay back on a heap of dried seaweed and wearily waved away Toby's questions. He and the others sat on barrels of hydrocarbons bound for orbital industries, while the train barreled deafeningly through narrow ice tunnels and past flickering flashes of siding caves and stations. Toby felt stunned; he needed some time to absorb the mere fact that his brother and sister were alive—and that Peter had apparently ordered him killed.

His denner provided a bit of welcome distraction, because he was fascinated by the train and all its rattling parts. The little guy kept hopping off Toby's shoulder to explore, stopping right on the brink of falling off the train. Alarmed, Toby went to pick it up several times; after hissing on the first occasion, it let him. With nothing else to focus on, he turned his frustrated attention to it.

Wrecks had seemed half otter, half cat. This one was more cat-like, but as the denner let Toby gently splay its front paws, he saw that they were more like little hands than feet. It could curl its half fingers around Toby's, and as it explored it picked up things to look at them. The shape of its legs and how it walked on them gave it the gait of a racoon, but its sinuous flexibility was all feline.

Jaysir noticed the attention Toby was giving to the denners and seemed a bit annoyed. "You want one of these," he said, slapping the side of his strange machine. "*Those* guys are crude by comparison. You've got half the hibernation mechanism inside you already. It's a set of synthetic organs that take care of all your natural systems, like temperature regulation, oxygen levels. It prevents shock and produces the natural antifreeze that keeps your cells from bursting when you freeze. All the cicada beds and denners do is take care of timing. Well, and they scan you as you're waking to make sure you're cooking evenly. Of course, the beds cook you, too. They supply energy while you thaw, microwaves to start with just to melt the ice around your cells. They talk to your synthorgans and send 'em the diagnostic information so the right enzymes and sugars can be produced to bring you round. Without all that, you're basically just a lump of thawing meat. But denners don't even do all that."

"Yeah," Corva protested, "but timing is the most important thing. You have to start the wake-up cycle at the right time. Exactly thirty years to the day after you go down . . . or whenever the McGonigals decide."

"What do you mean, when we decide?"

"I mean, the Cicada Corporation has a monopoly on the hibernation beds. They control the cicada technology and the synthorgan franchises and everything else that sets or depends on their timings. Only they can change the frequency. And they do."

"Corva," said Shylif. It sounded like he was warning her of something.

She shook her head. "Anyway, you're not a legal part of the lockstep if you're not using the beds. Which means we are not supposed to be here. Luckily, there're lots of ways people scam the system, and there're all the other locksteps and people from them who turn up unannounced, and . . . well, you get the picture. It's messy. There's a space in there for denners with cicada-type organs, on a very gray market."

Toby stared doubtfully at his new companion, who was rampaging among the barrels with Wrecks and Shylif's denner. "But how does he do it? Wake himself up from being frozen solid at exactly the right time? And then what's he got—a microwave projector in his head or something?"

"Basically," said Jaysir, deadpan. "These little guys have about as much energy stored in them as a good-sized bomb. Their quantum clocks still work even at three degrees above absolute zero, and they're their own cicada bed. *That* is part of their original design—it's what made the denners popular to begin with, the fact they could survive without the beds. Makes 'em cheaper than other pets, right? We stowaways just added some upgrades, is all."

He was talking about living creatures like they were machines. Toby didn't like that. As he was reaching out to his denner, though, the ceiling of the tunnel suddenly flew away and they were in open air—or was it open space?

Far above, the sky was a black circle. The train was slowing as it rolled along a landscape of ice that made up the floor of a very deep, very wide pit. It must be kilometers across and tens of kilometers high.

The whole space was given over to tracks, warehouses, and yards packed with shipping containers. These radiated out like spokes from the center of the pit, where five threadlike white cables, each as straight as a draftsman's line, rose up from the ice floor to pierce the domes and finally disappear in the circle of black above. These were space elevators, and based on what he saw rising on one, each was strong enough to support a vertical train.

"There's our ride," said Jaysir. "It'll get us to orbit and stow us aboard one of the freighters."

"As long as it's a freighter that's bound for Wallop," added Corva.

Jaysir frowned at her. "You're really gonna try it, huh?"

She gave a long-suffering sigh. "Jay, what choice do I have?"

The maker crossed his arms and glared at Shylif. "And what about you? You still think Coley was on that ship?"

Shylif shrugged impassively. "I have to find out."

Toby's thoughts were wavering unevenly between the shock of the revelation about his family and the idea that these people were proposing he ride a freight cylinder into orbit with them. Even apart from all the issues around hibernation, there was a pretty obvious problem with this plan. "Won't there be security? If Ammond or . . . or my brother, if they're really after us, won't they be watching the docks?"

"Of course there's security." Jaysir shrugged as the train slowed and shunted into a siding. "But there're legal limits on how much and what kind of technology they can use for security. That's one of your brother's policies. He wants to keep the lockstep at pretty much the tech level it was when you . . . uh left. The price of that is that people like me can hack their way past the security pretty easily."

The train bumped to a halt. "That doesn't mean we can walk around like we own the place," said Corva as she slung herself over the side of the car. "Don't let yourself be seen. Jaysir's only so good, and a lot of the bots here are still going to be under direct lockstep control."

Toby followed her down the side of the car with Shylif coming last. "You mean," he accused, "under Peter's control. You said Peter owns this world, right?"

"He owns Cicada Corp—the hibernation system," she said as they ducked between the shadows of stacked shipping containers. "That's the cicada beds and all the machinery that coordinates shutdown and restart for the cities, the factories . . . You can build your own cicada bed, for private use, but it's the whole industrial ecosystem around them that the McGonigals control. Supplies, diagnostics, repairs, emergency replacements in case of disaster . . . and the network that communicates with it all. It's a monopoly."

At ground level the freight yard looked like any one Toby had seen in any movie made in the past two hundred years: towers of containers, wide gravelly lanes between them, harsh lights and swiftly moving transport cranes like trucks on stilts. Bots walked here and there among the lanes, but there weren't that many of them. Jaysir was following a particular route through the maze; he seemed to be looking for something.

"There." He pointed at a stack that looked exactly like all the others. "They're going to be loading that one in an hour. We need a bribable dock manager. Wait here, I'll round one up." He scuttled away into the shadows; his behemoth of a bot didn't follow him.

"There's an overlay for that," said Corva sardonically. "Finding corrupt bots, I mean. There's a big black market in bot hacks, and a lot of people deliberately turn a blind eye when their bots get infected with black-market viruses. You can make extra money from a hacked bot and still deny any involvement if the police catch your bots at it."

Toby was thinking through the implications. "And Peter doesn't own the police?" She nodded, but that was all, and he threw up his hands in frustration. "You said you would tell me the rest! About Evayne, and Mom and Dad? Or is keeping Toby ignorant just as important to you as it was to Ammond and Persea?"

Corva shook her head quickly. "No no, I just . . . it's a big story. I've been trying to figure out where to start, is all."

He glared at her. "How about *anywhere*?"

Corva stared off at the distant walls of ice. She was chewing her lip, her eyebrows scrunched in thought.

"I guess it grew out of a tiny seed, like they say," she murmured at last. "But it's all so crusted over with legend and myth it's hard to tell. The fact is, the McGonigal family pioneered wintering over. They say your mother invented it so she could wait for your return from . . . well, heaven is usually the way they put it."

"Heaven?" He shook his head. "Heaven wouldn't be that cold. Or cramped."

Shylif covered a smile, and Corva's eyes widened before she turned away.

"What'd I say?" said Toby, puzzled.

"That's the core of the legend, right there." Now she was smiling, too. "That you were—are—some kind of genius at the least, or a divinely inspired prophet at most. That you preached a solution to all the problems of the world. You dropped hints but nobody would listen. Then you disappeared into deep space. Your mother converted and started wintering over to await your return, and people began following her. Peter and Evayne had this great conversion experience, too. That was how the locksteps started—and once they started, people began to realize that this was what you'd been preaching about all along."

"This? What 'this'?"

"*This*." She waved around at the general world. "A way to defeat time while remaining true to what it means to be human. Your mother unwittingly built a way for human civilization to become eternal—or as close as is possible. Fourteen thousand years have passed, yet only forty for your sister and brother!"

"Wait, you're talking about Peter and Evayne and Mom . . . what about my father?"

Corva looked uncomfortable. "There's no mention of a father, sorry. Though there're lots of stories about that, too—"

"I don't want stories! So Peter and Evayne are alive. And Mom?"

"Your mother is wintering over until you return."

He shook his head; that just didn't make sense. "Where? Where are they?"

"Evayne travels around. Peter rules the lockstep from Barsoom. Your mother . . . she's on a planet called Destrier, about half a light-year from here."

Toby scowled up at the black sky. "Then that's where I have to go."

There was no response from the others. When he looked down, he saw that they were standing several steps away from him, both wide-eyed. Spooked, he would have said, had there been anything nearby to scare them. He glanced around in case, but no, they were alone here.

At that moment Jaysir reappeared with a gangly chrome-plated bot by his side. "This one'll let us into the containers," he said. "But we have to hurry. The loaders are on their way."

He led them through the cargo stacks. Corva and Shylif hung back, whispering together heatedly. Toby shook his head and, growling under his breath, followed Jaysir.

The shipping containers were inflated cylinders with flat magnetic plates on top, bottom, and sides; the plates let you stack them under gravity or daisy-chain them in space. Each was about four by ten meters, and there were crude airlocks on either end. These were uncannily like the ones they'd had in his day, and Toby felt his steps slowing as he approached the one the chrome bot was opening. He knew these things had no windows, no propulsion, no power supply, no life support. They were just bags to stuff things in.

"See you on the other side," said Jaysir. He and his cargo bot headed toward another cylinder, leaving the three stowaways with the denners standing by the first one.

"He's by himself?" Toby watched him disappear into the maze of containers.

Corva shrugged; she seemed to have recovered her composure. "He and his . . . machine . . . weigh more than all of us put together. He'd tip the scales way over if we bunked together."

Toby turned his dubious gaze to the shipping container the silver bot had brought them to. "We're not seriously getting in that," he said.

She squinted at him, a touch of humor returning to her face. "What part of 'stowaway' didn't you understand?"

"But I thought . . . wouldn't you find somewhere inside the passenger compartments—I mean, in a closet or . . . ?"

She brayed a laugh. "Closets? You know there's no such thing. Oh, sure, in the smaller ships you could hack the glasses interface, make it so people and bots don't see you, but that only works until it doesn't work. This," she said, patting the side of the container, "always works."

"Almost," added Shylif as the bot did something beside the airlock door and it sprang open. "Quick, before the cranes get here."

He and Corva rushed into the container lock. Shylif offered Toby his hand. Toby hesitated.

"Go on back to the city, then," said Shylif, and he pulled his hand back.

"Wait!" Toby clambered up and into the square lock. Immediately, the doors slammed shut behind him. They were in darkness now.

The inner door opened and he heard somebody groping around for a switch. After a moment weak utility lights came on, back- and sidelighting a wall of plastic-wrapped merchandise that filled the cylinder right up to the airlock. Shylif and Corva let their denners climb down, and the little creatures slipped into crevasses between the packages, chittering back and forth as their humans crouched and murmured encouragement.

"Mrf?" Toby started as a little black-furred face appeared next to his. It looked at him, then after the other two. "Sure," Toby

said. "Go on." He didn't know whether the denner actually understood his words, but it got the sense of them anyway because it
hopped down and began exploring with the other two. Toby found
himself peering through gaps with Corva and Shylif, calling out
encouragement with them.

After a few moments, the denners had identified a few spaces
around the curve of the outer wall that a determined human
might be able to squeeze through. "There're always gaps in the
packing," said Shylif optimistically. "Like hidden chambers in a
pyramid."

The utility lights hinted at spaces back there, but still, Toby
shook his head. "There isn't even room to stand up. And what are
we going to do for *air*?"

"Another secret of these places," said Corva. She was burrow-
ing her way after Wrecks. "Emergency air supplies—they're required by law. Keep us going for a day or two on the other side, if
we need it." Her voice became increasingly muffled as she wormed
her way between boxes. "We won't need it on this end."

"But this is insane."

"Yeah," she shouted back. "That's why they never catch us at
it. Nobody in their right mind would travel this way. But really—
weren't those early ships of yours this cramped?"

He thought about the little tug that he had taken into the vast
empty reaches beyond Sedna. It really hadn't been much roomier
than this; it was just that its virtual reality and synthetic personalities had provided the illusion of unlimited space for its single
passenger.

Toby's denner poked its head out from between packages and
meow-chattered at him. "All right, all right, I'm coming." He took
a deep breath and began forcing his way through the gaps.

It turned out the denners had found a sizable chamber, and
with some shuffling and shoving, the humans were able to enlarge
it until all three could sit, knees up, with their denners perched or
draped on out-jutting boxes around them. Then Corva and Shylif
brought out several survival bags—sleeping bags, really, but air-

tight when sealed and insulated to withstand deep cold. Corva handed one to Toby.

"What about, well . . ." He waved a hand.

"Bodily functions?" Shylif laughed. "You should have thought of that before we left home! Seriously, we are going to leave some evidence of ourselves behind here. They'll know there've been stowaways. But as long as we don't damage the merchandise or tip the freighter's payload mass past its tolerances, nobody'll care."

Toby's heart was pounding. He had the momentary thought that these two people he was with were actually crazy. How could a trio of animals—pets!—keep any of them alive through being frozen and shipped like packaged meat ten or twenty times the breadth of the solar system?

It must have been visible on his face, because suddenly Corva reached out to put her hand on his knee. "We do this all the time," she said. "We really do! You have to trust your denner. What're you going to call him, anyway?"

"How—" He laughed, half hysterically. "How can I trust him when I haven't even had time to give him a name. And I'm expected to risk my life on his implants . . ." No, it was too crazy. Suddenly he knew he had to get out of there, and he turned and tried to stand up—and saw stars as he hit his head. "Ah!"

"Toby! Just keep it together!" Shylif and Corva held his hands and talked quietly, reassuringly, about how they'd done this before, and about how denner instincts drew them to curl up with sleeping people. In that space of shared mammalian warmth, the thrum of their purr would synchronize their metabolisms and keep both creatures alive. The denners' synthorgans provided energy and diagnostic data to guide the systems that supported the more massive humans.

Toby calmed down enough to know he was going to try to go through with this. But he still needed something to keep him from thinking about it. "Tell me more," he said to Corva. "About Peter and Evayne. Do they . . . are they . . . older?" She'd said something about forty years having passed in the lockstep, as opposed to the fourteen thousand that had gone by outside it. "Have they been awake all this time? Or did they winter over some of it?"

He could see in the dim light that Shylif and Corva were staring at him wide-eyed. "Amazing," said Shylif. "Just to hear you say those names as if—well, like they're your own family."

"They are!"

"But you have to understand," said Corva gently, "that we grew up hearing them spoken as names from legend. Like you'd hear about some ancient conqueror."

He shook his head. "They're just family."

There was a long silence. Then Corva said, "Right. Why don't I go on with the story, then, and you can judge for yourself when I'm done?" Cautiously, he nodded. She shot an uncertain smile at Shylif, who shrugged.

"Toby, I don't know what really happened, way back at the start. The fact is, your family figured out how to thrive out here between the stars, and they made sure they controlled the technology. Well, mostly. For centuries of realtime, all the action was around the stars. Empires rose, posthuman species came into being, there were wars and crashes and exploration and terraforming and everything you can imagine and lots that you can't. All the while that was happening, Sedna was growing bit by bit. Slowing down, too—we're pretty sure the lockstep frequency was small at first, maybe even 1/1. See, if you can winter over, you use resources more slowly, so if your bots can mine and manufacture slowly and steadily over all that time, you'll have so much more to work with in those times when you're awake."

He nodded. "But Ammond said that the big advantage was that you could trade more."

"Right! If you can travel to any of twenty or thirty thousand worlds overnight, it's a huge advantage. Because your potential trading partners aren't scattered around a flat map but in three dimensions, if you double how far you travel while you're asleep, you increase the worlds you can visit during that sleep by a factor of eight! They say you figured that out, and your mother took your message to the other Sedna colonists after you left . . ." He was shaking his head. "O-kay," Corva continued uncomfortably. "So anyway there was constant pressure to winter over for longer and longer times. While she was Chairman, your mother got us up to thirty years down, one month up. We've been at that since before I was born."

"And then she what? Went into sleep to wait for me?" He shook his head again. "That doesn't sound like her. I mean . . . sure, she'd miss me, but she wouldn't abandon Peter and Evayne. Or Dad. Just to wait for me. Something's screwy here."

"That's the story I know. Your mother began the locksteps, and your brother and sister control ours, the biggest one."

"Control it? Isn't Cicada Corp just a company? Why not just skim profits like the trillionaires always have and sit back and let it run itself?"

"Toby, if only a hundred people decided to immigrate to the lockstep every *real-time* year, there'd be three thousand showing up every lockstep month and, what . . . thirty-six thousand new citizens per *lockstep* year! But people in the wider world have known about the locksteps for millennia. Tens of thousands come to find us every year . . . *realtime*. Sometimes, millions. You do the math."

He thought about Sedna—but a Sedna without him and with a strange new custom pioneered by his mother. People hibernating, maybe just a few at a time at first, and not for too long. He could already see how useful that would have been: lower life-support costs, which would translate to a greater carrying capacity for the whole colony . . . more to go around. And then, blinking faster and faster forward through time, eventually the whole colony at once. Then people showing up, just a few at first, but soon floods. Three decades of colonization effort passing in one night: you'd wake and there'd be a new city next door that hadn't been there when you went to sleep. Whole worlds could appear that way.

"How could you possibly deal with a pace of change like that?"

Corva gazed at him, looking . . . sad?

"Simple," she said. "Peter and Evayne used *you* to do it."

He was trying to figure out what that meant and what to ask next, when suddenly the whole shipping container shook. All around the three stowaways, packages and boxes shifted ominously. At the first rumble Toby braced his hands and feet in alarm against the plastic-wrapped walls that surrounded him. His denner chirped and leaped to his shoulder.

"It's okay," said Corva. "We're just being loaded."

A sense of swirling motion made Toby push even harder against the walls. It went on for nearly a minute, then they were thumped down hard somewhere, and it ceased.

"Why now?" he asked. "I mean, why are they loading ships if there're weeks to go before everybody winters over? Wouldn't they wait until then to leave the planet?"

Shylif shook his head. "There's a sizable queue. These docks started running weeks before the population woke up, and they'll keep going for weeks after everybody goes to sleep. It's great for us—means we'll be off planet and asleep while they're still looking for us down here."

"Unless they look for us up there."

Shylif shrugged. "Then we're screwed." He reached out to ruffle Shadoweye's fur, then said, "Well, I'm going to find a stable cavity and retire. See you in thirty years." He and his denner clambered away through the jam-packed packaging.

Corva still wasn't meeting Toby's gaze. "We should, too. Toby, I want to tell you everything about your family and your . . . situation. But we need a better time and place. It's pointless to use up what little air's in here, because we won't have time for me to answer all your questions anyway."

"You keep putting me off—"

She clucked and Wrecks climbed into her survival bag with her. Toby could hear him purring.

"We have to do this *now*, Toby. Zip yourself into your bag with your denner," she said. "He starts to purr, you fall asleep, and you deep-dive: your metabolism slows by ninety percent, and so does his. When we get to space all the heat's going to leak out of here, so as the temperature drops he'll stimulate your body to produce the natural antifreeze and other substances that'll protect you in the next stage."

"Which is . . . ?" He thought he knew.

"You freeze solid and stay that way for three decades. Then, when we get to Wallop, our denners will wake up in anaerobic mode and start pumping energy into us. They're used to the rhythm of this lockstep, their circadian clocks are accurate to the millisecond."

"And you've done this."

Wrecks was purring even louder now. Corva smiled as she zipped herself up to her nose and settled herself back against the crates. "Enough times that I trust Wrecks with my life, yeah." She finished the zip-up and was completely engulfed in the survival bag.

His own denner sat at his feet, its tail coiled around its feet. It was looking up at him expectantly.

This was it. If he was going to get out of this death trap, it would have to be now. He could find a ride back to the city, maybe do some work for lazy robots like Shylif had been doing. He could hide out, learn what was really going on here. That was the sensible thing to do.

His denner was purring, a lulling, hypnotic sound. "Stop it," he said. "I don't even know your name."

And suddenly there were tears in his eyes.

Corva hadn't known anything about Toby's father. That could only mean one thing: Dad was dead. Funny thing—Toby had spent the past month knowing this as a fact, thinking that Mother was long gone, too, and Peter and Evayne. Suddenly the others were alive again, but Dad wasn't and somehow that made him . . . more than dead. Corva didn't even know he'd existed. He was gone, erased from history, and somehow that was so much worse than his simply having died long ago.

Peter, tyrant of seventy thousand worlds? And Evayne, did she know Toby was alive? Had she agreed with this insane order to have him killed? It was all crazy.

He shuffled his way into the little chamber where Corva now lay like a lifeless doll and climbed into his bag. The denner watched him alertly as he zipped the bag up to his chin. "I'm alone," he said aloud.

A little furry paw tapped him on the cheek. He turned to find himself staring into two golden eyes. His denner was small enough to be the runt of its litter and as lonely, maybe, as Toby.

Toby brought it into the bag, hugging it against his chest, and began to cry. "You need a name. You can't go to sleep without a name." Its purr was becoming hypnotic, and as had happened on the boat, Toby felt an answering vibration start deep within himself.

"It's gotta be good," he said sleepily. "Not Blacky or Midnight." He laughed at himself.

He thought about the gods and heroes of ancient mythology, many of whom had come to virtual life in the games he and Peter played. Which of them had gone between life and death? —A lot of those crazy Greeks, actually. Persephone would be perfect, except that she was a woman and this denner was male. Charon, the boatman of the dead? Too bleak.

The song of the denner was all around him now, and he knew its name. "You're Orpheus," he muttered. Orpheus, the hero whose music was so powerful that he used it to lull all the monsters of the underworld into sleep, allowing him to sneak into the afterlife and steal back his dead wife.

"All right, Orpheus. Let's go see Hades."

| Six |

THE AIRSHIP WAS A flying wing a little over two kilometers long, its transparent skin made of something so thin that you couldn't see it head-on; only in its outward curves could you make out the oily iridescence of its shape. It was as if the ion engines and passenger gondolas were suspended in midair. Toby had loved it—and why not? He was only fourteen.

They'd been on their way to orbit for two days now, circling Earth at ever-greater altitudes. The ionosphere was so thin here that satellites could plow right through it—but a light enough airplane with a wing this wide could use it for lift and fly all the way to orbit. This was the way poor people went into space. Mom and Dad had decided on a slow leave-taking, rather than a quick rocket to orbit and then on to Sedna. Until an hour ago, Toby had thought they were indulging an uncommon nostalgia.

But then, just after lunch as he'd been wandering the long galleries that looked down on the strangely patterned landscapes forty kilometers below, the ship had shuddered—just ever so slightly. Peter ran up, a blot of dark disheveled clothing and hair like a moving stain on the perfect white plastic surfaces of the corridor. "An airship just docked!" he'd cried. "An *invisible* one!"

"More invisible than this old thing?" But Toby was intrigued. Over the next twenty minutes they watched as the suborbital stealth rocket (now visible) disgorged cargo and passengers, each of whom Mom and Dad greeted with handshakes and serious expressions.

Peter had nudged Toby at one point. "I know that guy. He's Nate what's his name, the composer-thing guy." Ever precise, that was Peter—but Toby did recognize the long-limbed man with the easy grin. More than a composer, he invented whole genres and was famous for starting bands of startling and varied styles. He'd stay with one just long enough to propel it to international fame and drive a new trend into the spotlight; then he'd be off in a new direction. Like the McGonigals, he wasn't a trillionaire, merely rich and famous— which counted for everything, or nothing at all as Toby was learning. "But what's he doing here?" Peter stared as if he could burn the secret out of the man with his gaze. "Is he coming with *us*?"

The answer, which was yes, had come sometime after the stealth craft had broken off from the airship to plummet back into the air above the failed state of France. Toby and Peter were standing at the gallery rail, pointing out this or that detail along a filigreed coastline beneath their feet, when a shadow joined them. They looked up to see Nate standing a few meters away. He was gazing down, too, his expression more pensive than Peter's.

"Hey!" Peter went over to him. "You're that guy, right?"

Nate what's-his-name raised an eyebrow, then stuck out his hand for Peter to shake. "Nathan Kenani. You're Carter's boys, aren't you?"

"Whatcha doing?" Peter nodded at the passing landscapes. "You coming with us?" To Toby's surprise, Kenani nodded.

"I can't do it anymore," he said. "I mean, look at that." He pointed down. They were passing over southern China. Like everywhere else on the planet, it was divided into two kinds of landscape: sprawling city and empty, verdant parkland. The one was a gray mottle from this height, the other smooth green.

The gray was where billions of people lived all heaped atop one another, struggling to survive in the microeconomies they could cobble together from garbage and wind power in the ruins of their ancestors' dreams. The green was the estates of the trillionaires, who let in no one but their ecologists and a few people they wanted to reward or bribe.

The green was much bigger than the gray.

Kenani sighed. "I just wanted to look at it all one last time. Before they take out my implants, I mean." He tapped the side of his head.

"So it's true?" Peter was practically hopping up and down. "They say you got more than anybody!"

"Not really." Kenani smiled lopsidedly. "But I do have auditory augments, and visual ones and tactile. I can see seventeen primary colors and hear way down into infrasound and up past where dogs can go. But your mother says they're likely to kill me during her new hibernation process. Something about different expansion and contraction rates than human flesh . . . So I'm having them out."

"In Consensus, either everybody gets them or nobody does," announced Peter. "They're an unfair advantage."

Kenani looked puzzled. "Consensus?"

"It's a gameworld we've been building for . . . well, months and months," Toby explained.

Peter said, "No security without equality of opportunity!"

"Pete's just discovered socialism. Last week it was meritocracy."

Kenani laughed. "Well, that's cool." He gazed sadly down at the lands below. "I'd have everybody get them, then. I'm going to miss all this richness."

"But why?" Toby shook his head. "Why are you coming with us. Are you *sneaking away*?"

"Yes, I'm sneaking away, along with an assorted lot of criminals, subversives and dissidents, scientists, and whatnot." Kenani indicated the passenger modules behind the gallery. "Most of us are just fed up living in a world that's never going to change. Where there're no new frontiers. Everything's owned—I mean, there's not a centimeter of beachfront anywhere in the world where the likes of you and I can set foot! And every last bit of the solar system's been surveyed and claims staked. It's all we've got, and all we're ever going to have. And *they* own it."

Passing below was another area of city—but this one wasn't a roiled gray chaos like the others. It was more like an interconnected labyrinth of buildings, stretching on kilometer after kilometer, with no streets or windows to break the geometric perfection of its shapes. This place, and others like it, was where all the resources of the planets were funneled. It was a machine city, an entire economy dedicated to serving the needs and whims of the trillionaires. They had no need for human workers. They had their bots.

"In Consensus, nobody can own more than a hundred robots," said Peter.

Kenani snorted. "Good luck with that," he said. "Then again, why not? Make it Sedna instead of Consensus, kid, and I'll back you all the way."

THRUM, THRUM.

The sound was everywhere—filling the universe outside and roving through his belly and chest, his throat and his skull. Toby could feel it rattling down his arms and legs, awakening a painful tingle in them. He could feel it coursing up his spine, wrapping his jaw and tongue, penetrating his glued-shut eyelids.

He struggled to open those eyes, but when he finally did, he saw nothing. A groan escaped his lips and he felt his head loll forward. It came to him that he was sitting on some sort of surface, his knees bent up, arms lifeless at his side. And with him—

He felt the denner's fur brush his face. The little creature was climbing around and over him, nudging him with its head. All the while, its rumbling song vibrated through Toby, awakening his body from an impossibly long sleep.

He took a ragged breath. "How long," he tried to say. It came out as a weak croak, but Orpheus seemed encouraged. He butted Toby's cheek and the vibration became louder still.

Now Toby felt cold, too, a biting attack on all parts of his body at once. Something deep within him was fighting against it, a radiance like a tiny inner sun. He was running on battery power, he realized, much of it supplied by his own implants. Not all of it, though. Corva had said, with a straight face, that Orpheus would heat him to life using microwave energy.

Thinking of Corva brought home to him where he must still be: bagged in a shipping container en route to a world she'd called . . . was it Wallop? He could feel the survival bag wrapped around him like a blanket. In fact, even when he kept his head still there was a dizzying sensation of motion. Maybe it was simple vertigo. Maybe, though, the container was on the move.

"Corva?" Toby made a supreme effort and unbent himself, reaching up a hand to cautiously unzip the bag. Fearsomely cold air puffed in, waking him even further. He stretched his right arm out of the membrane and his fingers made contact with another bag. Corva wasn't moving, but he could feel the vibration coming from her cocoon: Wrecks was hard at work.

"Shylif!" There was no answer. Was it possible he was dead? And Corva, too? What then would Wrecks be up to?

No, there was another possibility, and however unlikely it seemed, it must be true. Skinny little Orpheus had managed to awaken Toby before the others.

He reached up to stroke the denner's fur. "You're amazing, you know that?"

At that moment he felt a falling sensation, and all around him the tightly wrapped packages shifted. He heard plastic wrap tearing— he hadn't been imagining movement after all. Then, with a bone-jarring *thump*, the container struck something and stopped moving.

"Corva?" he asked again. There was no response, just Wrecks's purring. Orpheus, he suddenly realized, had fallen silent. It was Toby's own shivering that was sustaining his body heat now, and that wasn't going to last long.

He felt terribly weak, as though he'd been sick and bedridden for days. This was nothing like the cicada beds, which pumped you full of sugars and nanotechnology that would fix you as good as new before you even woke up. Toby retched, but nothing came out; his stomach was empty and demanding to be filled.

He reached out again, found Corva's knee, and felt around for her backpack. Opening it was hard, and he toppled over twice, scraping his chin on the corner of a crate. But inside he found some food bars and a bottle of water.

He brought out the food and water and eagerly devoured a bar. Then he hesitated.

Corva and her friends had helped him, at no apparent profit to themselves. Then again, Ammond and Persea had seemed just as selfless at first. Maybe the stowaways had no agenda beyond simple human decency. Or maybe the fact that they'd tracked him between worlds, awaiting a chance to break him out of his captivity, simply meant they had their own use for him, yet to be revealed. Corva had hinted as much.

She had also promised to finish telling him about his family. Yeah, maybe—but now that he was free of Ammond and Persea's subtle censorship, he could surely find out the rest of the story himself. He didn't need Corva for that.

To hell with other people's agendas. There was one companion he knew he could rely on. He found another bar and offered it to Orpheus, who purred like crazy before attacking it. Toby gave a great sigh to quiet his inner arguers, and said, "Come on, Orph, let's see where we are." He groped around for the twisty passage through the boxes. After a moment Orpheus got the idea and with a chitter guided Toby into the correct gap. Moments later they were at the shipping container's airlock.

Toby patted along the side of the door until he found a control pad. As he touched it, a little keypad glowed green, startlingly bright and the first thing he'd seen for . . . how many years would it be?

After his eyes adjusted, he peered at it and saw that it was reading a breathable atmosphere outside. Now that he was standing up, he could feel the drag of gravity on him, too, and it felt . . . well, just about normal, despite his weakness. They were either on a rotating station somewhere, or this was a pretty sizable planet. He ordered the lock to cycle, and a few seconds later the outer door opened.

It wasn't too bright out there, but even so he had to squint. What he was looking at wasn't at all clear. Light percolated in from the sides, but right in front of him was a kind of wavering, streaky darkness. It seemed somehow familiar, but he couldn't figure out what it was.

Then a crooked line of white shot from on high down into plunging depths, revealing vast billowing clouds to all sides, and he saw that the streaks were runnels and beads of rain coursing down a transparent wall just a few meters in front of him. He only just had time to realize this before thunder banged off that wall; in the distance another bolt of lightning vaulted between two towers of cloud.

Toby was so busy gaping at the bottomless well of downpouring mist that he nearly toppled right off the lip of the shipping container. Swinging wildly, he managed to grab a frost-painted handle and looked down. He was three up on a stack of containers; five more loomed overhead. This stack was just one in a row of them. The place must be a warehouse.

Grumbling to himself, Orpheus was already climbing nimbly down. Toby spared one more glance at the transparent wall and was rewarded as a flash-flicker of lightning unveiled the scene for another instant. Clouds above, clouds below, blackness beyond them in all directions. And rain, rain in sheets and billows falling everywhere.

He made it—barely—down to the floor, and his landing rang it hollowly, as if it were a lightweight deck and not a floor at all. Everything in sight was made of plastic or the transparent stuff of the outer wall. Strange. Also strange was his sudden perception that the wall leaned out at quite an angle and curved gradually to either side.

"Where are we?"

"We're on Wallop, mate."

He whirled and nearly fell. Jaysir laughed.

Scrawny he might be, but right now Corva's friend looked a lot better than Toby felt. His complicated cargo bot stood a few paces behind him, hoses and wires trailing behind it. "You're the first up, are you?" Jaysir continued.

"Uh, yeah." His voice barely worked; he'd sounded worse on Lowdown, but that was because of the air. His whole throat felt dehydrated.

Jaysir pursed his lips. "You're not waiting around? Corva and Shylif could use a hand, I'm pretty sure."

Toby looked down. Until this moment he hadn't actually been seriously considering walking away. He met Jaysir's gaze. "I dunno. What would you do in my situation?"

"Hmm." Jaysir scratched his chin, then ticked some points off on his fingers. "Well, first of all, you don't know anything. You don't even know where you are. You don't know where you're going—"

"I'm going to Destrier."

Jaysir paused, one finger atop another. "You're going to *Destrier*? No crap?" Then he laughed and shook his head. "She put you up to this? Or was it your idea?"

"Totally my idea. Mom's waiting for me. That's what Corva said."

Jaysir resumed ticking off items. "And you haven't got a clue what that *means*."

"Corva told me about my family, Jaysir. That Peter's the Chairman, Evayne's alive too and my mom . . . she's on Destrier. So that's where I'm going."

"Maybe, but . . . listen, Toby, you can't just go from waking up to deep diving on the same day. It takes time to recover from hibernation. That's why the standard turn lasts a month. That's why nobody lives in the Weekly for very long. You can't just find a container bound for Destrier and climb in with your little guy. You're going to have to spend a few weeks in the city first—"

"I was only on Little Auriga for a couple of days! And you, too!"

"Actually, we'd woken up two weeks ahead of time, while the city was still thawing out. Corva figured we needed the time to get our bearings, recover, and find you. She was right. And you—you'd had days asleep in your cicada bed while they moved you from the ship to the docks. Cicada beds are a lot easier on the system than denners, man. You can't just bed down again today."

Toby turned and looked away through the ranks of shipping containers. Everything Jaysir said might be true, but the more

Jaysir tried to convince him to stay, the more Toby felt himself pulling away. "Okay sure," he said, waving Jaysir into silence. "Say you're right about all that. I've got some things I'm pretty sure I'm right about, too."

He imitated Jaysir, ticking points off on his fingers. "First of all, Jay, I'm not going to start trusting you just because you tell me you can be trusted. I fell for that once, I'm not going to do it again."

Jaysir made a kind of reluctant shrug of agreement.

"Second, you guys want something from me, but you're not telling me what it is. Tell me, and maybe I'll start trusting you!"

Now it was Jaysir's turn to look hesitant. "It's really up to Corva. This is her thing . . ."

"And you're what? Along for the ride?" Toby shook his head. "Third, I'm totally dependent on you, just like I was dependent on Ammond and Persea. If you were really friends, you'd help me get set up on my own and then *ask* me for whatever help it is you want."

Jaysir thought about it. "Okay, I can see that. Problem is, you've got no money, no idea how to survive on your own, and the instant you tell anybody who you are, you'll be jumped on by a hundred police bots."

"So *you* say."

Now Jaysir was starting to look a bit desperate. "Say I let you go. What do I tell the others? Corva . . . Corva needs you, man."

"I'll be around. You can call me—"

Jaysir was shaking his head. "We can't call you, you don't have a legal identity. Oh, I heard about this 'Garren Morton' alias, but you can't use it. And you can't use your real name, either. Shouldn't even say it aloud." He glanced around at the blank boxes surrounding them.

"Then tell me what I have to do to avoid getting caught while I sort myself out."

"Pfaw! Why would I do that?"

Toby stopped, gently set down Orpheus, then reached inside his tunic for the object he'd carried since bursting into the water on Auriga. He held it up in the cold factory light and was rewarded as Jaysir's eyes snapped to it with sudden intensity.

"This is a data block from Sedna. I don't know exactly how old it is in lockstep terms, but it was hidden in the back of a twentier—a bot from the original colony. You said you collect procedural computer code, Jay. I bet you've never gotten to hack something this old."

"Ah," said Jaysir. He hadn't looked away from the block.

"If you can help me get the data off of it, I'll give you whatever code's written into it. But only if you let me go."

Jaysir blinked and looked away. "What you need to do is buy a pair of tourist glasses. I'll give you our URNs and you can send me your glasses' address. So we we'll be able to contact each other, but we won't be able to track you, and don't have to use your URN or name.

"Don't open any accounts, don't buy anything virtually, or do *anything* that requires an identity check! I have a list of places you can stay that won't ask. And you're going to need a cash card." He rummaged in his baggy trousers and came out with one. Handing it to Toby, he said, "This should last you a day or two. But you can't just go running off to Destrier! You need to know where you are and what's going on first. And it's a hell of a story to tell."

With Jaysir's unique identifier, his URN, Toby would be able to phone, e-mail, or—if they shared services—locate him when needed. Jaysir was offering him a way to deal with him and Corva and Shylif at arm's length. Suddenly he felt horribly guilty about taking off like this. But Ammond and Persea had been prepared to kill him . . .

"Don't stick your head up, it'll get shot off." Jaysir turned away. "I gotta figure out what I'm going to tell the others. It won't be pretty, let me tell you."

"Thanks, Jay. I *will* call you."

Jaysir grunted. "It's a small world. It's not like you can go very far." Then he thought of something. "Hey, whatever you do, don't use any Cicada Corp equipment!"

"Why—"

"Just, just *don't*! I'll explain when I see you."

Troubled, but determined, Toby ducked his head in agreement and walked away.

DEALING WITH JAYSIR HAD worn him out. Toby felt tired and dizzy, and like his tongue and skin had been sunburnt. Even the dim lighting here was too bright, and as soon as he began to move he started puffing as if he'd just run a race. Cradling Orpheus, Toby plodded between the rows of stacked containers, peering about for a way out. With every step he took, he felt worse, and more guilty about leaving the others—especially Corva, whom he suspected would not be as understanding as Jaysir.

He'd seek them out as soon as he'd recovered from hibernation and felt a little safe and had some money, however one got that. Then he'd pay Jaysir back for the cash card. He might even help Corva with whatever it was she wanted from him—but he had to find out what that was first.

There were bots working in the warehouse. In his condition he couldn't have hidden from them if he'd wanted to, but they ignored him. Maybe he could subcontract to them, the way Shylif did.

The general traffic of robots, automated cargo carts and moving cranes gave him a direction to follow, and shortly he emerged squint-eyed into what at first seemed to be hot sunlight. He shaded his narrowed eyes with his free hand and looked up.

It wasn't sunlight, he wasn't outdoors, and this place was like nowhere he'd ever seen or heard of.

The warehouse entrance was one of a number of similar doorways that opened onto a circular plaza cluttered with shops and food stands, and crowded with people. So far, so good. Around the plaza, tiers of heavily forested cityscape rose up in a sweeping curve, so for a second or two he thought he was at the bottom of a small bowl-shaped valley. These weren't uncommon on Mars or the moon, where ancient impact craters made perfect circular depressions that could be domed over.

This landscape's curve became vertical, and then kept curving, inward now, to close a couple of kilometers overhead. He wasn't in a bowl, but a bubble. At its very summit, its north pole, brilliant sunlamps pulsed with light and heat. There was even a single little white cloud hovering in the middle of the space.

Tongues of forest and towers of glittering window and balcony swept up for much of the upper hemisphere of the bubble he was in, but gradually they gave way to buildings that seemed to sit on the outside of the sphere. These thrust elevator shafts and escalators through the bubble's skin—and that skin was transparent wherever it showed.

Flickers of lightning beyond it brought him glimpses of billowing cloudscapes far larger than this sphere. And, in the distance, he thought he could make out the ghostly outline of a mottled moon nestled in the clouds: another sphere?

Something broke the symmetry of the curve, and it took him a while to figure out what it was. With one of those figure-to-ground flips of perspective, he suddenly realized that what he'd thought was a flat circular formation high up on the sphere was a *hole*—a gap in the geodesic curve. Along its edges, escalators and walkways led from his bubble into another, larger space. He even spotted an aircar sailing out of there. And were those even bigger bubbles beyond?

Okay, he'd heard of aerostats—giant spherical living spaces that could be floated in the atmosphere. Before he'd left Earth, there'd been a news report about some of the trillionaires wanting to colonize Venus by building such things. That had been amazing, but this—!

The bubble he was in was at least a kilometer across, yet it was attached to an unknown number of others, like one soap bubble clinging to a raft of others. If a single bubble city could take flight, he supposed a knot of them could, too, and so this raft hovered high in the atmosphere of some vast, dark planet.

When he could pull his eyes back to ground level, Toby blinked at a vision of chaos totally unlike the majesty that presided overhead. Here, craft stalls, food and robot-part outlets were mashed together and half piled over one another; there were carpet salesmen here, and wood-carvers, perfumeries, neon-lit bars and shadier, slotted doors in ramshackle huts that were guarded by hulking military bots. People crowded everywhere, jostling one another and talking, shouting, arguing and haggling. And what people!

He and Peter had watched all the old movies set in galactic empires and ancient solar civilizations. They'd devoured sci-fi books from the dawn of spaceflight—and so, when they came to build the universe of Consensus, they had given it faster-than-light ships and a vast culture of aliens and evolving humans. All of that was impossible, of course: in the real universe, no such thing could ever exist, for traveling between the stars was a multidecade affair for even the most advanced civilization. No matter how much wealth you had, no matter how much power, there could never be, in the real world, a marketplace where denizens of thousands of worlds and hundreds of cultures met. Nowhere could dozens of species and subspecies of human and alien crowd together to meet and trade and celebrate an empire of reason and commerce vaster than any solar system.

Yet here it was.

Most of the humans in sight were ordinary enough, but some were incredibly tall and stringy, others short and powerful, like the man who'd kept the denners on Auriga. Yet others were green skinned, or scaly, or had become one with the machines that accompanied them. There were nonhuman shapes, too, though that was impossible: no intelligent alien life had been found within a hundred light-years of Earth . . . at least, not in Toby's day.

He found he was grinning. The fantasy had been made real, not on Earth but here in the vastness between the stars. The galactic empire he and Peter had dreamed about—as so many others had before them—had been built in the only place it could be and in the only way it ever could: in lockstep time.

But he was dizzy and nearly collapsed before he could make it to a nearby escalator. As he stood leaning on its handrail, letting himself rise through level after level of the bubble city, he brought out the list of hostels and hotels Jaysir had given him. When he spotted the sign for one, he gave Orpheus a tight hug and said, "We're home free. Just a few more minutes and I'll order up a room-service meal like you've never seen."

Provided, of course, he had enough on his cash card for that.

TOBY HADN'T HAD TIME to find the cheaper lodgings available in the city; he'd walked into the first hotel on Jaysir's list that he could find. He'd never stayed in a hotel by himself before, but he got through the strangeness of checking in without having to use any biometrics or produce ID. It turned out not be any more overwhelming than anything else that had happened to him lately.

The bed was deep and soft, the shower was hot, and there was plenty of good food available at the hotel buffet. He ate there alone and snuck some generous portions back for Orpheus, who roused himself from a sleep of obvious exhaustion just long enough to wolf it all down.

He'd wondered how to deal with the denner's bodily functions, but at one point Orpheus disappeared and Toby found him splayed precariously over the toilet. He glared at Toby and so his human companion retreated with a muttered "sorry." It was quite hilarious, actually, but he stifled his laugh. Orpheus, he had begun to realize, had a real sense of dignity.

His feeling of having been sunburned proved not far from the truth. Toby's body seemed to be shedding all manner of dead material, so his skin started to itch and flake, some of his hair came out in the shower, and his kidneys were working overtime. Orpheus wasn't much better.

Still, he was eager to take the next step. His family was alive— all except Dad. He had to get to them. Some kind of misunderstanding had made it seem like Peter had tried to have him killed, but that couldn't be right. He'd sort it out as soon as he figured out what was going on. Right now, the one place he knew to go was the planet Destrier, where Mom was apparently wintering over.

He needed to know more, but there were no TVs or other screens in this world; data, music, and entertainment flowed through people's glasses or implants. Toby had seen a stall that sold interface rigs down in the market, so once he felt able, he left Orpheus in the room for an hour while he went to buy a set of these.

Jaysir had suggested he buy a pair of tourist glasses. He did but found they did little more than highlight local sights and were constantly popping ads up for this or that restaurant or gaming room. Every time they did that he jumped or stumbled. He got back to the room okay, though, and plunked himself down next to a lethargic Orpheus. "Let's see if I can at least connect to you," he said to the denner.

Jaysir had mentioned in an offhand way that the denners had interfaces, and sure enough, when he looked at Orpheus through the tourist glasses, the denner sprouted icons and emoticons. His interface was pretty simple, actually: Orpheus could broadcast his location, could signify basic needs like thirst or a need to pee, and he had an alarm clock for setting hibernation wake-up times.

The clock showed that it had last been set by a user named Guest. That would be Corva, he reasoned. The heavy man on Auriga had left the primary account wide open, so he quickly set the security levels on the alarm so only he could use it. So. That was done.

Now for the other thing he'd wanted to do.

"Search word *McGonigal*," he said. It seemed the easiest place to start—but Toby had no sooner spoken the word than his vision was filled with plane after plane of hovering pictures and hot links to videos, movies, books . . . There were thousands.

He reached out hesitantly and tapped one of the virtual pictures, which spun and enlarged.

Who was this? Toby was looking at a middle-aged, bullet-headed, bald man with grim frown lines around his mouth. Next to him stood a similarly grim woman, of similar age, her face narrow and her eyes and mouth pinched and severe.

They looked like relatives, but from which side of the family? Had there been other McGonigals on Earth, who'd come to Sedna after Toby's disappearance?

Then he saw the picture's caption: *Peter and Evayne McGonigal inaugurating a new pilgrimage center on Cephus, Lockstep Year 32.*

A rushing filled Toby's ears, and the room seemed to bend around him. He sat back cursing.

It was them, and yet not them. Instead of his brother and sister, here were their strange ghosts—specters not of the past but of some terrible future of decline and severe disappointments. So they seemed, anyway, as they stared out at him: bitter, unsatisfied, even accusing.

He could barely breathe. The picture continued to hang there, perfectly still yet looming larger and larger in his vision. Toby tried to look Peter in the eyes, but it was like staring into the sun—after just a glimpse he had to turn away—and when his gaze fell on Evayne's face, the same thing happened.

His mouth was dry and he was panting as, with a frantic gesture, he wiped away the photos and the search term.

Who were those people? How many worlds, how many years lined the dizzying abyss down which he'd just looked? Years, decades of separation taunted him from just those two pictures.

He didn't know these people. He didn't want to know them; he wanted the family he'd had barely a month ago.

"*Mrph?*" He looked up, realizing he'd buried his face in his drawn-up knees. Orpheus's huge eyes held concern, and he reached to ruffle the denner's fur. "It's okay," he murmured. "We just need to . . . sort it all out."

He was doubly exhausted now and lay back. Before he knew it he was waking up in his clothes, apparently having not moved a muscle for hours. Orpheus was curled up next to him. When he put on his glasses he found it was six o'clock in the morning.

"Aw, crap." His croaking voice woke up the denner, who yawned and stretched in a very catlike manner, then stared at him expectantly.

They had breakfast, paid for the night's lodgings and, after that, they were almost out of money. Toby found himself sitting on the whitewashed hotel steps watching Orpheus nose around the base of the decorative hedges. He had nowhere to go now, unless it was back to Corva with his tail between his legs. He could call Jaysir, but he was reluctant to play that card. The data block was pretty much the only leverage he had right now.

Or . . . he should just walk right up to the town hall and tell them who he was. He was the long-lost heir to the entire lockstep empire, after all.

And yet, and yet . . . There were those faces he'd seen in the photo. What if Corva wasn't lying?

If she wasn't, then not only Peter and Evayne were alive. Their mother was waiting in cold sleep for the day when he returned.

That was a terrible thought. He had to go to her.

The glasses pointed only to local sights. Amazing as those were—dozens of city spheres made up a kind of raft continent— the glasses wouldn't tell him anything about how to travel to other worlds. Apparently you needed to buy an upgrade for that. He thought about this for a while, then went back into the hotel.

"Excuse me," he said to the bot at the front desk, "how can I find out about flights to, well, a planet named Destrier?"

"That's easy, sir," said the bot in its perkily helpful synthetic voice. "What you need to do is visit the pilgrimage center."

| Seven |

ORPHEUS WAS LIKE A lead weight wrapping Toby's shoulders by the time he found the place. It was a cathedral-like building sitting by itself in a plaza in one of the larger city bubbles.

Getting here had been a magical, if exhausting, journey. Though there was public transit throughout the Continent (as the locals called the raft of bubbles), it mostly consisted of slidewalks and escalators. Toby had been carrying his denner for over an hour now, buoyed only by the occasional vistas of the Continent that opened out before him. Some of the city bubbles were many kilometers in diameter, and each had others next to, above, or below it, so that the eye followed lines of city and forest up to dizzying perches far overhead or down to cavernous depths. Outside it was a permanent storm-lit night; Wallop, it seemed, was a nomad planet like Lowdown, orphaned somewhere between the stars. Yet it was a hub of commerce and culture for the lockstep.

Religion was clearly a major part of that culture. Men and women in white robes were lined up between velvet ropes, patiently waiting to enter the cathedral—if that was what it was. Toby could see none of the religious symbols he knew from Earth. The only repeating motif seemed to be carvings and statues of a seated man, perhaps a king on a throne.

The backdrop for the cathedral was a wall of tessellated glass that swept up a hundred meters or more. No lights glowed behind it, nor any lightning. He trudged over and shaded his hand to look through the glass.

Frost had painted the other side of it, but through gaps in this he glimpsed darkened buildings and snow-draped sidewalks. "Is that another lockstep?" he asked a passerby.

The man laughed. "Naw, it's the Weekly. It'll open up in four or five days."

"Weekly?" He was too tired to hide his puzzlement.

The man tilted his head and peered at Toby. "Where are you from that you don't know the Weekly? Lockstep 90/.25? Client to 360?"

Toby shook his head. "Sorry, I'm from a . . . a little station."

"Must be." The man shook his head and walked away.

The line of pilgrims started at a set of tents where tearful people were saying good-bye to relatives and friends. They entered one tent and came out the other side wearing robes. Apparently, they were required to leave their bots behind, too, because there was a fair number of these milling around the tents but none in the lineup.

Toby approached a woman who was directing people. "Excuse me, I was told I could get to Destrier from here."

"Ha-ha, very funny," she said. "You can get fitted for robes that way."

"Okay, but seriously, can I get to Destrier from here?"

She stared at him. "Where else would we all be going?"

"How much does it cost?"

"Pilgrimage doesn't cost anything!" She seemed genuinely offended. "Who told you it did?"

"Then I can just show up?" he said hopefully.

She nodded. "Just take the vows and find a role in the Order you're assigned to, and you can go."

Vows. Orders? He nodded politely but stepped backward. "Uh, thanks. Maybe, maybe in a bit." Sure, you could get to Destrier for free—provided you joined some religion or other. Who knew what that would involve?

Disappointed, he was turning away when he spotted a commotion near the line. Was that an actual fight?

A small group of people had approached the line and were apparently handing out printed (physical, not virtual) pamphlets of some kind. This was being taken very badly by some of the ones in the queue. Toby couldn't make out all the words, but the pilgrims were shouting something about blasphemy, and the pamphleteers were saying something like, "Origin is false!"

Everybody around the tents seemed paralyzed with shock or indecision. That wasn't really surprising; Toby had seen no real violence since he'd arrived in the lockstep. Even now, he kept expecting bots to step in and separate the men and women who were shouting at one another, yet it wasn't happening.

Suddenly a pilgrim vaulted the line and struck one of the interlopers. Fists started flying. Toby crossed his arms and watched, increasingly uncomfortable with the fact that nobody was doing anything to stop it. He'd had to step in between Peter and Evayne on numerous occasions; it was what you did if you were a responsible adult. So where were the adults in this crowd?

A flicker of fair hair appeared among the fighting people. It was a young woman, maybe a year or two older than Toby, dressed in street clothes and carrying a shopping bag. She'd probably just been passing by, but now she was caught up in the mob.

One of the pilgrims grabbed her by the wrist.

Toby shouted, then found himself running across the plaza. Orpheus dug his claws painfully into his shoulders, complaining loudly. The man who'd grabbed the girl had raised his hand to slap her, but Toby got there just in time to grab him by the wrist and elbow, like Dad had shown him.

The pilgrim let go of his intended target and tried to hit Toby instead, but Toby pulled down on the wrist he was holding and pushed on the elbow. The pilgrim went down on his knees just as a spitting Orpheus landed on his head.

"Run!" Toby caught a glimpse of the girl's face before she whirled and bolted. Then Toby, too, danced out of reach of the gabbling, shouting mob. He ran back to the tent area, but by the time he felt he was safe and turned to look back, the girl was gone.

AN HOUR LATER, TOBY and Orpheus sat together at a sidewalk café while he tried to recover his strength. The whole incident had taken only seconds, and he hadn't even been hit, but he felt like he'd run a marathon. Orpheus wasn't much better. With his dwindling money, Toby was trying to revive them both with hot food.

He was wearing the tourist glasses, so the landscape around him was tagged and labeled, and he'd come to ignore all that information—but now the universal symbol for New Text Message suddenly appeared in the upper right of his field of vision. Startled, he said, "Somebody just texted me," to Orpheus.

A WTF? icon appeared over Orpheus's head. Toby laughed, then focused on the message flag. "Should I open it?" There were only three people on this world who might be contacting him.

NEED CASH? GOT A JOB FOR TODAY. —SHYLIF

"Huh." Shylif, not Jaysir, and definitely not Corva. There was a kind of sting to that fact. She wasn't talking to him. Or maybe he was just making that up? "Oh, Orph, I'm getting paranoid."

It was true he was already out of money. Jaysir's list had provided some alternative choices of lodging, and Toby had looked at a couple of those while they walked. The cheapest was a stack of shipping containers just above the warehouse level; Orpheus had growled as they approached it.

He thought for a while, then shrugged and replied: OKAY. WHERE DO I MEET YOU?

Shylif sent a map, and a little later Toby found himself down at the dock level of the city sphere, which was crowded with bots and machines, and almost empty of living people.

He spotted Shylif and raised his hand to wave—then lowered it and nearly ducked behind a pillar before cursing and stopping himself. Shylif was talking with Corva. After a minute or so she nodded to him and walked off to join a more-or-less human-shaped bot that handed her a bag of grippies and morphing tools. It poured a bunch of hand-sized swarm bots out of another bag and they hopped and danced around her feet. Wrecks swatted at these as they moved away.

It seemed Corva was working, too.

Toby shrugged off his misgivings and went up to Shylif. "Thanks for the job offer," he said, then added, "and sorry about running out on you guys."

Shylif laughed, a rich human sound among the otherwise mechanical noises of the docks. "I totally understand," he said. "I'd probably have done the same thing."

"But does *she* understand?"

"Corva'll come around. She's a bit like you—she needs time."

Toby had no ready comeback for that, so he just followed as Shylif set off through the maze of gantries, cargo racks and rushing bots. Shylif seemed content not to talk, and soon Toby found himself saying, "So . . . what are we doing today?"

"Oh, just a little theft recovery from Lockstep 270/2."

It took Toby a moment to process that. "There's another lockstep on Wallop?"

"There're six that I know of. Two-seventy-to-two is a pretty big one, and it's also pretty aggressive. If you don't watch 'em, their guys'll raid our cities while we're wintering over."

"They . . . *raid* us?"

"Theft of resources and manufactured goods." Shylif sent him a sardonic look. "Yeah, I thought it was pretty weird when I first heard about it. But then again, everything about the locksteps is weird."

"No, really?"

"Locksteps raid one another during hibernation periods," Shylif went on. "There're treaties forbidding retaliation, but they don't forbid recovery of the stolen material if you can find it. Some of 360's missing supplies were spotted in one of 270/2's cities, so an expedition is being mounted to recover them."

"How did we get in on it?"

"I found a couple of bots that had been ordered to go after their owner's stuff," said Shylif. "They're city units, not really built for wintering-over conditions. So I offered to subcontract for 'em. We'll get paid one hundred fifty if we return with any of the bots' stuff and two hundred if we return with all of it. I've got a manifest— here, I'll share it with you." An itemized list blinked into visibility in the corner of Toby's vision.

"That's all there is to it?"

"Well, no." Shylif looked a bit put out. "It takes a lot of time and effort to find opportunities like this."

"Can you teach me how to do it?"

Shylif grinned. "I can."

"Thanks."

"The ship's leaving from Portal Eighteen in twenty minutes. You're gonna need pressure suits. Are you bringing your denner?"

"I have nowhere to put him. I checked out of the hotel. Where do I get suits?"

"Hmm." Shylif grinned. "Let's make that your first test."

Twenty minutes to find a suit? Toby looked around, cursing under his breath. Shylif was walking briskly away, seemingly ignoring Toby now that he'd given him a task.

"How the hell are we going to get suits?" he muttered to Orpheus. "I mean, maybe I can rent one, but you . . ." He tried to think of similar situations he'd been in, either on Sedna or in Consensus, but couldn't remember any. What would Shylif expect him to do?

Use the resources you've got. Which, right now, amounted to the his denner, the clothes on his back, and a pair of tourist glasses . . .

Of course! He lowered a mapping overlay onto his vision. He could see Portal Eighteen, about half a kilometer around the curve of the warehouse level. Toby did some queries as he ran after Shylif, and dozens of yellow flags popped up in his visual field, showing the locations of public pressure suit kiosks.

So Wallop was like Sedna: as with firefighting bots on Earth, pressure suits were one of those basic safety devices you had to have handy on a world like this. The atmosphere outside this bubble city was probably toxic, and you never knew when some accident or deliberate attack might pierce the city's skin. Suits were everywhere. All Toby had to do was pause at one of the brightly colored pillars and drag out the collapsed suitcase-like shape. There weren't any denner-shaped ones, of course, but he did find a bin full of survival balls. These were just sacks you could jump into and zip shut, but they had transparent windows and five or six grippies on the outside that could detach and act as hands or help you crawl.

"It's this or you wait for me here," he told the denner. Orpheus just blinked at him.

Portal Eighteen wasn't the solid metal airlock Toby had been expecting. Instead, when he reached the outer wall of the tall warehouse space where it was set, he found himself facing what looked like a giant heart valve: three flimsy-looking plastic flaps overlapped one another to cover a circular opening about ten meters across. As Toby joined Shylif under it he could hear wind whistling around the flaps. "Is that air moving out, or something else coming in?" he wondered aloud.

Shylif shrugged. "If it was coming in, we'd be dead now."

A heavy rail mounted in the ceiling ran through this insecure opening; hanging off the rail was a spindle-shaped transparent airship not much bigger than the shipping container they'd come to Wallop in. It was like some kind of deep-sea fish. He could see its internal machinery, and he could also see that there were no gasbags inside it—it was just a set of metal hoop-shaped ribs with plastic stretched over them. Maybe the whole thing was one big gasbag.

"Hey! What're you doing?"

They turned to find a man in a half-furled pressure suit striding up to them. He was tall and sticklike, with long limbs and a ratcheting way of walking. Loops of rope and belts festooned with fasteners bounced as he stepped up to glare at the only humans on the floor.

Shylif said nothing; was this another test? "We're here to work," said Toby, trying not to sound defensive.

"Oh, you're the replacements?" This from a woman who was standing about two meters above Toby. She'd been adjusting something at the bow of the airship. "We're on time, then!"

The man frowned at a point somewhere over Toby's head— reading his virtual tags, no doubt. "I dunno. The big one's flagged with a résumé as long as my arm, but the kid's got no credentials at all. For all I know he's never been outside before."

Toby stuck out his jaw and tried to look bigger than he knew he was. "I've done hundreds of hours on the ice on Sedna."

The skinny man started to say something, but the woman overhead guffawed loudly. "That mined-out hulk? What the hell were you doing there?"

Toby thought about it. "Growing up," he said finally. Shylif was now struggling to suppress a smile.

"Aw, let's give them a chance, Casson," she said. "If they've done cold they might be okay." She strode down the gangplank, and Toby could see she was wearing an outfit similar to Casson's. She saw Toby looking and lifted her loops of climbing line and let them fall. "You need a Personal Flying Device and some cords. If you're replacing the Segentry bot you'll be on my team, lucky for you but bad for me if you don't perform."

Toby nodded. "I'm . . . Garren."

"This one's Casson. I'm Nissa. PFDs're over there." Up close she looked fairly ordinary, except that her eyes were a striking pale mauve. She pointed at a heap of brightly colored bins on the warehouse floor below the airship. Then she blinked. "Hey, what's that?" She grabbed at Toby's backpack.

Orpheus stuck out his head and hissed.

Toby tensed, but all Nissa did was shrug and say, "It's like that, is it? He stays on board when we go in." She shot a sidelong look at Casson, who shrugged.

"Okay." Maybe these people had dealt with stowaways before.

"All right, now get goin'!" Casson jabbed a thumb at a line of bots that was marching up a gangplank into the open side of the airship, which apparently had nothing but ordinary air inside it. "We're leaving in five."

TOBY'S HEART HAD STARTED pounding when he entered the airship. The thing was so flimsy; it faced him with the reality of where they were about to go. He barely noticed the pressure suit building itself onto his body, and it wasn't until Orpheus gently seized his ankle with his teeth that Toby snapped out of his terror.

He bent to stroke the denner's head. "I'll be fine." When he straightened it was to see that they were already under way, sliding down the rail and through the city's sphincter. This was a disturbingly biological experience. Once the ship was outside, though, it bobbed comfortably in the air. Toby didn't know what made up Wallop's atmosphere, but whatever it was, ordinary air at room temperature was lighter. He dragged in a couple of deep breaths to calm himself, then took his first clear look at the planet he was on.

Right then he almost begged Casson to turn around and take him back. Since he'd climbed out of the shipping container he'd known, in an intellectual sort of way, that there was no surface to Wallop. Now, looking out the transparent side of the airship and down through clouds, with clouds below those, and basements of clouds on abysses of more clouds . . . he had to find something else to look at.

Shylif was sitting quietly, staring at nothing. Toby's eyes fell on Orpheus, who was also staring into the endless depths of coiling gray and black. If Orpheus had been a dog, his tail would be wagging. Toby had to laugh.

Shylif looked up, and Casson, who was up at the bow with Nissa, also heard the laugh and grunted. "Bots don't usually do that," he said. "Neither do first-timers."

"It's Orpheus," said Toby. "I think he likes it here."

"Orpheus? Good name. Maybe he always wished he had wings. Some of us are like that." Casson turned back to discussing the flight plan with Nissa.

Now Shylif came to sit next to Toby. He nodded at the darkness outside. "I spent most of my life on solid ground. Took me years to get used to these worlds."

"Plenty of them have surfaces, don't they?"

"Yeah, but . . . not trees, usually. Not forests."

"Ah." Toby looked down. "I miss Earth. Have since we left for Sedna."

There was a brief silence between them, then Shylif said, "You gotta know that lots of people go through what you're going through. Except that most of them know about the locksteps in advance. But that sense of being ripped out of your world . . . that's actually pretty normal."

He paused, thinking. "What hangs over your head is not being able to go back. Earth's not the same place as when you left it. There's nowhere to go but forward."

Was he hinting that Toby shouldn't try to go to Destrier? If he was, he was being pretty roundabout with it. Toby wanted to ask him about the dark past that Jaysir had described, but he wasn't sure how. "You came from outside the locksteps, right?"

Shylif nodded. "And now I can't return. The moment you step into this world, you give up everything you had before. It's like time burns it away before your very eyes."

"Then, why . . ."

"Why come here at all?" Shylif turned sad eyes on Toby. "Some people treat it like a train to a better future. They hop on, and when they hear about some world or civilization that's come up that appeals to them, they step off. Some people think it's a way of leaving mortal time altogether and becoming eternal, but that's ridiculous. We all die. And some . . . some just get tired of wandering the halls of the dead, calling out to people who'll never respond."

He started to walk away, but Toby said, "Hey, what's your connection to Corva?"

Shylif looked back. "She came to the docks looking for a way to get to Lowdown. Some of us stowaways were there—as well as other people who'd have eaten her for lunch. She needed help.

I . . . needed somebody to help." He shrugged, a motion barely visible through his suit.

"Help to do what?"

Shylif shook his head and headed aft.

There was no point in pressing; Toby knew he'd get no more from the man. With nothing else to do, he sat back with Orpheus, followed the denner's gaze into the darkness—and quickly became transfixed by what he saw.

He'd thought of the continent as self-contained, locked away from the environment it sailed through—but that wasn't the case at all. The piled-up bubbles sprouted gantries and balconies and docks and diving boards, and the air around and above them was full of darting, soaring shapes: airships, like the one he was in, but also aircraft and even winged humans. Some of these were nearby, so he could make out what they were doing—they seemed to be engaged in some sort of sporting event as they swooped and soared within a volume defined by six giant glowing hoops.

The continent was a collision of lanterns, or a surf of glowing pearls hanging untroubled amid Wallop's storms. The cities' curving sides cradled the white of towers and the green of cultivated jungles that raveled them like verdigris staining a glass ball.

Wisps of dark cloud began drifting across this vision as the airship picked up speed. Toby was too excited to be tired now; he tore his gaze from what was behind them, and as he did he spotted something. Far, far away, in the darkness beyond the Continent, a tiny yellow speck played peekaboo from behind the black skirts of a thunderhead a hundred times its size. With a jolt he realized that this tiny dot of light was another city. Now that he could use it for scale, the rest of the hammerheads and towers of billowing lightning-lit vapor surrounding him were suddenly revealed as utterly gigantic, way bigger than mountains—as big, it seemed, as worlds.

Way, way up above this cloud deck, lightning momentarily silhouetted a tiny black dot against the highest of the charcoal-colored clouds. Then the lightning was gone, leaving cutout thunderhead shapes against a velvet, star-spattered night.

With this he realized they'd been rising quite quickly; the continent was a smear of yellow far below his feet. They rose and rose through the stratified layers of Wallop's atmosphere, and eventually the stars became regular companions. They'd left the lightning far below, so it was by starlight that Toby came to see the horizon of Wallop. The little airship seemed surrounded by vast towers of black, but through gaps in these he could see similar thunderheads foresting the distance in smaller and smaller ranks. On any reasonably-sized planet those ranks would have lowered steadily to fall below the horizon line, but according to the tourist glasses Wallop was somewhere around the size of Neptune, so they simply became smaller and smaller until they merged in a blur at infinity. Staggered by distance and scale, Toby fell silent and just watched.

All the while, a distant city grew larger, like a blackened crystal ball, empty of prophecies. "It's not lit up," Toby said, and now he knew he sounded worried.

"It's wintering over." Shylif had returned and was standing next to him. "No need for lights when everybody's asleep. 'Course, its reactors are still keeping it warm enough to float. But the air up there is pretty calm; it's the best place to park a city if you want to avoid the storms for a decade or two." He pointed, and now Toby could see that the city sphere trailed hundreds of fine threadlike cables into the depths below it, like some technological jellyfish. "Those strips filter-feed trace amounts of metal and minerals out of the air. Takes decades to accumulate enough for a month's industry."

"Okay," Nissa called from the bow, "here's how this works. Those boys"—she nodded up at the black bowl of the sky— "intercepted some of our cargoes while we wintered over. The government doesn't care. It's a civil matter—lost property and all that. So the owners have to recover it. They've sent their bots to do that." She pointed her chin at the motley crowd of household bots and bulkier worker drones milling in the back of the airship. "Whatever it is they've lost is worth more than a bot or two, 'cause they risk

losing them and getting nothing back. Casson and I are along because it's against all kinds of rules, laws and treaties to invade
somebody else's wintering habitat using bots. Those same laws say
that you can't deny shelter and life support to a visitor. So we can
walk right in there and get the stuff, and the bots can come with us."

Toby frowned doubtfully. "What if they resist?"

"If they really wanted to resist, we wouldn't get within ten kilometers of the place," said Casson. "They don't want a war with
our lockstep. All they can do is bare-faced lie and say they don't
have the stuff. And since we know where it is, they can't stop us
walking in and taking it."

"Okay."

The city loomed overhead like a perfect thundercloud. Casson
switched on a powerful spotlight and they searched for a while
until they found a landing platform that stuck a good hundred
meters out of the city's flank. You could have landed an ocean
liner on it, yet Casson set their little airship down right in the center as if claiming the entire space.

As they drifted in Toby wondered how they were going to come
to a stop; he started as with a clang six bots fell or jumped off the
underside of the airship. They must have been holding on to it all
this time. They carried cables which they proceeded to unreel as
they searched for attachment points. There were plenty of these,
and in seconds they'd secured the airship.

Toby started to follow the others to the hatch, but Orpheus
stopped him by weaving in between his feet, causing him to nearly
trip. "Hey! Stop it. What—" Orpheus skipped back to the nose of
the airship, pressed his snout against the transparent plastic and
planted his paws on either side, for all the world like a little man
staring out. Toby paused, laughed, and went to join him. There
was a traffic jam at the hatch anyway; he had a moment.

The gameworlds he'd crafted with Peter had contained nothing
like this. The boys had plundered centuries' worth of science-
fiction and fantasy art to build their virtual worlds. They'd generated thousands of planets, from vast ringed monstrosities laced

with rainbows of clouds, to airless chunks of pure gold orbiting close to yellow stars and roaring with leonine light. They'd imagined desert worlds and water worlds, jungle planets and glacier-bound icescapes. Nothing they'd done had prepared Toby for the three actual worlds he'd seen since awaking in the lockstep. Nothing could have prepared him for what he was seeing now.

The airship looked like a glass tube lying on its side on a shelf that, no matter how broad it was, still seemed precarious. They were perched at the very top of this world's atmosphere. The delicacy and mesmerizing detail of a starlit cloudscape lay below them, all the more hypnotic because the peaks and outflung arms of vapor appeared perfectly still. It was like the entire world was wintering over.

Toby had a flash of vision then, an image of himself curled up and as still as this for the past thirty years—no, more: motionless and waiting, *for fourteen thousand* . . .

Just for that one moment, he felt equal to this place, for the city was doing only what he'd already done. Then Shylif called his name and he had to turn away.

"This way." He left Orpheus on the ship but made sure he was in his survival ball just in case. Then he followed space-suited human figures, and incongruously ordinary-looking bots, across the stillness of the platform and through a set of gigantic half-open doors. Apparently the city wasn't worried about maintaining its internal atmosphere right now; he saw other open portals at intervals around the curve of the dark interior.

Here were city towers, houses and trees, all in a very different style from the ones in the Continent. "They're sort of Mayan," he commented.

"What's Mayan?" asked Shylif.

"Before your time, I guess." Thankfully, it was hard to make out details in the darkness; he didn't really want to feel the oppressive gaze of all those empty windows on him. How many frozen human forms were curled up behind them, waiting out the years of what, to them, would feel like a single night?

That made him think of what Shylif had said earlier, about "wandering the halls of the dead, calling out to people who'll never respond." Jaysir said he had waited thirty years for his lost love to awaken again . . .

Chilled by the thought, Toby hurried after the others.

The fans of light cast by the bots' headlamps were easy to follow, so he jogged after them across frosted, snow-drifted balconies and ramps. Soon he saw where they were going: an incongruous heap of crates lay half submerged in snow near a frozen fountain. Without ceremony, the bots began rooting through the boxes, tossing aside the ones that, presumably, weren't owned by their masters.

"That's it?" Toby watched the free-for-all in puzzlement. "We just pick 'em up and go home?"

Shylif laughed shortly. "You want it to be exciting?"

"Well . . . maybe not."

"Anyway, it's not like they're not watching us." He pointed, and Toby, looking where he indicated, experienced a sudden heart-stopping shock. *Somebody was standing there, in the shadows.* It wasn't a bot, but a space-suited figure, human shaped. It stood as still as the icicles that hung above it like Damocles's sword, its metal arms crossed, feet planted wide, faceplate blank and dark.

"Wh-who's that?"

Shylif turned away. "A sentry, a keeper . . . call him what you want. This lockstep has them. They walk up and down the ramparts of the city, twenty years alone . . . If that one wanted us dead, we would never have made it this far."

"You boys got a manifest?" Casson's voice broke Toby out of his uneasy distraction.

"Yes," said Shylif. He called up the list of crates he and Toby were to haul. There weren't too many, but still, they'd have to make several trips. Toby cut a wide berth around the other bots, which were tumbling whatever they didn't want into a broad debris field around the central mound of boxes. He quickly found the first of the crates, heaved it onto his shoulder, and began to make his way back to the airship.

It was on his third trip that he began to realize how weak he still was. He'd just come out of hibernation, after all—and not your normal, run-of-the-mill thirty-year sleep, either. That wry thought made him laugh, and drop his crate.

He was sitting on it when Shylif came by, toting a much bigger box. "Tired?"

"I'll hire you to carry this one back, too."

Shylif laughed but didn't take him up on the offer. After hibernation, he was probably nearing the last of his strength, too. Toby took a deep breath and hoisted his box to follow.

This was a different lockstep from Peter's. Shylif had said that there were a number of them here on Wallop—and why shouldn't they be scattered throughout the universe? The name 270/2 described a timing ratio different from 360. Maybe they all ran on their own frequencies, and those might or might not ever sync up. Also, they might have been started at anytime during the past fourteen thousand years. Even a lockstep full of human beings just like himself might have a culture and traditions—not to mention language and technologies—thousands of years removed from Toby's. The mere thought made his head whirl, but all he had to do was glance around to know it must be true.

He struggled under the weight of the last crate on his shoulder and barely registered Orpheus's greeting when he reached the airship. The other bots all made it back with their cargoes, and Nissa cast off. Then she and Casson chattered on about the thieving habits of decadent locksteps as they turned the ship's nose into a canyon of open black air and began the long dive back to the Continent. Fatigued as he was, Toby barely heard them.

Shylif sat with him in companionable silence as they sailed back to the raft of cities. Somehow this easy quiet made Toby decide to trust the older man in a way he'd never quite managed with talkative Ammond. When they reached the city spheres and docked, Toby was able to unload his share of crates himself and took payment on the spot from Shylif.

Once they were out of their suits and the dock was behind

them, Shylif said, "Give me a call tomorrow. I'll show you how to find bots that want to subcontract."

Toby grinned. "Sounds good. And Shy, thanks."

"Don't mention it. Seriously, don't let Corva know." He rolled his eyes. "I'll talk her around. But give me a few days."

"Thanks."

In a kind of daze, he walked out of the warehouse district and rode an escalator up into the city. Orpheus chittered and danced about, obviously glad to be back on what passed here for terra firma. Toby smiled vaguely at him, but his gaze kept drifting. He was thinking about how vastly different the locksteps might be and how strangely familiar this one seemed. The people, the buildings . . . it was all bizarre and alien, this bubble city and the civilization it cradled—but there remained that strange familiarity.

It hit him when a woman passed him wearing a completely recognizable outfit of tunic and leggings. He spun, staring at her as she receded, and then he swore, and laughed, and swore again.

He'd seen that apparel just a couple months ago. In fact, he'd helped to design it.

In creating Lockstep 360/1, his brother Peter hadn't merely been inspired by the culture, customs and technologies of the gameworld he and Toby had created together.

Lockstep 360/1 *was* Consensus.

| Eight |

TOBY AND PETER HAD built a world together.

It hadn't been fun.

If you were the right kind of rich, and living on Earth, you could afford those things the rich needed: gated communities, 24/7 security bots, and human bodyguards who came with their own micro-armies of hand-sized flying guns and gnat-shaped spies. You could move through the world in your own little bubble of safety this way—if you were the right kind of rich.

The McGonigals weren't that kind of rich.

Dad had made his fortune in salvage—the deep-sea kind. His company hunted down methane clathrates and CO_2 sinks in ocean trenches, and converted their carbon to less volatile forms. Nobody wanted a repeat of the Big Belch, when the Arctic oceans had vomited up millions of years' worth of greenhouse gases in just a few short decades, undoing two generations' work in reducing CO_2 emissions. Temperatures had shot up to intolerable levels after the belch, and it was small consolation that the frantic international effort to build orbital sunshades had finally kick-started an offworld civilization.

Dad called himself a lowly greenhouse gas exterminator, but he'd made enough doing it to approach the threshold of being noticed by the truly wealthy. Mom was a garbage designer; it was her genius at optimizing the wastes of one industrial process so that you could sell them as inputs to another that had ultimately made possible the colonizing of Sedna. Nobody else could have built the superefficient resource management system that was the key to the colony's success. Toby's parents had skills that were perfect for settlers taking on a hostile environment at the edge of the solar system. But they had never planned to go there.

If Dad had become just wealthy enough to be noticed by the more condescending of the trillionaires, he'd also become just wealthy enough to be noticed by those who preyed on them.

So one bright spring day, Toby came home to find the front door of their mansion smashed in. The nanny was dead on the kitchen floor. Toby spent a long time staring at the blood matted in her long blond hair, how it stuck to the tiles, until he suddenly realized that Peter was missing.

All he could clearly remember now was that he'd run through the house, shouting Peter's name. Later, policemen and detectives had shown up—lots of them. Mom and Dad were there, and Evayne, too. Evayne had tightly clutched her plush toys, peering over their heads as they (minor robots as they were) also peered around. The toys had known something was wrong, and they'd gone into trauma-counseling mode as soon as the police arrived. Evayne had spent the next month listening to their soothing voices and talking to them, and with that and the right kind of pills, she'd come out of the whole thing just fine.

For Toby, the only thing that kept him from screaming himself awake at night was full participation in the investigation. He had to know everything that was being done, had to go with Dad to the police station to hear the latest updates. He learned all about the kidnapper culture that had developed out of the unholy marriage of interplanetary organized crime and a highly polarized society where you were either rich and independent, or destitute and indentured.

He remembered whole days of the search, entire conversations with his parents and with Evayne. But like the kidnapping itself, he could barely recall the day Peter had come home.

The kidnappers were dead. Peter had seen them go down in a

spray of gunfire. By the time that had happened, he'd been with them long enough that he'd started to bond with them, or so the psychiatrists said. Even though his captors promised to kill him if his parents didn't pay the ransom, Peter had begun to trust them, even grudgingly agree with their claim that they were justified in kidnapping him. The husband-and-wife team was poor, after all—deeply and irrevocably poor. There was no hope for them ever climbing out of that by legal means. Society was at fault here, not them, Peter insisted.

The kidnappers hadn't told Peter that they'd killed the nanny. Toby remembered the moment in the interview room when Peter found out. He'd been sitting there defiant, tears in his eyes, after screaming insults at the detectives. They'd murdered his friends, he accused. They were the monsters here.

"How can you say that?" the lead detective had burst out. "They killed Maria Teresa."

Peter had just blinked at him.

"Your nanny," the detective said. "They killed your nanny when they took you."

"Stop it, he's only eight years old," Dad said.

It was too late. Toby could see it in Peter's eyes, like a sudden crumbling. He'd gotten very quiet after that.

The quiet stretched for days, then weeks. Psychiatrists came and went. Mom and Dad had been distraught during the kidnapping, but now that it was over, a deeper despair seemed to be settling on them. Peter no longer smiled, and so neither did they.

Evayne was okay. She had her trauma-counselor toys. They tried these on Peter, and they helped a little. But nothing really worked, and Toby knew it even if Mom and Dad didn't. Somebody had to do something for Peter, and whatever it was, it would have to be just as huge as the kidnapping itself had been.

It took him four months of hard work before he was ready to bring Peter in. Toby had pressed Dad to buy him the very best sim-building software. Its distant ancestors had been a whole raft of game engines, 3-D modeling programs, and moviemaking packages. You could build entire universes with this stuff. But Toby had decided to start small.

"It's the house," Peter said. It was his first visit to Toby's world. For weeks he'd been practically climbing the walls from impatient curiosity. He'd known Toby was up to something, but his older brother wouldn't say what. Now he'd finally donned the link glasses (he wasn't old enough for direct implants) and had flipped into the virtual world Toby had made—and here was the very last thing he'd expected to find there.

They'd sold the house, of course. There was no going back to that place for any of them—and yet Toby had recreated it, in as perfect detail as he could remember. It sat alone on a gray plane under an equally gray sky. He and Peter were also standing on that plane, about thirty meters from the building.

"Why'd you do that?" Peter whined. "Why is *that* here?"

"Don't worry, we're not going in," Toby told him. He put a hand on his brother's shoulder. "You and I are going to make something."

"What?" Peter was still staring at the house, eyes wide.

"We," said Toby, "are going to build a world around this house. It's going to be a world where nothing bad could ever happen in this place. It's not going to be the world we've got now. It's going to be the world we wish we had."

Despite all his efforts, he hadn't thought this would work. Truth be told, he'd built the virtual house mostly to work through his own bad memories. Toby fully expected Peter to rip off the interface and not speak to him for the remainder of the week.

Instead, Peter said, "We need a wall."

"Maybe," Toby admitted grudgingly. "But what if we built a world where we *didn't* need a wall?"

Peter had looked at him, startled. Toby knew he had him hooked.

So Consensus was born.

TOBY'S FIRST RUN WITH Nissa and Casson netted him enough money to live for three days. He spent the time looking for more work and exploring the town. He felt vaguely guilty at avoiding

Corva and her friends, but he also felt inexplicably angry at them, like it was their fault that he had to feel guilty at all. It was confusing.

He'd lucked out and discovered a little bed-and-breakfast in the midlevels of the continent. It was a house, of sorts, reminiscent of the dwellings he'd seen once on the island of Santorini, before the family had left Earth. Narrow lanes and stairways led up the steepening curve of the sphere where apartments and condominiums piled up overtop one another. The bed-and-breakfast was at the end of a flight of steps that rose between two high walls. There was a little landing, and opposite the notch that led to the steps was a doorway surrounded by tangled vines. The proprietors looked like a pair of young, fit newlyweds—but they assured Toby they were both in their eighties, having immigrated to the lockstep from the inner solar system some six thousand (real) years before. They had led him to a very nice bedroom that looked out on the storm-ridden sky, told him supper would be at six, and left him and Orpheus alone.

He knew he should be learning more about the lockstep civilization, but where could he start other than with his brother and sister? Yet he had only to glimpse a photo or video of Peter or Evayne as grown-ups and his heart started to thump painfully. It was impossible to look at them. He didn't want to know they were real. So instead of broadening his knowledge of the year 14,000, he plotted how he was going to get to Destrier, where his mother waited for him.

Nothing would be easier than to announce his presence to the world. He should just get it over with, but his mouth turned dry at the very thought of telling somebody who he was. It wasn't the idea of suddenly being famous or important that terrified him, nor was it the possibility that Peter and Evayne didn't want him around for some reason. It was the prospect of actually being reunited with them—or, really, the colorless middle-aged versions who'd replaced the incandescent children he knew as Evayne and Peter.

Luckily, he had Orpheus. He and the denner were getting to know each other. Orpheus was very catlike, and he'd obviously made his choice where Toby was concerned. He'd romp away to

investigate some bush or staircase winding down the terraced interior of the city sphere, and when he disappeared from sight Toby
would be seized with a sudden terrible anxiety that he wouldn't
come back. But he always did—often with some pretty girl oohing
and aahing after him.

"Orph, are you trying to set me up?" he'd muttered after one of
these encounters. Orpheus had sent him an enigmatic stare, then
flounced away again.

The denner's own interface wasn't keyed to verbal commands or
gestures. It read Orpheus's pupil dilation, stance and other atten-
tional factors, as well as pheromones and major motions. It tracked
his circadian rhythms and energy use, and then translated all that
it saw into terms Toby could understand. He knew when Orpheus
was hungry—well, that was easy. But he could also piggyback on
the denner's reactions to the people around them. Orpheus would
scan the crowd with a quick twitch of his head, and then tags would
blossom over the heads of everybody in sight: green for those people Orph thought were trustworthy, red for those who weren't.
Other colors appeared, too, standing for assessments Orpheus had
made but that Toby couldn't now (and maybe never would) understand.

He'd been talking to Orpheus all along, but after a couple of days
with the interface Toby realized he was no longer saying things half
rhetorically, the way you did to pets. He'd stopped assuming that
Orpheus didn't understand him, because it was becoming very plain
that the denner did—just not in the way a human would. Orph saw
the context of Toby's speech, things like whether he was talking because he was nervous or socially cued by the situation he was in; his
emotional state; even, broadly, what it was he was trying to get out of
speaking. All without understanding a single word. And the glyphs
and icons that twirled around Orpheus's head like pain stars over a
cartoon character told Toby as much about him.

And so yes, it became obvious that when Orpheus dragged yet
another girl out from behind some bush or shop door, he really
was trying to set Toby up.

Now, even though he couldn't bear to open the books about his family or watch the many movies, Toby felt he was finally ready to explore the world he and Peter had built.

"THANKS FOR COMING." JAYSIR stood outside Toby's door, his bot—really less of a bot, more of a mobile contraption—taking up much of the hall behind him.

Noticing this, Toby poked his head out the door to look around. "My landlady doesn't like visitors. Particularly bots."

"Well, you shouldn't have said to meet here, then." Jaysir stood waiting until Toby moved aside, then came in and plunked himself in the room's only armchair. This left Toby the bed to sit on. Orpheus slunk as far from the cargo bot as he could get, while Toby rehearsed the things he wanted to ask Jaysir.

"Where is it?" Jaysir leaned forward eagerly. "You said you'd let me read it."

"Did you tell Corva where I'm staying?"

"No . . . but I might have, if I'd seen her this morning. She's not hunting you down or anything, you know."

"Of course not, I didn't mean—well, it's just that . . ." Toby decided to quit while he was ahead. "Anyway, I'm glad you came by." Toby brought out the data block and held it up.

Jaysir leaned forward to examine it without touching it. "Where'd you get it? Brought it with you on that little ship?"

"*They* had it. The people Ammond and Persea were meeting with on Auriga."

Uncomfortable with Jaysir's suddenly intense attention, Toby recounted the events in the underwater house on Auriga. Jaysir had him go through the sequence in detail twice. Then he sat back, thinking.

"It never struck you as odd that they tested your identity with the bot?"

Toby shook his head. "Why would it? The twentier was probably the only thing they could get that dated back to my time on Sedna. How else would they verify my ID?"

Jaysir snorted. "By telling you to command any bed anywhere on any lockstep world!" He waved at the one Toby was sitting on. "That one, for instance. Haven't you even tried to wake one up, reset its clock?"

"You told me not to." He had that feeling of things moving too fast for him again. "Why? Because it's a Cicada Corp bed, like—"

"—Like every other legal hibernation bed in the seventy thousand worlds. Which means you should be able to command it: start it up, shut it down, change its schedule to whatever you want. You sure you never tried?"

"No . . ."

"Good."

Toby got off the bed and knelt beside it. It looked like a standard pedestal bed, but the base had a label on it with some kind of iridescent insect shape. *A cicada, dimwit,* he told himself. There were various hatches and ports in the bottom, too.

"There're other locksteps, right?" he asked. "Do they use these?"

"Well, not these. Not McGonigal beds. Those are locked to our frequency. And using other beds in our lockstep is . . . well, not strictly illegal, but they make it damned inconvenient if you try."

Jaysir knelt next to him. "You don't have an interface for this, do you?"

"You mean in my glasses? No . . ."

"Well, that's part of the mystery, I suppose. But these things do have voice activation, too. Anyway, it's a good thing you haven't tried it."

"So you said. But why?" Toby got up, and this time he took the armchair.

Jaysir didn't seem to notice. "Why do you think those people who had you used the twentier to test you? And why do you think they did the test in that house, in an underwater room?"

"Well, I . . ." Auriga had been such a strange and exotic place, it had never occurred to Toby that meeting in the dockside house would be considered in any way unusual there.

"The bot wasn't connected to the Cicada Corp network, not then, and maybe not ever. It predated it. But it didn't predate your biocryptography. And the house was shielded, at least by the water and maybe by other countermeasures. It was a safe place to test you."

"Why safe? Safe from what?"

"Think about it. What would happen if you commanded the bed you're sitting on?"

"I don't know. I don't know anything about them."

"They're all networked, Toby. The first thing it would do would be announce to the rest of the network that Toby Wyatt McGonigal had just switched it on! Don't you think that little piece of information might just be . . . important to some people?"

"You mean they . . . that Peter and Evayne would find out where I was?"

"Exactly. And the fact that they used the twentier and not a bed means your brother may not know for sure that you're back."

"All this time I could have contacted them just by saying 'hi' to any old *bed*?"

"Which is the last thing you should be doing right now, trust me."

Toby crossed his arms. "Didn't we talk about whether I trust you? And the answer was . . ."

"Okay, okay!" Jaysir hopped up and down on the bed, looking agitated. "Just—just wait. Wait until you know more about what's going on. Please. If not for me, then for you."

Toby glowered at him, but somehow knowing that contact with his family was literally a word away made him feel safer—and willing, for the moment, to hear Jaysir out.

"So this is actually a hibernation bed?" It looked perfectly ordinary, until you examined the base.

"Stuff comes out of the hatches when you're asleep," said Jaysir absently. "You know, same way a space suit builds itself onto you. The bed'll build its cocoon on you and not even wake you up."

Toby remembered Ammond telling him that the nanotech and artificial organs that managed hibernation had been perfected over thousands of years. Now, though, he realized that while it might have been refined over aeons, probably every version had been commissioned and paid for by one client: the eternal Cicada Corp.

As far as the many civilizations on Earth and the other non-hibernating planets were concerned, the McGonigals had always been here. They predated the posthuman artificial life-forms; they'd inhabited these spaces before, during, and after the settling of all the nearby star systems.

"Jay, am I right in thinking that *this*"—he nodded at the bed—"is the most reliable investment in the galaxy?"

"Hmm? Oh, of course! Stable over thousands of years, and the McGonigals try to own or otherwise control the lockstep technology everywhere, no matter how many strange mutations of culture and biology it gets passed through." Jaysir laughed. "They can do this because they have the time."

"Then what about the denners?"

"When you're talkin' thousands of years, and thousands of worlds and cultures, *something's* gonna slip through the cracks. There are other empires with their own rules, and there're . . . things out there so powerful they can completely ignore the McGonigals. There's even better hibernation technology that sometimes finds its way back into the lockstep, in forms the McGonigals can't control. Denners are a great example of that. They came from Barsoom, their ancestors were cats whose genes were altered so they could tolerate ice age conditions. They could probably have survived on the prehuman Mars, if there'd been anything for them to eat. All they need to do the job of the cicada beds is a neural implant to improve their internal clock and an upgrade on their synthorgans to project heat for waking a companion. You could theoretically modify a human to contain all the tech and not use a bed at all—but the beds can detect that kind of mod, and it's illegal. You'd never be able to use a bed again if you got modded that way, and that's just not practical. But the denners—they give you the option.

"Anyway, lemme see that data block."

Toby moved it away. "First of all, what are you going to do with it? What if it's got stuff on it you could, well, sell? Or blackmail me with?"

Jaysir squinted at him. "Do you even know what a maker *is*?"

"Uh, yeah." Jay had told him a bit about them when they'd first met, and since then, Toby had looked it up on the public net. Makers valued personal autonomy over everything else. The maker ethos was to build everything you used and not to rely on money at all. Makers might own bots—even lots of them—but they tried to be their own microeconomies and microecologies. Toby wouldn't have been surprised if it turned out that Jaysir's walking contraption made food for him as well as serving as a mobile hibernatorium. Of anyone he was likely to meet, a maker was probably the least likely to want to steal something from him.

"I want to look at the firmware and design," Jay continued. "Maybe I can use it. I don't care about the data! But it's really old and probably incompatible with modern systems. Same with your original glasses, so hand 'em over, too, if you want them to work properly. Yes yes, don't be so reluctant! Why would I use a subtle ploy to track you or bug your stuff if we could have just knocked you on the head back on Auriga?"

Warily, Toby handed over the frames.

Jaysir folded his legs under him and put the block and the glasses on the bedcover. Then he waved over his bot, which began efficiently laying out various small instruments and tools in a half circle around him.

He started with the glasses. At first Toby tried asking him some of the other questions he'd been accumulating, but Jaysir just shrugged them off—he was concentrating. So with nothing else to do, Toby had to just sit back and watch.

After about half an hour Jaysir flipped the glasses back to Toby. "Try 'em now." He slid them on and tapped the arm to wake them up.

Tags bloomed into view everywhere: hovering (apparently) in the bed itself, in the walls and beyond, where he glimpsed a ghostly half-visible map of the city and continent. The mundane tags he'd seen through the tourist glasses were still visible, but now there was so much more as well. Jaysir's bot was festooned with tags and labels, as was Jaysir himself—social media hooks, mostly, in his case. Even the chairs had virtual labels that indicated who owned them, where they were, and warned of prosecution if they were taken off-site or damaged.

"Oh!" said Toby, trying to look around at everything at once. His former sense of the lockstep world being strangely unsophisticated was quite wiped away: the whole place was alive in the virtual realm. This really should have come as no surprise; Toby had grown up with virtual and augmented realities and had been missing them since he awoke here. Still, so much was strange in the locksteps. The lack of virtual layer had just been one more difference.

"Better, no?" Jaysir was attaching fine wires to the data block, so he couldn't see the expression on Toby's face, which Toby figured was probably a good thing.

Only a minute or two later, Jaysir hissed, "Yeess! I got it!" Even as he said these words, a virtual menu was coalescing above the block. "Data, data, you got data, Toby."

It was a confusing muddle, though. Toby saw dozens of giant backup files, each indicated by a translucent safe icon (complete with a little combination dial). Knowing twentiers as he did, he supposed these would contain endless video of the thing digging— digging trenches, digging holes, digging *in* trenches and holes. But there were other files, too.

He sucked in a breath. "It can't be!"

Jaysir had gotten to his feet. He turned and frowned. "What? You recognize something?"

"Some of these files . . . they're game saves."

"Games?" Jay shook his head. "Some games are on there?"

"Not just some games, Jay. *The* game.

"These are versions of Consensus."

TOBY HAD ISSUED HIS brother a challenge: imagine, then build a world where he could be safe. The first thing Peter made with the

Consensus tools was a cathedral of weapons, whose every brick contained a loaded gun barrel and every pillar, a bundle of blades ready to leap out and strike. It was munitions all the way down, and walls and locked doors, too, with roving sentry tanks and swarming drones and trapdoors. It was a magnificent hymn to paranoia, this cathedral, and outside its walls nothing grew: Peter had annihilated nature in this universe, just in case.

Toby had anticipated something like this, so he'd set the meta-rules by which they'd have to operate. As Peter was excitedly giving him a tour through the place, it came as no surprise when one of the sentry tanks failed to recognize Peter as the owner and blew them both to smithereens with one blast of its ion cannon.

It was more than a year before Toby was able to suggest (and Peter was able to hear), "Why don't you just build a world where nobody would have any *reason* to attack you?"

This had never occurred to Peter. In fact, it had never occurred to him that violence might have reasons.

Sometimes Toby had despaired of the lesson ever taking hold. But the revelation that there were Consensus gameworlds stored in the twentier's data block got him thinking about the game. He didn't open any of them after Jaysir left—they were from the years just after Toby's disappearance, and he was half afraid of what might be in them. This didn't prevent him from seeing Consensus everywhere he went, though. As he and Orpheus strolled the rich upper levels of the city, he found himself staring around in amazement—and pride. The streets and stairs of the continent were nothing like Peter's paranoid cathedral, but now that he'd realized who this world's creator was, Toby could see his brother's hand in everything.

Two days after Jay's visit, he was taking one of these strolls in the richer upper levels of the continent when suddenly Orpheus stuck his nose in the air, then took off. A virtual flag over his head signified he'd recognized something or somebody. In seconds he'd scrambled up a drainpipe and was running along the edge of a roof.

"Don't mind me," Toby shouted after him. "I'll just keep walking here, where it's slow."

Orpheus had his own maps of the city. To Toby, a chair was for sitting *on*, a table was for sitting *at*, and a potted plant was for looking *at*. Orpheus might consider sitting on all three, so they all had the affordance of "sitability" to him. It was the same with the tops of walls, with some of the narrow gaps between buildings; with banisters and tree limbs. To Orpheus, roof cornices were little balconies and drainpipes were subways.

Toby was still getting used to this fact of denner life. It had been this way all along, not just for denners but also for cats and dogs. Humans had just never had the ability to see them the way animals did. Orpheus's interface gave Toby that ability.

None of which helped him catch up to the denner. He jogged off in the direction he thought Orpheus had gone and, rounding a corner, nearly toppled over the young woman who was kneeling on the sidewalk and scratching Orpheus's chin.

"Whoa!" He stumbled and stopped.

She stood up, smiling.

"Oh," he said stupidly. "Hello."

"Hello again," she said. "I never got a chance to thank you the other day."

"Thank me? Do I know . . ." This was the girl he'd saved from being hit by one of the pilgrims during that miniature riot. "Oh," he said. "Yes."

Orpheus looked from Toby to the young lady, then back.

"I was happy to help," Toby said. "What . . . was that all about?"

"My friends and I were just trying to exercise our right to free speech." She stuck out her hand for him to shake. "I'm Kirstana."

"T-Toby." He'd been using an alias, but in the moment he completely forgot to give it.

She knelt again to scritch Orpheus's ears. "I think your denner likes me. What's his name?"

"Orpheus. Yeah, he does seem to have latched on to you." Toby scowled at the denner, but Orpheus blithely ignored him.

Kirstana put three fingers on the ground and leaned a bit, looking up askance at Toby. "What about you? You came out of the prep station, were you planning on going on pilgrimage?"

"No no," he said. "I was just touring around and walked into the middle of things."

"Touring, huh? Following the tags in those awful city guides?" She waggled her fingers next to her eyes. Toby had been wearing the tourist glasses, which must have been a dead giveaway. He grinned sheepishly, though he didn't know why he should be embarrassed.

"They're hardly a substitute for a *real* local guide," she continued.

"Well, I don't know anybody here."

"You know me."

Toby opened his mouth, then closed it. He'd never had this kind of a conversation with a girl—*woman*, for she was few years older than him. Was she *flirting*? Or just being friendly? He had no idea, just as he had no idea how old she thought he was.

"Well," he said. "I, um—"

The moment dragged.

Suddenly Orpheus leaped up, claws extended, and scrambled up Toby to perch on his shoulder. "Ow, ow!" He batted at the creature. Kirstana laughed.

"I could use a guide, sure," said Toby.

Orpheus purred loudly in his ear.

"You, I'll talk to later," he muttered.

| Nine |

LATE THAT EVENING, TOBY found he couldn't sleep. Things were finally starting to go his way, as he explained to Orpheus. On his haunches on the floor, he frowned seriously at the denner and listed his accomplishments on his fingers. "One: I know Mom's on Destrier. I just have to get there. Two: I've figured out how to make money so I can get there. Three: I met a girl. We're going out together tomorrow!

"And four: Jaysir's unlocked this for me." He waggled the twentier's data block. "Shall we take a look inside?"

There were two kinds of data in the block. It was mostly backups, which kind of made sense; what else would you stick in the bin of a bot like this? The backups were in turn partly stuff he didn't recognize, but some were Consensus Empire worlds, dated after he'd left Sedna. Peter's work, then.

He was as uneasy about opening these as he was about accessing the libraries' worth of information you could find online about his brother and sister. The way those library books took his family and turned their lives into dry discourses and reports, printed and categorized and cross-referenced . . . It was supremely creepy. The idea that these Consensus backups might reveal some side of Peter that he didn't know was also unsettling.

The second category of data in the block consisted of recordings made by the twentier itself. Shots of home: that seemed innocuous enough. So he linked the data block to his glasses and sat back against the bed.

Orpheus came to curl up in his lap. "Okay," said Toby, "here we go." And he loaded the first of the twentier's own records.

Ice and a black sky. He was looking at the horizon of Sedna. The twentier was crawling forward across the reddish plains, along with five or six others. Its scanning software classified the rocks (actually rock-hard water ice) and sand (smaller chunks of the same) as it went, so virtual labels kept popping up to obscure the vista. A faint murmur of radio chatter between the bots sounded like crickets chirping.

"Hmm." Toby fast-forwarded, getting a crazy zoom view of crater rims, giant rocks and plains, and the legs of space-suited humans flicking back and forth. Then the horizon disappeared, and it was all about digging.

"Well, crap." Digging. Then more digging. He zipped through hours and days and weeks of clawing, crumbling, heating and zapping as the twentiers excavated the Sedna homestead. A couple hundred meters below the surface, they hollowed out a vast circular cavern, and in this, other bots built a centrifuge. Sedna's gravity was minuscule, so they just pretended it didn't have any and made rotating habitats that spun to create centrifugal weight.

Toby remembered this time, and despite the lack of human faces and voices in the images, he felt a strange sense of nostalgia. He knew that tunnel and this rocky spire outside the entrance . . . wait, they were outside again. The twentiers were off to prospect.

Fast-forward . . . more fast-forwarding . . . It was all stars and rocks, rocks and stars. He was just about to give up when suddenly light and sound burst on him. "Ah!" Everything was moving way too fast and he scrambled to back up the picture to where the change had happened.

At first everything was a bright blur.

Then came sound, a voice: "Is it recording?"

Toby sucked in a sharp breath.

The blur receded, sharpened, and became a face.

"Yes, this makes us no better than our enemies," said Carter McGonigal, Toby's father, as he scowled into the twentier's little lenses. "But what choice do we have?

"Let's get started."

BOTH TOBY'S PARENTS LOOKED a little older than the last time he'd seen them. Mother, in particular, seemed careworn and tired. She was clutching a steaming coffee cup, and even though the twentier didn't record odors, Toby felt the pungency of its scent lighting up memories—so many of them!—of times she'd sat this way on Earth, and in the habitat.

That wasn't where they were now. His parents had lit some lamps in one corner of the vehicle bay outside the centrifuge and its meager comforts. Mother's backdrop was a wall of tools and machinery, and they both wore mud-smeared space suits.

"It's not just that you're talking about spying on your own friends," Mother said now. "It's a slippery slope. Where's it going to end, Carter? Isn't this exactly how the trillionaires got to where they are? One little betrayal at a time?"

"Yeah," said Father distractedly. He was poking at the air, obviously using an interface that probably connected to the twentier. "Same methods. Different goals."

Toby stared at his parents, mesmerized by the little differences he could see in them. They were older—aged, for him, literally overnight. The change wasn't so drastic as in those pictures of Peter and Evayne, and that somehow made it all more real. It was a bit like seeing pictures of them from the time before he'd been born—equally strange and unimaginable, yet obviously real.

Mother sighed. "So what do you want me to do?"

"Well. These twentiers are right at the edge of the network. They're the bottom-feeders of the colony, which makes them perfect. If the trillionaires really have planted a mole in our group— or more than one—then we can't trust the high-level network anymore. That's the first thing they're going to hack. So the Internet feeds, communications, entertainment—basically everything we use day to day in the habitats—is suspect. That's why I want to build a secure network of our own out here. Using these guys and the other infrastructure bots."

She knelt down to peer into the twentier's eyes; to Toby it was disconcertingly like both his parents were examining *him*. "What does that get us?"

"Well, security, for one thing. If we've been hacked, the trillionaires could send a shutdown signal to some critical piece of life support and kill us all in our sleep. Then they move in and jump our claim."

She reared back, obviously shocked. "You can't believe they'd do that?"

"Of course they'd do that," Toby's father said impatiently. "In a heartbeat. Which is why we have to secure all the low-level infrastructure. Gas supplies, electricity. Heat. Hell, the circuits that open the doors. Route that stuff away from the top-level computers and into our own network.

"The second thing it gets us is spies. We can monitor them, like they're monitoring us. Only we'll use the most basic pieces of equipment as our bugs. Let 'em have the TVs and e-mail."

"I see you've thought this through." She frowned in thought. "How do we secure it?"

"Turing-test biocrypto. Whoever issues a command to our equipment can't have only the right fingerprint, iris scans, or DNA. They'll have to have it all, and the personality markers, and more."

"So," she said, "you, me, and who else?"

"Peter and Evayne. Nobody outside the family. We don't know who the mole is."

There was a momentary silence while he worked at his interface. Mother was staring at him.

"What about Toby?"

Carter McGonigal froze, then slowly looked round at his wife. "Dear . . . if you want. We have his metrics. But . . . he's gone."

She stood up, and her head left the frame of the picture. "He's missing," she said flatly. "Not the same. *Not* the same."

Toby's mother walked away quickly, leaving his father staring into empty space, an angry expression on his face. After a long motionless minute, he stood up and walked away, too—but in the opposite direction.

The twentier sat staring at the wall, and the record didn't end until nearly a half hour later, when Toby's father came back and switched off the bot.

THERE WERE MANY MORE records in the twentier's data block. Toby didn't have the heart to look at them—at least, not tonight.

Even less able to sleep than before he'd accessed the record, he lay there in bed while Orpheus grumbled and shifted next to him. He thought about how the present had so suddenly become a distant past, and grew by turns tearful, self-pitying, angry and, at last, resigned.

Here and now was where he was stuck, unless somebody had invented time travel while he'd been away. That meant he had a date tomorrow, and at the rate things were going, he was going to show up bleary-eyed and disheveled. That wouldn't do.

"Get over yourself," he muttered, then turned on his side and mentally pushed away the past. "Tomorrow.

"Tomorrow . . ."

Reciting that mantra worked, eventually. He slept.

TOBY CAUGHT ONE GLIMPSE of Kirstana's house, but that was enough to tell him how important her family must be. She met him at her front door, wearing a combination of dark tunic and leggings, and a long dark cape whose hood was thrown back. The foyer behind her was actually a balcony at the top of a high open space; with a start he realized that the house clung to the outside of the local city sphere and was shaped like a drop of water, frozen in midtrickle down the aerostat's curve. Spiral stairways curled down to lower balconied levels within the drop. The big curving outer wall was one continuous sheet of glasslike graphene, so transparent that it seemed not to be there at all.

"How are you?"

"I'm good." Actually, he was. He had awoken feeling like he was doing the right things, however difficult it all was.

Kirstana had stepped through the door, and the large, hulking bot accompanying her closed it with a thump. "I hope you don't mind if I bring Barber," she said when she noticed Toby sizing up the bot. "After what happened the other day, my parents are giving me all kinds of grief for going out without a bodyguard."

"Will he rip my arm off if I get too close?" Actually, Toby wasn't intimidated by the thing; he and the other kids had grown used to having similar devices around after Peter's kidnapping. It was remembering those days, not so long ago really, that had given him momentary pause.

"Don't be silly." Kirstana set off with purpose down the street. "Meeting in person," she said as she walked. "One of those ancient customs that I just can't get used to. Back home, we'd be just as likely to send avatars and recover the memories later. After all, if you go yourself, you're, well, committing yourself to whatever experience you have in that place. That would have been so gauche where I come from."

"And where, exactly, is that?"

"Barsoom."

He'd heard that puzzling name before. "I thought Barsoom was a storybook name for Mars."

"Mars?" She rolled the word around in her mouth. "Maaaars. Never heard of it. But how can you not know about Barsoom? It's the capital—you know, the fourth planet of the solar system. Covered in ancient ruins and dried-out canals from all kinds of terraforming attempts. The water always drains away, but every thousand years or so somebody drops another comet on it and tries again. The inside of the planet's getting quite wet at this point!"

". . . Right. Of course I know it's the capital."

"But, that's the irony, isn't it?" She sighed. "Our family left before they moved the capital there from Destrier. We left because the place had become a backwater. It was dying. Again. But I remember it as a magical place. I'd get Barber to dig the sand away from some ancient doorway, and while he kept watch for the Tharks I'd crawl down in there with just a hand lamp to find ancient hieroglyphs and bar codes. I'd wonder what kind of people had lived there, so long ago. If they were people at all.

"There was one faded hieroglyph I'd run into in a bunch of different ruins, but I could never find the translation to it. One day I came downstairs and my parents were sitting at the dinner table arguing over a holo. And in the middle of the holo was that glyph.

"They told me it was one of the oldest symbols known to Man—as old as the symbol for computer, say. The symbol meant *lockstep*. And a lockstep, they told me, was a place even older than Barsoom, older than nearly anything, but still alive! The locksteps had been forgotten on Barsoom for centuries, but there were stories if you knew where to dig them up. And those stories went back . . . dizzyingly far, from our civilization through the one before, from language to language, back all the way to the beginning. I fell in love with everything lockstep, and my parents noticed. They were glad, because they'd learned about another family that had moved away, and people said they'd gone to the McGonigal lockstep.

"McGonigal!" Her eyes were shining as she said the name. "That name I'd heard, and I'd seen it, too. It was written everywhere, in some of the oldest religious texts put down thousands upon thousands of years ago."

"Religious texts . . ." He stopped, shoulders hunched, but Kirstana continued up the stairs, oblivious of his reaction. He hurried to catch up.

The bubble city Toby was staying in opened out onto another one at its top, and this one did the same to a third, higher one. Kirstana's house was near the top of this highest sphere, yet she'd been leading him upward since they left it. Now they were close enough to its sunlamps that big shades were needed to cool the stairs and galleries.

"Are we going to an aircar platform?" he asked politely.

Now she looked back and smiled, shrugged, and said, "What's the fun in sitting in some vehicle while you fly? I can get us something much better."

"What?"

"Wings."

The elevators and escalators continued on, until they reached a plaza—a broad balcony, really—that stuck out near the top city's solar lamps like a giant diving board. From here Toby could look out through the glass ceiling at the permanent storms, or down through widening and converging rings of city and forest, through a gap to more of the same, down and down.

A modest hut here rented angel's wings.

"They're just exos," Kirstana explained as she browsed a rack of furled feathered things as tall as she was. "You know, visitors from lower-g worlds wear them to amplify the strength of their legs and back, so they can walk here. These ones . . . well, they're *wings*. That's all."

Furled, they made up a tall, heavy backpack. Unfurled, they were huge; the black ones Toby chose had a wingspan of at least eight meters. Kirstana's were white. She chatted with the proprietor about the details of using them. Then, when properly strapped in, she simply walked to the edge of the platform and stepped off. Her security bot, Barber, stepped after her.

Toby shouted in alarm—but seconds later she reappeared, soaring so close to the sunlamps that she blazed white as if she herself were a lamp. Barber was riding on what seemed to be jets built into his shoulders. "Hoo-hoo!" shouted Kirstana. "Come on, the air's fine!"

He gulped at the proprietor. "You're good to go," said the young lady, slapping him on the back. Closing his eyes and trusting to the millennia of technological development that separated Kirstana's age from the one he'd grown up in, he ran and jumped.

The wings unfurled, and suddenly he was flying.

All you had to do was look the way you wanted to go, and tilt or shift your body that way; the wings took care of the rest. He learned early on that they had a mind of their own and wouldn't let you run into buildings or hit the glass wall of the city. Within those limits, he could do what he wanted.

In this way they spiraled down through the geodesic froth of the continent, pausing to perch here and there while Kirstana pointed to the sights.

"People come here from thousands of worlds to fly, both inside and outside," she shouted as they diverged and converged in the air. "There're tournaments and contests. Of course they trade, too."

The continent was mostly made up of Lockstep 360/1 cities, but not entirely. Some of the spheres attached to it were closed off and dark, and some of the 360 cities weren't inhabited by humans.

He gawked at the distance-blurred glitter of the first one she pointed out. "Aliens? There are *real* aliens?"

Kirstana laughed. "No, not real aliens, if you mean intelligent beings who evolved separately from us. Nobody's ever found those yet, I mean we've only been expanding into the galaxy for fourteen thousand years, we've hardly explored out to a thousand light-years. No, those ones there are uplifted chimpanzees. You'll also find apes and dolphins and—well, other things that are entirely new species unrelated to anything on Earth. And then there's artificial intelligences from the fast worlds, and augmented humans." She banked away, her voice fading as she singsonged the list: "—and mutants and heavy-worlders and hybrids and single-genders and neandertals and hypercats and . . ."

When they stopped for lunch in the heights of a jungle sphere full of mist and rainbow-colored birds, he tried to find words for how overwhelming he found it all. "We're in the middle of no-where between the stars, but this place seems as rich as Earth. Though that can't be. Earth, Mars—I mean Barsoom—they must be so much more than this. More than we could imagine . . ." Yet she was looking at him strangely.

"Earth? Barsoom? Oh, come on," she chided. "We have so much more than the fast worlds could ever have. Earth only has Barsoom and Jupiter and a couple of other planets and artificial worlds. Venus, sure; Saturn. What's that? Four or five trading partners? And then, the next fast worlds are four *light-years* away, that's *decades* of travel time—a one-way trip for anybody living in realtime." She shook her head. "No, Toby, the fast worlds are sad places, hopelessly impoverished. How could they ever have this kind of diversity? The richness? The vibrancy? And reach out and be able to actually touch it?"

"Heh." Toby was grinning again. *Way to go, Peter.* He noticed she was smiling, too. "You love playing tour guide, don't you?"

She shrugged. "We moved here when I was sixteen. I guess I've been exploring ever since. Every day when I step outside and look around I just . . . it's like I'm living in some kind of fairy tale. Even these words—'fairy tale'—the ancient idea of fairies, the language we're talking about them with . . . it's all so . . . amazing!"

He shook his head, puzzled. "The language? Why?"

"Because it's ancient and ever-present at one and the same time. So amazingly, impossibly old, yet still here. Living in a lockstep is like hopping in a time machine and shooting back to the dawn of history while simultaneously being shot into the far future. It's that incredible age everything has here—it's all preserved, the world as it was thousands of years ago."

Thoughtful, he put on his wings, and they looked for a convenient balcony to jump off of.

Suddenly Toby stopped. "What's Destrier?"

Kirstana stumbled. She looked closely at him. "You were in line to join the pilgrimage there. How can you not know?"

"I'm . . . not from round here either, remember?" He'd told her that his family was from one of the first lockstep colonies, a little comet world isolated from most of 360 for the past forty years. It was obviously time to embellish the story a little. "You know I'm from a second-generation world. But my grandfather moved us to a lockstep with much longer turns and . . . well, time got away from us. It's been a couple of generations since any of us were here. And Grandfather never wanted to talk about what he'd left. But he was, you know, one of the first generations in the lockstep. Which is where I get my accent."

"Destrier's the symbol of everything that's wrong with this place," she said darkly.

Toby was surprised. "But all this—" He tilted a wing at the wonders of the continent.

She shook her head. "Could be so much more, if it weren't for Origin."

Origin. Another word nobody'd mentioned to him yet.

"Is that the symbol for Origin, then?" he said. He pointed at the thing that had prompted his question.

She looked and scowled. "Oh. The shrines."

They'd mostly been invisible outside of augmented reality; from a distance this one looked like a simple niche in the wall that flanked the restaurant. Behind the wall, the outer skin of the city sphere curved down, very close here, forming a dark ceiling drawn with mazy rain patterns. Trees curled up to nearly touch the glassy surface. It was details like this that had been catching his attention since he'd arrived here, so he'd walked by little niches like this one many times without noticing them.

Up close he could see a human figure seated on what looked like a stone throne. A kind of sundial pattern formed the backdrop.

"Who's that?"

She reached out to touch the little throne with one finger. "The Emperor of Time." She gave an exasperated sigh. "He's been a major mythological figure for over ten thousand years, and you're saying he's new to you?"

He shrugged awkwardly.

"Right. Well, he sits on a throne, see? He's been sitting on it since the beginning of time. And here's the thing: he's perfectly free to stand up and walk away or run in circles or stand on his hands or whatever he wants to—free at any moment and every moment, and he has the power and everything. And every moment, every single moment since the beginning of time, he's freely chosen to stay right where he is."

Toby shook his head, puzzled. "Does he have a name?"

Now Kirstana laughed. "Of course! You know who he is. Everybody knows the Lord of Origins, the One Who Waits.

"He's Toby McGonigal."

SOMEHOW, HEARING THIS JUST made Toby feel really, really tired. He waved a hand and said, "I should have guessed."

But then, as he turned away from the shrine, a new and deep unease filled him. There were the houses and spiraling stairs of the city—a place modeled on Peter's design. "Whose idea was that?" he muttered, wondering. Then, to Kirstana, "Why're there shrines?"

She stared at him, perplexed. "It's the lockstep's official religion. People join the lockstep because it's eternal; that's why my parents brought me here. 'Cause even in twenty, thirty thousand years, this place will barely have changed at all. The Emperor remains unchanged, and we're supposed to model our lives on his."

"Lives?" He shook his head. "I thought Toby McGonigal was just lost in space."

Surprisingly, she looked uncomfortable. "That's not a very nice way to put it. He waits. And the lockstep unfolds according to His grand design."

"*His* design?" Not Peter's? Toby walked back to the railing that overlooked the tiers of the city. The sunlamps were tuning toward evening. "And who . . ." he groped for the word. "Who *enforces* this grand design?"

She *harrumphed*. He looked back; Kirstana stood with her arms crossed, hipshot. "Next you're going to tell me you've never heard of Evayne McGonigal."

Something inside Toby spasmed and he quickly looked away. "Sorry," he managed to say. "You've got an eleven-thousand-year advantage on me."

"No . . ." She leaned on the balcony next to him. "The advantage is yours. You'd be a celebrity on any nonlockstep world you cared to visit, you know. You're ancient, practically prehistoric. People would have, oh, so many questions for you!"

He was starting to realize what he was to her. "Like you have questions?"

"Well, yeah." She looked away shyly. "How often do you get a chance to meet somebody who remembers the beginning?"

"But I don't," he said hastily. "I'm third generation."

"Meaning your family moved to the locksteps only centuries of realtime after they began?" She shook her head. "The blink of an eye, in historical terms. You're still from right back at the beginning."

"I guess."

She looked away at the cityscape, a troubled expression on her face.

"I'm tired. Let's head back." She nodded, and they dove into the sky again, retracing their path but this time up and up through dizzying layers of city and black, rain-threaded glass.

They smiled but barely spoke as they parted. Both were exhausted, but somehow despite the awful news about this strange religion and Evayne's part in it, Toby was content for now. He felt like he'd accomplished something today, though he'd found no work among the local bots. He'd learned important things and made a friend. Also, he'd discovered a way his age could be important without all the politics and family complications that Corva and Jaysir attached to it.

Maybe he could hire himself out to explain the ancient world, say, at local rich people's houses. The thought was startling: could there be a career in being *old*?

Toby was still musing over this idea as he wandered back to the bed-and-breakfast. He was so absorbed in his fantasy of getting paid to talk about the early days of Sedna that he barely noticed as Orpheus suddenly bounded up. Only when a flood of icons popped up and he had to bat at them to dismiss them all, did he look up and see who was sitting on the step outside his lodgings.

". . . Haven't seen you in *days*!" Orpheus ran back to her, and she vigorously scratched his ears, making his head wobble. Orpheus stretched high and licked her forehead.

Toby just stood there, mind a blank, until Corva looked over Orpheus's head and said, "Hi, Toby. Fancy meeting you here."

Jaysir must have told her where he was. Well, it stood to reason: the maker had what he wanted now, why shouldn't he? "Uh, hi. You're, um, doing well? Getting work?"

Still scritching at Orpheus's ears, Corva tilted her head and peered at Toby. "I didn't come to this planet to work."

He'd just meant to be polite in asking that; now Toby was confused. "Oh," he said. "So then . . ."

"*We* came here because *I* needed *your* help," she continued, her face deadpan and her voice neutral. "There's no point in my being here otherwise."

He crossed his arms. "I never promised to help you."

"Well." She looked away. "That's true." After a moment, she set Orpheus aside and stood up. "I mean, all I did was save your life. It's not like you *owe* me anything." This was the first time he'd seen her through his revamped glasses, but unlike nearly anybody else he might pass on the street—and unlike Kirstana—she was not festooned with virtual tags and flags, other than the green-and-gray symbol hovering near the hollow of her throat.

"Ammond and Persea also saved my life," he pointed out. "What do I owe them?" She sputtered, but before she could say anything he added, "You won't even tell me what you need me for. That's hardly gonna win me over."

"Ah. Well, I guess that's kind of . . ."

He just stared at her, and after a couple of "but you sees" and "you gotta understands," Corva finally found the right words: "I couldn't tell you in case you screwed us over by telling the police, or got caught. If they found out . . ." She looked genuinely distressed.

"So this is where we were going. I guess you can tell me now we're here, right?"

She glanced upward. "Wallop was our destination. But yeah, I'm sorry. Of course I wanted to tell you! It's just . . . it's not you I don't trust. It's everybody you might talk to."

He thought of Kirstana and was suddenly uneasy. A glance around the street showed nobody lurking in any doorways—and after all, this was Peter's Utopia, a civilization modeled on Consensus. There were no hovering microbots spying and eavesdropping on every citizen. At least he didn't think there were.

"Come inside," he said. "And this time, tell me the truth."

| Ten |

AS JAYSIR HAD BEFORE her, Corva sat in his room's one armchair, and Toby perched on the bed. Orpheus looked from one human to the other, obviously torn; then he climbed into Corva's lap. She stroked his forehead and he began purring loudly.

"We came here to save my brother's life," said Corva.

The statement hung there; she didn't go on. Toby shook his head and said, "What?"

"He's in quarantine," she said. "On board a passenger ship from Thisbe." She said that name as if she expected him to know what it meant. He could have done a search on it, but that would have taken his attention away from watching Corva and the uncertainty and anger warring for dominance in her expression.

Toby took the bait. "Why do you need to save him?"

"Don't you know what quarantine means? *Your brother* has frozen him out of the lockstep!"

He jerked back at her sudden fury. "What do you mean, frozen out?" Even as he asked this, Toby had a flash of memory—of himself, standing on the outer hull of the tug and staring down at a black planet dotted with silent, frozen cities: unknowing that he'd arrived at a settled world, or that he'd awakened at the wrong time.

"All the 360 ports are closed to Halen's ship," she said. "They haven't got fuel to go home or to any other world, so they've been forced into hibernation until the ports open. And your brother's decreed that won't be for another six months."

Toby was shocked that Peter would do such a thing—but he was also puzzled. "That's . . . really bad. I guess. I don't know why . . . But if your brother's hibernating, all you have to do is wait. It'll take awhile, yeah, but he's perfectly safe, right?"

She shook her head, and for the first time since he'd met her, he saw Corva near tears. "It's not just that. He came here to try to find me, and because of that, they quarantined his ship for a year. And half that's done."

"Yeah, but—"

"But Thisbe! Thisbe's government wanted to trade with another lockstep. There's one on the planet that's even more successful locally than 360-to-1. It's called 240-to-1. The local council hacked the hibernation timing repeaters so we'd Jubilee with them—wake on their turns as well as ours. We could trade with both that way! But your brother found out and he . . . punished Thisbe."

A sick feeling, almost of watching from somewhere else, had taken hold of Toby. "Punished . . . how?"

"All ships from Thisbe are quarantined until it's gone three of our years at a ratio of 360-to-12!"

"Wait, what?" He had to sit back and think about that for a moment. "They've accelerated time on your world . . . by twelve times?"

She nodded rapidly. "All the McGonigal beds have shifted from wintering over for thirty years per turn to two and a half. For every month that passes for you and me, a full year passes back home. I came here to study for a year, before the quarantine. But it's been going for"—now her eyes scrunched up and she did begin to cry—"for eight months!"

Eight months had passed for Corva. Eight *years* were already gone by for her friends and family on Thisbe.

Those pictures of Peter and Evayne came to Toby's mind—the

ones that he couldn't look at—and there were all those books he'd been afraid to open that talked about the things that they'd done and seen, without him, in the past forty years. He should have known all about this, but he'd been afraid to investigate.

Corva sat across from him, crying, and he couldn't speak. He couldn't think of a single way to make it better for her.

But there was still something puzzling about the situation. "Why didn't you go home when this first started? You were living out here, I get that, but why stay here?"

"But that's the whole point, McGonigal!" She glared at him. "A lot of people from Thisbe travel, hell, half our economy runs on remittances from foreign workers! Of course we all want to go home, but who'll take us there? Any ship that goes back to Thisbe will be stranded there for at least a year! Travel's dried up—I couldn't get back—so my brother boarded a ship that was going to try to sneak around the quarantine. They got caught." Her hand went up, fingers half curling around her locket.

He was trying to picture the time in his mind. If you took a calendar and pasted it into just one month of another calendar, you'd have a year inside a month. But what they'd done to Corva's brother was take the bigger calendar and drop it into just one month of an even larger one. "Your brother's gone from living a year for every month you live, to living a month for your next year . . . while everybody back home lives twelve years . . . It's crazy. But why? Why do this extra thing to the ship he's on?"

She flung up her hands in frustration. "Because they tried to get around the quarantine by pretending to be coming from another world. And apparently it isn't enough to have everybody back home aging like that, they had to make any ships that left not come back for the full twelve years! It's a blockade, is what it is."

Toby swallowed. "Have they . . . have they done this before?"

She stared at him. "*Your family* has done this to other worlds, yes."

There was nothing he could say to that. He sat there, uncomfortable, until Corva said, "You're a McGonigal."

"I'm not my brother." It wasn't the first time he'd ever had to distance himself from Peter's behavior. After the trauma of the kidnapping, Peter had acted out in all kinds of ways, some pretty destructive. Toby had apologized for him more than once; he couldn't believe he was still doing it.

"I don't care about that," snapped Corva. "I mean, you've got your family's biocrypto. You're coded to be able to operate anything that's owned by the McGonigal family, right?"

"Well, I was," he said doubtfully. "Fourteen thousand years ago."

"Your mother refused to admit you were dead. Everybody knows she made sure you'd always be able to get back into the colony. There're stories about that—songs, epic poems. The very least of them has you returning from deep space while Sedna's sleeping and putting your hand on the doorplate and it opens for you."

"Epic poems," he said. "That figures."

"Toby, you can override the dock bots. You can wake the passengers. Just do that, and you'll never have to see me again. I'll go back to Thisbe with Halen and you McGonigals can sort things out however you want. Just . . . let us have our lives, too."

Had Jaysir told her about the interface they'd found in the data pack from the twentier? Or, more likely, it was Corva who'd put Jaysir up to helping Toby in the first place. As a way of discovering whether Toby really could do what he was rumored to be able to do.

He rubbed his eyes. Was there nobody he could trust? "Maybe I can do it," he said and shrugged. "I don't know. And anyway, won't the local government have something to say about it?"

"You're a McGonigal," she said, as if that explained everything. "They can't stop you."

CORVA INSISTED HE STAY invisible for the next few days. Maybe nobody could stop Toby once he publicly announced himself, but it was pretty clear that right now he was vulnerable. He could still be killed—or neuroshackled. So for now, he must pay for everything with cash, not take on any jobs that might get him noticed—and of course, tell no one his real name. He didn't bother to point out that he was already living that way, as per Jaysir's instructions.

Corva had to "make arrangements." Something about that made him nervous. Was there more to this than walking into the port authority office and commanding the bots to let her brother's ship disembark? He could picture himself ordering bots around, but people were another matter entirely. Every time he imagined himself trying to face down the city's masters, he thought of how easily Ammond and M'boto had kept him under their control. Whatever Corva meant when she used the name "McGonigal," Toby wasn't that. The instant he tried to bluff these people, everybody would know it.

So he tossed and turned through the night, and when he wasn't imagining himself getting thrown in some cell by the local police, he was thinking about Peter. Peter the tyrant.

He kept asking himself, *How could Peter do that to Corva's people?* But then he'd remember how Peter and he had built worlds and ruled them with fists of iron and otherwise. In Consensus, they had practiced tyranny, rehearsed it. Of course it was just a game, and this was real. Where, though, had the dividing line been for Peter? Had he woken up one day and thought, "I could actually build my perfect society"? Or had the steps shaded into each other so gradually that he never really stopped believing it was all a game?

Hideous thoughts. They chased Toby away from the comfort of sleep, and in the morning Orpheus whined at his haggard appearance.

He felt awful, but he still had to pay for his lodgings, and that meant finding some lazy bot whose job he could do for the day. It wasn't hard, because the robots that supported Peter's perfect world had a built-in sense of economy. They also knew, pretty much to the day, when their various systems were due to fail. Toby could stroll into a local factory and just loiter until one came up to him with an offer. This time around he found himself sorting plastic fasteners for four hours, a mind-numbing task that was somehow also soothing—provided you weren't doing it every day.

While he worked he listened to history lessons from the library. His original plan was to get some sense of what had been going on outside the lockstep, in the wider world that Kirstana had been born into—but that was impossible. Time had been on fast-forward in that world, to such an extent that any history lesson that touched on major events out there had to skip over centuries and even entire millennia, or summarize them with terms like "the gray ages" or "the second transhumanist efflorescence." You could spend days reviewing the highlights of just one little century out of those thousands of years, because all that history hadn't unfolded on only one world. There were thousands of planets, so take that original fourteen thousand years and multiply it by that much . . . Impossible.

All he could really sort out was that humanity and its many subspecies, creations and offspring had experienced many rises and falls over the aeons. Since they had the technology, and lots of motivations, people kept reengineering their own bodies and minds. They gave rise to godlike AIs, and these grew bored and left the galaxy, or died, or turned into uncommunicative lumps, or ran berserk in any of a hundred different ways. On many worlds humans wiped themselves out, or were wiped out by their creations. It happened with tedious regularity. The only reason there were humans at all, these days, was that there were locksteps. They served as literal freezers, preserving ancient human DNA and cultures. All kinds of madness might descend upon the full-speed worlds circling the galaxy's stars—expansions, contractions, raptures, uploading, downloading, mind control, and body-swapping plagues (quite apart from the usual wars, dark ages, and terraforming failures)—but everybody ignored those useless frozen microworlds drifting between the stars. Their infinitesimal resources and ancient cultures held no interest to the would-be gods of the inner systems. So once those would-be gods had wiped themselves out, the telltale silence from formerly buzzing stars would alert this or that lockstep, and they would send some colonists back. A few millennia later, the human population on Earth and the other lit worlds would again number in the billions or trillions, and some of those would return to the locksteps. And so Peter's realm survived and, in its own fashion, thrived.

He had better luck researching the lockstep laws; he began to understand why Peter might want to punish Thisbe. Locksteps were a kind of network—specifically, something called a *synchronous* network, where every node in the mesh sent and received messages at the same time. All the worlds shipped out cargo and passenger ships at the same intervals, and doing this put them all on equal footing. If a couple of worlds doubled or tripled their frequency, they could grow faster than their neighbors. Lockstep worlds were always tempted to do this, and worlds that did often made out very well indeed.

At first, Toby couldn't see why that mattered. Why shouldn't everybody just communicate as quickly or slowly as they wanted? Lockstep rates should naturally speed up over time until the whole system reset.

Part of the reason why Peter's lockstep was the biggest though was that he'd tuned its trading frequency to match the rate of production that the smallest outpost could keep up with. There were tiny colonies that didn't own even a chunk of cometary ice but harvested the impossibly thin traces of gas found between the stars using modified magnetic ramscoops. In an abyss so empty that there was only one hydrogen atom per cubic centimeter, the scoops filled their vast lungs like baleen whales filtering tenuous oceanic plankton. It could take them decades to fuel a single fusion-powered ship with enough hydrogen to visit their nearest neighbor. Yet even these little starvelings could contribute to the wealth of Lockstep 360/1, because its clock ticks were slow enough for them to keep up.

If you lived on a relatively rich world, like Lowdown or Wallop, you could harvest resources and manufacture goods as fast as you wanted to. You could leave the 360/1 lockstep for a faster one, such as 36/1, which experienced ten months for every one in Peter's empire. You'd think that this would provide a huge advantage to your industries because you'd be producing ten times as much as 360/1 in any given time period. Since you were awake ten times longer, however, you'd also *use* ten times as many resources.

More important, if you increased your frequency, you'd have far fewer "nearby" monthly trading partners than 360/1. It wasn't obvious why, but travel between the lockstep worlds took decades of realtime. Because Peter's lockstep slept for thirty years at a time, you could travel half a light-year while wintering over (if you were going at the average speed of a cheap fission-fragment rocket). One wintering-over journey between 36/1 worlds could take you only one-tenth that far—but that didn't translate into having one-tenth the possible destinations for the trip. Because the lockstep worlds were scattered through three-dimensional space rather than being on a two-dimensional planet, when you doubled the distance you could travel, you did far more than just double the volume of space you could access.

Lockstep 36/1 might have ten turns for every one in 360/1, but each 360/1 world could trade with *a thousand times* more worlds per turn.

So Peter's network was vast, and it ran on mutual trust that no one would take advantage of higher trading frequencies. Thisbe had broken that trust.

A couple of days later, he was listening to one of these historical programs as he walked home from work. As he turned the corner to his bed-and-breakfast, he saw a motley crew of people sitting on its front step: Shylif, Jaysir—and Corva. His landlady was visible in the front window, glaring at them.

Toby paused his program. Corva was poking at the ground with a stick, and Jaysir and Shylif were looking everywhere but at her. "What's up?" said Toby.

Corva stood up, brushing off her pants. She wouldn't meet his eye. "The plan's off," she said. "We can't get to the passenger module."

"You mean we can't get your brother back?" She nodded; she seemed to be on the brink of tears.

Toby knew he should be relieved, because what Corva had been proposing was both illegal and highly dangerous. He knew what he should be asking, too: *Will you honor your promise to show me how to get to Destrier?*

Instead he said, "What's the problem?"

Corva told him, the words coming out in a rush. As soon as she started to talk, the answer popped into Toby's mind.

He should just nod sympathetically and ask for what they'd promised. But Corva wasn't like Ammond and Persea; she really had saved his life, and if all she'd said about the McGonigals was true, she was taking a terrible risk in even confiding to Toby.

He said, "I know a way."

SIX HOURS LATER, THEY were descending between brooding mountains of cloud, down a single, endless cable that stretched from zenith to nadir through the awesome dark skyscapes of Wallop. The little elevator car, which Jaysir had hijacked for them using his black arts, had been moving for many minutes now. Just how far below the continent had the authorities hung the passenger unit?

"I still don't like it." Corva crossed her arms, glaring out the glass. "You don't know anything about this Kirstana person."

"I don't know anything about you, either."

"Yes, and look where it's gotten you." She glowered at him. "What does she know about you? About us? Probably a lot more than you think. You're not exactly very good at keeping secrets, Toby."

"What are you, my mother? I agreed to help you because you can show me how to stow away on a ship to Destrier. That's all." He turned away from her, ignoring the look Shylif and Jaysir were sharing.

He was still kicking himself for telling Corva how they could get down here. It turned out that the reason he hadn't heard from her for days was that she'd been agonizing about how to actually get to the quarantined passenger unit. It hung many kilometers below the continent's customs complex. The logical way down was by airship, but there was radar and other eyes to prevent that. The next logical approach was to simply board the elevator on the customs level—but getting into that would be next to impossible.

He'd had his chance to get out of having to do all of this. Instead, when Corva had explained the issue, he'd heard himself say, "I know a way. Why don't you just fly?"

"I told you, they track the dirigibles—"

"No, not by airship," he'd said. "With *wings*."

So it was that he'd called Kirstana and asked her about outdoor-certified exowings. Jaysir had modified them so that they would ignore proximity warnings and no-go zones. Jay couldn't bring along his beloved bot; he'd ordered it to wait near the docks. That was how they intended to return.

First, they would simply spiral down through the black air to a landing jetty and airlock at the base of the customs complex.

Simply? —Well, if donning a space suit and bundling their denners into airtight carrying cases, then relying on the artificial muscles and reflexes of strap-on wings in the hostile atmosphere of a gas giant was simple. The three stowaways had experience with similar environments—such as the oceans of Auriga—and Toby had walked the ices of Sedna at temperatures near absolute zero. Also, fourteen thousand years of refinements to the safety of the wings had helped. To his surprise, it had been fairly easy to skim close to the outside skin of the continent, so radar wouldn't catch them. The dark helped, making the danger of a fall more abstract than it would otherwise have been. But they could never safely descend all the way to the passenger unit this way. This elevator was still the only way to do that.

Now that the adrenaline-pumping flight was over, Toby was

actually kind of enjoying the elevator ride. It was clear that Corva, though, was having trouble with the precarious sense of being balanced above an infinite fall. She spent her time sitting in the center of the floor with her knees pulled up, Wrecks protectively wrapped around her ankles. Toby had tried to get her to talk a number of times as they dropped through the black, still air beneath the cloud deck. She just grunted or answered with a simple yes or no.

Orpheus was staring into the gray emptiness of the sky, as if those depths held secrets only denners could see. Toby knelt to pat him and after a minute of communing felt a bit better.

"You know," he said, to try to restart the conversation, "I kind of thought we'd be going *up*."

Corva tried to look nonchalant. "You can leave ships in orbit for decades at a time," she said, "but people . . . well, they get fried by the cosmic rays. So the passenger modules from Halen's ship are down here."

"And we're just going to waltz in and no one will notice?"

Jaysir smiled, rather falsely—he was trying to pace in the tiny space, with little success. He had also dressed uncharacteristically in drab clothing today and didn't look comfortable in it. "Well, *you* couldn't, but I can. We makers have our ways, you know."

"Yes," Toby agreed grudgingly. "So how are you going to get us past whoever's at the other end of this elevator ride?"

"Same way I got us into this elevator," he said. "By fooling the sensors. Nobody's down there anyway. It'll just be us."

Toby eyed him, thinking. "It must have been hard for you to leave your bot up top."

"It'll be fine." Jaysir looked away. "I don't want to talk about it."

The lights in the car came on suddenly. Corva grunted in surprise. "Turn it off! Turn it off? Am I the only one who doesn't like the idea of being the only lit-up thing for kilometers?" The sense of infinite monotony outside had disappeared; the windows were now just black mirrors.

"Hit it with my elbow," said Jaysir as he tapped a wall plate. The lights went off. "Sorry."

Corva gave a whoosh of relief and, gnawing at one fingernail, glanced at Toby. "And what about you? Sorry you came?"

"I'm sorry about the whole last fourteen thousand years. Why should today be any different?"

His eyes had adjusted in time to see her smile. He liked that smile. Then, "Look," she said, "more clouds."

Toby followed the faint indication of her pointing arm. Billows of black-on-black ascended silently outside. Suddenly a bright flicker silhouetted a bulbous thunderhead shape below them. "Lightning," Toby murmured. "There's another layer of storms down here?"

They watched in silent communion for a while, as the mist thickened, drawn in moments of white, and became rain.

Between lightning flashes, a faint glow became visible below them. They put their foreheads to the cold glass to try and see down. "Is that it?" asked Toby.

"Yes." Jaysir was staring at something invisible, probably some tag within his own interface. "Time is right."

"Why hang the passenger compartments down here?" he said after a moment. "Don't they want to keep them deep frozen?"

"I think they are." Corva touched the glass, snatching her fingers back as if it had burned them. "Somebody told me that when the cities are awake they stay in the only warm layer of air on the planet. Above that—and below it—it's far, far below zero."

Toby peered at the beads on the glass. "Then that's not water."

"God, no. There!"

A sliver of light had appeared below them. As they watched, it grew into a rain-dazzled arc. Toby puzzled over it for a while, until he realized he was looking at the top of a large geodesic glass structure, which must hang off the bottom of the elevator cable. The glass facets sparkled from within, breathing white and rainbow colors into the falling mist. Indistinct clouds reflected the pearly light.

Toby had time for one last glimpse of dark metal struts and glass angles dripping white or scattering spray into the swirling air before the lights came on again. He squinted at Corva, who shrugged. Behind her the window brightened, then a stanchion holding red running lights fled up and a sudden heaviness signaled their arrival. A framework of metal triangles rose around the car as it slowed to a halt. The faint vibration Toby had grown accustomed to in the past hour ended.

"Okay, Jay," said Corva. "Time to work your magic again."

He waved his hands in the air, for all the world like a stage magician preparing a trick, then said, "I'm freezing the heat sensors. They'll register the first person to step out but nobody else. And as long as that person doesn't go any farther, they'll stay in an infinite loop . . . So somebody will have to stay here by the elevator."

"You didn't mention that earlier." She was annoyed.

"Wasn't sure this would be the setup." He shrugged. "I'll stay if you want."

"No, we might need you. Shylif?"

The normally placid Shylif frowned. "I want to come."

"It's you or me," said Corva. "I could stay, I suppose . . ."

He turned away. "No. This is your show."

Jaysir pressed the key combination next to the elevator doors. Nothing happened for a moment, then the car shifted with a strange sucking sound, and the doors opened. A gasp of cold came in, followed by fresh warm air. The denners poked their heads out, Wrecks above, Orpheus below, and Corva stepped carefully over them. After the strange and wonderful skies of Wallop, and the weirdness of an elevator ride to nowhere, this vestibule lit by low lamps behind potted palms was jarringly prosaic. Shylif stepped out, and they all listened for the sound of alarms—ridiculous, really, since those might sound only in some security office kilometers above. In any case, nothing happened, and they followed him out.

"Shy, keep your comms open," Corva said to the big man. "If anything happens, we need to know instantly." He nodded.

After his initial surprise, Toby found the hum of the air circulation and the spotlit plants in the little antechamber reassuring. *Just do this one thing,* he told himself, *and then you can make a run for Destrier.*

Orpheus took off around a corner and, with a mild curse, Toby followed him. The denner was bounding down a long carpeted hall, at the end of which a set of shallow steps led down in a spiral. The only decoration in the hallway was a single table with a bronze buddha on it. Or was it the Emperor of Time—a Toby McGonigal? He was careful not to look too closely at it as he passed by.

"Stay in sight, damn it!" Corva and Jaysir had caught up. Toby saw how her lips were pressed together; she was scared. This was nerve-racking, but Toby didn't know enough to know what they should be scared of down here. He was curiously numb, in fact. He'd been through too many changes lately to really register a sense of danger here.

"Where the hell are we?" Jaysir was looking around.

"Top reception area," Corva said. The only way was down a short corridor to an arch that exited onto a broad curving balcony. Toby and Corva stepped onto this, with Jaysir and the denners following.

The gallery was suspended near the ceiling of a geodesic dome about thirty meters across. Toby looked down at a sculpted landscape of trees and pools lit by arc lights. The glass walls of the dome were an opaque black in this light.

"Oh yeah," said Corva. "Staging area for the elevators. I remember having lunch in one of these."

Toby looked at her. "You wouldn't be having lunch in a passenger lounge if you were a stowaway."

"No, of course not."

"Wallop is where you were going to school!" For some reason he'd assumed her school was on Lowdown.

She shrugged impatiently. "You only just figured that out? Why else would my brother come here if he wanted to find me and bring me home?

"Anyway, this isn't the same lounge as the one I came through. There're lots of these stations, but most of them are way up in the stratosphere. The only reason this one's down here is that it's on ice."

Toby could see potted orange trees down there. Looking at them, he felt achingly homesick for Earth. Wrecks and Orpheus were already on their way down a broad stairway that swept along the wall of the dome. "Come on," said Corva as she followed them.

"Some of the rich estates are built like this," mused Corva as she trailed her fingers along the dark glass of the outside wall. As he followed her Toby heard the faint drumming of rain and fainter murmur of distant thunder, filtering in from outside. "There are whole chandelier neighborhoods hanging down off the city spheres by the dozen. I thought it was so wonderful when I first came here." Her voice held something in between regret and disappointment.

Jaysir was staring around nervously and now pointed at a small grove of red-leafed maples. "Look at the trees! They're not green. They're red! Are they fake?"

Toby laughed. "No, they do that every autumn. Just before they lose 'em for winter."

"Oh, yeah, winter. They wake up the trees months before us, so it's always summer when we're awake. They spend a few months cooling them down after we go into hibernation, so maybe some of them lose their leaves then—but I've never seen it."

Toby walked with Corva under the canopies of red. The sound of rain receded, but the illusion of being outside was still hard to shake.

Jaysir had slept through all the autumns of his life. For some reason, this thought made Toby's heart ache, and he remembered leaving home for Sedna and how he and Evayne had both cried.

Peter had been silent.

Corva pointed out a set of low-lit steps that descended under the grass. "This should go down to where they dock the passenger modules."

They went that way, and neither spoke for a while; but something was on Toby's mind. He'd been thinking about it ever since he'd learned the significance of his family in this world.

Finally, during a short period while Jaysir was out of earshot, he asked, "What does it mean to you, that I'm a McGonigal?"

She darted a quick look at him. "I mean, that first time in the courtyard. Did you know who I was? And all that stuff about . . . about me being the Emperor of Time, this cult figure, you knew about that . . ." He shook his head. "Are there really people out there who think I'm some sort of god?"

She'd drawn her shoulders in and wouldn't look at him. "You have your sister to thank for that," she said curtly.

"I'm asking about what *you* believe."

"I was raised to believe you never existed at all."

"You mean that the Emperor of Time never existed. But what about me?"

"You? As a person? A human being?" Now she met his eyes briefly. "Toby, *nobody* thinks about you that way."

He didn't ask any more questions, and she didn't speak either.

At last they stood in the final, lowest chamber. This was a hexagonal, metal-walled drum with a suit locker in one wall and an airlock built into the floor. The sound of running, dripping rain filled the room.

"This is it," said Jaysir. "The passenger module's behind that door. Fire up the interface, Toby."

He tapped the side of his glasses and awoke its augmented reality interface. "I still think we should have tested it before," he said. "We might have been able to do all this from the city, through the net—"

"Bad idea, I told you," said Jaysir. "If it didn't work, and the network trapped your query, we'd have been caught. Safest to do it from here, 'cause I know we're close enough that you can get a direct link to the module's timer."

Toby sighed. "All right. I'll try." He pinged the ship's hibernation system.

Instantly, a bank of colorful rectangular buttons and data windows popped into view. They seemed to float, translucent, half a meter in front of him. "Hmph. Well, I do have something." He peered at the virtual console. "It's . . . it's a passenger manifest."

Jaysir did a little dance. "Hot damn! What about the frequency? The timing?"

Toby examined the virtual board. It was actually quite ridiculously simple. There were some clocks showing current time and a kind of alarm—strangely, rather like Orpheus's setup. Of course, since this was a three-dimensional and virtual display, the interface elements also had little tags. He reached out to tap a little red flag attached to the main timer, and a larger window opened.

It read, OVERRIDDEN BY EVAYNE MCGONIGAL, 38.2/14372.2.

Toby swore.

"What is it?" Corva was gnawing at her fingernails again. "Is something wrong?"

"No, no, it's fine. I just won't know if I can reset the clock until I try."

"Toby . . ." He glanced over at Corva. She was looking more distressed by the second. "Can you check . . . is he here? Halen, I mean. Halen Keishion?"

He looked at the manifest—momentarily distracted by the discovery that he could apparently reset individual cicada beds or select some or all at once—and ran his finger down the air until he saw it. "Yes, Corva. He's here. His bed's registering green. He's okay."

She blew out a heavy sigh, smiling weakly.

"How about Sebastine Coley?" It was Shylif's voice, coming through the open link. Toby glanced down the list.

"Sure—" But Jaysir and Corva were both waving their hands and Corva was shouting, "*No!*"

Toby blinked at them, then remembered the story Jay had told him about Shylif's past. Something about a woman, and a man who had lured her into a lockstep fortress . . .

"Shy? Shy? Answer me!" Corva stared at Jaysir in horror. "Oh, no," she whispered.

"What?" Toby looked from one to the other. "What's happening?"

"The alarm's been triggered," said Jaysir. "Shy's left his post. He's on his way down here.

"To kill Sebastine Coley."

| Eleven |

"I DON'T LIKE POLICE," Peter had told Toby once, as they were arguing over yet another point of design for Consensus. "They're people, and how can you trust people? But I hate cop bots, too, 'cause, well, they're *not* people." In their next version of Consensus, he'd provided a solution to both problems.

Toby sat on the floor with Corva and Jay, looking up at that solution.

They had raced up from the bottom of the facility, hoping to head off Shylif. Toby couldn't believe he was intending to kill one of the passengers in the module, but Corva had confirmed it. "He joined us because he was hunting this man Coley and he'd tracked him to Thisbe," she'd said as they ran. "I never thought he'd actually *find* him!"

Apparently, now that he had, all other considerations had ceased to have any meaning for him. So he'd left his post, and in that instant the alarms that his presence there kept suspended had gone off.

It had taken surprisingly little time for the police dirigible to arrive.

In Consensus, red lights on the heads of bots like these four meant they were being "ridden" remotely by professional law officers. Telepresence had been decent in Toby's day; he had no doubt it was perfect now. The people remotely controlling these bots would feel they were right here and had to be aware that they stood two heads taller than any normal human and had enough strength to tear off an airlock door with their bare hands—if their robot bodies would let them.

The bots had overrides to prevent their human drivers from killing or badly injuring anyone. The humans, in turn, had overrides on the kinds of simple assumptions a bot might make about what kind of situation they were in. Peter had thought it was a nearly perfect solution.

What made it actually perfect was the fifth bot that hung back from these four. Its headlights were green, meaning it was being ridden by a civilian observer, who would also be recording everything that happened here.

The cop bots didn't seem too concerned about that fifth guy. One of the red-lit ones crouched with a gnashing sound in front of Toby. "Facial's not getting a match on this guy. They must be stowaways."

"They had denners," said a second one, which stood with crossed arms over Corva. "Saw 'em scamper off that way."

What about Shylif? Toby exchanged a glance with Jaysir, who gave a tiny shake of his head. Had they found him up top? Or was he hiding somewhere?

"Denners . . ." The first cop leaned toward Toby. "Is it true what they say? Those things're altered to work like cicada beds?"

"I wouldn't know," said Toby.

"Shut up," snapped Corva. "They've got lie detection built into those suits. You just said 'yes,' you know."

"Oh." He felt himself flush.

"Ha," said the cop bot, tilting its head to one side. "Good readings off this one. So, kid, who are you, and where are you from?"

Toby looked the cop in its lenses. "I am Toby Wyatt McGonigal, I was born on Earth fourteen thousand years ago, and I own this lockstep and everything in it. Including you."

There was a second's pause, then the cop bot stood up, shaking its head. "Detector's not working after all. It says he's telling the truth!" There was a general laugh at that idea. The cop bot shook its head again. "What he said about the denners might not be admissible. We'll have to catch them."

"Hell!" said another cop bot. "I'll get 'em." It raised its arms, much like a professional wrestler showing off his muscles, but in this case the maneuver just made room for two cat-size bots to detach themselves from its torso and leap to the floor. They shook themselves and then flitted silently away.

Corva shouted, "Don't hurt them!"

"Call them, then," said the first cop bot. "Save us all a lot of trouble."

Corva sent him one of her most withering glares. It was the first time, Toby reflected, that he'd seen that look directed at somebody other than himself.

"On your feet, then. We'll catch up to them." The cop hauled Jaysir up and reached down a metal hand for Toby, but he brushed it off.

"They're down this way," said the cop whose cat bots were on the hunt. He stalked off into one of the corridors and everybody followed him in a tight group.

"So," said the first cop. It had hooked its white metal thumbs into the conspicuous holsters at its waist and was sauntering next to Toby like a man with his hands in his pockets. "You came here to do some looting, then? —No, no, don't answer, it happens all the time, and, hey, I wouldn't want to put words in your mouth or anything."

"Yeah," said Toby. "That's why we came."

The cop bot shrugged at the civilian observer. "Don't know what's wrong with this detector."

"Has this happened before?" asked the observer. Unlike the flat artificial voice of the cops, its was clearly human. Female, mature, perhaps even elderly.

"What the—" The cop whose body parts were hunting Wrecks and Orpheus paused. Then he swore and started running. From somewhere up ahead came a strange swishing sound.

They caught up with him in a big industrial kitchen. Everything was chrome steel and ceiling-mounted chef assemblers. These were all dormant, but there was a lot happening at floor level.

The cat bots were trapped back-to-back in the middle of the room. Careering and hopping around them were six spinning pin-wheels of white spray: pressurized dessert-topping bottles whose valves had somehow come loose. They were coating every nearby surface with white topping, and the cat bots had gotten a liberal layer. The things were back on their haunches now, scrabbling at their cameras to try to clear them.

And then, with majestic slowness, the heavy industrial fridge behind them began to lean in their direction.

"Hell!" The cop bot leaped forward but skidded in the icing and ended up on its back just as the fridge came down like a hammer on it and the cat bots.

The fridge bounced once then settled a few centimeters. The cop bot lay on its back, arms and feet splayed and its head under the heavy fridge. Suddenly it crossed its arms and ankles, and Toby heard a muffled voice say, "Well, this is just great."

"Get it off him," said the lead cop. It was impossible to tell, but Toby imagined his voice sounding tired.

Two other cops lifted the fridge as if it weighed nothing, and the one on the floor clambered to its feet. Its head was a bit lopsided, which was nothing compared to the state of the two cat bots.

The civilian observer shook her head. "But how did they . . . ? Oh!"

Behind the fridge were boxes and a long metal tray that must have been used as a lever. Toby felt a prickle up his spine as he realized that the denners could have had only a few seconds to improvise this trap.

He looked to the others. "Are they as smart as . . . ?"

Jaysir shrugged. "Best not to worry your head about it."

A couple of meters away, an icing-smeared cop bot was trying to fit two squashed subunits into slots in its torso. They wouldn't fit, and finally it threw them away in disgust. "I'm gonna kill those little freaks," it said.

Another cop gestured from a nearby doorway. "They went up," it said. "They're somewhere in the greenhouse."

"On *civilized* worlds," said the iced cop, "they make crime impossible."

Corva quirked a smile at it. "Where would be the fun in that?"

It cursed and walked away. Instantly Corva's smile disappeared. She turned to Toby, and he could see the worry and disappointment that were her true feelings.

"Time to let you earn your pay, *heir to the lockstep*," she murmured.

"What?" He nearly tripped as they were hustled up a flight of steps to the open, window-wrapped greenhouse. "You think I can—?" He nodded at the cops.

"I really think you can," she said, and next to her, Jay nodded. "If you are who you say you are, you can override any Cicada Corp equipment." When he just stared at Corva, she rolled her eyes and said, "These bots are *Cicada Corp bots*."

Toby swallowed. If he ordered these bots to shut down, he'd reveal himself. There was no going back from it. These cops would be kicked out of their system and find themselves back at headquarters, and they'd see that it was a McGonigal override that had taken them out. As if that weren't enough, they'd have it in his own words: *"I am Toby Wyatt McGonigal . . ."* There'd be no hiding anymore; he'd be meeting Evayne and Peter soon, but too soon, far too soon.

Corva hissed at him. "What are you waiting for?"

Toby called up the Cicada Corp console. He could see the activation symbol hovering over the heads of the cops. All he had to do was tweak that, and they'd fall right over. Similarly, he could open the doors. He'd been prepared to wake the dead just now . . . He could do this.

"Uh-oh," said the lead cop bot. They were walking across the greenhouse, and it abruptly stopped and turned to the others. "Did you get that? One of *them's* come in person."

The iced cop swore. "Why?" It turned to Corva and Toby. "What did you do to attract the attention of the Guides?"

Corva gasped. Toby was about to ask Jaysir what a Guide was, but there was no time. Corva turned to him, suddenly frantic. "Do it!" she hissed.

"Do what?" asked the cop even as Toby focused his eyes on the virtual glyph over its head. With a slight squint he turned it from green to gray, and the cop bot froze, its torso leaning back in a skeptical pose, its head tilted to one side.

The others hadn't noticed yet, so while the leader was saying, "They're not even going to tell us what it was all about," Toby shut them down.

"Are they just gonna take over like they always—?" The last cop bot suddenly realized it was alone. "Hey—" Toby shut it down.

"Why didn't you do that before?" Corva was wavering between outrage and delight.

Using the console felt like cheating. It felt criminal, like an assault on the legitimacy of the whole lockstep. But he couldn't say that; she wouldn't understand . . . and he would sound like a Mc-Gonigal. He just shrugged.

Corva grimaced. "Come on! We've gotta find the boys."

A few calls summoned the denners from where they'd been hiding. They seemed very pleased with themselves, especially Orpheus, who pranced around Toby's feet before climbing him to hang off his backpack. Wrecks was circling the immobile cop bots, obviously curious as to what had happened to them.

"Hurry!" Corva mounted the steps three at a time. Toby couldn't understand her sudden panic; in fact, now that he'd crossed the bridge of actually using the console to control his surroundings, he felt strangely elated. Sure, it was a cheat, but he hadn't hurt anybody, just cut the remote connection to some people in a distant building. With luck they wouldn't even be able to tell that it was a McGonigal override that had done it.

Since he was thinking this way, Toby wasn't at all unnerved when they reached the gallery level and found the corridors crowded with bustling military bots.

"Oh, crap." Corva shrank back as dozens of weapons were raised and aimed at them—but Toby just squinted, and the guns drooped.

He strolled through the frozen combat units. "It's fine," he said. He wanted to laugh. "These guys can't touch us!"

"Oh, *they* can't," somebody said.

Standing in the middle of the corridor was an armored man. One of his metal-sheathed arms was crooked around Shylif's throat, and the other hand held a gun to his head.

"But I sure can," he said.

". . . McGonigal."

TOBY AND CORVA EXCHANGED a glance. Jaysir looked at the floor. Then Toby sighed.

"Really, does everybody know about me now?"

The man with his gun to Shylif's head barked a quick laugh, then said, "I don't know what you did to my bots, but I can't afford to have you take them over. If any of them so much as twitches, I'm shooting your friend here."

"That leaves us at a bit of a standoff, doesn't it?"

"Not really. Elevator's this way. Come on." He backed in the direction of the antechamber.

"I'm sorry, Corva," mumbled Shylif. "When I heard the name I started off without thinking—but then I changed my mind, and I came back but it was too late and . . ."

Toby had always thought that Shylif was a powerful man and might be a formidable fighter. Indeed, he was the same size as the man whose arm was around his throat, but his own space gear was strictly commercial. The other man's had a military exoskeleton built into it; he could have squashed Shylif's throat with a simple twist of his arm.

They disappeared back down the corridor, and Corva, Jaysir and Toby reluctantly followed. The man's voice floated back from up ahead: "Glad to see you haven't lost your sense of humor, Toby. It's what I always liked about you."

Toby blinked. "Wha—"

"He's a Guide," whispered Corva. "One of the original Sedna colonists. You didn't think your family were the only ones to use the locksteps?"

The idea hadn't occurred to him, like so many other details about this mad future that, once someone mentioned them, be- came blindingly obvious. He shook his head. "Too much going on." Then he called out, "Hey! Who are you! It's been forty years, you know."

"That it has, Toby. Come in here." He was waiting for them by the elevator. Four more military bots were standing by its doors.

"Get in the elevator." The man was nervously eyeing his own bots. Toby knew he could take those over, but he couldn't be sure he could do it without being noticed. All it would take would be one of them nodding or saluting and Shylif would die. So he marched into the elevator and Corva followed. Their captor edged in, still pushing Shylif ahead of him.

"You spent so much time in those goddamned games that you probably wouldn't remember me if your life depended on it," he said as he gave a glance-command to the elevator to start. "I'm Nathan Kenani."

Toby peered into his face and suddenly saw the younger man in this careworn face. "Nathan!" It was he and Peter had first met on their way to Earth orbit, the composer.

"Nice to see you again, kid." Suddenly Kenani shoved Shylif over to stand coughing next to Toby and the others. "I'm glad you remember me."

"Of course I remember you! You know, Peter and I used your music in our games."

"I know you did. Your brother made a goddamned anthem out of one of my pieces. Now every time I hear some innocent young thing belt it out with tears in her eyes, I get the creeps."

"Sorry about that," said Toby. "But it's not really my fault."

"Isn't it? You got him started on all this." Kenani made a wide wave with his gun. "You and your game therapy. Oh yeah, I remember all about that." He grinned, the drawn skin of his face suddenly giving him a sharklike aspect. Behind him, lightning flickered.

He eyed Corva. "She know about that?" Toby shook his head minutely. "They don't know anything, do they? Hey, Toby, you remember sheep? Peter and I, we joke about that sometimes. These people have never heard of sheep. If they had, they might be better at recognizing their situation."

Toby felt sick. "If this world's so awful, why do you put up with it? There must be others—the whole first generation. Did you all just decide to blindly follow Pete into . . . this?"

Kenani shook his head. "Some of them fought, but there was a side that was always going to lose, and I decided not to be on it. Us, we're all that's left. And, no, this future's not 'awful' at all."

He glanced up at the approaching cityscape but kept his pistol steadily aimed at Shylif. "You know what a Guide is, Toby?"

The word had popped up frequently in his library, but so had dozens of other terms; Toby had been overwhelmed by all the details of lockstep history and hadn't known what to skim and what to research deeply. "Sounded like thought police when I read about it," he said.

"If you don't like the lockstep, you can leave anytime you want," Kenani snapped. "We just have standards for those who stay. It's pretty simple: if you want to live in Peter's lockstep, you have to assimilate. That means accepting our way of life—*your* way of life, Toby, you and your family's, and mine, and all the originals'. We've got millions of people immigrating every year, did you know that? For the most part they come from worlds that are separated from the culture you and I share by more than ten thousand years. They speak languages that share no common words or grammar with ours. They have totally different ideas about basic things like family structure, morality, clothing . . . If we let them keep their ways, the whole place'd come apart at the seams. And hell, people arriving this month have 360 years of history separating them from those who came from the exact same place one year ago lockstep time.

"We're the only thing they have in common. The Guides are there to teach people how to live in our culture, is all. That's why they call us Guides."

"People worship you like gods," Corva accused. Her face was pale.

"Not something we encourage," Kenani retorted. "Unlike your sister," he added to Toby with an ironic smile.

"Evayne," said Toby, and his heart was in his throat. He was as responsible for her as he was for Peter. When she ran through the halls of the gray Sedna habitats singing, his heart lifted and he felt he could relax for a minute. When she was silent or had locked herself in her room, then Toby prowled the halls thinking of how to break her out of her shell through some game or gift or clever word. Evayne and Peter, he juggled the happiness of both.

"How is she?"

Kenani blinked at him in surprise. Then he laughed. "You're probably the first person to ask after her like that in ten thousand years. And nobody'd be more aware of it than her."

"I want to see her!"

Again the surprise. Then Kenani laughed. "That's actually what I had in mind."

"Wait, you can't," interrupted Corva. "You're a Guide, you work for Peter McGonigal."

"Do I now?" Kenani appeared to consider the proposition. "If that's the case, then I guess I should do what Brother Peter told me to do . . ."

"What did Peter tell you to do?"

"Why, kill you, of course."

"No!" Toby stepped forward, his face hot and his hands balled into fists. "You're lying! He wouldn't hurt me!"

Now the old man just looked sad. "You're right, he'd never hurt his brother, Toby Wyatt McGonigal. But the Lord of Time? The One who Waits to return and deliver the universe to perfection after fourteen thousand years of buildup and expectation setting? He'd kill *him* in a heartbeat."

"But I'm none of those things. He knows it. You know it."

Kenani tried to shrug in his suit, but its shoulders barely moved. "You know it, I know it, some of the other Guides know it . . . and that's about it. The rest of the human race and a goodly chunk of the nonhuman intelligences in this part of the universe see you differently. Peter knows this. He knows what's at stake if you reappear."

"I don't want to reappear! I just want to go *home!*" He bellowed the last word, and he was standing toe to toe with the Guide. Kenani hardly blinked.

"There's no home to go back to, Toby. I'm not here to kill you. But if I don't do that, my only alternative is to hand you over to Evayne. Then, she might kill you, but at least it won't have been me who had to do it."

He couldn't believe Evayne would hurt him either, but longing for home had reminded him of something. "You do have another choice," he said, stepping back. Outside the elevator car, the rain had stopped, the clouds had parted, and the rainbow-colored clouds and glowing spheres of the Continent were lowering toward them.

"You could bring me to my mother."

Kenani's eyes widened, and he gave an involuntary hiss. Then, "She went crazy after you disappeared, Toby. There's a reason none of us has woken her in thirty years."

Toby crossed his arms and sneered. "I don't believe that. She went into cold sleep to wait for me. That's what all the stories say."

"Stories?" Kenani laughed. He glanced up at the rapidly

approaching cities. "All you know is the stories, isn't it, Toby? Since you woke you haven't spoken to anybody who was there. You haven't been told what really happened."

Trying to keep his voice level, Toby said, "Then why don't you tell me?"

WHEN THE ELEVATOR DOORS opened in the customs complex, Nathan Kenani holstered his pistol and waved his three prisoners out. A sizable crowd of human soldiers and military bots was waiting; the men all bowed as one as Kenani appeared.

"I know you've got the McGonigal overrides, Toby," he said, putting a hand on Toby's shoulder. "You could probably cause some serious mayhem if you took over these bots. But my men would fight. Probably a lot of them would die, and you might, too—after all, they don't know who you are."

Toby shrugged off the hand. "What if I told them?"

"Anyone that believed you would probably faint. The rest . . . well, they've heard *that* one before. My point is, don't try anything, please. It'll just end badly."

"Where are you taking us?" Now at the head of a very large and intimidating retinue, they entered a maze of hallways behind the spaceport's customs hall.

"My original plan was to load you on my ship and take you back to Peter. Let him deal with you. But with everything . . . and considering you want to see her anyway . . . I've decided to turn you over to Evayne. So we're not going anywhere."

"Why?"

"Because she's already on her way here. She's coming through the official differential, so her ship'll be here at the start of the next turn. We'll winter over here and wait for her. It's just easier that way."

Corva had been silent for a long time, but now she said, "You must have arrived through the Weekly lockstep."

Kenani nodded. "We do that a lot—shift differentials to move around quicker. Peter, though—he stays on this time. Means he's even younger than he used to be." Now that Corva had reminded him that she was there, he eyed her and Shylif. "By the way, Toby, what do you think we should do with these friends of yours?"

"Let them go! They have nothing to do with any of this."

"But they know who you are?" Toby had no reply to that. Kenani sighed. "I'll let you hash that one out with Evayne."

Toby glared at him. "You said you were going to tell me what really happened. At least do that before you let me see Evayne."

"Let you see her?" Kenani shook his head. "You're still living in the past. *She* will see *you*—and then only if she chooses to. She may not bother."

"I can't believe that!"

They'd come to a long low room with about twenty cicada beds. They looked like half-melted plastic seedpods, black and glossy under amber and mauve lights, with blue telltales dotting their sides.

Kenani gazed pensively at the beds. "There was a time when I wouldn't have believed it either. But now . . . well, listen, and then tell me what you think." He waved at the human part of his retinue and they retreated, leaving only forty or fifty armed bots surrounding them. Kenani had one drag over a recover couch from the far wall, and he sat down on it, legs planted widely apart and his hands on his knees like a Chinese emperor. He frowned at Toby.

"Once upon a time," he said, "fourteen thousand years ago, a family that used to be rich had its last holdings bought out by the nasty hyperrich who'd taken over the solar system. They had enough money from the sale of that last business for one, maybe two generations to live in some comfort. But their grandchildren were going to be wage serfs like everybody else. There was no hope for them.

"Unless they did something crazy. The trillionaires had plowed under all the laws that might have protected the worlds of the solar system from exploitation. It was a winner-take-all situation, and asteroids and even planets belonged to whoever could get to them first." He turned to Corva. "Toby's parents knew that all the worlds in the solar system were claimed already—but way out past Pluto, there were other places.

"The parents pooled their money and made an offer to some other idealistic or desperate people—like me—to join them in homesteading Sedna. We spent all our money on a couple of ships and basic life-support and mining supplies. Other groups had done this, but they hadn't had the resources to make it as far as Sedna. But this family was different. They'd pioneered a new kind of hibernation technology back on Earth. It was originally intended for battlefield and emergency use, but they figured they could use it to minimize their life-support needs on the long trip out.

"One day, the family's eldest son was lost when his ship . . . well, it just disappeared. He'd been on his way to claim a comet for the colony. They knew where his ship should be, but if he'd been knocked off course, that straight line became a cone of possible trajectories, and the space they'd have to search in widened with each passing day.

"There were . . . arguments. His mother and the other kids wanted to send their remaining ship to search for him; his father said they couldn't spare it and they should use long-range radar and telescopes first. Most of the colonists agreed with him, but as the days and weeks passed, they found nothing on the scopes. His mother's frantic anxiety turned to bitterness and resentment. The family was . . ." Suddenly he stopped, glancing sidelong at Toby.

"Look, Toby, I'm sorry . . ."

"What? What happened?"

"They grew apart," said Kenani. "Your mother and father. He ended up on one side, trying to keep the colony as a whole together, and your mother, your brother, and your sister were on the other side, convinced that not enough was being done to find you.

"Finally, he relented and they used precious resources to send a small probe after you. The rest of us weren't happy. It was going to take a year just to reach your last known position. Your dad made the decision, then went back to work. He had a colony to run, after all. Your mom, and Peter and Evayne . . . they watched and waited."

Toby tried to picture the situation. Yeah, Dad would be steady in the face of a crisis like that. It was painful to think this, but he hoped that Dad would just mourn him and then carry on. It would have been the right thing to do.

"As the months wore on, your mom and Peter found it harder. Peter . . . he checked out of day-to-day life. You'd built this crazy online virtual reality together, and he became obsessed with perfecting it. Your mother went farther. She declared that she was going to winter over until the probe reported back. And over your father's objections, she did."

So that's how it happened.

Kenani gazed off at nothing. "That time, it was for a year. She revived in time to learn that the probe had found ambiguous readings. Maybe it had seen a sign of your ship . . . maybe it was just a comet. That was far worse than a simple yes or no answer would have been. She became obsessed with finding out what had happened to you, and because you'd gone into hibernation yourself before your ship disappeared, she was convinced that wherever you were, you were still alive.

"It turned into a war between your mother and father—she trying to scrape together enough resources to send an expedition after you, he insisting that the colony couldn't spare anything, that it was riding the knife-edge of failure anyway. This went on for . . . I dunno, a year or two?" He shrugged.

"And then . . . your mother thought of something. She'd seen the life-support projections. The colony couldn't support its full population for much longer. She went to your father and made him an offer. It's now the most famous, most studied deal in history."

He paused dramatically.

Toby scowled at him. "Come on!"

"No, really. She said, 'I know we don't have the resources to send out an expedition. But we would if we had fewer mouths to feed. If I and some of my friends go into hibernation for another year, it'll take the strain off the colony and give scavenger bots time to gather more ore and the manufactories time to grow more food. In return, you promise me that some of those resources will go toward building another probe to hunt for Toby.'"

A painful knot was growing in Toby's gut. He didn't want to hear any more, but at the same time, he had to know. He knit his hands together and stared down at his feet. After a moment, he felt Orpheus shift in his backpack, and the denner nuzzled his neck. He reached back to scratch Orpheus's chin—and had a sudden idea.

He turned his attention away from the story for a moment.

Kenani was completely absorbed in his narrative, and so were Corva and Shylif, who had doubtless never heard their history told this way before. "So . . . well, she did have some volunteers. There were enough cicada beds because they'd used them on the trip out from Earth. Anyway, she deep-dove and . . . she convinced Peter and Evayne to go with her."

Toby snapped to attention again. "They left Dad alone?"

Now Kenani wouldn't meet his eye. "Twice: once while he gathered the new resources, and again to wait for the new probe to report back. Two years.

"But . . . but here's the thing," he went on quickly, "it worked! With them wintering over, the strain on the colony was reduced. The bots could do most of the work. When they came out of cold sleep, they pitched in and worked hard—it was almost like the colony had seasonal workers it could call on when needed and then send home when they were done. They could actually afford to send out a probe, and then later another.

"The colonists began to talk about it. If they wintered over during times when they weren't needed, then they could supply labor when it was needed, and reap the rewards. They'd be richer than they'd imagined they could be, and the colony would grow . . . So more and more of them began following your mother's example. This went on for a few years, and your dad fought it every step of the way. Eventually, he gave up."

Toby gave an involuntary yelp that combined anger, grief, and surprise. His father *never* gave up. It was his iron will that had made the Sedna expedition possible. Kenani was talking about a man Toby didn't know. "What did he do?"

"When the colony could afford it, he came to us—the other original founders—and asked us whether we'd join him. Some said yes, and he and they . . . went back to Earth.

"Listen, Toby, it wasn't a retreat! They needed to go back to complete their claim on Sedna. By doing it, your father made the Sedna colony into an official world within the Solar Compact. He brought in investments and new colonists. And he brought all of you into the society of the trillionaires—he made it so you could *own a world*."

"But he didn't come back." Toby had figured that out already. He was also acutely aware of how Kenani's version of events didn't match up to the fragmentary records he'd pulled from the twentier's memory.

"No, Carter didn't come back to Sedna," said Kenani. "He . . ." The Guide grimaced. "After a few years, he remarried. He lived a long life. I don't know if he was happy. He was a pretty private person."

Remarried.

Okay, he wanted Kenani to stop talking now.

"Meanwhile, your mother had discovered that the longer she wintered over, the more resources her mining and refining machines could accumulate to use when she woke up. Also, the probes that were hunting you were going farther and farther, and taking longer and longer to report back. Her sleeps became longer and longer, and she convinced more people to join her in them. New colonists arrived, and some of them followed the new pattern, too. Peter and Evayne . . . they were growing up, and they knew the colony needed a McGonigal to be present at all times to ensure their sovereignty. So they started alternating—leapfrogging forward through time while your mother slept more and more.

"Your mother's probes had photographed and mapped other nomad planets, far past the orbit of Sedna. It was she who realized

198 | KARL SCHROEDER

that if an expedition visited one of those while everyone back home was wintering over, it would be as if those worlds were right next door. She encouraged an expedition to a planet that was two years away, and when that worked, she put together a colonization program.

"Here's the thing, Toby: the new colony couldn't have survived if they'd run all their machines and life support all the time. They wintered over three-quarters of the time; that's what allowed them to survive. But they did more than that! They thrived. And when regular flights between the two worlds became possible, they decided to coordinate their hibernation times with the people back on Sedna.

"That is how the locksteps began."

"NOW I'M AFRAID I'M going to have to separate you from those traveling companions of yours," he said, motioning for one of the military bots to come forward. "Don't worry—we've got cicada beds for all kinds of clients."

Corva held Wrecks so tightly that he squeaked in protest. "But they always winter over with us!"

"They'll be nearby," said the composer. "I know you kids love your *pets*." He emphasized that last word without irony—in fact, he had a strangely serious look in his eye, and his attention was focused on Toby as he said it.

Something wasn't right here. He should know what the denners were. The military bot took several carriers and put them on the floor. As Toby and the other two coaxed their denners into them, Toby was watching Kenani. There was an expectant, almost anxious look in the old colonist's eye, as if there was something he very badly wanted to say, but couldn't.

Toby looked at the ranked military bots. The eyes and ears of Peter? Or even Evayne? When he glanced back, Kenani caught his eye and nodded, almost imperceptibly.

Corva and the others looked stricken, but there was also an underlying grimness to Corva, a steely determination. Kenani had said nothing about the passenger carrier; was it possible that neither the police nor he had figured out that it was why they'd been in the chandelier station to begin with? No, he decided, it wasn't possible: Kenani must know. He was probably pretending to be kind to cover the fact that he was going to send Orpheus and the others to be studied, maybe even vivisected.

"Bedtime, kids," said Kenani. He pressed his thumb to the locks of three lozenge-shaped cicada beds in turn, then stepped back. Toby ordered his suit to unravel, then climbed into his bed. He sat there for a moment, watching as Shylif, then Jaysir, then Corva slammed the lids on theirs. Then he faced Kenani.

"I'm still a McGonigal," he said. "I can't believe Evayne would hurt me. And if she doesn't—if I'm still here in a month or a year or ten years—"

Kenani made a shushing motion. "I know," he hissed. "You don't think I know? Stupid boy. But she *will* kill you, there's nothing *I* can do about that." Again that odd emphasis in his words, and his eyes were fixed on Toby's with fierce intensity.

Toby nodded. "I'll remember," he said.

Then he lay back and shut the bed's lid.

| Twelve |

HE'D FELT THIS BEFORE.

Thrum . . . thrum thrum. Pause. *Thrum . . .*

Not so far away, though, and never so weak. Toby struggled to move—even to open his eyes. He felt like a lump of stone neglected by the sculptor. Buried in a hill. Lost in time . . .

He could feel the source of that faint vibration: a small, heavy body sprawled atop his. Orpheus was struggling.

Toby remembered the first time he'd awoken in between destinations. He'd been confident, had no idea that the tug had missed its target and wandered for thousands of years. He'd fallen down a well of centuries and not even known it. And this time? How long had it been?

But this wasn't like that time. Orpheus was with him. Yet Orpheus was dying, he could hear it in the weakness of the vibration that traveled up and down his body. Dying, and it was Toby's fault.

He couldn't move, but after a profound struggle he was able to crack his eyes just enough to see that the lid to his cicada bed was closed. Its transparent surface was mostly frosted over, but outside, dim blue light showed the ceiling furred by the same white frost he'd seen in the tug. Frozen air, Sol had called it. The internal telltales of the bed were active and registered red: emergency power-up. Orpheus must have tripped them when he climbed in.

Orpheus and the bed were fighting: he was using all his power to try to revive Toby, and it was using its to push him back into hibernation. There was no question which one would win. This bed wasn't set up to care for a denner, though; Orpheus would die if he stayed here. He couldn't possibly have enough energy left to wake himself again.

"Go . . ." He tried to say *back to sleep*, but his jaw wouldn't move. If only he had his glasses, he could contact Orph through his interface, tell him to reset his clock—

Interfaces . . . didn't these beds have their own internal controls? Of course they would. He twisted, flailed around in the narrow space, and felt a keypad near his right hand. He mashed his numb fingers against it and was rewarded as data windows blossomed into existence in the crystal canopy.

The display showed that the bed was drawing on an inexhaustible well of power from elsewhere in the city. It was programmed to push Toby back into sleep, and it would keep at it until it succeeded. After all, he wasn't due to wake up for another twenty-two years.

Why twenty-two? Then he remembered it all: Nathan Kenani's strange hinting statements and Toby's own desperate plan. The order he'd sent to Orpheus just before they'd been sent to their beds.

"This is . . ." His voice was a ragged whisper, but he had to try it. "This is Toby Wyatt McGonigal. Wake me up."

The indicators in the data window changed, and seconds later Orpheus's drone ended. He felt the denner collapse into the gap between his arm and his body. Around them both, the bed was now humming into action.

Rest, Orph.

THIS TIME, TOBY AWOKE refreshed. He blinked lazily at the distant frosted ceiling, then remembered everything and turned on his side, gathering Orpheus into his arms. The denner was limp.

"Oh, no, no." He hugged Orpheus to him, crying. The bed had

woken Toby, but it had ignored the denner. Maybe it wasn't too late, though. Cicada beds could perform medical wonders, and reviving creatures from the brink of death—or beyond—was their specialty. And somewhere nearby was the bed Orpheus had been in until today.

Toby went to lift the bed's lid but got an alarm in response. "Toxic Atmosphere" and "Fatal Temperature Differential" were just two of the indicators that flashed red. He could lift the lid, but the first breath he took would freeze his lungs into solid cages.

"What do we do now, Orph?" From his position on his side he could see through the bed's lid; most of the frost had cleared off it now. The beds containing Corva and Shylif were right next to his. Beyond them, the room was dark except for the blue telltales indicating where infrastructure machinery, designed to operate in hypercold conditions, was maintaining the ideal hibernation conditions for the city.

It was incredible, but Orpheus had survived that environment. Toby had known the denners could survive without air, and in deep subzero temperatures, for a little while. They had to have those abilities to be able to wake themselves from cold sleep. They were biological, but had been seriously genetically engineered at some point in the past.

He craned his neck to look down at the floor and saw little denner paw prints crisscrossing the thin snow that covered everything. There were broad drag lines through that snow, too. They seemed to start at a set of lockers in the dim corner of the room and ended up below Toby's bed. What had Orpheus put so much effort into hauling over?

He couldn't see it, but suddenly he knew. "Orph, you're a genius," he whispered to the lifeless body he cradled. "Hang on, hang on, I'll get you help."

Toby took several deep breaths, then, holding his breath, slammed the bed's lid back.

The cold hit him like a hammer. He barely had time to roll off the bed and make a grab at the balled-up environment suit; then he couldn't move. His fingers were painfully cramping into claws, and he just managed to reach out and cradle the suit's helmet before his hands went numb.

The suit woke and swarmed up his arm, built itself over his head. It felt like he was plunging into an icy lake as the pieces conformed themselves to his arms and shoulders, covered his face and mouth, and ringed his torso. The thing flipped him over as it finished its work, and just as he was seeing spots and about to faint, he felt a blast of cool—but not cold—air shoot down his throat.

Coughing, frostbitten by the material sheathing his whole body, Toby rolled, thrashed, and banged his head on the base of another bed. Then he was able to sit up. The air rushing into him was getting warmer and so was the metal touching him everywhere. The suit was trying its best.

More coughing. He crouched there for a long time, until the painful tingling of reawakening nerves settled into mere clammy chill. Then he levered himself to his feet and looked around.

Half the room's beds were showing amber telltales. They were trying to wake their sleepers. Toby stumbled over to one and scraped away the frost to reveal the face of a grim middle-aged man within it. One of Nathan Kenani's soldiers, no doubt.

"Go back to sleep," he said. The beds' indicators flickered and then changed. Quickly, he gathered Orpheus into his arms and crunched through the frozen air to the denner's original cicada bed, which he found by following Orpheus's paw prints into the next room. The pet beds were little boxy affairs suitable for cats and dogs, set along the far wall. It was easy to find Orpheus's—it was the one with the open lid, whose lights were flashing red while it beeped in alarm. He set Orpheus carefully inside and commanded it to start emergency treatment.

Next he had to take care of Kenani's bots—which were, after all, McGonigal bots. Several stood in the darkened corners of the main room. These were watching Toby. They'd probably been awakened by the alarms that had gone off when Orpheus tried to override his bed. They were doubtless programmed to wait for the human soldiers to wake up before taking any action.

"You're mine now, all of you," he told them, and his voice overrode their settings. "Find my glasses and warm them up."

He went to the other boxes and commanded them to awaken Shadoweye and Wrecks. Then he returned to the main room and gave the same order to the beds where their masters slept. One of the bots handed him his glasses, and he pushed them against his faceplate until the suit understood and built itself a mouth to bring them in. It fitted them onto his face, the interface sparkled into life around him, and he activated the Cicada Corp Console.

And then . . . there was no more to do. He found himself turning around and around in the middle of the room, adrenaline making him swing his arms and curse—but the beds were working. He was done here.

Toby left the main room to find a window. The suit's interface said it was hundreds of degrees below out there, and what atmosphere there was, was hydrogen and very thin. The normally bustling spaces looked postapocalyptic with snowdrifts covering the carpets and frost on the dead video signs. Here and there, faint telltales glowed from dormant equipment. He soon found a door to the main spaceport hall and walked over to one of the transparent outer walls of the city. Outside, he could see the other spheres of the continent, vast dark curves breaking up the starscape. Stars meant the city must be very high in the atmosphere, and indeed, when he ventured a look down, he saw nothing but black.

Yet kilometers overhead, attached to the side of the dark spheres was a fantastical lantern. Glowing warm yellow, the single solitary city sphere cradled greenery inside it, while little bright dots of flying machines drifted lazily around its curving side.

The Weekly lockstep was awake.

Toby sagged against the clear wall. For a second he thought he was going to faint, but at least now he knew there was somewhere to go once they got out of this room. They could even find a hot meal up there.

He hadn't really thought this would work. The only thing that made him set Orpheus's alarm for seven years less a day, just after Kenani got the drop on him, was his memory of Corva and Shylif talking him into sleeping in the shipping container. That kind of hibernation had seemed impossible, but they'd done it. More than that, they claimed to do it all the time. If they could perform such routine miracles, why couldn't Toby do something as simple as set Orpheus to wake in seven years' time instead of thirty? He'd guessed that the pet bed couldn't override Orpheus's own internal clock, and based on what he'd seen in the kitchen downstairs, Orpheus should have no problem getting out of it. His modified biology should let him survive long enough to open Toby's own bed and climb in. And then he could wake his human.

Simple enough, but so many things could have gone wrong. Even a basic mechanical lock on the pet bed would have killed the plan—and probably Orpheus. Toby certainly hadn't factored in the lack of air. It had been Orpheus's own idea to drag a pressure suit over to Toby's bed, though he couldn't actually lift it in.

Toby turned his head. He could see Orpheus's icon through the wall, or so the glasses made it seem. The indicator was no longer red, but amber.

He wanted to dance in a circle and shout his elation, but there was still something to do. This task was the biggest and, after bare survival, the most important by far. A responsible man wouldn't be wasting his time jumping around. He'd be acting.

Toby selected a dozen or so military bots and told them, "You're coming with me."

With them thudding through the snow behind him, he headed for the elevators.

EVEN WITH THE HEATERS going full blast, the passengers were shivering as they entered the terminal lounge. Most looked around

in sad confusion; they'd expected to be awakened on normal lockstep time, and it was clear that hadn't happened. Some were angry, and a knot of these approached Toby where he sat at the exit.

At the far end of the hall, the elevator was just disgorging the
latest of the refugees from Thisbe. Toby quickly scanned the faces,
but nobody there seemed likely to be the one he was looking for.

He turned his attention back to the five angry men now standing before him. One of the military bots flanking him shifted
slightly, and distant Weekly city light slid liquidly over its armor.
One of the men glanced at it nervously.

"See here," said the one in the lead. "Why're we off frequency
again? We know we were quarantined—"

"You tholes rolled over for the McGonigals," said another. "It's
disgusting—"

"But why this?" The first waved at the creaking walls and
wreathes of subzero vapor that coiled and flanked the passengers
like cobras. "It's a mess!"

Toby cleared his throat. He'd had plenty of confrontations with
angry characters and usually dealt with them well—in gameworlds.
Generally those characters didn't all talk at the same time, as these
guys were doing, nor did they egg their bot companions on to pos-
ture threateningly in front of combat bots that could squish them
instantly. If combat bots had any sense of humor, Toby was sure his
were laughing on the inside.

Suddenly he, too, had to laugh. The men glared at him.

"What's so funny?"

"If you're all like that on Thisbe, then I see where Corva gets
it," he said.

"Corva?"

Toby turned. A man not more than a few years older than Toby
himself pushed his way through the encircling crowd. He had
piercing dark eyes, black hair, and familiar high cheekbones. He
wore a multipocket jacket and baggy trousers, had a collapsed
pressure suit knotted around his waist, and a satchel slung over his
shoulder. "Did you say Corva?"

"Corva Keishion of Thisbe sent me," Toby said. "Who're you?"

"Where is she!" The young man stepped forward and half raised his arms, maybe to grab Toby's arms. The combat bots shifted, and he didn't complete the gesture, but he said, "She's my sister. I'm Halen."

The other men had fallen silent; they were looking around themselves in a new way—appraising, even hopeful. "We're outside the lockstep," said one.

"You're in the Weekly," corrected Toby. He pointed at the distant lantern sphere hanging kilometers overhead. "Or you will be, as soon as we get up there."

"But they won't have us!" It was the first man who'd spoken. He had the same wealthy air that Ammond had exhibited, and he had a whole team of bots to carry his luggage. "It doesn't matter if it's 360 or the Weekly. We're banned for twelve months!"

"You were," said Toby. He was beginning to enjoy this. "As to the Weekly, leave it to me."

"And who are you?" demanded Halen.

"Somebody whose life your sister saved." It looked like the last elevator had unloaded, and the lounge was now full of scared but defiant-looking people.

Toby turned to the five men who'd confronted him. "Can you keep a lid on things here for an hour? There's an . . . important reunion I want to arrange."

They glanced at one another, and then a sly grin appeared here, a brusque nod over there. "You're going to take us into the Weekly?" said the rich-looking one. "We could visit it back on Thisbe, but not stay or pass through—"

"This time is different." *I hope.* Toby didn't know what power he might have over the Weekly's government, but unloading the passengers into the Weekly had been part of Corva's original plan. She must think it would work.

"Come on," he said to Halen and stepped into the fearsome cold of a connecting corridor. As they walked, Toby couldn't help glancing over at Corva's brother. He was tall and strong looking.

Toby was acutely aware of how pale and scrawny he looked in comparison. What did Corva see when she looked at him? Certainly something substandard, if Halen was what she was used to.

"Where is she?" her brother repeated. "And how did you wake us up in the middle of winter?"

"I've . . . got an interface to the McGonigal clocks," Toby told him as they slid carefully down an ice-sheeted ramp. "I was able to override them."

"But . . . but nobody's ever been able to do that! How—" Halen had breathed the dangerously cold air too deeply and started coughing.

"It's a long story. I'll let your sister tell you."

THE McGONIGAL BOTS LET them into the high-security area, and Toby led Halen to the chamber where Kenani had imprisoned him and the others. When he opened the door, Orpheus came bounding up and in his usual style climbed Toby with his claws out; luckily Toby was in the suit, which the denner's claws wouldn't penetrate. Still, Toby said, "Hey, watch it!" and only when he had the denner settled on his shoulder did he see it wasn't just the denners who were awake. Shylif and Jaysir stood over Kenani's bed. Shylif was pensively sipping a steaming cup of something. And Halen . . . where had he gone?

Corva sat on a crate in the next room, one hand tightly clutching her oval locket. Halen knelt in front of her and was speaking to her in an insistent way. Toby hesitated a moment in the doorway, then backed away to give them their privacy.

Jaysir noticed and grinned. "You did this, didn't you? But how?"

"Nothing magical," mumbled Toby, trying, while trying not to be obvious about it, to eavesdrop on Corva and Halen. Distractedly, he continued, "I just set Orpheus's clock before we were separated. He woke me up."

Jay nodded, and a grin battled against Shylif's serious demeanor. "But your bed wouldn't have let him do it," said Jaysir. "Not unless you overrode that. Ours, too."

Toby shrugged. "The secret was out the instant I reprogrammed the passenger unit. I can't stop the McGonigal network from broadcasting my presence—it already did it, seven years ago."

Of course, Peter and Evayne had already known. Were there others, though, like Kenani, for whom the news would just be arriving? He didn't know how public the log-in details on the beds were. Or who might be monitoring them.

He stole a look at Corva and her brother. She seemed heartbroken. Why? Did Halen seem older? She'd spent all her effort to rescue him and the rest of her family, but now that it had actually happened, she would be faced with the reality of how time had already altered them.

Had it been too late all along? What was lost in time couldn't be returned, and here in the locksteps, any innocent sleep might cleave you from those you loved by years, by generations. Toby hugged himself and turned away again, tears starting in his eyes. Finding a bench (all its frost gone now, he noticed with some remote part of his attention), he sat.

He gathered Orpheus into his lap and sat there hunched over until murmured conversation arose behind him. He turned to find Corva, Halen, and Jaysir standing there. They were all looking at him. "What?"

"Toby," said Corva, alarm sharpening her voice, "where's Shylif?"

PEOPLE WERE YELLING IN the passenger lounge. As Toby and the others ran in, he saw that a knot had formed over by the elevator doors; someone there was bellowing louder than anybody else. Around this cyclonic eye, other passengers milled like frightened clouds. The bots he'd left to guard the place were ignoring the chaos. As long as nobody tried to leave the lounge, they had no orders.

"*Coley!*" It was Shylif's voice but transformed by rage into that of a stranger. "*Sebastine Coley?*"

Toby pushed his way through the encircling crowd to find one man standing in the open space at its center. Shylif was glaring down, fists balled, at a man who crouched at his feet. "Please—" this man whimpered. "I'm not—"

"You're Coley! You said you were Coley!" Shylif's denner, Shadoweye, was slinking back and forth behind Shylif's feet, wailing and hissing. His tail was fluffed out, like a scared cat's would be.

"Shylif, stop!" Corva stepped unafraid into the ring. "You don't want to do this."

He spared her an indifferent glance. "I've waited forty years to do this." He reached for the man at his feet.

"He's not Sebastine Coley!"

The voice was thin, barely audible over the jumble of voices surrounding them. But Shylif paused and looked over.

"*He's* not Sebastine Coley," repeated the very old man who stood, his weak legs braced by an exo, with a group of women and children.

"I am."

Shylif blinked at him, and in that moment of indecision, Toby suddenly realized what he should have been doing all along. "Bots! Restrain this man!" Shylif straightened and began to turn, but the security bots were faster and he was lifted off his feet before he could even uncurl his fists.

Toby went to stand next to Corva. He offered his hand to the man on the floor, who hesitated, then took it.

"I . . . I'm Miles Coley," he said, ducking his head and looking around at everyone but Shylif. "This man said he was looking for a Coley, and I said, 'I'm a Coley.' Then he knocked me down!"

Toby turned to the old man. "You're Sebastine Coley?"

"He's my grandfather," said Miles in a surprised tone. "Granddad, what's this about?"

"I . . . I don't—" But the old man wouldn't look at them.

"You know." It was Shylif, still straining against the implacable grip of the security bot that held him. "Her name was Ouline. You stole her from Nessus."

"Ah. Ah!" The old man suddenly wilted, and he would have fallen over had his exo not compensated to prop him up.

"You lured her into the lockstep fortress and stole thirty years from her—from me!" Shadoweye was clawing at the security bot's ankles, wailing. The bot ignored the denner, but Corva knelt down and clucked at him. Reluctantly, he climbed into her arms.

Miles Coley had joined his wife and daughters; they formed a protective wall in front of the old man. One of the women was comforting Sebastine, who had burst into tears at Shylif's accusation.

Shylif's struggles had slowed. It seemed it had begun to dawn on him that he wasn't facing the callous young man who'd stolen his life but a pale ghost at the end of his own. He stared at Coley, and as he stilled, Corva came to him and let Shadoweye slide onto the metal shelf of the security bot's enclosing arm. Shadoweye butted the underside of Shylif's chin, but for the moment, he was ignored.

"She died, Coley," he murmured. "She took her own life."

The old man's sobs intensified. His grandson gaped in astonishment, turning from him to Shylif and back again. "Granddad? Granddad, what's this man saying?"

Coley stammered. The moment stretched, and though all eyes were on this scene, Toby knew that the long unfolding of the drama behind it wasn't going to be resolved in the next minute, or the next day. He held up his hand.

"We're going to deal with this, but we can't do it here," he announced. "We have to get out of here while we can."

There was a startled silence, and then people's gazes began to shift from Coley and Shylif to Toby. One of the men he'd spoken to earlier said, "Where is it we're going, anyway?"

"Back to Thisbe," Toby told them, "to reset your clocks. But to get there, first of all, we're going to have to go through the Weekly."

ORPHEUS RODE TOBY'S SHOULDER as they strode under geodesic glass ceilings that revealed black skies and, ahead, the looming lantern glow of a city sphere. This was the one source of light in

Wallop's cloud continent. The passages they'd come through were eerie and silent, and though he'd ordered heat in the main thoroughfares that led to the lit city, now and then he caught glimpses of side corridors where hoarfrost still painted the walls and where the floors were drifted with oxygen snow.

Though still weak, Orpheus fired off happy emoticons and his head bobbed back and forth as they reached the outskirts of the Weekly lockstep. Toby should have felt similarly triumphant—he'd just escaped one of the lockstep's most feared cultural enforcers, after all, and had rescued an entire shipload of people to boot.

The confrontation between Shylif and Sebastine Coley had deeply disturbed him, however. Not just for its own sake, but because it made him wonder, even more, what it would be like when and if he ever set eyes on his own brother and sister. Lockstep time wrenched you back and forth, and after Shylif's experience he was beginning to realize just how unpredictable and brutal it could be.

They had only one encounter during the long walk through the frozen utility corridors linking the docks to the Weekly. About five minutes after they exited the customs area, Jaysir's bot came stomping out of a side corridor, streaming vapor and with flecks of frost dripping off it like dandruff. Some of the passengers shied back in alarm, but Jay visibly relaxed, and after inspecting the monstrous thing, he gave a sharp nod and let it fall into step behind him.

Shylif was accompanied by bots, too, but in his case he walked head down and eyes glazed, and his bots were an armed escort. A few steps away, Sebastine Coley trudged in much the same stance, while his family fluttered nervously behind him.

It took awhile to get through the airlocks. These were set up to protect the Weeklies from the dangerous cold and toxic air permeating the rest of the continent, and normally nobody came through them until Jubilee, which happened every four weeks, local time. Visitors from 360/1 being unexpected in between times, bots and humans were now working furiously on the far side of the transparent glass walls, trying to get more doors to work. Meanwhile a trickle of humans cycled through, three or four at a time.

There was a lot of hand waving and emotional conversation happening with the workers and security people on the other side. The cover story Corva had come up with was that an explosion had vented some of the 360/1 habitats. Those gesticulating men and women had better be sticking to that story: they'd be telling the Weeklies that the bots that watched over the 360/1 cities during their long sleeps had woken a small army of emergency drones and backup systems when they detected a blast, and had evacuated everybody from the affected area. There was a problem with the power, though, and they were unable to find enough safe beds for the residents of one particular neighborhood. So here they were, arriving at the airlocks to the Weekly lockstep with just a few household bots and some luggage.

The story should hold long enough for them to pass through the Weekly and take passage back to Thisbe—which seemed to be most people's plan. It helped that these "refugees" were accompanied by numerous official 360 bots, including an impressive military escort. When Toby finally cycled through a lock himself, he left that escort behind, but even so nobody asked him any questions.

The hubbub was subsiding by the time the last bots brought their masters' luggage through the locks. Many of the refugees had bulled their way through the emergency responders and by now had lost themselves in the crowds of the city. That was a good idea, Toby thought. Since nobody seemed to need him anymore, least of all Corva Keishion, he eventually screwed up his courage and began walking into the tiered city himself. He'd find some sort of job, make some cash, and figure out how to get to Destrier. That had been the plan. It needed to be the plan again.

"Where do you think you're going?"

He turned to find Corva glaring at him. She was clutching her brother's arm, but all her attention was on Toby, and Wrecks sat at her feet glaring down his nose in imitation of his mistress.

"You got what you wanted," he said. To his own surprise, Toby found himself feeling resentful and, before he thought about it, added, "though you nearly got us all killed doing it."

"So you admit your sister would have killed us?"

He flushed angrily and turned away. "Good-bye, Corva."

"Toby, wait!"

He didn't stop, but she ran to his side. He waited for the next cutting comment.

"I'm . . . I'm sorry," she said.

He stopped, blinked at her.

Corva stood with one foot twisted, toeing the pavement she was staring at. Her hands were clutched, all knuckle. Wrecks sat on his haunches, watching this performance in obvious surprise. "You didn't have to do any of the things you did," she said. "I know you risked everything for people you'd never even met. And setting Orpheus's alarm like you did—that was a terrible risk you both took and I'm just . . . I'm amazed at it all, that's all."

He'd never seen her like this. "You asked," he said. "I helped, is all." Oh, but he knew that wasn't all, not by a long shot. The thing was, Toby still hadn't absorbed the implications of what he'd just done. Walking away right now would probably have been best. He needed time to work through it all. Strangely, though, now that he had Corva's gratitude he was finding it made him even more uncomfortable than the indifference of her countrymen.

He had to laugh at his own words. "I guess it was kind of a superhero thing to do. It's just . . . that's not me, Corva."

"I know. It wasn't me a year ago either."

"Corva Keishion, exchange student," he said with a smile.

"And then subcontractor to bots, then stowaway, criminal, revolutionary . . ." She shook her head ruefully. "I could try to say that one thing led to another, but that really doesn't begin to describe it."

Now they both laughed. After a moment, though, Toby's smile faded. "What are you going to do now? Go back to Thisbe?"

"I guess," she said. "Though, you know, the basic problem remains. The blockade . . . the punishment frequency."

"I can't reset your whole world's clock."

She looked him in the eye, and that steely look was back in hers. "Are you sure about that?"

"No. I don't know. I haven't exactly had time to find out what I can or can't do. But anyway"—he turned away from her again—"I don't want to."

"I get it," she said stiffly. "You don't want to take on your brother and sister."

It wasn't that at all. The fact was, waking these people, evading Nathan Kenani and taking over the lockstep bots—it had all been way too easy. Disturbingly easy. It was like playing Consensus in God mode, except that this was reality. You could blow up whole planets without a second thought in the game. Nearly anything he did with such powers in Lockstep 360/1 was bound to hurt somebody.

"Look, why should I stick my nose into any of this?" he demanded. "I don't know anything about anything here, you said so yourself the first time we met. I've been trying to catch up, but how do you catch up? It's impossible. Now you're asking me to rejig time for an entire world? How am I supposed to tell if that's a good thing to do or an evil thing to do? Corva, if I can't tell, then I'm not doing it. That's all there is to it."

At some point in the argument Corva's brother had come up to them, and a small half circle of refugees from Thisbe had gathered a few more paces back. "You're right," said Halen, putting his hand on Corva's arm. "You have no reason to take our word for anything. Why don't you see for yourself?"

Toby grimaced. "By going to Thisbe with you, I suppose?"

Halen's lips twitched into a smile, with the same reluctance Toby saw in Corva. "If you're feeling insecure," he said, "you can bring that little bot army of yours."

"But really," said Corva, "how are you planning on getting to Destrier? Evayne and Peter have to know that's where you're headed. They'll be waiting for you with an army of their own, and it won't be one you can switch off."

"And you can get me there?"

"Maybe. If you help Thisbe, you'll have an entire planet on your side."

Corva had lowered her voice and was glancing around, and Toby was also growing uneasy with the listeners. He started walking, and she and her brother fell into step beside him. Wrecks was gamboling around Corva's feet and attracting a fair amount of attention from passersby, but they soon left her curious countrymen behind, and the crowds of the Weekly were diverse and strange enough that the three of them didn't really stand out.

Once they were out of earshot of the commotion around the airlocks, Toby said, "How much have you told them—your friends from the ship?"

"Obviously I told Halen. Some of the others know you brought us out of hibernation early, but not how. They might suspect, but the whole idea of you being a real McGonigal is so . . ."

"You think they'll figure it out when I retune your whole planet's frequency?"

There was a momentary silence; Corva and Halen glanced at each other. Then Corva sighed. "How do *you* want to do it? I mean, you're going to reveal yourself at some point. Right? So when? And how?"

Toby's bravado collapsed. He'd actually been trying not to think about that, just as he'd been trying not to think about how his brother and sister had changed, seemingly overnight, from familiar friends to hostile strangers.

"What happens when I do?" he asked, spreading his hands. "I have no idea. You have to tell me." *And I have to trust you.* But could he?

"Well," said Corva. "Some people think the world will end. You'll bring us all to paradise, because your return will be the fulfillment of time itself." She saw his expression and quickly looked down. "I know, it's crazy. But even the mildest interpretations . . . you have to understand, according to all our traditions—the stories, the religious orthodoxy, and about a billion books and stories—you're the *heir*. The eldest son of the McGonigals and the original designer of the lockstep system."

"Which I'm not," he pointed out. "Kenani said that Mom created it."

"But who knows that, other than a few people like him?" She shook her head. "It doesn't matter, Toby: you're the heir. The Creator and Savior of the locksteps. If people thought you'd returned, they'd turn away from your brother and sister instantly. Many would follow you without question. And some . . ."

When she didn't continue, Halen nodded to her, as if she'd just agreed with something he'd said. "Some would follow Thisbe out of the lockstep."

"Not some," said Corva flatly.

"A lot. Many. Most, maybe. Would you let that happen?"

Toby shrugged; he had no idea.

"More important, would Peter let it happen without a fight?" Halen leaned back, frowning at Toby. "Come with us to Thisbe and see what people really think of the McGonigals. Then tell us what you want to do. Though, I warn you, you might not like what you see there."

"I don't like any of this," said Toby. There was no question he was trapped. With Peter and Evayne after him, he had nowhere else to go. Even so, the idea of pretending to be the messiah the legends said he was, was profoundly disturbing.

He sighed.

"I'll go. But not as Toby McGonigal."

| Thirteen |

TOBY STEPPED ONTO THE soil of Thisbe, stopped, and began to cough. Tears filled his eyes and he had to step away from the others and cover his face for a moment. Orpheus climbed up to perch on his shoulder and said, "*mrrt?*"

It was years since he'd breathed the dust-laden, mold-and-bug-filled air of a real planetary biosystem. It was like fire in his lungs. There was more to the shock than that, though.

Blazing sunlight sent waves of heat into his face. The air was hot and felt free of the heaviness of the subsurface domes and close metal passages he'd been condemned to after they left Earth. When he squinted his eyes open again, he beheld a wilderness of rolling hills, green grass, and trees nodding in the breeze. Blue sky presided over it all, where white clouds reached for and overtopped one another. He could smell the grass and wildflowers. The buzz of insects sounded from nearby. It was all so beautiful and overwhelming, so like Earth.

"Wh-where are we?"

The sun flickered and went out. Toby blinked and ducked with a shout of surprise. "Damn," he heard Halen say.

Then the light came back on, only now it was a lurid, monochromatic blue. Everything was suddenly electric and strange, the trees pale parodies of themselves, the sky white. "What the hell—?"

Corva glanced up and shrugged. "Glitches. They happen. You'll see. I don't actually mind the blue ones. It's the red I hate."

Toby put his hand up to his face—but no, he hadn't absent-mindedly donned his glasses. This was no virtual world. He could still feel the heat of the strange sunlight on his face and smell the flowers. The bugs were still zizzing in the warm air. "That's not a sun?"

Jaysir and Shylif were with them, and now Jay laughed. "Welcome to the Laser Wastes. Or, at any rate, their slummy edges."

Behind them the Travelers' Rest was a long low building on the edge of a fairly conventional, if overgrown-looking, spaceport. A few bots were struggling to cut down young trees that were blocking some of the buildings' exits, and only one runway was clear; the others sprouted grass and more small trees through cracks in the pavement.

In the other direction, past the hills, Toby could now make out the towers of a sizable city. "I don't understand," he said, shading his eyes and peering upward. The light source was as bright as the sun, but it was a tiny dot, too intense to look at. "What *is* that?"

"About eight thousand years ago some civilization or other built this shell of energy harvesters around Proxima Centauri. That's the nearest star to Earth," Jay said.

"I know that."

"Right. Well, a few thousand years after *they* died off, one of the locksteps made a devil's pact with the things that had inherited the harvesters in return for a little fraction of that power. They built thousands of these asteroid-size lasers—red, blue, and green, to make white, you know?—and aimed them at some of the nearer nomad planets. Like this one."

"Wait—we're, how far from Proxima Centauri here?"

"Oh, a good two light-years away. You couldn't even see it with the naked eye. But the laser light reaches us, and it's enough to heat the whole planet to livable temperature."

Toby knew he was staring, slack-jawed, at the sky. He couldn't help himself, his mind had gone blank. Finally Orpheus head-butted him in the cheekbone and he stammered, "O-kay. How many worlds did you say?"

"Thousands. But they're not lockstep worlds—well, except for a few discards like Thisbe. They're too hot. Too *fast.*" He nodded at the overgrown runways.

Corva nodded in agreement. "They've gone strange, a lot of them. Alien and dangerous, and they don't communicate with the outside world anymore. The Wastes, that's what we call them."

"And Thisbe is . . . ?"

She shrugged and jabbed a thumb at the sky. "Far out on the edge—and glitchy. So not worth the effort for your average self-respecting civilization. Perfect for us, though."

"—And with that, here's my ride," said Jay. He waved at an older man and middle-aged woman who were strolling toward them across the landing field. The man was accompanied by a cargo bot like Jay's, which balanced an impossibly tall pile of machinery on its back. The woman was surrounded by a . . . Toby squinted . . . a flock of some kind of glittering metallic things. Behind her stalked a tall, willowy, and sinuous bot, not quite human formed but beautiful.

"Makers?" said Toby. Jaysir nodded.

"We're not loners, you know. There just weren't any on Wallop. We love to get together, we just refuse to engage in social relations that are based on material inequity. Anyway, I've got a lot to talk about with these guys. About what we should do next."

"You're not going to tell them who—"

"—You are? Not until you give me the all-clear." Jaysir grinned at him. "But you understand, I need to . . . set them up for it, so it's not a complete shock when you do. And you'll probably want to know whether we can help, when you make your move."

"I don't know that there're any moves to be made, Jay."

"You just keep thinking that." With a cheerful wave, the maker walked off to meet his kin.

Halen had flagged down an empty aircar, and they piled their few belongings into it and set off for the city. A few minutes into their flight, the "sunlight" went from psychotic blue to eerie green. It stayed that way for a minute, then flipped back to yellow-white.

Now that he could properly see, Toby realized that their car was part of a regular stream converging on the core of the city; the awakened passengers from a dozen ships were on their way into town. The sky would probably have been dark with aircars, he supposed, if it weren't for the blockade.

As the shock of seeing and feeling sunlight faded, Toby remembered his nervousness upon awaking today. He and Orpheus had used cicada beds on the flight out, so woke refreshed, and he'd been instantly aware of the ordeal that was to come.

Today, he was going to meet Halen and Corva's parents.

It didn't help that Shylif was guesting with them as well. Corva had invited him to stay at her parents' place until the Thisbe courts heard his case against Sebastine Coley. At first he'd been reluctant but had finally agreed just this morning. Toby was simultaneously cheered and uneasy that he'd accepted. After the incident on Wallop, he wasn't entirely comfortable around Shylif anymore.

Having Shylif there when he met Corva's parents might help to defuse the tension. On the other hand, it made Toby seem like yet another possibly disreputable member of her rogues' gallery, and he was eager to counter this impression. He rehearsed his words as buildings of alien architecture, and occasionally the Consensus style, flicked past below. *"Pleased to meet you, sir, ma'am,"* he'd say, or something like that. *"Yes, I saved your son."* Or, *"No I didn't save anybody, your daughter saved my life."*

Or maybe, *"Hi, I'm the brother of the man who's oppressing your entire planet."*

"Am I Garren Morton today? Or Toby McGonigal?" he'd asked Corva before they went into hibernation—last night, or so it felt like.

She'd frowned. "Let's start with Garren and work our way up," she'd said.

"Ah, Orph, what do I do?" He put his face next to the denner's and scritched the fur between his ears. Orpheus made a bouquet of smiley-face emoticons to go with the purr he gave off. He seemed quite unconcerned with the strangeness of this new world. Toby wasn't so comfortable.

Corva's brother was some kind of revolutionary. They'd talked a few times while he and his older, gray-haired companions from the ship had worked to secure them a ship back to Thisbe. That wasn't the only ship they were after: more than half the men and women Toby had rescued from Wallop's frozen clouds were on their way to other worlds, where they claimed they intended to do "business."

Ammond had been doing "business," too. Even if the strange quarantine of Thisbe was unjust, Halen and his friends seemed to be doing more than just trying to undo it. Halen, at least, hated Peter's lockstep. You could hear it in his voice when he said even the most innocent thing about it. He wanted to take down Peter's world.

So should Toby help him do it? The towers of the city swept slowly by below them. The place looked postapocalyptic: the building façades were cracked and vine choked, the streets overgrown with grass and trees. Various big machines were struggling to cut it back, and bots were working to fix the damage to the buildings. Still, the place looked busy, with crowds of people in the streets and lots of aerial vehicles hopping between the districts. The aircars from the spaceport thinned out, most landing on this or that downtown platform. Theirs was one of the few that kept on into the forested suburbs.

"The city's not under a dome or anything," he suddenly realized. "Do you get any winter here?"

Halen shook his head. "It stays subtropical most of the time—except when the sun has an outage. Those can last for weeks, and then the whole world'll freeze over. It's brutal. The rest of the time, everything's constantly growing, so while we're hibernating it just takes over." He nodded at the grass-choked streets. "Normally that all gets cleaned up before we wake, but the bots can't keep up with the blockade schedule. Too many turns too close together; they're breaking down."

"Home," said Corva. Her voice was tense.

The aircar settled on the overgrown lawn of a fairly modest-looking stone house. The place was ringed with trees, and only narrow paved footpaths wound between those to the neighbors and beyond. Apparently, out here in the suburbs they'd given up on keeping the streets clear of invading vegetation.

Toby stared at the trees. He hadn't seen so many in one place since he'd left Earth. They made him want to cry, and he felt a pang of intense envy for Corva and her family, who were lucky enough to live among them. Although, they probably never had time to get used to them. A sapling this month would be a stout adult after just one turn and dead after a few more.

People were coming out of the house. Halen pushed up the aircar's canopy and bounded out. Corva followed, but as she approached her family her footsteps slowed, and then she stopped. Suddenly she burst into tears.

"You're *older*!" she exclaimed. A man and a woman rushed over to her, along with a younger man and woman. She let her parents embrace her but pushed away the other two.

"No! It's terrible, it's terrible!" With a sob she burst past them and ran into the house.

Toby sat in the aircar, clutching Orpheus and feeling sick. Finally Halen seemed to remember him and called, "Garren! It's okay, come meet Mom and Dad!"

He didn't want to get out of the car, but Orpheus squirmed from his grasp and leaped down to the grass, where he proceeded to roll back and forth in delight. Toby put a shaky hand on the canopy bed and climbed out. With slow steps he walked up to Corva's family. They were debating who should go after Corva.

"—Rescued us from the time lock! He won't say how he did it, but he agreed to come with us." Halen was grinning, but his eyes were cold as he looked over at Toby.

His parents weren't like that, they were practically in tears themselves. Corva's other brother and sister looked to be about Halen's age; all seemed older than Corva, but a sinking feeling in Toby's stomach told him that, no, *she* must be the eldest.

"I'll go to her," said Corva's sister.

"No," Toby heard himself say.

Halen's grin froze. "What?" he said in a slightly strangled tone.

"I'm sorry." Toby bowed quickly. "I'm Garren Morton. Corva and I are just friends, but, the thing is . . ."

"What?" Halen said again. His smile was gone.

"It happened to me, too," Toby blurted. "Having years stolen like . . . like's happened to you. I know how she feels. My own brother and sister are . . . well, they're a lot older than me now. And my parents are dead. For me, they were alive just a couple of months ago, but it's been . . ." Halen's eyes widened in warning, and Toby shrugged. "An impossibly long time.

"I know you want to run to her," he said to Corva's sister. "She looks the same to you, but for her, you're an entirely new person. It's going to take her awhile to get over that shock."

Her father sighed. "It's what I said would happen. The same thing would have happened to you," he said to Halen. "You shouldn't have risked it all like that, son."

Halen was now the target of their attention. With another quick bow, Toby moved around them and entered the house, where alert bots offered him orange juice and biscuits. He stared at them, sidled past, and called out, "Corva?"

He hesitated but didn't really feel like he had to tiptoe about; the household bots were there to protect the privacy of the family and would simply bar him from anywhere he shouldn't go. Or so he supposed, until he saw that half the butlers were sitting silent in dusty corners: broken-down, like so much of the city.

He started up the stairs, and they didn't stop him.

She was facedown on a bed in one of the bedrooms. This was a girl's room, its walls tuned to shifting washes of yellow and peach; pictures of family, places and people tumbled and sailed slowly up and back in that dimensionless space. There were wooden boxes under the bed and chests of drawers whose tops overflowed with jewelry and dozens of toys, some of which had broken down and sat forlornly while the rest all crowded at the edge of the surface, watching Corva weep with concern on their tiny faces.

"Evayne's room looked like this," said Toby from the doorway. Corva stiffened, then turned her head enough to say, "You've got to be kidding."

"She's my little sister, Corva. At least, she was last time I saw her."

Corva lay very still for a long time. Then she rolled over and sat up. She wouldn't meet Toby's eyes. "I was hoping to totally redo this room before I showed it to any young man. I haven't lived here in years."

"You were at school."

She nodded. "Studying architecture! How to design buildings to last thousands of years. Ruin design, it's called." She wiped her eyes with the back of her hand. Suddenly, something seemed to occur to her, and now she did send Toby a puzzled look. "What about you? You got lost because you were away from home for some reason. There're a billion stories about why, but most of them are ridiculous—"

"We had to seal our claim to Sedna by visiting all its moons. One was stupidly far away. Rockette, we called it. I got lost on the way there."

It was strange. What had been his immediate experience yesterday was something he could talk about as being in the past; it was a story he could tell. He grinned and shrugged. "That's really all there was to it. I didn't want to go, but Mom and Dad weren't home, and Peter and Evayne weren't old enough."

Corva frowned, thinking. "That must have been tough on all of you."

"Toughest on Peter. He hates change, he's afraid of his own shadow. He cried for days when he found out Mom and Dad were going."

"What about when *you* left?"

Toby shrugged. "We had this gameworld we shared, called Consensus. I promised I'd meet him in it every day. He was fine with that."

Corva gave him a long measured look. "Are you sure about that?"

His heart was suddenly hammering again. He shook himself angrily and scowled at her toys. They backed away, all except for a little warrior with a sword that stood bravely with its thumbnail-size weapon raised.

"We can't talk about any of this without tripping over it, can we?"

"Tripping over what?" He thought he knew, but he wanted her to say it.

"The change. How we slept, and overnight they got older. And . . . how it's all around us all the time. These cliffs of time you could just fall over accidentally at any moment. Lose a day, lose a century . . . I hate it."

He was surprised. "You want to leave the lockstep?"

"That would be worse. To be stranded in realtime? Left behind by everybody you ever knew?" She shuddered. "No, it's just so unfair how a year can be snatched away from you like that. Or . . . or a whole life."

He found himself sitting on the bed next to her, and she leaned in to him. As he had so many times with Evayne, he put his arm around her, but this was different and he knew it. Corva buried her face in his shoulder. "I'm sorry," she said, voice muffled.

"For what?"

"For using you the way I did. For being mean. I just . . . didn't think I could trust you."

"But you can."

She was silent. Then she pulled away. "Toby, we have to face them some time. For me, it's today I guess. For you . . . do you really know what'll happen when you do that?"

He clasped his hands and looked down. "No. I guess not."

"Then don't make any promises, okay?"

Fair enough, he thought, though her words had hurt him. He stood up briskly. "Come on. They're waiting for you. I think you need to make the first move."

"And . . . how I feel? About seeing them so different?"

He gave a short laugh. "Maybe you should hide that for a day or so. See how it goes."

Corva stood, too, and blew out a deep breath. Then she smiled. "Nobody else could have said that to me, but maybe you're right. I'll pretend for a day and then . . . see."

They almost joined hands, but she turned away first, and they went downstairs.

THE KEISHIONS WERE LOUD. They had definite opinions about everything, and every single one of them needed to be right all the time. Their arguments started at breakfast, continued all day, spilled out onto the lawns, and echoed through the forest around the house. At first, Toby just stayed out of the way, but gradually he realized that they appreciated his opinions, and he began to relax. Most important, they knew he was an ignoramus when it came to the lockstep worlds, so he felt comfortable asking them the dumbest questions—about Thisbe, about the locksteps, about their family, and sometimes—when he could appear nonchalant—about Corva.

Like him, she was the eldest—or had been. She still won the most arguments, and the others deferred to her despite the age gap. What she had lost to them in time, she'd more than made up in experience.

Corva was no help at all during his first few days in the house; she was too busy getting reacquainted with everybody else. Halen hung around the edges, brooding and watching Toby. Meanwhile, outside the permanent pitched battle of the Keishion household, Thisbe was fully awake now and working hard to catch up with the damage from the frequency shift that Peter had wrought on it.

Toby found it natural to help the bots clearing the underbrush and fixing years of storm damage. Orpheus spent all day outside anyway, and Toby loved the fresh air, too, but also in some ways it was like being back on Sedna, where there had always been building or repair work to be done. He loved fixing stuff, and while doing this absorbing work, he could completely forget his troubles for hours at a time.

(Although, on those rare occasions when the "sun" changed color, he came crashing back to reality, at least for a minute or two.)

Gradually, he noticed that Corva was often nearby while he was working. She would bring him water, or simply be seen reading in the crook of a tree while he was hacking at the underbrush. Then she began perching, not far off, on a newly repaired wall or a lawn chair she'd dragged over; and since, well, they were in the same space anyway . . . they talked.

"I had a denner when I was growing up," she said as they watched Wrecks and Orpheus chase each other around the ragged, but finally mowed, lawn. "Chauncey was his name. I was pretty lonely at first when I went off to school, so I looked into getting another one, but you couldn't get them on Wallop. I wasn't going to let that stop me, so I kept asking people and pushing, and that's how I found out about these people on Lowdown who bred them."

Toby was startled, and then it all made sense. "Ammond and Persea!" They'd bred denners.

She nodded. "They owned the operation, they didn't do it themselves. They had them implanted with the cicada-bed tech for shady customers. Total gray-ware stuff, it's just barely acceptable to the lockstep monitors. Anyway, I had no intention of using Wrecks that way, it seemed wrong, but these were the only denners you could get. Then the blockade happened. My money got cut off, I couldn't go home, then I found out that Halen had tried to run the blockade and was trapped in stasis. I had to sell my bots for food, I couldn't afford to travel . . . but I'd heard about the stowaways when I got Wrecks."

She told Toby how she'd met Shylif and how they'd stowed away on a flight back to Lowdown, where, with the last of her money, she'd bought Orpheus. "He was for Halen, you see. I had this crazy idea of sneaking into the quarantined ship and getting him to wake Halen up. I had no idea how it was going to work, but I was damn well going to try."

So far, this made sense. Toby watched the denners roll around, play fighting, while he thought through what had happened. "But how did you find out about me? Or did you even know who I was?"

"Actually, we had a pretty good idea. See, we were stowaways. We were living a bit off frequency anyway, and spending time in spaceports and warehouses. So we were watching when Ammond's tug bots brought down your ship. They did it a week before everybody was supposed to wake up; but we were already awake, 'cause we'd set the denners' alarms to get us up well before there would be people nosing about. So we saw them shrouding this incredibly old radiation-fried ship in orange plastic sheeting and walling it up in a warehouse space off in a far corner of Ammond's operation. And then we saw them bring you out.

"I was really curious at that point, so I looked up the lettering on the side of your ship. I expected to get a hit off the lockstep ship registry, but instead, all the hits were from books on ancient mythology . . ."

He frowned in thought. "So when I saw you in the courtyard that first day . . ."

"I was there to buy Orpheus—but I was also there to look for the boy we'd seen them take out of the ship. And when you came running out I freaked. First, 'cause I knew who you might be, and second, because Ammond's guards had told me they'd cut off my nose if they caught me sneaking about."

He nodded. It all made sense. "And when you woke me up on the way to Little Auriga?"

"You'd only just gone under. Your hibernation was still reversible—like in the boat, remember? Oh, you mean how did I get to you?" She shook her head quickly. "Ammond thinks of himself as a criminal mastermind, but his security's really lame. Thisbe is habitable all the time," she said, gesturing around at the rich trees and long grass, "and there're other locksteps here. *We* are good at security, at locks and vaults and alarms. We have to be. So Shylif and I didn't have much trouble breaking in while your ship was on the ground waiting for launch clearance. Shylif had already taught me how to break into a ship; you need to know how to do that if you're going to be a decent stowaway. I needed to learn how anyway, if I was going to get Orpheus to Halen."

"But you followed me to Little Auriga. You didn't have to."

She looked uncomfortable. "When I woke you up to warn you, it didn't seem like you understood me. You were all dopey and 'huh?' So . . . we argued about it and decided to go after you."

"'Cause I was a McGonigal and worth a lot?"

She glared at him. "'Cause I thought they were going to kill you. Or worse."

"Worse, yeah." He shuddered. "Thank you. —Though, really, it was Orpheus rapping on my window who showed me the way out."

She laughed. "Anyway, I'm just glad it's over. I suppose it's what they call an adventure, but to me it was just one long panic attack. If that's what an adventure's like, I never want another one."

Away on the other side of the lawn, Halen was chatting with one of the neighbors. Toby nodded at him. "Halen never got his, you know."

"His what?"

"His adventure. He never got to have it. He started out to save you, and you ended up saving him instead. He never even got a proper look at Wallop. Went from ship to ship, sleep to sleep, and now he's back here."

Corva gaped at Toby. "What are you trying to say? That he's *disappointed*? Mad at me for saving him?" Toby shrugged. "Oh, come on. Is that how boys think about these things?"

He nodded. "That is how boys think about these things."

"Well, it's stupid."

She changed the subject, and soon Toby went back to working with the bots. After that, though, they spent a lot of time together. And they talked.

The rhythm of life in the locksteps was starting to become clear to him, and talking to Corva helped give the abstractions flesh and blood. She described the parties that happened at the end of every turn—every month, that is, by human reckoning. Whatever resources the household or the city or planet hadn't used during its four weeks awake had to be able to hibernate or else had to be used up. Some things were too fragile or temporary by nature to winter over. So you used up all the food in the fridge and broke up, burned, or built mad sculptures out of other transient things. In some places the neighbors vied for extravagance and shock value—although, since the ritual happened so frequently, some people just ignored it and went to bed early, trusting the household bots to clear away the deteriorated and decayed objects by the next waking.

More ceremony was lavished on people who might be traveling. At the very least you wouldn't see them for a month. If they were on their way to the other side of the lockstep, or somewhere exotic like Earth or Barsoom, then it might be a year or more. Leave-taking parties were major events in any neighborhood.

Next morning—at start-of-turn—the trees were bigger, or completely cut down, and even entire landforms like hills might have shifted slightly. The climate might be different, too—Thisbe's was none too stable. Most important on such mornings, though, was the fact that ships from a thousand worlds crowded the skies.

Corva talked about visiting the port on the dawn of a new turn and watching exotic, weirdly dressed strangers step blinking into the lurid daylight of her planet. They brought crafts and gifts as alien as themselves, and stories and pictures from around the lock-step and beyond.

The longer a world slept, the more ships could appear during that special night. As Toby had learned, if you doubled your sleep you would far more than double the number of worlds whose ships could reach you in that time. Modern fusion or fission-fragment rockets could get you about half a light-year in thirty years, and nomad planets were spaced about one every tenth of a light-year in this part of the galaxy. A world that slept for three decades couldn't visit just five times the number of worlds as one that wintered over for one-fifth the time; it could visit *five hundred* more. The longer you slept, the more opportunities for trade you'd have.

Lockstep 360/1 was about five light-years across, and within that space there were more than seventy thousand worlds, ranging from little moon-size ice balls to a couple of planets as big as Jupiter. All were easy to get to from even the smallest outpost, provided you could spend thirty years at a time accumulating fuel for the journey and wintered over.

And yet Thisbe had gone against the sensible rules of the lock-steps and been punished for it. The blockade remained.

Corva patiently explained why. "Thisbe's really a fast world. See," she said, pointing to where some bots were repairing a roof, "there's a huge cost in wear and tear to wintering over here. There's a trade-off between how much you can produce while you were awake and how little you'll consume if you sleep longer. There's also a trade-off between the bigger manufacturing and agriculture potential of fast worlds like this and the bigger trading opportunities you get if you winter over longer. There're other lock-steps on Thisbe, you know, and they get by on higher frequencies 'cause fast worlds like this do better at manufacturing than trade."

Corva took Toby on walks through the neighborhood, where some houses were sealed up and silent. These were neighbors she only saw on Jubilee, which happened only once or twice a year. They were the ones who were more often awake, though—it was really Corva and her people who were usually the silent, sealed-up mysteries.

During one of these walks she told Toby what had happened. "The government wanted our Jubilees to synchronize with more of the other locksteps. Those locksteps wanted it, too. They don't use McGonigal cicada beds," she added, nodding at a silent estate whose lawns were overgrown with weeds and young trees. "So there was a lot of talk about scrapping our beds and using theirs. That would cost a huge amount, but more important, we'd break the lockstep agreement."

"What's that?" He'd read enough to know it was some sort of service agreement between the McGonigals and the 360 worlds.

"The agreement says we promise not to change the frequency except during emergencies. In return, we get access to all the

360-to-1 worlds without port taxes, immigration reviews and all that. Dad calls it a 'level playing field.' It's useful, 'cause among other things it lets all the worlds trade using the same currency and know what its value is from turn to turn.

"The government thought of a way to bend the rules. The cicada beds all have their own timers, of course, but they're coordinated by a timing signal sent from centralized servers. One of those is here, on Thisbe, and it sets the exact frequency and times for a couple hundred worlds whose only connection to the rest of the lockstep is through us. We're the gateway. If we hack our timer to shift our frequency just a little—add a year here, drop one there—we could go into Jubilee with our neighbors a lot more often. Barsoom might complain, but they wouldn't come down on us. And since we were the server for all those other worlds, they'd follow us. There's a whole bunch of different locksteps near the Laser Wastes that would come into Jubilee. So with one stroke Thisbe could double its trade potential."

Toby nodded. It was brilliant. That overgrown estate, normally silent, would be awake more often. More ships would crowd the sky. "It's perfect! Why would it be a problem?"

"If they let us get away with time shifting, everybody might try it. Then there'd be chaos, because the value of money couldn't be predicted anymore and ships leaving port for their farthest trading partners couldn't be guaranteed to get there in time. What happens if I've got a crucial trading trip planned with a world that's a twenty-nine-year journey away, and they decide to slip their schedule and come awake after twenty-seven years so they can Jubilee with somebody else? I get there and they're wintered over. I have to wait another turn to do my trading with them. Instead of one month lockstep time, that trip's taken at least two. It's crazy."

He was puzzled. "You think your people were wrong to do what they did?"

"Yes!" She threw up her hands in frustration. "It was stupid. But it's more stupid what Barsoom did to punish us! Way too extreme."

He had to agree with that. Corva had lost eight years of her family's lives to the blockade, and could have lost four more. Shifting Thisbe's frequency into high gear like this was a brutal overreaction. The global economy was depressed, with resources that normally could accumulate for decades being used up faster than they could be renewed. Trades that had happened once a month now occurred only every year, and the Jubilees were totally screwed up.

"I'm surprised you put up with it," he said. "Better to leave the lockstep entirely than suffer like this."

"If only it were that easy," she said. "Leave 360 and we slash our trading partners. If we permanently speed up, we'll lose dozens or hundreds of worlds as next-day neighbors. But we can't go on this way, either. It's unfair. It's evil."

So there it was. She didn't say the words, but Toby heard them in his head as in her voice: *You're a McGonigal, maybe you can stop this.* He had no idea whether he had the power, yet also unspoken was another accusation: the fault lay not with the lockstep system but with the fact that it was ruled by the McGonigals.

The peaceful setting, combined with Corva's comment about her adventure being over, had been making Toby wonder: could his own be over, too? If he'd escaped Nathan Kenani, maybe he'd escaped Evayne as well . . . and maybe he didn't need to ever confront her or Peter. They were different people now; his beloved brother and sister were lost forever to time. Wouldn't the sensible thing be to just accept that and find a life for himself in this wondrous and strange world his family had built while he slept? But things were far from perfect here. Corva was right: what was happening to Thisbe was unfair.

It was hilarious in a way. Evayne and Peter were acting up again. It was time for the eldest brother to clean up the mess as he had so many times in the past. He had to laugh.

"What's so funny?" She sent him one of her special glares.

Toby shook his head. "It's all been going by too fast for me to keep up," he said. "But that's got to change.

"It's time I started planning my next turn."

| Fourteen |

SHYLIF WENT EVERYWHERE NOW with a guard of McGonigal bots. These were entirely under Toby's control, and Shy knew it, yet he hadn't complained. In fact, he seemed oddly cheerful, despite the fact that Toby—and the Thisbe government—were keeping him from confronting Sebastine Coley again. Coley's whereabouts were known, but so far, the Thisbe authorities couldn't charge him with anything. The alleged crime had taken place on another world, and thousands of years ago in real-time terms. The odds of Shylif achieving actual justice seemed very long indeed.

Yet he'd come to see Toby one morning and said nothing about any of that. On the contrary, he'd volunteered to help Toby catch up on his history. After all, as he'd put it, "I had to do all this reading, too, once."

Thisbe's public records were open to Toby, and he'd finally summoned the courage to confront those images and videos of his brother and sister taken after he left. After what he'd just done on Wallop, it seemed silly to keep avoiding a few pictures. Yet as the days passed and he combed through old news stories, he found very little that made the new Peter and Evayne come to life for him.

"Look at this!" he said in exasperation. He and Shylif had their glasses on and were sharing a set of research windows. "Says here about half the original Sedna colonists are still alive—which I kind of figured after meeting Kenani. I mean, it's been forty years since I left, after all. You'd think they would have written memoirs, made documentaries, said *something* about the early years."

"Not if they're being threatened," Shylif pointed out reasonably. "Obviously, the Chairman wants to keep his secrets."

"Yeah." Toby didn't try to hide his disappointment. Had Peter learned nothing from Consensus?

"But there's another reason, Toby," Shylif went on. "You're kind of uniquely positioned to not see it."

"What do you mean?"

"Lockstep time is strange. This history you're looking for, at one and the same time there's nothing to it—only forty years!—and way too much of it—fourteen *thousand* years. Both at once. How are you supposed to think about that?"

Toby didn't know. The official records were disappointing, being merely a litany of massive immigrations, explosive economic growth and the conquest of new worlds. There were about a million pictures of Peter standing on some podium or other, waving and smiling. It just went on and on.

But he had another source. The archive from the twentier contained chaotic and fragmented records from Carter McGonigal's surveillance of the Sedna colony. Toby went back to these.

There were two kinds of records. One was the surveillance footage itself, which came in giant terabyte dumps from hundreds of cameras and listening devices, mostly standard bots eavesdropping while they went about their business. Toby assigned this to some game personalities in his local copy of Consensus, telling them to review it for relevant items.

The other kind of record, though, was much more interesting. Carter had recorded family meetings held in a cramped little closet, where he and, initially, just Mother, had talked about their fears and suspicions. Toby's father was convinced the trillionaires had planted one or more spies or saboteurs among the Sedna colonists. Months went by, and nothing turned up to confirm that worry. Toby watched it all anyway, fascinated and sorrowful at being so close to and still so far from his dearest people.

One day it wasn't just Mom and Dad meeting. Peter and Evayne were there, too. And Peter wasn't happy.

"You're doing *what*?" He stalked back and forth, his head and eyes turning to remain fixed on the open surveillance windows in the physical control panel at the focus of the room. "Isn't this what *they* do? Why are *we* doing it?"

"Listen," their father said tightly. "You're going to have to know how this stuff works. I'm not going to be around . . . well, for a while. I have to return to Earth, there's a challenge to our claim. While I'm away, we're going to be vulnerable. If something's going to happen, it'll be while I'm en route, do you understand? You have to be ready."

"It's wrong! I'm not doing it!" Peter stopped still and glared at his parents, and Toby found himself smiling. He wasn't sure of the date stamp, but at this point Peter must be almost as old as Toby had been when he set off for Rockette. That meant he'd be pretty much as old here as Toby was now. A kind of twin, yet Toby could still see the boy in him. He could see the man, too—the density of Peter's bones was making itself known in the angles of his face, the round solidity of his skull—but he still seemed so young. It made Toby wonder whether he, too, seemed as young to the people around him.

Evayne walked over and put her hand on Peter's arm. "I get it," she said. "It's how things are, Pete, we can't change it."

"Why don't . . . why don't you just treat this like it was a Consensus scenario? Play it through? I'll help."

Toby skipped ahead, taking giant steps through time—weeks, months, a year. After his father left for Earth again, the records became unevenly spaced. At last he came to the final one.

The shot was of Sedna's landscape. Nearby everything was utterly black, and out at the horizon it was, too, with only the sky blazing with stars to indicate up and down. In the middle distance was a cratered plain, and on it bright flashes of light created a stroboscopic impression of bots—big mining units and smaller, human-formed ones—locked in combat. The flashes were explosions and electrical discharges. The scene was, at first, utterly silent.

Then Peter's voice came on line, perfect and stereoscopic. "We're going to be hiding this backup as soon as I'm done. I just wanted to record what's happening . . . in case what we're going to try doesn't work.

"The trillionaires have made their move."

The camera pulled back. The image was taken near ground level and had the quality of the twentier's own cameras. Amplified starlight illuminated a sheltered ring of rocks where several space-suited figures sat, surrounded by bots, butlers, and weapons both makeshift and purpose built. One of the space-suited figures stood in the center of the space, and although its faceplate was blank, it moved with the jittery intensity recognizable as Peter's.

That suit knelt now in front of the camera. "We woke up today to find the colony bots running amok. They tried to kill us in our beds. Luckily this surveillance network my parents set up isn't connected to the main Internet. We were alerted by that surveillance system and were able to get out. The bots we'd committed to it are still on our side, who knows for how long? And they're all fighting it out down there." He pointed, and the camera obligingly turned to take in the sight of the distant silent battle.

"It's pretty clear what they're trying to do. They've ruptured the colony's oxygen tanks, blown up the greenhouse—"

"I saw a pack of them going into the food stores before we got out," said someone else. The camera turned again, this time revealing who else was on this rise above the battle: everyone, it seemed. There were hundreds of space-suited figures sitting, standing, and pacing here. Only a few bots, mostly twentiers, squatted among them.

"We've nearly mopped them all up, but the damage is done," Peter went on. "They targeted essential life support, in order to take us down as quick as they could. Whoever's running the operation doesn't care if all his bots get wiped out in the end, because we're already good as dead. We can't survive without those supplies. The plan's pretty simple, eh, Mom? Destroy our air, water, heat and food supplies, and we die. Call it a tragic accident, hold a big memorial service back on Earth, and after a while drum up support for a new expedition to seed a new colony. That'll take a few years, but hey, they've got time, right?

"It's a plan so simple it can't fail. Except that it's going to, right Mom?"

"As long as they don't target the cicada beds," she said.

"And it looks like they haven't. Whoever they are, they don't know about your experiments. They certainly didn't know about the secondary network. So they have no idea what we're going to do."

The camera returned to Peter, who now loomed above it, a silhouette whose backdrop was the twisting banner of the Milky Way.

"Dad's network is still operating, but it was always pretty simple and I was able to take it over long ago. I'm pretty sure *they* are not able to control it, even if they knew it existed. That network will coordinate the bots we've got left while they repair the life-support systems and rebuild our supplies. That could take months or years, but it doesn't matter. We'll all be asleep.

"We already proved we could double the size of the colony by having half our people winter over—isn't that what you're calling the hibernation, Evie?—while the rest of us are awake. We don't have enough beds for everybody, so what we're going to do is cycle through them a few at a time. When those ones are frozen solid, we're going to store 'em in the hangar and put the next group into the beds. When the crisis is over, the bots will bring us back the same way, one batch at a time."

Peter gazed in the direction of the battle. "Looks like things are winding down. We might be able to go back soon. We're not going to broadcast any distress signal. We'll let 'em think we're dead. Then, in a few years, we'll be back up and running, and waiting for them when they send their own colonists.

"Funny thing is, we might be even better off by the time we wake up. The longer the bots have to fix things up, the more resources they'll have ready when we revive. Everybody ready?"

The camera swung again, showing the colonists standing, turning, gathering together facing Peter and two other suited shapes—Evayne and Mother, no doubt.

Suddenly Peter turned to look into the camera. "You! Twentier! Take this record and hide it. You're going to ground now, too. I'll find you when we're done.

"All right, everybody, single file, and watch out for—"

There was nothing more in the twentier's memory.

THE KEISHION FAMILY BOTS were repairing each other now. There wasn't any more work to be done around the house, and the Keishions had settled into something that Corva said was a lot like their normal routine. Supplies and resources were thin these days, but they were industrious people. They were getting by.

Toby spent whole days away from the estate. He could be seen walking in the hills, talking to nobody apparently, but with his glasses on. Sometimes a small swarm of butlers and grippies followed him, and together they would act out dramas and battles in the parkland that wove its way through the city. Corva and Halen stood together one morning watching this spectacle and shaking their heads. Later that day Halen marched out and stepped between Toby and the butler he was talking to.

"Toby, what are you doing?"

"Oh, hi, Halen, what's up?"

"I dunno. Just a blockade, and all of us aging ten times faster than the rest of the lockstep. Or hadn't you noticed?"

Toby was holding a grippy like it was a pistol. He let go and it dropped, changing shape and twisting like a cat to land on sudden little legs. He lowered his glasses to look over them at Halen.

"Why don't you come in here?"

Halen frowned minutely. Then he snapped his fingers and one of the bots that always hung around him walked up and handed him a pair of glasses. He put them on and Toby synced their interfaces.

The hills wavered and were suddenly overlaid with an entire army—thousands of mechs and armed bots, scurrying reconnaissance mice and stilt-legged snipers. Off in the sky, the blued-out shapes of vast rounded forms stood half out of the atmosphere.

Halen peered at one of these. "Nothing like that exists," he said.

Toby had been wondering how Halen would react to this simulation and decided now that he'd pretty much gotten it right. "Not in the real world, no," he admitted. "This is Consensus. It's a game."

Halen's lips thinned and he looked away for a moment before saying, in a tightly controlled voice, "You're playing a *game?*"

"Yes, I am. You wanna play?"

"No. No thank you." Toby could see that Halen was working his way up to some sort of outburst, so he decided to stop toying with him.

"It's called Consensus. Peter and I designed it."

The air visibly went out of Halen's anger. "What?"

"After the kidnapping, Peter needed therapy. But we'd come all the way out to Sedna instead, and we didn't bring any human psychologist. All I had to go on was the 'pedias and psych avatars. So—"

"What kidnapping?"

Toby shook his head sadly. "Something that never made it into the history books, it seems. Peter was kidnapped when we were kids. It was horrible for all of us, but him—he built this shell, and none of us could get through it. So I made Consensus and lured him into it."

Halen turned around, examining the martial vista. "This is a military sim."

"I set a challenge for him, I said, 'Design a world where what happened to us could never happen.' We were still designing the place when I got lost. This is what a lot of the early versions looked like."

"Wars? How's that safe?"

"I played a little trick on Peter," Toby admitted with a shrug. "I populated the gameworld with nonplayer characters who acted like real people, not like entertainer bots. Pretty easy to do when you can just order your programmer bots to swap out the usual game character minds with libraries of personality types based on centuries of sociology and psych studies. I'd make millions of pseudopeople and then we'd plug in whole new governments and economies and see what they did. It was mostly really bad. Mostly, they ended up like this." He nodded at the army.

"The thing is, Consensus isn't perfect. As a simulation of reality, I mean. Nothing is—there're always assumptions, shortcuts, and if you started with some detailed sim of a particular moment in time and played forward, the game would diverge farther and farther away from what actually happened.

"The point is, if you treat reality like a game, it's going to show in your decisions. I'm . . . checking something."

Halen nodded slowly, but he was frowning again. "You're studying your brother. That makes sense. But if you're looking for strategies, Toby . . . there's really only one. You know what it is. And Peter and Evayne are terrified that you'll use it."

"Wake Mother, you mean?" He shook his head. "I'll do it for my own sake, but seriously, what's she going to do? Scold Evayne for becoming a murderous high priestess in the cult of Toby?" He laughed.

"You don't get it," snapped Halen. "I knew you didn't get it. It's not about you, or her, or Evayne. It's about what other people believe about you. You're a god, Toby. Evayne made you into one."

Toby shook his head. "People in the lockstep can't possibly believe that. I only disappeared forty years ago. I know thousands of years have gone by outside—"

"Toby, most of the citizens of the lockstep are *from* outside. The number of people here from your time is so incredibly small that they don't even register. Three-sixty is a lockstep of immigrants, and almost all of them come from worlds where your cult's been cultivated for thousands of years."

"Cultivated . . ."

He had fully intended to read up on this, but there was so much else to cover, he hadn't gotten to it yet. Toby did know hints of the story, so he wasn't entirely surprised when Halen said, "Evayne visits worlds on the down cycle of their civilizations. Postapocalyptic places, failing terraforming efforts, places ravaged by posthumans or tailored plagues or whatever. She lands in a big splash of glory and music and hands out gifts, things like self-reproducing fab printers and med bots. Then she tells the grateful people that she's the messenger of the boy god Tobias McGonigal. She sticks around long enough to get the right stories stuck in their heads and get them used to the icons—you know, the statues—then she leaves. But she comes back, every few centuries, to reinforce the cult and draft the most fanatical members into her little army.

"Don't you see? Everything she has is built on *you*. You're the god of her religion. If you return, she's immediately retired, and she knows it. Every single member of her army will go down on their knees to you the instant they find out who you are. All you have to do is announce yourself. What other strategy do you need?"

Toby gazed out over the ranked masses of the game's latest army, and he felt sick. He and Peter had both tried such gambits in Consensus, and not just once or twice but numerous times. He knew such scenarios could end in absolute triumph, even in societies where Peter's kidnapping would be impossible. But to get to that, you had to make other things impossible, too—like independent thought, free speech, and self-determination.

You could play through it, and it looked great—but reviewing Consensus now with new eyes, he could see the flaws. It wasn't just the sheer amorality of it—the bloodbaths and pogroms that necessarily went along with successful religious conquest. Those alone should have ruled out the strategy. Yet on top of that was the simple fact that there was no way to simulate all the many ways that the strategy could go wrong. Just because something worked in Consensus—or in Halen's imagination—didn't mean it would work in the real world.

"Evayne can't afford to have you announce yourself. Or, if you do," Halen went on eagerly, "she'll have to make sure that you're not returning as a messiah."

Toby appraised Halen. Corva's brother obviously thought he understood Evayne. What to him was reality, though, sounded like just another Consensus scenario to Toby, and he more than suspected it would be the same for Evayne. But if it wasn't a game for her anymore; if she had convinced herself that there was only one way things could play out . . .

Then Toby might have the beginnings of a real strategy.

"Go on." He crossed his arms, stepping back from Halen's intensity.

"There're two ways for a world to end, Toby: in glory or in fire. If Evayne can't profit from you bringing glory to the people, she'll make sure they think you're bringing *fire*."

The words hung there, and the moment stretched out. Toby took off his glasses, and the ranked armies vanished; his generals became butlers; his weapons, grippies. There was only him now, standing on a hillside with Halen Keishion.

"So you see," Halen murmured, almost apologetically, "you can study the past all you like, but it doesn't matter. You really only have one choice.

"You have to become the god that the people think you are."

IT CAME AS SOMETHING of a relief when, the next day, Corva told Toby that the courts had agreed to hear Shylif's case against Sebastine Coley. "I'm going to be a character witness," she said. "We . . . haven't talked about you to the court. I hope that's all right. But I'd like you to come."

Law had been one of those ideas Peter detested. "There's no such thing as two identical acts," he'd told Toby. "All actions have different outcomes. I steal a diamond necklace from a rich guy who's forgotten he owns it, nobody cares. You steal a loaf of bread from a factory that makes millions of them every day, and you get sent to prison. It makes no sense. Every act should be judged entirely on its own."

In the world before artificial intelligence, this had been impossible, so there was law. Justice, however, was one of the few places in Peter's utopia where he allowed AI, so Shylif and Sebastine Coley found themselves standing in a marble courthouse but not in front of a traditional judge or jury. Toby and Jaysir sat in the visitors' gallery and watched as the two were made to stand in front of a man who looked for all the world like a real judge. "He's not," Jaysir muttered. "He's a cyranoid. He just recites whatever the AI whispers into his ear. He's not allowed to speak on his own."

Court officials read Shylif's complaint, and character witnesses came forward to speak for him and for Coley. Corva had her turn, and described Shylif's deep well of sorrow, how he preferred working with bots in the warehouses and factories of the lockstep to spending time with humans. Coley's family described a loving father and grandfather. It turned out he'd become the patriarch to quite a large clan.

When all of this was done, the judge asked Coley whether Shylif's accusations were true.

Coley nodded, and the faces of his family members crumpled in shock and disbelief. Toby had never seen anything like this in real life before, and witnessing it was utterly unlike watching a court drama. This was not an entertainment; it was just sad.

"I'm sorry," Coley said. He hung his head.

Shylif's lips curled in a sneer. "Is that all you have to say for yourself?"

Now, unexpectedly, Coley raised his head looked Shylif in the eye. "No. No, it's not.

"I did some terrible things when I was a young man. That's over sixty years ago now, for me. I know it's less for you. Either way, it's time that's gone, and so much has happened since. I was saved by a woman who became my wife, and she made me into the man I am now. But I know I can never escape who I was or what I did."

He looked up at the judge, and now Toby understood why the AI that presided over the courtroom was given a human face. Coley knew he was addressing a presence that dwelt behind the man in front of him, but at times like this one needed to put a human face on the moment. "Sir," he said, "I'll face justice for this, and for the other things I did. It's time, I guess. But you have to know"—and now he turned back to Shylif—"what that means."

Jaysir and Toby exchanged a glance, and both leaned forward to hear better.

"What do you mean?" said Shylif suspiciously.

"I'm not doing this to salve my own conscience," said Coley. "I'm too old and too much time has passed for remedies like that. And don't think that any outcome will make you feel better, because we both know it won't.

"I'll accept the judgment of the court. It won't do any good. It won't bring Ouline back, it won't right the wrongs, it won't heal the wounds.

"It's . . . just one of those things that have to be done."

Silence descended on the court. Shylif stood like a statue, while Coley's family squirmed in their seats. Suddenly, the judge picked up his gavel and its descent made a clap of sound that echoed through the space.

"Sebastine Coley," he said, "how many descendants do you have?"

Startled, Coley said, "Uh . . . I have five children, and they're all married. They've each got three or four kids and some of those've got kids now, too . . ."

The judge nodded sharply. "Sebastine Coley, I sentence you to recount the story of what you did to harm the people beloved of the man Shylif, one at a time to each and every member of your family who is old enough to understand the tale. You will do so in the presence of Shylif, the complainant, so that he can be assured that you do not lie or leave out any detail. Every person in your line will know from your own lips exactly what you did." He banged the gavel again, and the court was dismissed.

A look of horror had come over Coley's face on hearing these instructions. Now he collapsed to his knees, sobbing. But Shylif, standing over him, lowered his head in thought for a long moment, and then nodded.

"I am satisfied," he said.

| Fifteen |

ONE DAY TOBY LOWERED his glasses down his nose and frowned at the sudden appearance of heavily laden carts on the neighborhood footpaths and cargo quadcopters over the trees. They all buzzed about with a sense of excitement, and many of the neighbors were out on their porches watching. Bots ran to and fro as well; some were setting up tables on the lawn of the Keishion estate.

He dismissed the scenario he was exploring and walked over. "What's going on?"

A bot bowed to him. "Tomorrow is end-of-turn, sir. We are preparing a potlatch party."

"Tomorrow?" He'd really lost track of time. It felt like the city had just gotten back on its feet. If this was how turn's end felt after wintering over for only two and a half years, what was it like when the turns took their usual thirty?

He skittered around nervously, too, until he ran into Corva. She was sitting in one of her favorite places, the stone wall that ran into the house, and she was reading a book.

"Oh, just ignore it," she said when he pointed at the organized chaos going on around them. "It's just turn's end. Join in or not, it's entirely up to you."

"Oh."

So he tried, not very successfully, to be nonchalant; he'd experienced this gigantic transition only a few times so far. Corva had grown up with it, had seen it literally hundreds of times. He couldn't help but imagine himself a week from now, silent and still as a dead man and lying in a cicada sarcophagus. He'd be behind locked doors in a hermetically sealed chamber, the house's solar heat exchangers keeping his body so cold he'd freeze solid if not for the antifreeze in his veins. This was normal? He'd done it on the flight to Sedna, and again on his way to Rockette. Since then he'd experienced hibernation—what, five times? He would never get used to it.

Time had flown while he brooded over what Halen had said. Toby hadn't come up with a good answer to Corva's brother. He'd just started avoiding him. The whole idea of the god gambit preyed on him, though. It was so fundamentally dishonest he didn't even know where to start to say why. It was creepy. Halen thought it was the only way to go.

All of it—turn's end, the god gambit, the inescapable fact that ninety-nine percent of the people living in the lockstep were from civilizations that had come into existence while he slept—forced him into an awed awareness of *time*. Saplings would grow in the yard while he slept tomorrow. If not for the acceleration of the blockade, entire trees would appear during that one night. The grass would be long and weed-shot between the closing and opening of one's eyes.

So much had happened, too, in recent weeks, and yet Wallop was still asleep. Nathan Kenani had only just closed the lid on Toby's bed, as far as the traitorous Guide was concerned. Kirstana had only just said good-bye to Toby, probably in full expectation of seeing him when she awoke. So it was on seventy thousand other worlds. They were all wintering over simultaneously, billions frozen solid, waiting the tick of a new turn. Between one beat of their hearts and the next, whole lives would flash past on the fast worlds near the stars.

People did pause to think about it, he knew. Evayne tapped into the wonder and terror that lurked under the sensible façade of the locksteps; the myths and the cult Toby channeled those feelings in directions that were politically useful to Evayne and Peter.

Toby was curious, and the turn's end parties sounded like fun, so he convinced Corva to go out with him, and they house-hopped through the neighborhood. Everywhere they went, people pushed food and drink on them. They ate a lot of fresh fruit. Everybody also seemed to have one or more big pieces of machinery they couldn't fit into their vaults. These were doomed to sit under the rain and weather for more than two years if nobody claimed them. Corva offered advice about how to store them based on her studies in ruin design, and they moved on to the next house.

It was fun, and a good distraction to the prospect of imminent hibernation. When they got home, it was very late and nobody else was up. The house's windows were sealed with metal covers, and now Toby could see how the place was built with a bright and relatively open outer layer and an inner core containing the bedrooms and cicada machinery. After stripping off her shoes, Corva headed in that direction, but he hung back.

She looked around, frowned. "What's the matter?"

"It still seems unnatural to me."

She laughed in surprise. "But you hold the record for the longest hibernation of all time!"

He crossed his arms and looked away. This wasn't funny to him at all, and after a moment Corva seemed to realize it. She tilted her head at the kitchen. "Let's sit up awhile."

They shared the last juice in the fridge. Bots were quietly boxing the house's contents after photographing the exact position and orientation of every stray sock and data pad. They'd recreate the scene with perfect fidelity in two and a half years.

He felt nervous and edgy, and also utterly weary, so balanced on the kitchen stool as if it were the top of a tree. Toby hadn't told Corva what Halen had said to him, and he didn't know how to talk about it now. Instead he said, "My mom's slept as long as I have. Almost. I have to go to her, Corva."

She didn't reply. They both knew Destrier would be crawling with Evayne and Peter's troops. They would be waiting for Toby. Going there was his obvious next move.

"She'll keep."

He blinked at her; to his surprise Corva blushed.

"Gods, Toby, she's waited for you for fourteen thousand years! She can wait a little longer."

"What are you talking about?"

"I mean you could . . . you could stay here." The last word was almost inaudible. She still wouldn't look at him.

"Corva, I can't be your house guest forever."

"That's not what I mean." Now she was seriously blushing. "Oh, hell." She jumped up and made to move away, but he grabbed her hand.

"I'd like that," he said. "I didn't know if you really wanted me around."

"What are you, stupid? Of *course* I want you around!" She hadn't pulled her hand away. "But you have some world or other to save, and the Empress of Time to wake, and things like that. I never thought you'd want to . . ."

He was afraid of meeting his mother again. Something had happened to her, something had broken, he was sure of it. Who would abandon the rest of her family—her whole world!—to wait for one lost son to come home? The thought that she'd done that made him profoundly uncomfortable. Once again, he had no idea how to explain that to Corva.

So he didn't try.

He kissed her instead.

ORPHEUS LAY ACROSS TOBY'S belly like a thousand-pound weight. The denner was snoring, a faint but reassuring sound.

The knock on the bedroom door came again. Toby blinked and raised his head to look groggily around. He'd slept . . . that's right, he'd kissed Corva last night. It had been hard to get to sleep after that, thinking about her, and also about—

—More than two years passing in one night.

He sat up, rolling Orpheus aside. The denner crawled into some bunched-up blankets and went still again.

"Garren?" It was the voice of Corva's father. The knock came again.

Toby looked around, then down at himself. There was no sign that more than an ordinary night had passed. Intellectually he knew this was the result of vast amounts of work by bots and biomedical systems; if he'd slept for two and a half years, it was mostly in a semifrozen state. The room would have been warming up for weeks, the bots and hibernation systems working day and night to restore his body and reverse all signs of decay within the room. He shuddered at the thought, then said, "I'm here!"

"Can you come outside, son? Something's . . . well, we've got visitors."

Toby had been climbing out of bed; he stopped and stared at the door. Then: "Give me five minutes."

There was no point even wondering who it would be. Whoever it was, things were out of his control again. All he had that was his were his few minutes of freshening up in the suite's little bathroom. He could pick out his own clothes, ruffle Orpheus's fur. Then he took a deep breath and put his hand on the door latch. Time to let go of the dream he'd spun with Corva last night.

The Keishions were waiting in the hall, faces grave. Toby walked past them and downstairs. Corva stood by the front door, hands clenched in front of her. They made eye contact, then he stepped outside.

Ranks and ranks of military bots stood on the Keishions' lawn. He'd seen this kind of vista before, but never in real life. Armed quadcopters hovered in the air above the mechs, and farther off gray airships sat in the sky like condensed clouds.

A delegation of men and women stood in front of the bots. There must have been at least twelve of them, all in fancy uniforms. A woman in the center stepped forward, her face shining with some kind of excitement, and as she bowed deeply to him, so did all the others. As did all the bots. The copters dipped as well. Past these dipping heads, Toby could see the astonished faces of the neighbors he'd been partying with last night.

"Welcome," said the woman in a husky voice. "Welcome, Tobias Wyatt McGonigal, to the lockstep of your creation and to the world of Thisbe!"

And all those in sight murmured their wonder and bowed even lower.

| Sixteen |

THE LUXURY AIRCAR WAS whisper quiet, and this made it awkwardly obvious that nobody was talking. Outside the tinted windows, the sky suddenly went bloodred, as if to reinforce Toby's mood.

During all the bowing and speechifying in front of the Keishions' house, Toby had spotted Halen lurking about on the edge of the delegation. Toby had ignored the bowing multitude and walked up to Corva's brother.

"You just had to tell them, didn't you? You just couldn't wait for me to make up my own mind what to do. You had to force my hand." Nobody else but the immediate family had known his identity—except for Shylif and Jaysir. Somehow, Toby hadn't doubted for a second that it was Halen who'd told the government.

He didn't even try to deny it, simply stepped back and shrugged. "I told them, yes, but they'd promised to leave you alone."

"*This* is leaving me alone?" Toby swept an arm to show the massed army and the groveling politicians.

"I know," said Halen. "But something's changed."

Toby glowered out the aircar window now, thinking furiously about what to do. Halen's betrayal was trivial—and maybe justified—given what he'd told Toby next.

Evayne was on her way to Thisbe. And according to the government telescopes, she was bringing a whole fleet.

"Where are we going?" he demanded of the senior government official who sat opposite him.

"It's a place called Leaning Pines," she said brightly. "It's a resort. It's the best environment we could find. I hope you like it."

"*Like* it? What am I supposed to like about any of this?" He glared at her, then Halen, who sat next to her; then he felt Corva's hand on his arm.

She leaned in close and whispered, "Can't you see she's terrified?"

Toby blinked and suddenly got it: these ministers and representatives, seated chatting but glancing at him every few seconds—they weren't escorting him as a prisoner, much less a guest. Toby was a McGonigal; they were all *his* guests, for Thisbe was his world. They were desperate to make a good impression on an absentee landlord unexpectedly making an inspection.

"I'm sorry," he said to the woman, who smiled uncertainly. Equally uncertain, he stuck out his hand. "I'm Toby."

Her face held wonder as she let him shake her limp fingers. "Calastrina de Fanto Esperion," she said. "Appointed proxy of Demographic Twelve of the Great Byte." The Byte, Toby had learned, was Thisbe's C-shaped southern continent. That made Esperion the representative of about six hundred million people.

"Appointed proxy?" He'd worn his glasses and could do a search on what she'd just said, but these people knew who he was and would expect his ignorance. "Not elected?"

To his surprise, Esperion blushed. "I'm a proxy, not a representative. I didn't want the appointment, but it turns out that I vote, mod, and buy exactly like about fifty million other people. I can be relied on to think and vote the way they would if they were in the council. At least until I get jaded or compromised. I'm only here for another year," she added, as though apologizing.

So this place was based on one of the démarche models. He probably should have studied local politics earlier, but for a change his mind had been on the bigger picture—the whole history of the locksteps and the place of the McGonigals in them. He looked out the window and sighed, a little ruefully.

They circled a long, sinuous mountain lake. A collection of truly huge tents lay tumbled across one end of it. "The resort," Corva said, when she saw where he was looking. "They keep it boxed while we winter over and rebuild it every time. The landscape changes too much for a permanent installation."

"It's pretty." The curving sheets of tenting were colored in a whole rainbow of tones.

Corva was very close to him; he could almost feel the heat of her skin on his cheek. "Toby?" she said quietly. "Why did you insist that I come?"

Again he sighed. "Because you're the only person who knows who I am and isn't afraid of me. —Well, except for Shylif and Jaysir, maybe."

She laughed and sat back. "And Orpheus." But she seemed pleased with his explanation.

They landed on a gravel beach next to a cold lake—but a real lake, under a real sky, even if that sky was fluorescent green right now. Toby had brought Orpheus with him, and together they crunched down to the edge of the water, distracted by its reality and beauty. The air was crisp and cold.

"M-Mister McGonigal?"

He turned to find Corva hiding a smile, and past her a half circle of dignitaries were waiting patiently for him to get over the view. Halen was frowning, his arms crossed, but Toby could tell he was excited, too. Well, this was what he'd wanted.

"Okay," he said, walking back up the beach to stand next to Corva.

"What can I do for you?"

"YES," HE ADMITTED A few hours later. "I can override every cicada bed on the planet."

They sat at a huge curving oak table inside a vaulted hall with translucent sides. There was wine and coffee and sweets, and for a very long time now Toby had sat listening to one after another local governmental official give speeches in his honor.

He'd used much of the time to refocus his eyes inside his glasses' view; he'd been learning how the Thisbe government worked and who these people he was sitting with were. About half the ministers consisted of professional politicians, the rest being made up of randomly chosen citizens like Esperion. To qualify for sortition you had to be a high-ranking player in one of a number of different political or economic games; Esperion must be very good indeed. About half of them were really here—the rest were represented by their avatars. There were political parties, but they were ad hoc and lasted for only one sitting session, which was four years. During that time, the ministers ran sophisticated simulations based on their own or their constituents' biases and beliefs, and tried to enlist support for initiatives based on the results. Even then, there were no direct votes; the ministers played matching games of the would-fixing-A-improve-B-would-fixing-B-improve-A sort.

All of this was familiar to Toby, because he and Peter had explored these possibilities. The plan was that Sedna would eventually become a full-fledged nation, and Father had emphasized that it would need a well-designed government. This was a major reason their parents had tolerated the many hours Toby and Peter spent in Consensus.

Now, having admitted he could directly control Thisbe's frequency, Toby tried to gauge the reaction among the politicians. They were all stone-faced or smiling, of course; luckily the political translation layer they'd given him provided a different view through his glasses. Some of the politicos were literally turning green—not with envy but with approval, which subtitles translated in various ways: that fellow over there was happy that Toby was telling the truth, while the woman to the left of him had just had her worst predictions confirmed. Other ministers were yellow, still others crimson, and several had turned black, apparently signifying that they were not psychoculturally capable of actually absorbing the meaning of what he'd just said.

Above them all, the interface was showing a disklike balance-of-power meter, which was currently tilting around like a top. Everything was in play, apparently.

This was all amazing and showed how far government had come since his day. To Toby, though, it just confirmed something that had been obvious since the day he awoke here: the whole Consensus plan had been flawed.

Thisbe could organize its government however it wanted. It didn't matter, if private individuals like the McGonigals controlled just one critical utility. On Thisbe, they controlled time itself.

"I can change the lockstep frequency," he continued once the power meter had stabilized a bit. "But I can't give the power to do that to anyone else. It's locked to me, somehow."

They all nodded politely, and orderly waves of change moved through the political model—except that somebody somewhere said sarcastically, "That's convenient."

Toby looked for whoever had spoken. Finally, somebody who wasn't going to be creepily polite! "Probably designed to keep us alive," he said. "Otherwise, you could torture me into giving you superuser status, then kill me." *Or you could just neuroshackle me.* He really hoped they wouldn't think of that.

"Sound planning." The speaker was an elderly gentleman with a flat face and high cheekbones, and a dry, sardonic voice. Through the glasses, he appeared amber-colored right now, and his subtitle read LONG SEVILLE, MINISTER OF SECURITY.

"Look, I'd give you all superuser access if I could," said Toby. "This isn't where I want to be right now. I just want to get to Destrier and find my mom . . ."

The entire assembly had turned black and red and green, except for a couple of amber holdouts. One was Long Seville.

Toby appealed to him. "What did I say?"

The old man sighed and sat back, crossing his arms. "You, the Emperor of Time, just announced that you intend to fulfill the ancient prophecy by throwing open the gates of Time itself and awakening the Mother of All. What did you expect to happen?"

"It's my family," he said sullenly. "I just want to be reunited with them."

The old man took off his glasses. Toby frowned, then took off his own. Freed from the intricate political interface, they were now just two people seated at a table. Everybody else was talking, gesturing, looking around inside a shared virtual space. It was as if Toby and this minister were in their own little bubble of reality.

"Not supposed to do this," Long said, holding up the glasses, "but you're obviously new to our way of doing things. Listen, kid, most of the room didn't even hear what you just said, because their translation systems couldn't figure out a way to have it make sense in their worldview. Thisbe's a pretty sophisticated world, but everybody here was still raised on the myths and legends about you. For the most part these people don't believe them, but you just said they were true! What you have to do now is back up and start over, only this time, please try to avoid pushing any religious buttons, would you?"

They put their glasses back on and Toby said, "What I meant was . . . I don't want to run the lockstep. Everybody has these ideas about what I'm going to do now that I'm back, but nobody's thought to consult *me* about them."

This got through, largely. Encouraged, he continued, "I know my brother changed your frequency. That was wrong, and I'll talk to him about it when I see him. I'll reset it for you." He turned to smile at Corva, who was watching him stone-faced. "All I ask in return is a little help with . . ." Was there any way he could say "being reunited with my family" without pressing those "religious buttons"?

". . . with settling into my new life."

They heard that. The interface's feedback layer flooded him with restatements of his own words: he knew what he'd just *said;* now the interface was telling him what each minister had *heard*— what the words he'd said meant to them after being filtered through their stated expectations and hopes, known prejudices and biases, cognitive deficits, and so on. The interface proposed a set of rewordings that it thought would custom-translate his meaning for them, but it was a bewildering jumble that he had no time to review. He signaled *yes* to it and the rewordings went out.

This politics stuff was harder than it had seemed in Consensus. It still came down to one thing, though. They were haggling.

"Look, I was told Evayne's on her way here, but then everybody clammed up about it. I need to know. Is she coming? When's she going to get here? Can I meet with her? Or is that . . . a bad idea?"

Some of this got through. The political interface swirled through a whole spectrum of colors and the balance of power tipped and swung for a few seconds. Translations and interpretations flew back and forth, and then the whole room stabilized green.

Long Seville nodded and stood up. "Can we get a . . . yes, thanks," he added as a set of windows opened in the interface. They were all dark, but if Toby squinted he could make out little points of light in one.

"This," said Long, "is a telescope view into Sagittarius. Those bright stars there aren't stars. They're the engine flares of a whole fleet of ships. They're aiming for a full stop at Thisbe, and there's little doubt who's leading them."

Toby was unconvinced; he supposed he was giving off subtle body stance and facial cues that would make him look amber right now. "How do you know it's her?"

"Because we'd been tracking these dots. They were on their way to Wallop, but they changed course right about the time you left."

"Ah. How many ships?"

"A hundred forty."

They couldn't be that big, individually . . . but still, each one could have the nuclear power to wipe out a few cities.

Toby stared at the display. He, Peter and Evayne had deployed fleets like this in Consensus many times. Of course, that had been a fantasy world of faster-than-light travel. Still, he remembered Evayne's attitude toward military solutions. She'd never hesitated.

Long was talking, but Toby wasn't listening anymore. He was remembering how they'd divided empires among them and how passionate Peter had been about the game. It wasn't a game to him, it was his lifeline, his only route to feeling secure about the world.

Redesign it. Make it perfect. Then make sure it stayed that way.

Evayne had been too young to understand Peter's passion, but she'd certainly picked up on it. And now? They both ruled a real empire, and they'd been doing it for decades. It wasn't a game anymore, the stakes were real, and the one person in the world who could destroy everything they had built had just reappeared.

For the first time Toby got it—he understood how Evayne could really be on her way here to kill him. All he had to do was stop imagining the Evayne he'd known, the little girl, and imagine an older woman whose childhood was a blur now and whose reality was rulership.

His mouth dry, he said, "How does this work?"

People had been talking, but his words stopped everyone.

"What does she do when she gets here?"

Long cleared his throat. "We'll be wintering over. The whole world will be hibernating, at least all the McGonigal beds will be. Normally ships arrive at different times, and they all go dormant until start-of-turn. But in a case like this . . . you want to be awake first. So they'll take action as soon as they arrive."

"What action?"

He looked uncomfortable. "Land in force, wake us up and demand that we turn you over."

Toby nodded slowly. Advantage went to whoever woke first. "Can you just stay awake until she gets here?"

"We can leave a military force awake, but it'll cost us. We could also set the force to wake up a month before she arrives. We've got a lot of non-McGonigal cicada beds, but not enough yet for a real defense. Either way, it ends in a confrontation, and she can threaten millions of innocent lives. Most of the population will be wintering over, so they'll be helpless."

"Not if I wake everybody," said Toby.

"Exactly."

"And we know when she's going to get here?"

"We know the earliest date she can arrive, yes."

The tables would be turned if all of Thisbe was awake and ready when Evayne arrived. She had to know that, but she was coming anyway, and that made Toby uneasy. Did she really want to kill him? If not, then why bring a whole fleet with her? It made no sense.

He looked around the room, and his gaze fell upon Halen Keishion. Corva's brother was watching him in return, and he had a smile on his face that could only be described as smug.

There would be no more doubts about who he was if he changed Thisbe's frequency. Only a McGonigal could do that. There might be rumors and leaks coming from the Thisbe government now, but if he repelled Evayne word would spread instantly through the lockstep. People would wake at the next turn to the news that the Emperor of Time was returned. Sooner or later he would go to Destrier and wake up the Great Mother. And then time—or at least lockstep time—would come to an end.

There was going to be panic and mass hysteria. Millions would flock to Toby's side, believing that somehow they would be saved by him. Others would side with Peter and Evayne, especially if they abandoned the myth and revealed the truth that Toby was just an ordinary person. There would be chaos and civil war if Thisbe didn't give Toby to Evayne.

Halen knew this. He'd planned for it.

And he was smiling.

TOBY HAD BEEN BOMBARDED with options, proposals, and facts and details for days now. On the third afternoon, mentally overloaded, he managed to break away from the crush of subdued but frantic officials for a few minutes. He hunkered down on his haunches to toss pebbles into the cold lake.

"How am I supposed to know what to do?" he asked. "There's just too much to take in."

"I disagree." It was Sol, invisible but audible through the earpiece in Toby's glasses. About halfway through the day of meetings, Toby'd had the brilliant idea of waking his two favorites Consensus characters. Sol and Miranda had been listening in since then, but until this moment they'd been silent.

"What do you mean?" He picked up another smooth pebble and gave it a toss that he hoped would skip it. It sank immediately.

"Before all of this happened, you were following where your own research took you." Now it was Miranda, speaking in his other ear while Toby groped for another pebble. "You've been reviewing the records from the twentier. But they're not the only source available to you, you know."

"Huh. I guess." Summoning the courage to watch the twentier's records had been exhausting. Because of how difficult those had been, he'd been holding off exploring the other aspect of lockstep life that had made him most uneasy. Obviously, he was out of time with that one.

"Show me Destrier," he told the glasses.

As always, the amount of information on offer was overwhelming, so Toby had learned to start with kids' picture books. He found one in the Thisbe Internet and flipped to a page captioned THE GRAND PROCESSIONAL.

In the picture, a sea of pilgrims—he recognized the robes he'd seen at the pilgrimage center on Wallop—were caught midshuffle as they moved down a vast, seemingly endless avenue. The scene was lit by a dozen or so little suns, probably orbital light platforms.

The stones of this grand avenue were worn into smooth grooves by millennia of sliding feet. According to the book, they were replaced every few centuries. The stones of the pyramidal towers that lined the avenue were also replaced on a rotating schedule, such that out here, at least, nothing of the original building material remained. The holy city renewed itself like a living body, shedding cells continuously. —Maybe, but everywhere Toby looked, the surfaces were smoothed and sculpted into natural-looking contours. It was uncanny, as if by wind and rain Nature had sculpted something that looked like a city yet was entirely natural.

The book proudly told how this shuffling procession had been inching forward, reciting one particular chant without pause, for over ten thousand years. Supplicants from all over the galaxy came here; not all were human. They gave up fortunes, families, entire lives to endure decades, even centuries of travel, simply for the chance to put on a coarse robe and parade, just once, down this avenue. Some fainted on the way and others died—just for the opportunity to spend a few precious minutes in the presence of the divine.

The domes of the city looked out on a plain of dazzling white frost dotted with towering spires. It was illegal to walk there, and to the discerning eye that plain should have been far more awe-inspiring than this little road. Those spires had stood, unmoved and unchanging, for eight billion years. Next to that, the centuries of wear and tear visible around the Great Mother's resting place were nothing. Less than an eyeblink.

Sol and Miranda were reading along with Toby as he flipped through the book. "It says here," said Sol, "that all of Destrier experienced time within the 360/1 lockstep, except for the domes in these pictures. They're in realtime."

"So those people there . . ." Miranda's forearm and finger appeared in Toby's virtual view as she pointed to a bald-headed man in one of the shots. "His family's been helping pilgrims into their robes for hundreds of generations."

"Wow," muttered Sol. "So if we took the whole of written human history up until the day Toby first set foot on Sedna, this city's records are five times longer."

"It's got its own languages, its own cuisine and modes of dress," said Miranda. "But the only reason the city exists at all is to guide visitors to the place where they can—how does it put it here?—'glimpse the Great Mother resting forever in her crystal coffin.'"

"Quiet now," Toby told them.

The only photos of his mother's resting place were long shots taken from at least a kilometer away. Way over there, the procession entered a ramped slot that led down below the vast oval dome covering Mom's cicada bed. They would shuffle into a narrow chamber containing a single quartz window, through which the blurry shape of the Great Mother could be seen. From here, the dome appeared more like a rounded hill, though it was scrupulously kept clean of vegetation by the same hereditary keepers who served the pilgrims. The dome hadn't eroded, really, it had just settled gradually and imperceptibly over the centuries, even while the spires that surrounded it were fervently rebuilt.

The landscape beyond the city might well be impossibly old compared to this place, yet Toby had never in his life seen a place that felt as *ancient* as this.

And this, of course, was the point. This was the gift that Evayne and Peter had bestowed upon humankind: the gift of permanence.

History roared ahead on the lit worlds. Civilizations rose, but they fell, too, and maintaining one at a starfaring level was very difficult. On the worlds circling the stars of the Local Group, humanity and its various offspring had fallen many times in the past fourteen thousand years. Every time it did, the locksteps had been waiting, ready to pick it up again.

Toby got it now. 360/1 and its siblings were like a seed bank; they were insurance. They lived so slowly and were so dispersed that they were ignored. Yet they were always there, had always been there, and, as long as Evayne and Peter had their say, always would be there.

He took off the glasses, once again finding himself squatting by the cold lake. Reaching to pick up another round stone, he hesitated, unable to complete the gesture without wondering just how old this little rock was. "Shit!"

"I beg your pardon?"

Corva stood next to him, hands on her hips, head cocked quizzically.

"Sorry. I was . . . thinking."

"Out here? You'll catch one of those ancient diseases. Influenza. Or scrapie or something."

"They don't work that way." Then he held out his hand. "Wanna walk with me?"

He saw her nearly glance over her shoulder, then think better. She took his hand and they scrunched through the wet gravel. The pink clouds stuttered and turned gray, and as his eyes adjusted, everything slowly washed into normality. He could be on Earth for all he knew.

"Are you feeling all right?"

He shrugged. "I'm okay. They want me back in ten minutes."

"But you've been negotiating for three days! When is this going to end?"

"Soon," he said curtly. The government had been making offers, and they'd been running vastly detailed simulations covering all sorts of plans. In some, Evayne somehow got past the orbital defenses and rained down fire from orbit. In those cases, the government admitted it would have to give Toby up without firing a shot in return, in order to save its own people. The simulated Evayne played much like he remembered her doing in Consensus. She rarely chose such a brutally direct option. More often, based on Thisbe's historical records, she would land and seek to capture her target personally.

Toby was not her first, apparently. There had been many pretenders over the ages, all claiming to be the returned messiah. Some had raised huge armies, but none had been able to crack the biocrypto. They couldn't prove who they were. None had made it to Destrier, though the more deluded—those who truly believed they were Toby Wyatt McGonigal—swore that if only they were given the chance to lay their palm on the circular lock to the Great Mother's chamber, it would turn for them.

Evayne usually left them to the Guides, but in particularly troublesome cases she would intervene directly. So far the sims showed her behaving exactly as she had in those cases.

Last night, Toby had sat with Corva in front of a fire under the vast peaked roof of the tent house they'd given him. He'd dared to say to her then what he couldn't say to Halen and the other angry opponents of the McGonigals: "Maybe she doesn't know it's really me."

Corva hadn't replied. They'd been sitting close together but not touching. They hadn't kissed since that first time before the last wintering over. He hoped it was because events were just rampaging ahead too fast; there were always people about. They hadn't had a chance to talk about it and, well, he felt awkward.

Her silence now had seemed like a blow, though. He'd wanted her to agree. He wanted somebody to tell him his sister wasn't a monster. But it hadn't happened.

Now, holding her hand on the cold beach, he glanced at Corva and had to smile. Under her black bangs, her face was fierce with concentration. Thinking, always thinking, that was her. She didn't know the first thing about rendering sympathy, but that didn't mean she didn't care how he felt.

Suddenly she looked up. "Where were you, just now?"

"I was visiting Destrier."

She shuddered and let go of his hand. "That place is creepy. I can't believe you want to . . . I mean, I know why, it's just that . . ."

"Nobody's more creeped out than me. But it's not some weird goddess they've got under glass there. It's my mom."

"Not *just* your mom."

"*Just* my mom." When she sent him one of her skeptical looks, he growled. "Corva, she's slept almost as long as I have. She doesn't know that Evayne made her into the Great Mother, any more than I knew I was this stupid Emperor of Time! The world's not going to end when she wakes up. She's not going to make some mystical pronouncement that will change history. She's going to . . ." *Ask where her children are.*

That, of course, was where Toby got the creeps. It wasn't those millions of worshipers lapping against the sides of Mother's stone dome that bothered him. It was the question of what he would have to say when he woke her:

"Why did you abandon Peter and Evayne to wait for me?"

What she'd done was wrong, it was sick. He'd been dead, as far as any of them had known. Why would she entomb herself to wait for a child who would never come home?

Corva sensed his discomfort and shrugged. "I don't know how

you'd even get there," she said lightly. "Destrier's better defended than Barsoom. If Evayne and Peter don't want you there, you'd need an army and a navy as big as the whole lockstep's just to knock on the front door."

"Yes, well, talk to your brother about that," he said. "He's figured out how to get one."

"What do you mean?"

"Come," he said, "I'll show you." He began walking back up the beach.

"We've been running sims for two days now." He waved to one of the bots that stood near the largest tent complex, and it waved back. "In a situation like this it's all about who can strike first. Evayne's hoping to get here while we're all asleep. If I'm not the real Toby, then she's certain to be able to, because she's going to arrive in seven months, realtime. We'll be wintering over."

Aircars had been landing all morning in the fields behind the tents. There were crowds of people everywhere, of course; the whole resort was crammed with ministers, analysts, and spin doctors. Corva might not have noticed the new arrivals yet.

"Either way," he went on, "she has to catch us napping to get the upper hand. The government wants me to wake the whole planet just as she arrives—when she's committed to landing her people but before she can consolidate her position. Then we'll ask her to stand down."

Corva shook her head violently, tossing beads of dew from her black mane. "You know I hate that idea. We should just run. We escaped her at Wallop."

"Those sims don't work, Corva. Any ship leaving Thisbe is going to blaze like a star. It'll be easy to track. —Not that we shouldn't send out a few decoys anyway. She'll have to split off a few ships to follow them. But *all* of them will be caught."

There was a mumbling murmur coming from up ahead, where the largest of the vaulting tent structures stood. Toby headed in that direction.

He grimaced and ran a hand through his hair. "Anyway, what

happens after we've had our showdown with Evayne? I've promised to restore Thisbe's frequency, but as soon as I do that, the
whole lockstep will know I'm back."

"No no!" She stepped in front of him, putting a hand on his
chest. "All we have to do is say it was Evayne who did it, while she
was here! What's she gonna do, deny it? It's perfect!"

"And then what? She'll be watching Thisbe, searching every
ship that leaves. Even if we drive her away this time, she'll just return with a bigger force."

"Unless we defeat her and *then* escape."

"She'll just keep searching for us, wherever we go." He gently
took her hand and started walking again.

He mounted the concrete platform where the edges of the giant
tent were fixed. The murmuring was loud now, and Corva heard
it. She snatched back her hand and stepped away from Toby, but
only now did she see that the two of them weren't alone anymore:
a half circle of men and women stood silently on the path behind
them, along with some McGonigal lockstep security bots. Hands
clutched under her chin, sneaking looks left and right and behind
her, Corva reluctantly followed Toby as he strode toward a sweep
of tenting that formed a kind of archway.

"Don't worry," said Toby as he stepped into the dim space beyond, "there is another way."

A spotlight pinioned them there, and within the vast space of
the tent, a thousand people gasped and murmured and, just as the
government ministers had done in front of Corva's house, all bent
their heads and knelt before the Emperor of Time.

He turned to reassure Corva further, but the look on her face
froze him. He would never forget it.

"*McGonigal!*" Corva threw down the word like a curse.

Then she turned and ran.

| Seventeen |

*"**THE RULES OF A** lockstep standoff are simple,"* one of Thisbe's generals had told Toby. *"Wake before the other guy and capture him in his bed."*

"That's it?" Toby asked.

"No. *The more resources you have, the higher the frequency you can set for your troops—or the more troops you can keep awake on a rotating basis. The more you push this, the more it costs you. If you have to go all the way to realtime, and don't sleep at all, then you've probably already lost."*

Toby stood on a stone balcony in one of Thisbe's mountain fortresses, gazing out at a stunning vista of white-capped peaks and roiling clouds. The air was thin and bracingly cold.

In the valley below, Thisbe's army was burying a bunker full of supplies. The whole planet had only enough food, energy and industrial capacity to stay awake for a few weeks. It was a lockstep world, its whole infrastructure based on the slow accumulation of resources during winter-over. Even with nanotech and orbital industries, there was no way they could stay in realtime for long. Soon, the entire world would have to sleep.

The jets screaming across the sky and the busy soldiers and bots in the valley were all trying to balance an equation whose terms weren't all known. How long to sleep? That was what it all came down to. Everybody knew when Evayne's ships would arrive, but that wasn't the problem. Every day the Thisbe defense forces stayed awake in anticipation of her landing was a day's rations used, a day's energy. If Evayne was smart—and Toby knew she was—she wouldn't stage a landing when she arrived. She would go to sleep and wait for a while. Six more months, a year. She would slumber, unassailable in far orbits, while Thisbe bled itself dry waiting up for her.

The defense forces had come up with a rotating watch that allowed them to keep a standing army ready at all times. The problem was, it was small. Evayne had the advantage, and everybody knew it.

"You have quite the way with women," somebody behind him said.

Toby turned to find Jaysir and Shylif standing by the metal doors that led to the mountain tunnel. "You made it!" Toby exclaimed. The generals hadn't wanted to allow these two civilians—stowaways, no less!—to visit their precious bunkers. Toby had been insistent, but he hadn't been sure until this moment that his stubbornness had done any good.

Shylif stepped forward and shook Toby's hand. Jaysir grinned and slapped him on the back. Toby frowned into Shylif's eyes. "How are you?"

"Actually . . . better than I expected." He smiled, and there was a twinkle in his eye that hadn't been there before. "Can't say the same about Coley. But he'll live."

Toby nodded and shot Jaysir a guilty look. "Corva hates me. I know."

Jaysir shrugged. "Well, you did the one thing she didn't want you to do. You sold out to your legend. I'm actually kind of surprised that you called for us. You hardly need our help anymore, do you? You've got the whole planet to play with now."

"Tactful as always, our Jay," rumbled Shylif with a frown.

"So I didn't live up to her expectations." Toby looked away across the windswept valley. "The problem is, everybody has *expectations*. I had to decide who to disappoint, didn't I?"

Shylif looked away, pensive. "That, I understand. But why did you ask us to come?"

"Two things, one of which Jay already knows about—" At that moment a call came through on Toby's glasses. He held up a finger to Jay and Shylif, and turned away. "Hang on a sec. Yes?"

"Sir." It was Long Seville, who as minister of security had been charged with the thankless task of planning the defense of Thisbe. "We've received a message from your sister. It's for . . . well, it's for you."

He turned back to Jaysir and Shylif. "It's Evayne. Can I have a moment? You know, family stuff." Wide-eyed, the two backed away. Toby walked to the stone balcony and took a deep breath, bracing his hands on the cold granite. *Okay. You can do this.* He opened the message.

The woman who appeared, as if hovering in the air before him, could have been some long-lost aunt. She looked *so* much like Mom it was agonizing. Evayne was now older than Peter, or so the stories said, because she had changed her frequency so many times in the pursuit of state business. Still, she looked no more than thirty—an imperious queen in green robes, beautiful and terrible in her wrath.

"What the hell, Evie," he muttered.

"To the people of the planet Thisbe," she declared, "I give my greetings, and a warning. You will release to me that person who falsely claims to be my brother, the holy Emperor of Time, Toby McGonigal, Who Waits. Bring him to your seat of government, and I will descend to claim him in six months, realtime. If you resist, you will be destroyed.

"To the impostor, I appeal to you to save your countrymen at least from the fate that awaits you. Come forward of your own accord, and we may be lenient. Hide, or attempt to fight us, and not only you, but all whom you love will share your fate."

The picture blinked out.

"Long," snapped Toby, "I'm replying."

"What are you going to say?" There was tension in the minister's voice.

"Don't worry, I'll send you a copy so you know what I said."

With a barely perceptible sigh, Long agreed.

Toby stood for a long time staring down into the valley. Then, when he realized he was just putting things off, he shook himself and said, "Reply.

"Hey, kiddo, how's it going? Haven't seen you in ages, you look great! I haven't talked to Peter yet, but I hear he's doing good, too.

"Yeah, I got your message. Don't make me prove that I am who I say I am. I mean, after all, I know more embarrassing stories about you than anybody alive. Well, except maybe Mom.

"Yes, it really is me. So you see, there's no need to unload any more crap on these people, who've already had to put up with a lot from you. We're gonna reset their frequency—either you or me, I don't care which of us does it. Then you and I are going to sit down and have a conversation—long overdue, I think. Deal? Great. See you in six months.

"End."

His smile slipped, and he tilted his head back to glare at the clouds. "Stupid, stupid." Well, but how was he supposed to handle this? Like an adult? He was seventeen years old, and Evayne knew it—but she hadn't seen him in forty years. If he'd acted any differently than he used to with her, she might not have recognized him.

She, on the other hand, had looked and sounded nothing whatever like the little girl he'd loved as his only sister. He closed his eyes and his face twisted into a grimace of pain.

After composing himself, he went back to where Shylif and Jaysir were standing together at the tunnel entrance. Well, it was more like they were *huddling* together, the way they looked. They were scared, and Toby didn't like the idea that it was him they were scared of.

"You need to hide her," he said. "From everybody, but most of all . . ." He didn't say Halen's name; he shouldn't have to with these two.

His friends exchanged a glance, then Shylif smiled. "That's a *good* idea."

Corva's brother had styled himself as the right-hand man to the new messiah. He was bursting with ideas—what Toby should wear, the uniforms his new staff should wear. He wanted to design a symbol for Toby's new movement (really, Halen's movement), something that could be printed on banners and hung off buildings. Toby had refused to let news of his return spill out of government circles, so naturally rumors were flying everywhere, and he was sure Halen was eagerly spreading many of them. Halen couldn't wait for the moment when Toby would step onto the stage of some gargantuan amphitheater and command a crowd of tens of thousands to go down on their knees before him.

"And then," Toby went on, "you need to do the same yourselves. Shy, you take care of Corva. Jay . . . remember what I asked you to look into? —That is, if you're sure no one else is listening."

Jay laughed. "If they are, their ears just pricked up."

"Are they?"

"They're trying." He shook his head. "But this conversation is private. You knew I'd be jamming our personal space, didn't you."

"No. I hoped . . ." He had to smile, though; Jaysir was clever about these things.

Jay had perked up, positively enthusiastic for a change. He said to Shylif, "Toby wanted me and the makers to look at the code from that data block I told you about. He thought we might find something useful."

"And did you?" asked Toby.

Jay made a noncommittal gesture. "Well, we found something, but I don't know if it's useful. It's about your biocryptographics."

"How easily that word rolls off your tongue," observed Shylif.

"What did you find?"

"We know how it works for everybody else who uses Cicada Corp devices. We all have user accounts and we sign in biocryptographically. But that's not how your commands seem to work. You don't have an account—you don't need one."

Toby was puzzled. "What do you mean?"

"Back on Wallop, I just assumed you were a superuser—that you had an administrative account on the Cicada Corp system that let you change major settings and stuff in the system. But that's not what you've got. There is no superuser, as far as we can tell. The Cicada Corp system is self-administering and can't be accessed by anyone from outside. That's what the code on the block seemed to say, anyway. If you'd given us access to the data itself . . ."

But Toby was shaking his head. "Yeah, I thought not. Toby's data is encrypted with the same biocrypto," he told Shylif. "I copied it, but without the same combination of DNA, voice, iris, fingerprint, and brainwaves I can't get at it. Anyway, you've got major power over the Cicada system, but not as an administrator."

Toby shook his head. "If I'm not a superuser, then how am I able to command the system?"

"It turns out you're not commanding it at all. You're voting."

"I'm *what*?"

"You're voting because, Toby, you're not an *administrator* of Cicada Corp's systems.

"You're a shareholder."

TOBY NEVER GOT USED to how noisy it was at night. The crickets brr'd at one frequency, other bugs at others, and night birds called, this species a high note, that one a low. The wind in the trees roared intermittently but deafened everything when it did. Daytime was even worse: cicadas boomed, monkeys and birds exchanged insults in the treetops. The frequency spread of animal calls widened until every band that could take a signal was filled. Any given morning, sitting listening to this vast symphony was a lesson in just how impoverished the Earth had been when he'd been growing up. Only on a world with a fully recovered ecosystem, or a terraformed lockstep world wintering over, could you hear the world as it had sounded before the advent of Man.

Tonight the familiar constellations were out. Thisbe had no moon, and on cloudless nights like this it could get pretty cold. Toby was used to that now, just as he was used to walking in the dark while Orpheus prowled ahead. Sometimes they'd scare up tomorrow's dinner. Sometimes they encountered the sleepy, slow-moving harvester and repair bots that were the only part of This-be's industrial system awake right now. He did his best to avoid such encounters, because you never knew whether their industrial Internet had been hacked by Evayne's people. Any of those boxy grain tenders or flood watch spiders could be spies for the enemy.

There was no sign that any had been in this area, though. He moved cautiously but confidently through tall grass and between young trees. As he went he counted the low blocky shapes of the houses lining what had been, and someday would again be, a street.

He hadn't known that the bots shrink-wrapped the houses after everyone was asleep. All that neon-pink plastic was torn away and recycled by the time the humans inside awoke. Right now, any tears or punctures in the material would be instantly visible to the monitors that overflew the houses on a weekly basis. If anything were seen, investigation and repair bots would be sent out right away. That meant Toby had to be careful when he broke in.

"Seven . . . and eight." He whistled for Orpheus, then moved around the abstracted house shape, searching for an overhang or tree-shadowed spot where he could cut through. "Over here!" Orpheus bounded into view as Toby was rummaging in his backpack for his shears. He'd found an indent beneath what was probably a dormer window, where a cut wouldn't be visible from the air. Orpheus watched with his usual attentive curiosity as Toby stabbed at the hard plastic again and again, until finally the blade of the shears went through.

It took awhile to cut a hole big enough for Orpheus to slither in. Though it was completely dark inside, the denner moved quickly between the taut pink material and the walls of the house, and called back when he'd found a path for Toby to worm through. That was the claustrophobic part; he always had one or two moments when he was sure he'd become stuck. He'd be found, years from now, mummified against the side of the house like a squashed cockroach. Tonight was okay: he reached a window in a couple of minutes, and with a little prying got the old-fashioned thing open. Orpheus flowed inside; Toby got in by falling noisily.

After cursing and dusting himself off, he finally lit his windup flashlight and took a look around. The silence in here was disturbing, especially after the cacophony of the night. The air was stale but breathable. The rooms on the main floor were empty except for a few big heavy crates that were also plastic wrapped. Lifeless bots were chained together in places. He barely glanced at them. As soon as he found the stairs to the house's lower core, he put on his glasses and went down.

The hibernation chamber was a concrete bunker with a vault-like door. The edges of that door were sealed with rubber caulking, which he peeled away with a knife. While he did that, he pinged the chamber's systems through the glasses.

After the third ping, a wire-frame diagram of the vault's interior blossomed in his glasses' display. It showed three cicada beds. All were occupied; all stasis indicators were green.

He read the names. The first he didn't know; the second, he frowned at. He sighed with relief when he saw the third.

With a command through his McGonigal account, he ordered this bed to wake its occupant. Then he slid down the wall to sit on the floor. Orpheus came up, and Toby scrunched his ears and playfully wobbled his head.

"Okay, Orph. This is home for a couple days. Might as well make ourselves comfortable."

He got up again, leaving the backpack by the door, and went to see if he could unwrap a couch to sleep on.

"AM I THE FIRST one up? Where is everybody?" Corva stumbled into the living room, wearing a long ratty housecoat, her hair a tangled nest.

She froze when she saw Toby.

He'd cleared a couch and was sitting with Orpheus in the light of his flashlight. Now that she'd seen them, Toby let Orpheus go and the denner ran to her. Corva knelt, opening her arms to him. Wrecks was still asleep in her bed.

"They were watching us," he said. The words just hung in the air between them; her expression didn't change.

"Watching us and listening. You didn't seriously think we could talk about anything at the lake without the government and your brother's friends hearing every word?"

Corva stood up and went to the blank window. "We're off frequency. You woke me up . . . Halen's still downstairs. Are you going to wake him up, too?"

"That's up to you." He sat forward, clasping his hands between his knees. "I'm sorry that I couldn't tell you what I was planning. I had to make it seem like I was going along with them, and I knew that Halen, at least, would be watching *you* to see if I was faking. You couldn't know that I was. I did it because I . . . I was afraid they'd neuroshackle me and turn me into their puppet if I refused. Or worse—do that to *you* to force my compliance."

She sucked in a quick breath. "Halen would never—"

"Are you sure about that? You know I got a message from Shy at turn's end. Shy said he'd tried to get to you, he was going to ask you to winter over with him instead of with your family. He couldn't get near you, but he did talk to Halen. You brother said he'd pass the message along. Did he?"

She started to protest, but the words didn't seem to be coming. The certain fury that had been on her face a moment ago had disappeared. She turned away.

"Neither of us knows Halen." He glared at her; he wasn't going to relent now. "Time stole the brother you knew, just like it stole mine. Who can we trust? Certainly not those scheming, spoiled brats I apparently have to call my family. If I can't trust my own brother and sister not to try and kill me, why should I trust yours? Why should you, when he's years away from the person you knew? And anyway, there's the government. They claim to be all democratic and rights respecting, but what do I know? You said it your-self when we met. I don't even know what I don't know."

She traced her fingers down the blank glass of the window. "What have you done?"

"Nothing. Not yet. I'm going to take care of Evayne, but I'm going to do it my way, not theirs. Not as the . . . the messiah of the locksteps, or whatever they're trying to call me. Not as some god returned from an eternal sleep.

"I'll do it as her brother."

She turned to look at him now, but with less suspicion in her eyes. "How?"

"I know her." He stood up and came to her hesitantly. She didn't back away. Encouraged, he said, "I read the histories and I saw the strategies and tactics she's used. It's exactly how she played Con-sensus, and how she was with Peter and me. The thing is, no-body's ever provoked her in the right way. But I know how. I know how to push her buttons."

"Why?" Corva shook her head. "Why make her mad? Won't she just retaliate?"

"That's the thing. We're not going to give her anything to re-taliate against. She'll hate that."

"But she's threatened the whole population!"

Toby snorted. "Bluff. She's never followed through on a threat like that. If you check the histories, you'll see. She's got *some* sense of justice, though she tries to hide it. She only strikes against those who are directly responsible for stuff. And in this case, that's just me."

"Just you? What are you—are you *alone*?"

"Except for a few defense force pickets, you and I are the only people in the world who're awake right now. Maybe the only peo-ple in the whole lockstep. Unless you tell me you want me to wake Halen now. If you do, I will."

Now she did back away. "But why did you even wake *me*? After everything—"

"Same reason I'll wake your brother if you tell me to. Because I trust you. You're the *only* one I trust."

"I don't understand."

"Yeah, I know. But this'll probably help." He held out his glasses. Corva looked at them dubiously.

"What's in there?"

"The recording I made of the talk I had with Evayne when she first got here. I think you should see it . . . if you want to understand what it means to be a McGonigal."

Corva was staring at the glasses as if they were some sort of poisonous snake. Then, reluctantly, she took them from Toby and put them on.

SHE WORE WHITE THIS time. The resemblance to Mom was still uncanny, and Toby's stomach had knotted the instant he saw her, but he'd been determined to not let his anxiety show. "Hey, sis. Welcome to Thisbe. I guess you're coming in to land?"

It was a warm evening and he was sitting under a giant oak tree on the edge of the capital city. Thisbe's Internet was awake, so it had been easy for Toby to route the call from his glasses to a transmitter halfway around the planet. Before he'd donned the glasses to make the call, he'd watched as one after another, reentry trails from his sister's ships had scored bright lines across the dimming sky.

She nodded cautiously. "Hello."

Toby sighed. "You're thinking that I'm surely recording this, and that you'd better mind what you say in case I spread it all over the galaxy. Does that mean we can't have a real conversation?"

She half smiled. "We wouldn't have that problem if you'd just meet me face-to-face."

"Not going to happen."

She shrugged dismissively. "It doesn't matter. Anything we said to each other would be taken as a Sign. I've been playing this game a lot longer than you have. I know what would happen if you broadcast this conversation. Half the lockstep would believe it, half would think it's a fake—and that you're a fake. Can you tell me that you know which half would get to you first?"

For all her brave words, Evayne didn't look as confident as she had in her first message to Thisbe. She must have accessed the planet's lockstep system and seen that he'd reset the frequency of all the McGonigal cicada beds on the planet. It was now twelve years until Thisbe was due to awake.

"Peter and I are so sorry about the whole Lowdown thing," she said now. "We didn't think it was you. Why would we? There have been so many pretenders over the years . . ."

The knot in his stomach tightened even more. He wanted to believe her so much, but— "Ammond and Persea had my ship. If that wasn't enough, all they had to do to prove that it was me was ask me to command any piece of Cicada Corp equipment. I've wondered why they waited until we went to Little Auriga to do it. It must be because somebody ordered them not to try it. Somebody . . . didn't want them to know." He shook his head. "That would have been Peter or you. And I'm sure you talked about it."

"But they tried to kidnap you—"

"They ran because Peter ordered me killed!" The knot was unraveling and in its place he felt a rushing fury that made him careless of what he said now. "And you went along with it just as casually as if this were still Consensus and it was just another move!"

She shook her head quickly. "No no, he didn't tell me—"

"Evayne. I *know* you knew."

He hadn't known, not for sure, but her silence now told him the truth. She didn't reply, but she didn't look away either. He remembered that defiance from when they were kids. He'd always known how to wear it down—but would the old ways work now?

"*Why?*" Damn it, his voice had cracked saying that. He bit his lip and sat tensely, scared of saying even one more word.

She crossed her arms and—a small triumph for him—broke eye contact with him. "You said it yourself," she murmured. "We're *not* playing a game here."

"What do you mean?"

"You think you can just reset Thisbe's frequency, and there'll be no consequences?" She shook her head and laughed bitterly.

"That wouldn't work even in Consensus! The ripples would spread. Other worlds would be emboldened, they'd flout the lockstep rules, too. Toby, you don't know how close it all is to breaking up as it is!"

"You called me Toby," he said bitterly. "That's something, I guess."

"You think you can just come back? If you did, you'd always be a pawn. I'm sorry I set it up that way—we really did think you were dead. It is what it is: if the world finds out you're back."

"Evie! You tried to kill me before I'd done *anything*!"

She opened her mouth, closed it.

Toby hurried on: "The solution to this whole 'Toby the messiah' thing was obvious all along. All you had to do was bring me in and declare me as your son. Raised in secret in another lockstep, so you could say you only had me like a month ago. So I'm a McGonigal, well, it's still a big deal, but I'm not *the* McGonigal. Why the hell didn't you do that?"

She started to answer, but he cut her off. "Why not just come to me? Take me home? Didn't you know that all I want to do is come *home*?" His voice was cracking again. He was on the edge of tears.

"Toby." He was startled at the huskiness in her own voice. "Toby, do you know why I never had kids?"

He shook his head. "You used to talk about having a family when you grew up."

"I would have, too, but we got too busy, Peter and I. First it was running Sedna with Mom. Then, when her lockstep scheme was so successful, it was all about keeping that going. It wasn't easy. People flooded in from everywhere—at least that's how it seemed to us, sleeping for thirty years at a time. Whole cities would spring up overnight, new colonies of people speaking new languages, even biologically different! Posthuman, or barely human. We had to wrangle it all, find a way to make them fit, or the whole thing would collapse."

She laughed drily. "There were already legends about us. People were starry-eyed when they met Peter and me. They stammered, practically wet themselves. And they always—*always*—asked about you."

"Why?"

"'Cause you'd disappeared mysteriously, and Mom had spent so much time and energy trying to find you. Understand, by that time she'd been searching for *centuries*, realtime. Word got around. You were the big secret at the heart of the lockstep. And it started to get out of control."

"So you decided to steer it."

"Toby, I was way too late." Her expression was fierce and unrepentant. "By the time I knew what was happening, I couldn't be seen in public with any man other than Peter without the rumors flying that it was you, secretly returned. There were no men who didn't treat me like some unattainable goddess anyway, except for the original Sedna settlers. They all had similar problems, and what, was I going to marry one of them? They were all like uncles . . . it was never an option."

"But you could have rewritten the legends," he insisted. "Could have said I'd been found, dead or something . . ." But she was shaking her head again.

"By the time I realized I had to act, there were these cults, sects, which had developed their own stories. There was one that prophesied that the great sign of your return was going to be me announcing that you'd been found dead! And there was another one . . .

"Toby, there's a whole branch of the religion that believes I'm going to announce I've got a son, and I'll reveal him and he'll be already grown up. And I'll say . . . I'll say"—there were tears in her eyes now—"I'll say I only just had him but hid him away in another lockstep where he's grown up. But I'll be lying, because it'll really be you. *You* returned!

"Don't you get it?" She was leaning forward, very close to the camera. He felt he could almost reach out and touch her, and the stricken look on her face made him want to hug her to him. "You can *never* be seen with me, except as a prisoner, an official impostor.

Any hint that you're not that will be taken by someone as proof that you're the Emperor of Time returned to end the locksteps. Toby, you can't return. You can't abdicate. You can't keep a low profile, you can't adopt an alias and try to disappear. It's all been anticipated, it's all expected and watched for, and any hint of this or that prophecy coming true will spark revolutions and pogroms. Peter and I aren't just the most famous people in the local universe. We're the most watched, most spied upon. You can't just come home.

"You can't be here at all."

The idea echoed around in his mind for long seconds: *trapped, we're both trapped in this,* but then . . . Something about Evayne's expression sparked a memory. He could picture her so clearly standing with her hands behind her back, solemnly swearing to him that she hadn't taken his favorite hall flyer. Yeah, he remembered that look, and he'd seen it other times, too. Toby laughed.

"I almost fell for that. You've gotten good."

Her eyes widened. "Wh-what—"

"You're trying to weasel out of something, just like that last time when you and Peter were planning to wipe out my colony on Jaspex—remember, in Consensus? You gave me the same kind of bullshit speech that time." He scrunched up his mouth and tapped his chin. "Now, what would it be that you're avoiding this time . . . ?

"Mom." He could see from her expression that he'd hit the mark. "I'm not Toby the Messiah until I go to Destrier and wake her up. All this stuff about pogroms and revolutions—that's all theoretical, isn't it? There's something else going on here."

Evayne glared at him. "Oh yes? Well, tell me you weren't on your way to Destrier next."

She had him with that one. He ducked his head. "With nobody around to tell me the rules of the game, what else would I do? You stacked the deck against me, Evie. I want to know why."

Now this older woman, who looked so much like some long-lost aunt, looked away and said, with real sadness, "It's far too late for that, Toby. I wish we'd had a chance to finish growing up together, I really do. But that chance is gone. This has to be good-bye." She made a throat-cutting gesture and her image vanished.

"I CAN'T BELIEVE IT," muttered Corva as she took off the glasses. "She's . . . Toby, she's awful."

He sighed heavily. "Family, huh? Seriously, I'm starting to get over the shock of it all. That Evayne . . . is not my Evayne. *My* sister's gone, Corva."

Then—because he couldn't put it off any longer—he said, "So what about it? Do we stay here an extra day while we wake Halen? Or do we leave him safe where he is, for now at least?"

He held his breath. The look on Corva's face was heartrending. She bit a fingernail and stared for a long time back at the stairs to the underground vault.

"We go," she said, almost inaudibly; and in that moment it was as if she'd taken a giant step, over countless choices and possibilities, to a place from which there was no going back. She hung her head and without another word followed Toby out of the house.

They climbed out of the plastic-wrapping into bright sunlight, hot air, and the buzzing of cicadas. Corva hugged herself and looked around. "Whoa. They did a bad job on the street." She'd noticed the unkempt wilderness that had sprung up around the pink house shapes. Wrecks had, too—he sat up on his haunches, whiskers twitching, almost quivering with alertness. Orpheus sat nearby, watching Toby with the air of a worldly-wise traveler observing a tourist.

"This way," Toby said. "I've got a pack and supplies for you." He began walking through the tall grass. Corva hurried to catch up.

"Where are we?"

"Not far from where we left things." He watched the denners scout ahead. "It's funny, I have to do the math every now and then to keep it straight." He counted it out on his fingers for her: "The main lockstep hasn't started its next turn yet. Kenani's been asleep on Wallop for eighteen years realtime, so he's still waiting for Evayne to arrive so he can turn us over to her. One more week has passed in the Weekly since we left there. And two years, realtime, have passed since you went to sleep."

She grinned. "Yeah, it can be confusing. You'll get used to it." Then she lost the smile. "How long have you been awake?"

"A few months. Long enough, like I said, to get over certain things."

"And in all this time you've done . . . what?"

It was his turn to grin. "I've been driving Evayne out of her mind.

"Do you want to help?"

| Eighteen |

"IT'S ALL ABOUT THE interface," Miranda was telling Corva, "and the things it can do for you."

"'You' being a McGonigal," Corva pointed out.

"Well, yeah. Which is why I can only show you this mock-up. Toby can't share it with anybody else. It's the biocrypto, you know."

Toby watched them out of the corner of his eye as he kicked through the remains of a recent battle. Having spent several weeks together now, the two women were chatting like old friends, despite the fact that one of them was a fourteen-thousand-year-old game personality. He'd found a way to port data from the government strategic models to Consensus and had given Corva an account in that. Now they both could see the whole vast network of Thisbe's planetary civilization spread out around them, icons and pointers and information flags standing like giants over the horizon; or they could zoom it all into a handheld map. They could manipulate the time lines, slide back to review or forward to project outcomes—though only he could enter any commands into the real interface.

"I can't believe the army gave you an account," she'd said when he first booted it up for her.

Toby had laughed. "The alternative was letting me blunder around with no firm data. What would you have done?"

"Here," said Miranda now. "See how you can monitor the cicada beds? There's health status, power levels, number of sleepers . . ."

"I don't see any names. How can you tell who's who?"

"You can't. That information is in the government's emergency database, which you, and Evayne, don't have access to."

"And that was the key to the whole plan," said Toby; but he wasn't watching the other two anymore. He had knelt by the remains of a burned-out bot to examine its design. "Damn."

The bot was cylindrical, not human shaped at all though it did have legs. It was about the size of a refrigerator, but he couldn't tell whether it had been armed. Of course, it was hard to tell much from the landscape of churned ground and twisted metal that spread over about a square kilometer of grassland. The forest fire started by the battle was still going, a few klicks east of here; Thisbe firefighting bots were water-bombing it with monotonous regularity. If they didn't get it under control in the next day or so, the lockstep system would be forced to wake up everybody in the neighboring town so they could evacuate.

Which would be perfect.

"Did you find something?" Corva came over, her feet crunching on the burnt, black ground.

"I can't tell what model this was," he said, poking at the downed bot with a stick.

"And that's a problem because . . . ?"

"It's a problem if Evayne's got a reserve of non-McGonigal bots. That would mean she can get around the network problem."

"I still don't get that," Corva said to Miranda.

"It looks as though Toby has an administrator's account to the lockstep system, but Evayne is just a user," said Toby's virtual shipmate. "He's been able to override all of her commands to lockstep technology. That includes any of Evayne's systems that he can communicate with."

"Which is why she cut herself off from the planetary network," Toby said. Standing, he brushed ashes from his knees and looked around for more clues. "She can't take over my bots, but I can take over hers. I could even have taken over her ships and shut her down in orbit, if only I'd known about this sooner!"

"I'm sorry," said Corva sarcastically, "but why *didn't* you?"

"It's the interface." Miranda shrugged. "It's kind of . . . cryptic. Lots of things it doesn't tell you. Like, for instance, the identity of a given sleeper. There are emergency systems that can track who sleeps where and can wake a sleeper remotely. For example, you can set an alarm to do that if somebody close to you dies or some other personal emergency happens. Your ship's manifest cross-referenced names with the cicada beds the passengers were in. But by themselves, the beds don't keep that kind of information."

"Which means I've been able to use both Orpheus and the beds to winter over. Doing it with Orph is incredibly exhausting for both of us. If I was able to use only denner hibernation, we wouldn't have been able to just randomly jump through time the way we're doing. Like I said, that's what makes this plan possible. And, I mean I can't be positive, but this"—he gestured at the mechanical carnage—"sure looks like it's working."

Bots had fought bots here: networked Toby machines versus locked-down marauders from Evayne's ships. Hers had been on a search-and-sweep of the local town, breaking into houses and reading IDs off the cicada beds. Evayne had human troops doing the same thing, but Toby didn't go near them—and, so far at least, Evayne hadn't harmed any of the helpless Thisbe citizens whose homes she was invading.

"I was expecting a tug-of-war," he said. Orpheus and Wrecks were waiting at the edge of the burnt ground, and Toby's denner sniffed dubiously at Toby's pant cuffs as the humans met them. He and Corva shouldered their packs and waded back into the tangled brush.

"I thought we'd both be issuing orders to the lockstep system. She'd command it to do one thing, I'd tell it no, she'd say yes. I was expecting a game of global Whac-A-Mole, but it hasn't worked out like that."

"Whack-a-what?"

"But it sort of has," he went on, oblivious. "Better, really. I wake up a whole town, Evayne freaks out and sends her people to find out if it's an army group assembling. Random beds come awake all over the planet, and she can see that in the interface but not who it is who's up. She never knows whether one of them might be me, so she has to send somebody to investigate each and every one. Which takes fuel and people—and means she has to have people awake all the time. But *I* can sleep for years if I want."

He'd expected that he would have to manually wake people, because if he scheduled wake-ups ahead of time, Evayne could find them in the interface (though not *who* they were) and investigate before they woke, or just reset them. Toby's plan had involved being awake more than sleeping. As it turned out, that hadn't been necessary. He had Evayne's forces dancing to his tune all over the planet, which freed him to mess with her in other ways.

Corva shook her head. "Sooner or later she's going to start killing people. She's gonna call your bluff. What are you going to do then?"

"If she pisses me off, I'll wake the whole damned planet. She knows that." He could tell she was far from satisfied by that answer, so he said, "How's the story end? There're a bunch of possible ways:

"If I wasn't Toby, but let's say some pretender who'd convinced the local government I was the messiah, then Evayne would have waited until most of the planet was wintering over. Thisbe just doesn't have the resources to replace all the McGonigal cicada beds in time. So she'd be able to dig in, take out the military's installations, and threaten whole cities with destruction unless they turned me over. That was your brother's nightmare ending to the story.

"But if I really am Toby McGonigal, then I can have the whole planet up and running before she can get herself established. Then we have enough force to put up a good fight, maybe even win. In that case, the outcome's not certain—and that means there'd probably be a pitched battle. I might die, you might die, but probably Evayne would lose. If she survived, she'd end up our prisoner. And with her as our hostage, the road to Destrier's wide open.

"That's Halen's dream version."

"That's the one you agreed to," she pointed out.

"Corva, a lot of people die in that case, and me . . . I end up just like Evayne, locked into playing my role in a myth I didn't invent. It sucks, I was never going to do that, and I'm sorry I had to let you think I would."

"Okay," she said with a slight smile.

"The thing is, this thing about me being able to override her commands changes the story. But for this twist on it to work, I had to make sure she committed herself now, when she doesn't have that extra force. I had to lure her in.

"So when she arrived, the planet was wintering over. She thought it was safe to come out of orbit, so she set some ships down by the capital and headed in with a big force to wake up the government and throw down her ultimatum. A force of soldiers was waiting there—the ones who hadn't been using McGonigal beds. There was a confrontation, but I'm sure the Thisbe soldiers were confused and demoralized at that point. They figured I'd betrayed them. So they were facing each other tensely in the middle of the Grand Plaza when one of Evayne's aides came running up to her. I wasn't there, by the way; I watched it all later on the security footage. Couldn't quite make out the expression on her face, though, when her people told her that McGonigal beds all over the planet were starting to wake up—including other army bases.

"If I'd wakened the whole planet, we'd have been in Version Two of the story again—a pitched battle. But it wasn't like that. There were just enough Thisbe military awake now to keep Evayne from safely leaving the planet. Also enough to put up a good defense if she tried some stunt like threatening to wipe out a town."

"Wait—but why?"

"It was a message from me to her."

"Yes, but *why*? What did you think she was going to do?"

"Exactly what she did do. I know Evayne. If you dangle some-thing just out of her reach, she'll keep jumping at it until she col-lapses. She's always been like that, but who knows it aside from me and Peter? In forty years, nobody's ever done this to her. She's probably totally forgotten that this is her vulnerability. So I made myself the bait, and said, 'Here I am, come get me.'"

"You set the rules of the game! If she breaks them by escalat-ing—"

"Then I escalate, too. If she hurts anyone, I wake the bombers, the mechs, and missile battalions. She could play a different game, but only by denying her essential nature—"

Corva reached out and gave Toby a hard shove. As he stum-bled, she shouted, "That's crazy dangerous! She could swoop in and catch us at any time! Then what?"

He laughed. "Then I lose everything. But only me."

"And me, you jerk. You dragged me into this."

"Are you saying you thought you were *safe* when you came with me?"

"Well, no, but—"

"Evayne may know about denners, but she doesn't know we have Orpheus and Wrecks. She suspects I'm using non-McGonigal beds; some models don't have to report their status to the lockstep network. I know she thinks this because she's got her people scour-ing the planet looking for those beds. She rousts anybody who's in one and then destroys it. Meanwhile, she's watching the network. Any McGonigal bed that's activated—either waking up or going under—could be me. So she has to investigate. And that's sapping her strength. Even worse: it's using up *time*."

"Are you saying," and now she was shouting, "that there're thou-sands of people out there who've had their beds destroyed? That they're stranded in real time?"

He shook his head. "You know the lockstep laws. They can use any available bed if they can't get to their own. Although the other thing Evayne's doing is disabling all the empty McGonigal beds she can find, to deny me a resting place. She's got enough for the refugees—but she thinks she can tighten the noose around me this way."

A little calmer, Corva nodded to the denners. "Except we don't need the beds."

"Right."

They walked together for a long time, Corva with her head down and hands behind her back while Toby broke the trail for her. He was headed for a road that led to the next town. It was going to take a couple of days to get to it on foot, but he'd been learning patience recently. He could afford the time.

"How does it end?" she said suddenly. "This version of the game?"

He looked back at her, grimly satisfied. "Peter and Evayne started something they think they can control. They can't control it—but I can.

"The game doesn't end on Thisbe. This is just the opening move."

THEY'D BEEN SLEEPING IN houses, but there were none here between the towns. He was pretty sure Evayne had no automated hunters in the sky right now (the Thisbe ground forces having shot most of them down) so he decided to risk a fire.

He and Corva sat side by side on a log and roasted some stringy rabbit that Wrecks had caught. It was comfortable and even romantic for a while. They talked about their vastly different childhoods, finding so little in common that it was amazing to both they could relate to one another at all. After a period of companionable silence, though, Toby noticed that Corva was staring at the sinuous river of stars that crossed the sky. After a time she stood up and put her back to the fire. "I've never seen this," she murmured.

"What, the Milky Way?"

"No. That." She nodded at the horizon.

Under the sky, there were no lights at all. Beyond the small circle of orange cast by the fire, everything was utterly black and still. The sawtoothed cutout of trees on the horizon reminded Toby of another time he'd stared into black like that. It was on his first waking in orbit around Lowdown, when he'd turned away from that same vision of the Milky Way to find sight absorbed by the vast circular blackness of the planet. He remembered what that had felt like, and coming to stand next to her, he felt a bit of it now.

Except for the occasional crackle from the fire, there was no sound at all. It was as if they were standing at the border to the land of Death, nothing ahead of them but perfected stillness.

Corva shivered. "Is this why we did it?" She turned to nod in the direction of the town they'd left. "Did we have a million years of being faced with . . . with *this* every night, and did we invent fire and weapons and clothes and culture and art and houses just so we wouldn't have to look into it? —That awful emptiness?"

He nodded. "I guess you never camped out."

She turned to him. "You're not afraid of it, are you? Not the way the rest of us are."

Toby shrugged. "I've seen it before, I guess."

"You want to rub her nose in the horror of realtime?"

"Or her men's noses. Every second that ticks by while they chase me, they age, while the people they left behind remain . . ."

"Perfect."

He laughed. "Imagination does funny things. Especially when it's faced with something like this. Right?" He shouted that last word into the night.

There was no echo. Silence and blackness ate the word and remained untouched.

"Don't do that!" Corva sat down again, now resolutely staring into the fire. Toby noticed she was playing with her little hologram locket.

He sat next to her. "What is that, anyway? You've worn it since I've known you."

It had been a while since Corva had given him her I-can't-believe-you're-so-stupid look. "You're kidding. You're playing this complicated mind game with your sister's people, and you don't even know how they think about *time*?"

"I know they're afraid of it. Else why run faster and faster into the future?"

She gave a heavy sigh. "Yeah. Okay, there're two visions of time—of what it is. The first is the oak in the acorn. You know what that is?"

He wracked his memory, trying to remember how Evayne's official religion worked. "That everything's predestined, unfolding according to some kind of plan?"

"Oh, it's more than that. It's the idea that the only true creative moment in all of time was the first one—the big bang. Everything that's happened since is just working out the implications made possible in that first second. The engine was built before time, and now it just runs. Your sister's taken that idea, applied it to human civilization, and put *you* at the heart of it. Toby," she said, now struggling to keep a straight face, "you're the big bang of the locksteps."

"Great. Another title to add to my list."

"The story is that you saw it all in a flash of vision—I mean, how humanity could cheat time and become eternal, even if our individual lives are still short. You built an eternal city of sorts, a real Olympus that would abide no matter what happened on Earth or the other fast worlds. One of the things that means is that there can be nothing new added to the locksteps. No innovation. No revolution. No change of any kind."

"Kenani's job," he said with a nod. "To keep things from changing."

"Nothing new. And nothing to look forward to. In other words, nothing to hope for."

"Ah." He reached out to touch the locket. He understood its shape now: a miniature tree inside an acorn. "But if that's not what you believe . . ."

"I wear this to remind myself that I *don't* believe it. I look at time a different way. It's physics based. See, when the universe was emerging from the primordial fireball—"

"It's not every conversation," he interrupted, "where you get to use the words 'primordial fireball.'"

"Oh, be quiet. As the . . . the bang cooled, things began to crystallize out of it. Quarks and leptons, electrons and protons. They weren't there before and *never had been*—and then they were. Before they existed, they couldn't exist, they were impossible. They weren't stored somewhere in some kind of seed form before the bang. They were impossible, and then they were there.

"Same thing with life," she said. "Before life existed, how could some immortal observer from outside the universe have seen it coming? It wasn't one of those things that matter did—until suddenly it was doing it. And then consciousness played the same trick on life . . .

"The point is," she said, gently taking his fingers off her locket, "time isn't the working out of a predesigned destiny. Time is the possibility of *surprise*."

Toby had a sudden startled image of the two types of time: one that *pushed*, with all the terrible weight of the iron-bound laws of history behind it; and one that *pulled* you forward into a future of limitless possibilities. "So what does believing in surprise get you?" he mused, looking up at again at the stars.

"What do you think, silly? It gives us the one thing that the oak in the acorn never can:

"Hope."

TOGETHER, THEY DRIFTED THROUGH a landscape empty of any of the agendas of human civilization. In the tangled brushlands, along the edges of overgrown roads, and under the canopies of untended trees they met instead countless beings busy with the tending of their own lives: hurrying bees, chirping beetles, lazily waving rushes in the shallow waters. The frequent lurid changes in color that washed the sky didn't affect these creatures, who'd adapted and moved on. In time, Toby got used to it, too, only occasionally reflecting on the unimaginable power hinted at by the laser sunlight.

He and Corva moved from place to place, keeping as many steps ahead of Evayne's searchers as they could. They would curl up on cold concrete in front of some randomly chosen house's hibernac- ulum and sleep for weeks or months at a time. When they emerged, the lawns would be more overgrown, the plastic wrapping of the houses a little more frayed, and the Internet news services full of automatically generated alerts and bot-authored reports of Evayne's activities.

After resting and getting their bearings, they would set out for the next safe position from which to prod Toby's sister into wast- ing her energies.

It was among the towers of the capital that Toby's plan fell apart.

They'd come here because both of them were tired of the wil- derness. Toby's straggly new beard was filling out, and with no bots to give them a proper haircut, both had hacked-up pageboys. They'd stolen clothes as they went, but under them they were flea- bitten, darkly tanned, and covered in little scars from brambles and broken branches. It was just a matter of time before one of them broke a leg, or developed a major infection too far from a ci- cada bed. So they'd infiltrated the shrink-wrapped towers near Corva's home, where the bot count was higher but there were also more places to hide. For the turn of a few weeks, and a winter-over of nearly a year, they enjoyed the fabulous luxuries of houses and condominiums whose inhabitants slept like fairy tale princes and princesses, just meters away.

Then one evening as they were crossing a plaza on their way to their latest nest, Toby heard a faint sound above the chirping and buzzing of the insects. He stopped walking and put a hand on Corva's arm. "Wait."

The denners had heard it too: a kind of quiet ripping sound, coming from nowhere and everywhere at once.

Toby shouted a curse and began to run, as sleek silvery aircraft suddenly wove between the towers ringing the plaza. They shot past and disappeared, and Toby and Corva managed to make it to the overhang of a sealed subway station. Corva crouched down, watching the sky. "Did they see us?"

"I don't think so."

She cautiously stepped out from under the overhang. "Maybe they were on their way somewhere else." But she ducked down again as four more craft soared overhead. These were bigger: troop transports from the look of them.

Toby's heart sank. "They're doing a spot check. And we're going to show up like bonfires in their thermal cameras. We're the biggest life-forms in the city."

"We make for the outskirts," she said, "or maybe hide in the subway. If we deep-dive there—"

He shook his head. "There's no refrigeration in the tunnels. We'll be eaten by centipedes."

"Then what—"

Toby had fished his glasses out of his backpack, but when he put them on he growled. "No signal here. We need to get into one of those residential towers. Once I'm on the net, I can wake up the city."

She leaned out, searching the skies. "I think we're safe for now. We'd better run for it." The sound of jet engines echoed off the buildings; it sounded like the big transports were landing.

They were about to sprint for the nearest residence when Corva grabbed Toby's arm. "Wait—wake *how much* of the city?"

"Corva, the instant I start any beds, Evayne is going to know I'm here. Our only chance now lies in numbers.

"We're going to wake everybody."

| Nineteen |

THE FIRST STIRRINGS WERE in the form of lights. As night fell, small pinpricks lit the darkness, high up in the towers and scattered along the roadways where there had been none before. Above them, the soaring shapes of aircars and flying bots—busy hunters—eclipsed the stars. It was a curiously slow and anticlimactic event—if you didn't know what you were looking at.

Toby and Corva watched the slow rousing of the city through the glass outer wall of an empty condominium, high up on its seventieth floor. Even from this height, Toby didn't feel they were safe, so they didn't go near that window but instead viewed the city through the crack of a doorway to an inner room. They kept the lights off, and once or twice hovering shapes drifted past outside, dangerously close, and they crouched behind the place's (active but empty) cicada beds, hoping these would block their biosignals.

Evening turned into night, night into morning: the city awoke slowly. By the time the random rainbow of dawn painted the eastern horizon, there were lights on in nearly all the towers. Traffic— mostly bots—was running in the streets below in increasingly strong pulses.

Feeling a bit safer now, Toby ventured to the glass wall to look down. It was only when he spotted the first human forms emerging from neighboring towers that he finally felt safe enough to sleep for a while.

"Let them try to sort *this* out," he said as they lay down on the carpet between the beds. "Once the crowds reach their max, we can slip through their lines and go into stasis in a house they've already searched."

Corva nodded. "They'll know the beds aren't being used, but as long as it's cold . . ." House insulation around the hibernation core was very good; with the denners, they should be able to deep-dive safely for a month or two even in one that had had its power shut off.

He wrapped his arms around her and murmured, "Safe," into her ear. They kept their clothes on and their packs ready at hand, though, as they drifted off to the faint sounds of a city waking.

TOBY AWOKE COUGHING. SOMETHING abrasive—an awful chemical odor—was in the air. He sat up blinking. On the other side of the room Orpheus and Wrecks were scrabbling frantically at the door.

"What's happening?" Corva levered herself onto her hands and knees, and at that moment the room shook to an ear-piercing alarm. "FIRE, FIRE," said an impersonal voice from some hidden speaker. "PLEASE EVACUATE THE BUILDING THROUGH THE STAIRWELLS. MOVE IN AN ORDERLY FASHION TO YOUR DESIGNATED ASSEMBLY POINT IN THE—" The voice suddenly cut out.

Toby had thrown open the door. In a glance he took in the fact that it was evening again—a perfectly blue one tonight—and the additional fact that a swarm of black somethings was dipping and diving around the tower. Still coughing, he went up to the transparent outer wall but jumped back as one of the things shot past only a meter or so beyond the glass.

"They've cut the power," Corva called hoarsely. "We can't stay here."

"It's no fire," he said, gathering up a frantic Orpheus and grabbing the strap of his backpack. "They're pumping something through the air system."

"Easier than"—she paused to cough—"go door to door themselves."

Efficient. Not like the Evayne he'd watched grow up, but just like the Evayne she'd become in his absence.

The corridor outside was filling with anxious people—men, women, children and pets, including other denners. Many of these people had no idea they'd been woken out of turn, and some stopped, blocking the way while their neighbors attempted confused explanations. Even those who'd checked the net and knew that the city was waking alone didn't know why. There was no mention of Toby McGonigal; the government had hidden the truth of the situation well. As they moved down the stairwell, Toby did hear the name Evayne spoken, first just once, then over and over again. The rumors that she was coming to punish Thisbe again had been impossible to suppress in the days leading up to their last sleep—not with all the civil defense forces being put on alert.

They were afraid, and the fear was contagious. By the time they spilled out into a grass-tangled lot behind the building, Toby had become just another mote in a swirling stream of panicked people. They passed shreds of plastic sheeting that had wrapped the exit, catching fractured glimpses of people darting to and fro under a swooping flock of black things, and then spotlights came on and blinded him.

"MOVE AS FAR AS YOU CAN INTO THE PLAZA," roared a bot voice. People stumbled and fell; kids were crying. Toby reached for Corva and put his arm across her shoulder to keep her close. Unable to see clearly, buffeted by others, they made their way toward a line of tall shapes half visible behind the spotlights.

"Mechs, Toby." Corva pulled back.

"Doesn't matter how close we are," he said. "They'll see us. And hear us—" He stopped talking. If Evayne had recorded his conversation with her—as she surely must have—then she would have his facial and voice biocrypto fed into all her bots. He had to hope his longer, lank hair, sunburnt features and new beard would confuse them. But his voice . . . Corva looked up at him, and he just shook his head.

"Where are the defense forces?" somebody shouted.

"They'll be here! Give them a chance."

They would, Toby knew; he'd woken them, too. There'd be some resistance, somewhere—but not right here, right now, and that was all that counted.

He'd lost. He couldn't say it, couldn't speak his fear, but his grip on Corva tightened as they staggered to a stop near the ranked forms of the military bots that ringed the lot.

These weren't McGonigal bots but some standard military model. Evayne wouldn't make the obvious mistake. Ditto for the half-meter-size quadcopters that flocked overhead. None would obey his commands.

Halen had been right. Better that he should have hidden behind an army of co-opted McGonigal bots and an even bigger force of fanatical Toby worshipers. He imagined the sky dark with his own ships, Evayne's forces on the run, and an unstoppable militia flying his banners behind him as he stepped onto the soil of Destrier. That whole world would fall on its knees before him. They'd been waiting, after all, since the dawn of time. With Evayne helpless, he could have strode to their mother's strange resting place and put his hand on the lock there, the one that only he in all the universe could open.

These . . . things, that his brother and sister had turned into—they'd be on the run then. He was never going to get his Peter back, nor his Evayne. But at least he could have driven those dark changelings out of the universe. He could have set things right, as he was supposed to. Now he'd never get the chance.

"WOMEN AND CHILDREN TO THE GREEN AREA!" Laser light described a square near the building.

"Why are they separating us?"

"What's going on?"

"*We're not going to harm anyone!*" It was a new voice, not the mechanical claxon sound of the military bots but a human man.

He stepped out from between the mil bots, one of Evayne's senior officers in a black-and-silver uniform.

"We're searching the city for a criminal!" he went on, raising one hand to try to still the cries of outrage and fear coming from the crowd. "If you're not him, you can go home. I'm just going to split off the obvious noncandidates to get this over with as quickly as possible!"

Slightly emboldened, some of the men pressed forward. "You have no right to do this!" one shouted. "The lockstep laws—"

Three milbots stepped toward him, the thud of their footsteps reverberating through the ground. "You don't seem to understand," said the officer. "Nobody will be hurt if *nobody* resists."

Some of the men looked ready to fight despite their fear. A terrible feeling of helplessness was building in Toby's throat. Barely aware he was doing it, he took a step forward.

Corva pulled him back. "What are you doing?" she hissed in his ear.

"I can't let them be hurt for no reason—"

"Stop it!" She hauled at his arm.

But the moment had passed. The men who were thinking of resisting now found themselves washed with air from a dozen or more drones that hovered just above their heads. None of them could have taken a step without being knocked down, either lethally or by one or another stun technique.

"Women and children into the square, please," the officer repeated. Reluctantly, the crowd began to dissolve into two parts.

Toby took his arm away from Corva's shoulder and gently shoved her after the other women. "Take Orph, will you?"

"No, Toby—"

"It's fine. I'll just be a minute." He disentangled Orpheus from his shoulder and handed the denner to Corva. Orpheus struggled, chittering anxiously.

"Go!" He stepped away from them. Corva backed away, then turned and fled through the maze of grim men, into darkness.

Abstractly, Toby noticed that lights like these spotlights were

shining around other nearby buildings. This same drama was being played out throughout the neighborhood.

The officer began walking along the front of the crowd of men,
a bot about his own size striding with him. This one flicked a light
into the face of each man as they passed. "No," said the bot, and
the officer would pull the man forward and point him at the other
crowd, the one with the women and children. "No, no, no, no . . ."

With terrifying speed, they peeled back the front lines of the
crowd, getting closer and closer to Toby. He knew they'd find him;
why not just step forward and get it over with? But he couldn't move.

"*Orpheus!*"

Corva's voice jolted him out of his paralysis. Toby whirled, saw
her standing with the other women, a hand at her neck. Orpheus
must have bitten her, because here he came, bounding through the
tall grass that separated the two groups.

Toby took a step toward him. "No! Get back—"

Lightning flashed from one of the swooping black drones, and
Orpheus wasn't running but tumbling, once, twice, then flopping
utterly still in the dark grass.

"No!" Toby ran to him, or tried, but suddenly a milbot loomed
in front of him and a metal hand rammed him in the chest. His
breath knocked out of him, Toby sat down hard.

The officer strolled over and tilted his head, frowning. "I'm so
sorry," he said. "Your denner?" He crouched in front of Toby, peering into his face. "No, I don't think . . ."

His bot had come up behind him and now it bent down, too,
flicking its light in Toby's face. Toby had just a moment to look
past it to where Corva stood stricken with the others, Wrecks
crouched at her feet with his hackles raised, then the officer's bot
said,

"*Yes.*"

THE FLIGHT OF EMOTIONS across the officer's face would have
been hilarious at any other time: disbelief, panic, triumph all battled it out in the few seconds that he crouched frozen in front of

Toby. Then he reached out quickly; Toby flinched, but he was offering his hand.

"I'm so sorry, sir. Can you come with me please?"

Toby ignored the offer of help. He wanted to turn and look, see if Orpheus was okay and if they'd realized that Corva was with him—but anything he did, a flicker of the eyes, a half turn in that direction—might alert the watchful bots. If they'd been recording everything then there was nothing he could do anyway; but if not . . .

"Yes," he said, "I'm coming," and he stood and resolutely walked away from Corva and the dear friend who lay so unmoving in the grass.

The officer was talking excitedly, doubtless advising the other search units that they could stop their sweeps. The milbots broke ranks, milling about for a moment and then falling into formation around Toby and the other human. Black shapes swooped and soared triumphantly over it all, morphing into hinted silhouettes as the milbots flicked off their spotlights.

"This way, sir," said the officer. "We have an aircar waiting. It's not much, but I hope you won't find it too uncomfortable."

This comment startled Toby out of his shock. "Uncomfortable? What do you think I've been—" But there was no point, and anything more he said was just going to turn into screaming anger. He shook his head, but the officer was practically running now, the mil bots pushing from behind, so Toby had to say, "What's the hurry? We've been at this for years, a few more seconds isn't going to matter."

"It might, sir."

"And stop calling me sir."

"Yes, Mr. McGonigal."

Four big boxy troop transports waited on the other side of a stand of trees, along with a smaller staff car, which could seat eight or ten people. Four bots similar to the one that had revealed Toby stood next to it. The officer stepped up to them and said to Toby, "In, please."

Reluctantly, Toby complied. He couldn't help himself and spared a glance back at the lot where he'd left Corva and Orpheus. All was dark there, just a confusion of moving shapes as the people from the tower belatedly realized they'd been set free.

The bot that had accompanied the officer moved to step into the aircar, but the man put his hand on its chest. "Wait here a second," he told it. Then he slid past it and into the car.

"Sir, I—" the bot began, moving forward.

The officer reached up and yanked down the aircar's clamshell door, banging the bot on the head and knocking it aside.

"Lift! Lift!" He practically screamed the word as he slammed into the seat next to Toby. The aircar surged upward, but the officer was already reaching for the manual override. As he took control they slewed sideways and then dropped. Toby was suddenly weightless, and he shouted as he braced his hands on the canopy. Black cutout shapes of trees shot past, and suddenly the sky was full of laser light.

Some part of Toby's mind was registering that real laser shots didn't look anything like those in the movies and games he'd seen—they were diffuse, tremulous, and wavering, full of sparkles as the beams exploded stray motes of dust. But the tree next to them erupted in orange flame as one caught it, and then they were clear—

—For just a second before something slammed into the canopy, making Toby shout again. They took another hit, then another and a quick fusilade: bangbang *bang!*—with the last one cracking the windshield.

"Damned drones," muttered the officer as he steered the aircar around the apartment building. Toby glanced back in time to see a sumptuous living room explode in fire as more laser shots tried to cut through the building.

"Don't worry, they're not trying to kill us."

Toby reared back, staring at the man. "How can you tell?"

"If they were, we'd already be dead. But if they think they're actually going to lose us, they might get serious." He dove at the ground and, scant meters above the road surface, they dodged through the streets. Everywhere around them, vehicles and drones were rising into the sky. There were more laser flashes, only . . . "Hey, they're shooting at each other!"

"Some of us are loyal," said the officer. "Some would die for your sister even after learning how she's betrayed you."

"Ah." A tumble of emotions flew through Toby then: fury that this man had been an ally all along, despair that Orpheus had been hurt or killed for no reason; relief that Corva was out of danger and, over it all, a savage sense of triumph at the carnage playing out across the cityscape. Bots were fighting bots, aircars and drones weaving around one another while people ran to and fro in the streets. Divided loyalty was shattering Evayne's ranks, just as Toby had planned.

All his good intentions had evaporated but he didn't care anymore if people got hurt. He laughed bitterly. The officer glanced over and something in Toby's eye made him say, "I'm so sorry if—"

"Carry on," snapped Toby. "This is perfect."

THEY SHOT BETWEEN TREES that passed so close the branches whipped the side windows. Yellow blossoms of fire erupted behind them and Toby's stomach flipped over repeatedly as they maneuvered.

It's nothing you haven't seen in Consensus, he told himself—or tried: none of the virtual battles he'd fought with Peter had included actual g-forces and vertigo. He gritted his teeth and tried to remember what a commander was supposed to do in situations like this.

"Where are we going?" He was glad his voice wasn't quavering or squeaking. The officer grunted but had to pull some extreme banks and turns before he answered.

"We've been in contact with your people for years," he said as they entered a slot between tall towers, and he opened the throttle. "Almost since we arrived."

"My people? What are you talking about?"

"Your army," said the officer. "The one we'll be taking to Destrier."

Toby slumped back in the seat, shaking his head. The cult of the Emperor of Time would surely have their own denners and non-McGonigal beds. Just like the Thisbe defense forces, they could skip a certain number of people through time on their own frequency. Toby hadn't known how many of the recent firefights and ambushes had been engineered by the defense force and how many had been Halen's cult; he hadn't really cared. The one possibility he hadn't considered was that some of Evayne's own people would be highly motivated to find out.

"How many of you are there?"

The percussive sounds of battle were fading behind them. The officer sat back, too, grinning now. "We've had to be very careful about recruiting. Our core is over a hundred men, but at least half of the soldiers may take their orders from your sister only because they think she's acting on your behalf. They've been spinning their heads around trying to reconcile the Great Lady's actions with that loyalty. If you'd declared yourself before, you could have had sixty-five ships and almost five thousand men at your command . . . instantly. When you do declare yourself, I'm sure most of the others will come around."

"Declare myself?"

"Announce your true identity and your intention to march on Destrier."

"Oh that," said Toby.

"Everything's going to change after tonight," the officer went on excitedly. "Her forces will crumble away; they'll all defect! Then we'll have her and you can fulfill your purpose."

Toby decided not to ask the officer what he thought Toby's "purpose" was.

"What about my brother? Isn't this just part of the lockstep army?"

The officer shrugged. "They'll try to defend Destrier. I mean, the total lockstep army is seven million men and women, and hundreds of thousands of ships; nobody knows how many bots there are. But the same thing is going to happen then as is happening now. They'll come around."

But not without a fight. Toby's angry satisfaction was draining away, replaced by dread. *This is Halen's plan.* Just as surely as he knew that, he knew it had been M'boto and Ammond's plan as well—with the tiny difference that they had intended to be the puppeteers pulling Toby's strings.

Of course, you didn't need to neuroshackle somebody to make him your puppet. All you needed was to know that person's currency. To have leverage over him . . .

Corva. He'd left her behind—and where would she go now? Back to her family.

"Crap." He twisted in his seat to look back. The city appeared absurdly festive, but the fireworks were going off strangely close to ground level. There was no returning there, at least not tonight. "Crap crap crap."

"Sir? What's wrong?"

"Nothing. Stay on course. I need to think."

It was all unraveling. He didn't know how many of Evayne's human forces were awake, but she could concentrate all her bots here while they awoke. For his part, Toby would have to depend on whoever on his side was awake at the moment—and it sounded like it was the cultists. He could start thawing the rest of the defense force, but it would take more than a day for them to become operational. By that time everything would probably have been decided, one way or the other. It didn't seem like he had much choice.

"Fly lower. I need an Internet signal."

The officer barked a humorless laugh. "We're about as low as we can go without slowing down. There're still drones on our tail."

"See what you can do."

His glasses signaled intermittent connection to the net. Thisbe wasn't set up to provide global high-data coverage while wintering over; typically the repeaters and antennae went into hibernation like everything else. They'd have to get lucky enough to find an industrial unit that was coordinating the slow harvesters. If he could stay in contact with it long enough to issue some commands, the whole mesh could wake itself—and the army.

The trouble was they were being herded past the city outskirts. An occasional bullet or laser shot past, and the officer had to keep them almost at ground level, while bots fought bots in the air above and behind them.

A hill loomed ahead, and they were up and over it in seconds. Spread out before them was the black plain of a wintering world— except that far off near the horizon, other city lights glittered.

"What's that?" He shook his head and blinked, looked at it again. "I didn't wake that city."

"It's Lockstep 180/1, sir. They share Thisbe with ours."

"Can we get there?"

He looked shocked. "We can't involve them in a civil war. The treaties—"

"*I* didn't sign any treaties. Besides, they can't turn away refugees, can they?"

"What are you saying? You want to go in there *alone*?"

"You were thinking I was going to take our army in there? Defend ourselves with 180 as a shield?" Toby shook his head. "Of course not. So yes, I aim to go in there alone."

"With respect, sir, for you to stay they'll demand you winter over on their frequency. All your sister has to do is post a guard to prevent you leaving. Once you're bottled up and living on a different frequency, you're no threat to her."

". . . And bottling me up would work great for her—if the rest of Thisbe let her do it. This is how we win or lose: you get me a signal long enough for me to wake the rest of the army, and then we head straight for 180. Got it?"

"Yes, sir!"

They swept in a tight turn around one of the city's last towers and began to hunt for a repeater tower while bots and aircraft converged on them from every direction.

. . .

A WEEK LATER, TOBY stood with the officer, whose name was Ourobon, and the administrators of the city of Equinoct. They watched as a small group of human figures passed through the new checkpoint that 180's own defense forces had set up on the edge of town.

Lockstep 180 spoke a different language and all its customs and culture were different. Thousands of years separated them from 360, and they had no Guides to make them conform. Toby had used the meager information in his glasses to negotiate with them.

Using Equinoct as a neutral meeting place would never have been a viable option before now. The generals had agreed that involving a different lockstep would have played into Evayne's hands because it was the McGonigals who had the treaties with all those other civilizations. They wouldn't have given him the time of day, until he could convince the local city fathers that Evayne was on the run.

Which he could now do.

He still wasn't sure he could trust them. Nobody stopped him, though, when he strode out to meet them. Their backdrop was fields of green dotted with troop transports and tents: the ragged remnants of a once-great military force. Way off in the sky, speckling the white clouds like a flock of distant birds, a much larger force approached. Everybody involved knew what that meant.

The new arrivals had been disarmed. As soon as they passed the checkpoint they were officially in Lockstep 180, foreign soil for anyone from Thisbe's dominant culture. Lockstep 180 wasn't large or extensive, but it had its own army and fleets; it had no intention of getting dragged into a McGonigal family squabble. Anybody carrying weapons across the invisible line at the checkpoint would feel the full force of 180's wrath—and so would 360. Evayne had to worry about how many other locksteps would join 180 if it decided to punish Peter's empire.

So it was that Evayne approached Toby weaponless and with her hands out. "Brother!"

He suppressed a sarcastic laugh. *So* now *I'm your brother?* Yet he really did want to see her, and so it was with undisguised eagerness that he stepped forward, took her hands, and then threw caution to the winds and hugged her.

Her whole body went rigid, then after a moment she relaxed a bit—just enough for her to gently take his arms and disengage herself. "I don't deserve that," she said quietly.

"You're the only sister I've got," he said. "And we're kind of in this together, even if you don't think so."

She glanced back at the forces massing in the sky. "I do *not* think so."

Toby thought of that distant squadron as Halen's new army, though he was sure Corva's brother had little power in it. A mixture of Thisbe defense forces, native Toby cultists, and turncoats from Evayne's forces, it was rapidly taking control of the planet. In doing so it was eating up vast resources; a lockstep like 360 lived lightly on the land and had few stockpiles. The whole planet would be going back to sleep soon, to awake on its normal schedule as Toby had commanded. Big changes would be waiting for those citizens who'd slept through the last few years.

"That," said Toby, nodding at the approaching force, "doesn't obey me. It obeys the mythical Emperor of Time, who's got an agenda."

Evayne made a skeptical noise, crossing her arms. Right now she looked so much like their mother that Toby was astonished. "You can't tell me it isn't your agenda, too," she said. "Next stop: Destrier. Right?"

"It doesn't have to be now," he said.

"But every day you wait, the bigger *they* become." She jabbed a thumb at the new army.

Toby shrugged. "What's your point? Evie, it's over. You had your run as pope, but now you gotta step aside. I don't care how we spin it, but one way or another the universe is going to find out that I'm not a god. They're going to have to deal with it."

She shook her head. "Toby, I know you think Peter and I have been totally corrupted by power. But it's not like that. I wasn't lying when I said the myth took on a life of its own. There's nothing for me in promoting it—Peter and I are already the most powerful people in history. Hyperrich and immortal—well, it can't get much better than that, can it? But we're as trapped by your myth as you are.

"There is no easy way to end this, and you know it. You're going to arrive on Destrier carrying fourteen thousand years' worth of baggage. Whatever you do, there'll be social upheavals on countless worlds."

"So all you want to do is keep a lid on it?"

"Keep a lid on potentially limitless levels of religious violence, yes."

He snorted. "As you can see, it's too late for that. —Not my fault, by the way. I was trying to keep this between you and me. You forced my hand."

"And you're about to force mine," she snapped. "I told you before, this isn't a game anymore. The stakes are too high to turn back now."

"Uh, Evie, last I saw I was the one who had your troops surrounded. You had me trapped here for a while, but unless you want to drag 180 into this, too, you can't touch me. And as soon as my army gets here, you're my prisoner. Unless you head for orbit and leave Thisbe with your tail between your legs. And in that case, you're letting me go."

"No! There's another choice. Your only real choice, Toby. You have to renounce your identity. Declare yourself an impostor. We'll come up with a plausible story about how you controlled the cicada beds here on Thisbe. You become just another Toby impostor, the latest in a long line. You never interfere with the lockstep frequencies again, you never command a McGonigal bot to do so much as sweep the floor—and this all dies down. We go back to the way it was."

"You've got to be kidding!"

"Come on, you know it makes sense. It's the only way."

"And what's going to happen to me? Haven't you executed all the other impostors?"

"Well, most of them took their own lives in the end . . ."

"And if you don't do it, some Toby cultist fanatic will come after me sooner or later. You're telling me to make myself a marked
man forever—and you're saying we never wake Mom up! Is that
your plan?"

"Toby, at this point, letting her sleep is the lesser of two evils."

She gave him a sad look, then shook her head and started to walk
back to the checkpoint. "About Mom . . . this time it's you who's
being unimaginative. You think we only have two options with
her: let her sleep or wake her up. But there's a third, and if you
don't do as I say, I'll have to do it."

A queasy feeling of horror was welling up in Toby's throat.
"What do you mean? Evie, what you are talking about?"

She paused at the checkpoint. "I've got about an hour to get
offworld before your little army makes it impossible. So I'm leaving. You come with me now, Toby, or else when you get to Destrier, you'll find that our mother can't be awakened." She saw his
expression and sneered. "You can't possibly believe that Peter and
I never discussed this? —That we wouldn't have built a switch into
her bed that would make it look like she's hibernating, long after
there's nothing left to revive?

"You've got an hour to grow up, Toby. I'll wait as long as I can,
but you made this deadline, not me."

She turned and crossed the line into her own camp and ignored
everything that Toby shouted after her.

Only after she disappeared behind a tent did Toby cough and
sink to his knees. He nearly retched, and only Ourobon's hand
on his shoulder kept him from sinking all the way onto the grass.

Thisbe's artificial sun chose that moment to change color, from
solar yellow to bloodred. Toby stared at his hands in this light,
shaking his head.

"Sir! What did she say?"

"She . . . she's leaving."

"We can keep her here," said Ourobon. "It'll be hard, but—"

"You'll have to shoot her down. You'll probably kill her. Anyway, it doesn't matter. If she thinks we're going to stop her, she might give the order from here."

"We're jamming her."

"And can you guarantee you'll be successful?" Toby brushed off Ourobon's help and stood up. "No, let her go. She's not going to do it until she absolutely has to."

"Do what, sir?"

"Never mind." At the far end of Evayne's camp, her remaining flying bots were rising up and arrowing in the direction of the incoming squadrons. There was going to be bit of a dogfight before Evayne got out, but she had enough firepower left to get at least one lander back to orbit, where her ships waited.

"Ourobon, whose side are you on?"

The ex-officer in Evayne's army looked startled. "Why, yours, sir."

"Then I need you to gather some people you trust. People who'll do what I say, not what the leaders of that army want me to say."

Ourobon nodded slowly. There had been spotty communication in and out of 180; Evayne's jamming transmitters fought with Thisbe's, but there was little she could do to stop point-to-point laser comms. So Toby knew that Corva Keishion's whereabouts were "currently unaccounted for." He knew what that meant: she'd gone back to her family, and Halen or one of his friends had been waiting for her. Once Evayne was gone and her local forces mopped up, Toby would be able to walk through that checkpoint a conquering hero—or so it would appear. There was that little matter of leverage, though. If Halen's people had Corva, if they threatened her . . . he had no illusions that he would be able to resist.

"I need a ship and a loyal crew, and I need to go straight from here to there. No interruptions, conversations, or debriefings."

"A ship?" Ourobon looked puzzled. "You're taking a single ship to Destrier?"

Toby shook his head. "Not to Destrier.

"I have unfinished business somewhere else."

| Twenty |

NATHAN KENANI SAT UP, blinking, and swung his feet over the edge of the cicada bed. He rubbed his eyes, looked around the chamber, nodding in satisfaction as he apparently recognized where he was. Then his gaze fell on Toby.

"Hello, Nathan."

To his credit, Kenani didn't miss a beat. "And a fine good morning to you, too, Toby. I see you've been busy." He squinted, taking in the deeply tanned and weatherbeaten skin, the new beard, and the uniform. "Been a long night, has it?"

His eyes were shifting around the room again. He'd registered the troops; now he noticed Shylif, and Jaysir, who slouched in one corner. He looked around some more, appearing puzzled.

"Where's your girlfriend, Toby?"

"She . . . went home." *Damn him!* thought Toby. Kenani was dangerously astute. Even freshly awakened from thirty years' sleep he was able to instantly zero in on Toby's single weakness.

He couldn't have known about any of the events on Thisbe, much less anything about the veiled threats that had been radioed to Toby's ship. Those messages suggested that Corva's life could be made a living hell if Toby didn't return there. He'd commanded his men not to acknowledge the messages in any way. The instant those who'd sent them knew he'd received them, he'd be on the hook of the Toby cultists.

Halen had given Corva up to them. That fact had provided Toby with the final lesson—as if he'd needed it, after Evayne—in just how badly family could treat family.

Toby couldn't turn the whole planet over looking for her. He had known where Jaysir and Shylif were wintering over, and when he'd waked them he'd pleaded with them to look for her. To his surprise, they had chosen to come with him instead.

"You've not finished what you came here to do," Shylif had explained. "Getting that done's the best way to get her back. And, let's face it, you're no expert on the locksteps yet. You'll need help."

"Well, that's what you wanted, wasn't it?" Kenani was saying. "To help her get home?" He crossed his arms. "I'm a little cold, and hungry, Toby. Do you have . . ." Toby had looked back and nodded, and now somebody came forward carrying Kenani's folded uniform. A bot entered the room pushing a rolling cart stacked with hot food.

Kenani stared at this little performance. "Huh. I always wondered how much like them you'd turn out to be when you grew up."

"Them?"

Toby assumed Kenani was talking about his brother and sister, but the Guide said, "The trillionaires. Those bastards we left Earth to get away from. Seems you're coming along quite nicely, the way you handle the servants and all."

"You're not my servant, Nathan, and I haven't come to kill you or anything—in case you were wondering." Toby smiled at him. "Look, I did my homework; there're decades of news reports about you and the things you've done in the service of the lockstep. There's nothing horrible—you're pretty much the same man I met on that airship back when I was fifteen. I'm pretty sure you've been trying to keep everything together, just like your job description says."

"Well." Now it was Kenani's turn to look uncomfortable. "Thank you."

"Nathan, you've got integrity, that's why I came back to you. I mean, you deliberately gave me a chance to escape, last . . . last night. Didn't you?"

Kenani shrugged. "Let's just say I decided to be a bit sloppy . . . I knew what those denners of yours could do, but most of my men hadn't seen them before. So I just . . . overlooked something and neglected to warn them about it, too. I wanted plausible deniability in case you did get away . . .

"Hell, what am I saying? I thought you deserved a chance is all."

"That's good enough for me." Toby gazed away at the awakening city, thinking.

After a few moments, he was able to summon the courage to ask the question he'd come here to ask: "Mom didn't go to sleep to wait for me, did she? At least, not the last time."

An ironic smile played across Kenani's lips.

"Just tell me."

Kenani looked put out. "I didn't lie to you, boy—well, not entirely. She did start wintering over to wait for her search probes to report back. And that is what got the whole lockstep thing started." He frowned even deeper. "What makes you think that last time was any different for her?"

"It's a little discovery I made on Thisbe. It seems I can override Evayne's commands to the lockstep system."

"Really, now?" Kenani looked genuinely surprised. "I never thought she'd done *that*."

That told Toby part of what he wanted to hear. "You're not surprised that she *could* do it. Only that she *did*."

Kenani pretended to be absorbed with the difficulties of dressing himself. Toby let him get away with his silence for a minute or so, then he said, "Tell me how it happened. How did my mother end up being trapped in hibernation like that? It wasn't her own choice, was it?"

Kenani began to tuck into his food. He was obviously thinking about his options—what he could say, what he could leave out, what he could get away with. Finally he sighed and said, "I don't know for sure what happened that day. None of us were there, just the three of them. But they'd been arguing pretty fiercely, that's for sure."

"About what?"

"This myth about you being some kind of messiah was part of it . . ." Kenani hesitated, then took the plunge. "But not all of it. Fact is, your mother'd been overriding their commands to the system. There were some new worlds that had joined the lockstep—this was, what, about eight years in, our time—and they wanted to use their own cicada beds. Break the McGonigal monopoly. Peter and Evayne were having none of that, let me tell you. So many services are tied to the beds that they could shut whole cities out of the system—and they did. Your mother brought 'em back in. She wanted to change the way the lockstep operated, but somehow the other two weren't letting her do it. She wanted a democratic system, they wanted to keep control.

"Here's the thing, Toby. If Evie did something, Cassandra would just shut it down; she could do the same with Peter. If both Peter and Evie both ordered something, Cassie couldn't override them. But neither of them alone could override her, either."

"Ah," said Toby. It was as he'd thought.

"I don't know how they got her into the bed. Might have knocked her on the head for all I know. But anyway, she wasn't able to counter their command when they put her under. They came back and told us she was wintering over to wait for you, like she had in the past. We were suspicious, but what could we do? The time stretched out and she didn't wake up, and then we found out Evayne had been sending people to worlds outside the lockstep, feeding them this rubbish about Toby being the messiah and Cassie some mystic figure waiting for the end of time. It was pretty clear at that point what had happened."

Toby sighed, then glanced back at his people. Some of the former officers in Evayne's private army were looking extremely uncomfortable. Well, if they hadn't figured out yet that he was just a human being like them, then they'd better wake up fast. Things were going to get real uncomfortable for the Toby myth, real fast.

"Thanks for being up front with me. You're nobody's servant, Nathan. I'm not going to do anything to you, or order you to do anything . . . But there is *one* thing you could do for me—as a favor."

Kenani looked relieved but cautious. "What?"

"You're a Guide. That means you've got a direct line to Peter, right?"

Kenani nodded slowly. "Any messages I send will go straight to him. Anybody else'll have to go through the bureaucracy."

"Right. So you can forward a message to him for me."

Kenani gulped. "You know, they sometimes shoot the messenger."

"Don't worry. Anyway, I'll keep it short."

Toby had been thinking about what to say to Peter, and he'd rehearsed several different speeches and declarations—but now he found he didn't like any of them. "You know, Evayne, she . . . she fled Thisbe after we defeated her there. She said she was on her way to Destrier to kill Mom."

Kenani blinked and went very still for a second. Toby watched him carefully, then said, "Now here's the thing . . . she changed course. She's not going to Destrier at all. It looks more like she's on her way to Earth."

"Ah. Really?" Kenani was visibly fighting to keep his cool look.

"I know my mother's not on Earth, Nathan. But I also know she's not on Destrier. She never was, was she? Destrier is a honeypot. It's a trap to catch Toby pretenders. It's a pit for drowning navies. She's so sure I'm going to go there that she doesn't think she has to show up herself. But she's just worried enough that she's on her way to where she and Peter really hid Mom."

"Well, obviously, the capital is Mars now," stammered Kenani. "They call it Barsoom these days, isn't that hilarious?"

"I said it looked like she was on her way to Earth, but really, there're a lot of worlds between here and there. You don't know which one it really is?"

Kenani said nothing, but he was pale and just shook his head.

Toby shrugged. "I think you do—after all, you've been part of

Peter's inner circle from the start. If Peter and Evayne never actually moved her, then she's where she had become accustomed to wintering over. I'm pretty sure I know where Evie's going. I want you to send this message to Peter:

"Tell him Evie's threatening to kill our mother, and tell him I have a better idea. Tell him I'll meet him and we can work that out."

"Meet him where?"

"Just say I've gone to finish the job I started."

He nodded politely to Kenani, then (still stung by Kenani's comment about servants) picked up his own chair and carried it to a nearby table. He clapped Jaysir on the shoulder, nodded to Shylif, and together with their officers in tow, left Nathan Kenani sitting with his forgotten breakfast.

"I CAN'T BELIEVE IT," said Jaysir a few days later. "*This* is the most heavily defended place in the whole lockstep? I never even heard of it!"

Toby smiled sadly at the irregular, faintly starlit shape that they could just barely make out a few kilometers from the ship. "You know what they say," he said. "Some are born great, some achieve greatness, and some have greatness thrust upon 'em. Everything important about *that* thing was thrust upon it.

"Welcome to Rockette."

Jaysir, Shylif and Toby hung weightless in front of a large curving window in the officers' lounge of Toby's ship. They were alone for now, as the crew bustled about reviving the vessel's systems. Toby had chosen the fleet's fastest courier vessel, and then they'd stripped it of its armor and weapons, sawed off and discarded the cargo container, even thrown out most of the furniture. With extra boosters bolted on, the fusion engine could edge them up to an impressive ten percent light speed. Even if Evayne were throwing her own furniture out the window, she hadn't taken a particularly fast ship and had only the fuel she'd left Thisbe with. Peter had to come all the way from Barsoom, after a delay because of the time it would have taken Kenani to relay Toby's message to him. Toby had the advantage over Evayne in speed, and the advantage over his brother in timing. So he'd gotten here before either of them—but just barely.

"Sir?" The captain had appeared in the door of the lounge. "They can destroy us, sir, if they want to. We have no defenses."

Toby smiled at her. "I know. This was never going to be an even match."

"But what is this place?" She ventured into the room. The woman was as intimidated by Toby as was the rest of her crew, but at least she wasn't a fanatical Toby worshiper: she was worried about the safety of her people. "Sir, I've been in the lockstep navy for twenty years and I never heard so much as a rumor that this . . . this *fortress*"—she nodded at the window—"existed."

"I expect if you looked it up, you'd find that Rockette was private property," said Toby. "Owned by my family. And I doubt there's a single human being manning those lasers and ships." They were invisible to the naked eye, but radar had revealed thousands of them, as well as mines and missiles, forming a cloud around Rockette far larger than the comet itself. "Rockette's important to the McGonigals. That's all I can tell you right now. But tell your men they're safe. None of that firepower is directed at us."

"Very good, sir." She bowed in midair.

"Could you get a boat ready? My brother's arriving soon and I want to meet him on the comet."

"Yes, sir!" She flew gracefully out of the room.

"Hmm." Jaysir scratched his head. "None of it directed at us? Yeah, I kinda think it's *all* aimed at us. And anybody who finds out this place exists."

Shylif was taking it all in calmly; after Sebastine Coley's trial and punishment, nothing seemed to faze him. "But Jay, you yourself said we'd be safe."

"Yeah, and you believed me? How long have you known me, Shy?"

Toby grinned at them, but he was hugely anxious. He'd made a guess on Thisbe about why he was able to override Evayne's commands to the lockstep systems. Jay agreed that he'd guessed rightly, and now as their little courier ship had approached Rockette, Toby had issued a command to its defenses to stand down. If his guess was wrong, then yes, they really could be blasted out of the sky at any moment.

Even if it was right, he was safe only while it was just him and Peter at Rockette. When Evayne arrived in a few days, he'd be helpless.

He might be heading into a tearful reunion with his siblings—or an interrogation. Knowing them as he did, Toby suspected this meeting would be a bit of both.

"Tell me again," he said to Jaysir, "why this is going to work?"

The maker shrugged. "I never said it would."

"Yes, but—"

Jaysir tilted his head from side to side, noncommittal. "The McGonigal security system is a black box. People have been poking at it from outside for thousands of years, but beyond a certain point, we just don't know. Your mom built well."

"Yeah." Toby let out a long, ragged sigh. "Thanks. Can I have a minute or two alone before I . . . ?"

"Oh, sure." Jaysir pulled Shylif toward the door. "You know I'd say good luck, but that would just be stupid. How about, don't get 'em any madder at you than they already are?"

"Great. I'll remember that."

They all laughed, and the other two left.

So there it was: the little comet he'd been on his way to when he got lost, fourteen thousand years ago. It didn't look like they'd built much on its surface, which was still painted crimson by radiation-baked organics. Those took millions of years to build up; in its tiny gravity field, he was sure he could find two little stones balanced precariously atop one another somewhere, that had been balancing that way since before the time of the dinosaurs. Next to the inhuman aeons that passed between a pebble wobbling and falling on Rockette, all the events of the last fourteen millennia were nothing. As far as Rockette was concerned, Toby wasn't arriving late at all.

He shook his head and turned away.

Nobody spoke to him on his way to the little inflatable lifeboat, and he made eye contact with no one. He felt like an intruder; they were well rid of him. Surely if Halen had been here, he would have organized banners and speeches and a photo op, and would have demanded of everyone present that they swear some weird blood oath or brand themselves to mark the occasion. That was the sort of thing you did with living gods. Toby was far happier sneaking out.

In the red light of a tiny utilitarian airlock he let a suit build itself onto him, as he had so many times before. Doing his checks and cycling through the airlock made him feel much better because the familiar chore reminded him of days—not so long ago, for him—when he'd cycled himself through Sedna's airlocks to attend to some minor repair problem on the little world's surface. Funny thing was, he'd always grumbled about leaving Consensus to do those chores. As he settled into the ship's little lander, he found himself smiling, just a little.

The next few minutes passed in silence, too, save for the occasional radioed flight plan update from the ship's bridge. He acknowledged with a terse yes or no and kept his eyes on the approaching comet, where a landing field was now lit in pinpricks of light. When he did set down, nobody human was waiting for him, only a few bots that directed him into a deep slot in Rockette's regolith. Down there was another airlock.

He never remembered, later, going through that lock, nor could he recall removing his suit or sailing down the long, dark passages into the heart of the comet. Toby was running on automatic, absolutely sure of what he was going to find here but his thoughts shocked silent by what it would mean.

As he'd expected, all the passages led to one chamber, a spherical room in the most protected heart of the comet. There was nothing ceremonial or even comfortable here, only coils of frost-covered hose, tangles of faintly humming machinery, and, tethered in the very middle of the space by wires and cables and pipes like the kernel of a seed, a single closed cicada bed.

Toby drifted up to it and, after a momentary hesitation, put out his hand to rub the frost from the top part of the canopy.

"Hi, Mom," he said.

TOBY COULD TELL IT was Peter in the doorway because of the way he moved. Forty years had bulked him up and slowed him down a little, but Toby could have picked him out of a crowd even if he'd been facing the other way.

That bullet head, though; it still threw him. "You look good," Toby called, his heart meanwhile threatening to go off the rails. "Shame about the hair, though."

The Chairman was accompanied by some milbots, mostly big human-shaped types with guns. "You know I thought about doing that," said Toby, pointing to them. "I guess if I didn't know it was really you, I might take precautions."

"Yeah, well I *don't* know who you are," said the Chairman. He started to say something more but stopped when he saw the status indicators on the cicada bed. He swore and moved down with surprising agility for (Toby tried not to think it) an old guy. Placing both hands on the bed's canopy, while his bots encircled Toby, he swore again and then commanded it, "Shut down! Go back to sleep."

The indicators didn't change. "That's interesting," said Toby. So his guess had been right; the tightness in all his muscles loosened just a bit.

"I found out about this on Thisbe," he said, "when Evie tried to block my commands in the system. Turned out she couldn't. I wondered whether it'd work the same with you. I guess it does.

"Bots! Stand down!"

As one, Peter's military bots folded in on themselves and went still.

Peter whirled, gasping. He grappled a pistol out of the closed fist of one of his guards and pointed it at Toby. He didn't look like Peter now, just like a hostile older man with a gun. All Toby's bluster evaporated. "You—" Peter looked from Toby to the bed and back again. "You're waking her up!"

Despite the gun pointed at him, Toby told himself, he had to go ahead with what he'd planned. "Yes," he said, "and you can't change that. She's a few hours away still, but she'll be back before Evie arrives. Which means, little brother, that you have to make a choice."

Peter's eyes were wide. "What—"

"See, I'm not armed. I wasn't about to mess up Mom's bedroom with a gun battle. That means you've got me right where you want me. You can kill me before she wakes up. But you can't stop Mom from waking . . . and you alone don't have the power to put her to sleep again. Do you?"

Warily, Peter grabbed a handhold on the cicada bed and settled himself opposite Toby. "Evie told you about the share system?"

Toby shook his head. "Evie didn't tell me anything." He didn't try to disguise the disappointment in his voice. "She's become rather good at following orders." Now the anger was slipping out. "Is that her, or did you twist her that way?"

Peter didn't say anything, but the pistol was still pointed at Toby.

"You know, when I found out what I could do, I figured Mom had given me a superuser account on the corporate system. It made all kinds of sense, but the question was, did you guys have the same privileges? You must—unless . . . she didn't entirely trust you."

"We had our disagreements," said Peter. "But you were out of the picture."

"So if she was the superuser, holding the administrator's account to the whole lockstep system, then you two might just have ordinary user's privileges. And if she didn't like how you were scheduling worlds in the lockstep, she could block you, or cancel your actions entirely.

"But that's not how the system works, is it?"

Peter had been staring at Toby with a kind of fascination; now he shook himself and seemed to snap to attention. "Why does it matter?" he said. "Evie caught enough of your people on Thisbe to learn what you're up to. It's the whole messiah thing, just like we foresaw."

This time it was Toby who started to object and Peter who overrode him: "Come on! They love you there! You came down from the sky and promised to reset their frequency, and last I heard, you were building a nice little army to storm Destrier." He sneered. "Don't get high and mighty about family stuff now, Toby."

In that moment, Toby knew they were brothers again—even if Peter wanted to kill him, he'd just acknowledged who Toby was. As when Evie had done it, it made all the difference. Suddenly all the armies, lockstep bots and expectations of the outside world were irrelevant; the universe had closed down to just him and Peter. Him and his brother, fighting.

In that case, he knew what to say next, like he usually did with Peter. "If I was really playing the messiah card, I'd have brought my army here, wouldn't I? But I didn't. I wanted to talk to you."

He could see that this had hit home, because the pistol finally wavered. Because this was Peter, though, and because they'd argued their whole lives, he couldn't resist adding, "And who set up the whole messiah thing, anyway?" He matched Peter's glare. "It's your script, Pete. You guys jammed it into my hands, and that whole damned planet wanted—demanded!—that I follow it.

"Only I'm not going to do it, because the messiah plan is a red herring, isn't it? You were never *afraid* I'd try it if I came back. You were counting on it."

"The religion . . ." Peter's lips thinned. "That was Evie's department."

"But it had a purpose, didn't it? Over and above keeping people in line, I mean. The prophecy's a honey trap for would-be conquerors. I hear it's worked pretty well. And me, well"—Toby spread his arms—"of course I'd run back to wake Mom if I returned. The second I tried, all the people whose loyalty to you might be shaky, and everybody who'd been plotting behind your back, they'd all jump on my side. They'd all be exposed. We'd troop on over to Destrier, and then you'd crush us all there.

"Pete, that's just so . . . so Consensus." Toby shook his head in disgust. "And vicious. And what I could never figure out was, why in hell would you be so vicious to me? How could I ever have threatened this grand empire you've built? If I came back, don't you think I'd want to celebrate it with you?"

Peter's eyes shifted, ever so slightly, but he wasn't meeting Toby's gaze anymore.

"Even if you thought I'd disapprove, what would it matter? My disapproval wasn't going to topple your empire. It was a puzzle with no answer. Peter, you tried to have me *killed*."

"Shut down," Peter McGonigal said to their mother's cicada bed. Its lights stayed green.

"You can still shoot me, by the way." Toby waved at the gun in Peter's hand. "At least now I know why. Cicada Corp's systems recognize four shareholders, right? You, me, Evie, and Mom. We don't own the same *number* of shares, though. You and Evie each have one. Mom has two—and so do I."

"I couldn't believe it when she told me," said Peter. "She'd given you two—you! You'd been gone for years. And she kept two for herself, just to keep Evie and me in line."

"Yeah, and when that got too inconvenient for you, you guys trapped her in here and voted her to sleep. Permanently. Except you didn't kill her."

"No." Peter reared back, outraged at the idea. "We wouldn't—"

"But you'd kill me."

"That's—"

"Different? *Why?*"

That one question hung in the air, while silence stretched between them. Finally, and to Toby's surprise, Peter jammed the pistol into his belt and crossed his arms. "You really don't know?" he asked skeptically.

Slowly, Toby shook his head. They remained that way, in a standoff, for a long minute. Finally, Toby said, "It had to be something that happened before I left. I've been thinking about that. I don't think it was anything I did on Sedna. So earlier . . .

"Guess what," he said suddenly. "I've got backups of Consensus in my glasses. I was going through them the other day, and I found something. You might want to see it. You've got implants, I assume?" Guardedly, Peter nodded. "Then let me share it with you." Slowly, in case Peter went for his gun again, Toby reached up to tap his glasses awake. He uttered several quiet commands, and a virtual environment blossomed around himself and his brother.

Peter gasped, then stared. *"That?"*

"The very first thing I did in Consensus," said Toby. "I showed it to you that first time we went in together. Our house."

It was the house Toby had grown up in, where Maria Teresa had died trying to protect Peter; the place they had never returned to as a family after the kidnapping. Toby had built this virtual copy as a healing exercise for himself, but he'd shown it to Peter and issued a challenge: *Figure out a way to prevent what happened here from ever happening again.* Build a better world.

Peter reached out, very slowly, and took the handles of the model to rotate it. He zoomed them in and suddenly he and Toby were inside, hovering above the landing where Maria Teresa had died. Peter stared at the tiled floor for a while. Then he said, almost inaudibly, "I could hear them talking."

Toby waited. Haltingly, his brother said, "There was this spot near the back of the room where the kidnappers were keeping me. There was an air vent in the floor, and if I put my ear to it, sometimes I could hear them. It was too faint for me to make out what they were saying, but I knew the voices."

Now he looked up at Toby. "One day, after I'd been there for, oh it must have been a couple of weeks, I put my ear down there and heard them talking to somebody else who was there. I could feel the footsteps through the floor, and I heard his voice.

"It was Father."

Toby blinked, and suddenly his thoughts were sliding all over, trying to catch each other. "What?"

"Our. Father." Peter had come around the cicada bed and was closing in on Toby, his eyes wide. "Our father was there. He was part of it. It might even have been him who let them in—him who killed Maria Teresa—"

The words came out in a rush now. "Why would they need to

kill her? They could have tied her up, they were wearing masks so she wouldn't have seen their faces and I didn't see them kill her, I didn't even know about it until after. But if she'd caught *him* helping, if he'd been seen, then he couldn't let her live, could he? It would have ruined everything."

Toby was too horrified to speak. He wiped away the virtual model of the house, and so it was just him and his brother, eye to eye in the cold machine space of the chamber. "But . . . why . . . ?"

"Why?" Peter's brows crunched into a sarcastic expression; he'd made that as a boy, but it had never drawn so many wrinkles with it in the old days. "Why? *Sedna.*

"The kidnapping is what convinced Mom to leave Earth. Same with nearly everybody else who came. The whole incident galvanized an entire movement, remember? Maybe you don't. Money came in from everywhere to pay my ransom, and afterward, it hung around, because suddenly Dad had a plan. He went back to all the people who'd helped and told them, 'Look, there's something better we can do with this money. We can't trust Earth anymore, either the trillionaires or the poor. We've got to get out.' *My* disappearance, *my* being tied up in that room, *my* seeing them killed in front of me and learning about Maria Teresa—all that was *just part of the plan.*"

He was trembling now and had shed all the years that separated them. He was just Peter now, just Toby's little brother.

"And I knew it," he said. "I knew it every step of the way—from when we left Earth to setting up the colony, to after you abandoned us to when he did, too—"

"I never abandoned you," objected Toby.

"You two were close, you and Dad. After you disappeared, all I could think was, 'He's snuck back to Earth, to make way for Dad's return. Where they'll be trillionaires with the Sedna wealth . . .' Because, well, you were always the one who measured up. I was damaged goods after the kidnapping, a bad reminder, and anyway, if I hadn't been expendable to begin with he'd never have used me for it."

"Wait, what are you trying to . . . you think I knew about this? You think Dad *told* me?"

Peter lowered his head, looking up past his brows at Toby. "You're saying he didn't?"

"I . . ." There'd been that conversation on the rooftop . . . Peter was beginning to smile; he was taking Toby's hesitation as a yes, so Toby said, "There was something!" He recounted that conversation and their father's words to him. *I'm going to do something to help change things, and it could get rough for us for a while. You may not understand everything that's happening.*

"That's it," he finished.

"That's it?" Peter was glaring at him. Toby stared him down.

"The only reason you think I knew is that I disappeared, and because . . ." He wanted to deny Peter's other assertion, but he couldn't. "Maybe he did favor me. I was the eldest. But that didn't mean he confided in me. Do you really think I would have kept it together if he'd told me? Maybe I was the oldest, but he didn't spend any more time with me than he did with you and Evie. Meaning, almost none. You were the ones I knew. He was my dad, he was important, but my life revolved around you guys!

"Look, Pete, you've got the tug I left Sedna in. Your forensics people have to have gone over it. You know it really was adrift for fourteen thousand years. You know what happened to knock it out of commission. You may have spent the past forty years thinking I abandoned you, but you *know* now that I didn't. It was an accident. I got lost. And now I'm home."

"And I knew nothing about . . . what you just told me."

It was unbelievable, horrible, couldn't be true—but even as Toby was thinking these things, his imagination was fitting it all together. His awakening on Lowdown, the order from the Chairman, and all his discoveries about the locksteps and the Toby cult and the Guides. They all spun in his mind, a whirlpool with its center at that single moment in the past, when Peter crouched on the floor of his cell listening at a grate.

"This . . . all of this . . . you've been running ever since." And not just Peter, but Carter McGonigal, too—fleeing from his crime on Earth and pulling his family and friends with him. Had Mom known, or suspected? She, too, jumping forward through time, each leap farther than the last. Telling everyone all the while that she was hunting for that moment when her lost Toby would return to her, when really she was trying to *get away* from something else, some knowledge she couldn't unlearn.

"Evayne . . . does she . . . ?"

Peter nodded. "I told her, oh, thirty years ago I guess. Long after you'd left. She never really came to terms with it, I think."

Toby hung his head. Everything had changed, and he wasn't ever going to get back what he'd just lost.

"Sorry, Toby," said Peter. "It's funny—you know there was a day, long time ago now, when I suddenly realized you weren't my older brother anymore. That I was the older one. I'm older than Dad now, did you know that? Older than Mom, too. The family's on my shoulders now. I'm not yours to command."

It came to Toby then that Peter really had intended to kill him on Lowdown, and just now when he'd brought out that vicious looking little pistol, Toby had been within seconds of dying. A wash of adrenaline hit him, and he hid his suddenly shaking hands behind his back.

He tried to pull himself together. For a moment he'd forgotten why he'd come here; he was adrift and at the mercy of the Chairman. Then his gaze caught the green telltales of their mother's cicada bed, and he clutched at the purpose and idea that had brought him here.

He looked up at Peter again, all his cockiness gone. "I get it. And you're right. By the time I got to Thisbe I thought I knew what was going on. I was the big brother, come back to set you guys right." He laughed humorlessly at himself. "Yeah, that was totally wrong, wasn't it?"

Peter nodded. "You see, things have changed. You'll understand why later, but right now, Toby, you have to shut Mom's bed down again. Put her back to sleep."

Toby sucked in a deep breath, looked him in the eye, and said, "No."

Peter blinked and started to speak, but Toby said, "This part of it I understand perfectly. You and Evie have locked yourselves and the locksteps into a pattern you can't get out of. You're riding a whirlwind that's roaring into the future, and you think you have to *steer* it. You think you can play Consensus with seventy thousand worlds—actually, you think you *have* to. Evie's terrified that it'll all fall apart if you don't keep your hands on the wheel. So are you, right?"

Peter shook his head. "You don't understand—the politics, the—"

"Oh, I do understand. You've run off a cliff and as long as your legs keep pedaling, you're going to stay up. The instant you stop, you fall. But it's not the lockstep that'll collapse, is it? You've just told me . . . about Dad," Toby coughed and had to stop for a second. "You have to keep running or *that* is going to catch up to you. But you don't need to keep pulling the lockstep along with you."

"You don't get it, we built it like a machine, Evie and me. The Toby cult, the whole Emperor of Time crap, the Guides, the messaging to the fast worlds, how we handle immigration . . . It's a system, Toby. You can't break it. *You* can't return, or the whole thing falls apart. Mom can't wake up, or the same thing happens—"

"Isn't it really that you're afraid we'd outvote you? 'Cause, you know, we will."

Peter fell silent. Toby floated over to rest his hand on the warming cicada bed. "We're back to arguing over how many possibilities there are. You're saying there're only two: the status quo you and Evie spent so many years building, or a catastrophic collapse. But you know that's not true."

The Chairman of Cicada Corp watched Toby warily, saying nothing.

"Mom'll be awake in a few hours," said Toby. "Then we're going to wait for Evie to arrive. And then . . . the shareholders of Cicada Corp are going to hold a vote."

He raised his hand. "All in favor of issuing one share per cicada bed user, say aye. All opposed . . ."

Peter still said nothing. Toby shrugged. "There're four of us, and six shares. One vote per share. Mom built the system, she knows how to make the necessary changes. Was this what she was proposing when you guys tricked her into this last sleep? Don't answer that, I don't want to know. It doesn't matter anyway. The fact is, you and Evie have a chance to redeem yourselves now. We can make the vote unanimous."

"One vote per bed . . ." Peter was practically strangling on the words. "That'd be democracy!"

"Yeah. Worst system of government except for all the others, right? But it's not like the people of 360 don't know how to handle it. They're mostly free anyway. I mean I saw how the government on Thisbe handles things. Peter, *they* have built the world you and I tried to build with Consensus. You can fool yourself into thinking you've been the guiding hand, but really, it was them, them all along." He thought of Corva's fierce passion, and even her brother's determination to right the wrongs of the world. They weren't passive subjects of Peter McGonigal. They didn't need him.

"The only thing standing in their way now is Cicada Corp and our stranglehold on the lockstep frequencies. We are going to give it up—you, me, Mom, and Evie. Take our hands off the wheel and watch the ship steer itself."

Bravado and determination had kept Toby going this far; he'd said his piece, done what he came to do. Now that he had, he found he was trembling, practically fainting. It was all catching up to him.

His voice cracking with exhaustion and sorrow, he held out his hand to his brother and said, "Peter, I just don't want to run anymore.

"And I don't think you do, either."

| Twenty-one |

"HEY, TOBY, OVER HERE!"

He looked up from the shard of blue pottery he'd dug out of the dirt. Sol was standing framed by two pillars that once might have been straight but had been sculpted by the wind for aeons, until now they looked like twisted tree trunks.

Miranda's head popped up from below Sol's feet. "You really should see this," she shouted. "I think it's an intact chamber!"

Toby dropped the potsherd and picked his way through a landscape of tumbled stone blocks and irregular red earth. He had to climb around a fissure that separated him from his two friends, and he momentarily stood higher than Sol's head. From here he could see down the long slope behind the twin pillars, to where irregularly joined pools of water sketched the direction of an ancient canal. Hazy distance veiled the rise of other plateaus—green on their lower slopes, Martian red on the summits where ruin after ruin teased at the sky. Noctis Labyrinthus, this region was called—the Maze of Night—and it was one of the most ancient settled parts of Mars. Barsoom, as it was called now.

Miranda stood up, dusting herself off. If Toby had taken off his glasses, he'd have seen her as she really was: a gangly tour guide robot like the one pretending to be Sol. Through his interface, he could pretend they were real people. He'd given these bodies the personalities of his game characters but let this one retain the tour bot's database of historical data. So it wasn't surprising when Miranda said, "Six different cultures built here. This whole hill is a rubble pile, who knows what's at the bottom?"

She knelt again. "I think we might be able to squeeze in there. There's a tiled floor, it might date from the second Thark Flowering."

Toby wasn't listening. His fingers had strayed out to stroke the side of one of the pillars. It was so old it had lost all sign of being artificial. It reminded him of Stonehenge—and then, uncomfortably, of the grand avenue on Destrier. He snatched back his hand.

"It's going to take awhile," he said with a sad smile, "to catch up."

If Miranda and Sol had been human, they might have caught his irony and laughed, or expressed some sympathy. As it was they just smiled and nodded.

Toby knelt to look through the gap Miranda had found. It was dark in there. He doubted he could have fit through, but it would have been easy for Orpheus.

He stood up again, gazing out at the dying canals.

At least this landscape didn't change in an eyeblink, like Earth's did. Toby had been on Barsoom for six months now; for three before that, he'd lived in a lockstep fortress in the Amazonian uplands of what had once been Brazil. He'd wanted to be around green and real sunlight, but every thirty days, the landscape hiccuped and changed completely. New trees, a new tributary to the river below the fortress, or a new town full of people who barely remembered those whom he'd gotten to know over the past weeks. He'd hated it there, and Mom convinced him to come back to Mars.

Barsoom was practically homey compared to the rest of the solar system. Mercury didn't even exist anymore; it had been eaten and its constituent matter spread out to form a vast Dyson cloud that gathered sunlight to power starship launchers and other less comprehensible machines for the posthumans who'd taken over much of the place. Venus was fully terraformed now, a world of shallow oceans that forbade any locksteps from settling there.

Space itself was crowded with artificial worlds, some inhabited, many ruined and silent.

Considering the godlike powers possessed by the posthumans, Toby had been a bit surprised that humans—or conventional life-forms of any kind—still existed. When he'd expressed this to Peter, his brother had just laughed. "Technology can speed up evolution, but it can't do anything to give it a direction. What these AIs and robot cultures keep forgetting is that purpose comes from vulnerability. Give people the power of the gods, and they'll eventually run down like wind-up toys for lack of reasons to go on. It's happened around here so many times that the posthumans finally figured out that they need us. We're kind of the bottom-feeders of their ecosystem—a necessary evil. Humans are optimized to care about things, and the posthumans feed off our passions. Without us, they just speed-evolve into useless lumps. The solar system's crowded with those.

"It's not a flattering role to have in the grand scheme of things," he'd added with a shrug, "but it's a living."

Peter could always make Toby smile. He'd developed a hard crust of cynicism, decades of learning and incident having weathered his heart like the wind had done to these pillars; yet he was still Peter. It was as if the brother Toby had known was a bright light that still managed to shine through all the brambles and encrustations time had wrapped around it. Even the revelation about Dad.

It was shocking how little Peter remembered of his childhood with Toby and Evayne—even though that time had made him who he was. When the melancholy of time began to coil around Toby's soul, he only had to spend ten minutes with Peter for it to entirely lift.

It was a good thing Toby had discovered his brother in the Chairman, because unexpectedly, he'd lost his own childhood when Peter told him about their father's part in the kidnapping. He still didn't believe it—not all the time, anyway. He would struggle with that, he knew, for years.

He knelt again next to the little cave entrance and was seriously considering squirming in there when a message tone pinged in his ear. "Toby," he answered curtly.

"Where'd you go?" It was Mom—Cassandra, as she liked to be called now. "I looked all over the grounds!"

"Sorry, I was . . . restless. I'm just doing a little exploring."

"Hmmph." He could hear the distaste in her voice. Cassandra couldn't understand Toby's interest in the ocean of time that separated them from their previous lives. Maybe it was because she'd had practice skipping forward before Peter and Evayne had locked her away. She had deliberately turned her back on everything she'd lost. "Well, the last of the delegates is here. There're some from that world where you argued with Evayne. Thought you might want to know."

"Ah! Thanks. I'll be right there."

He didn't dare hope. Thisbe had been one of the last holdouts in Peter's drive to create a lockstep parliament. The cult of Toby was raging there—in various flavors, he'd heard, who fought one another in the streets over minor points of doctrine. Halen Keishion was a major leader in one of those factions, and the rumor was he was trying to set up his own lockstep. Toby had sent Jaysir back to try to locate Corva, but try as the makers might, they'd so far been unable to uncover any information about her whereabouts.

The cults were entirely focused on Destrier. Cassandra and Toby had found it surprisingly easy to adopt new identities on Barsoom, with easy access to Peter. He supposed it was inconceivable to the cultists that Cassandra might not have been in her imitation Taj Mahal on Destrier all these millennia—and therefore inconceivable that she might have been quietly awakened somewhere else, to exit the historical stage into an ordinary life.

One result was that there were few security milbots monitoring his progress through the ruins. Toby had felt free to come here almost unaccompanied. He bounded back to the Martian aircar, ducking under its cartoonishly big lift fans, forgetting Miranda and Sol. They quietly dissolved back into tourist bots as the aircar whined into life.

"Oh, and your sister's here, too," added Cassandra as two military bots ducked under the closing clamshell doors of the aircar to sit behind Toby. He didn't miss the chilly sound in his mother's voice; she and Evayne were still not talking.

"Thanks." His mother rang off, and Toby pensively watched the ruined palaces of Noctis dwindle below him. He tilted the aircar east, toward Valles Marineris and the triple cities of Ius, Calydon, and Louros. Home was Peter's sumptuous palace on the north slope of Ius Chasma, but it was in Calydon Fossae that all the action was happening.

As he approached the vast canyon complex, he could see aircraft buzzing over the city like a cloud of midges. Delegates were arriving literally by the boatload, from the farthest reaches of the lockstep. They were here to hammer out a lockstep-wide scheduling policy now that Peter and Evayne had made their one-bed, one-share public ownership offer in the lockstep monopoly. Calydon's minareted streets were crowded with democrats, autocrats and cybercrats, monarchists, panarchists, and demarchists. All were bravely stepping into realtime to debate and deliberate for as long as it took to come up with the new lockstep government. It might take months, or years—but in lockstep time, it would all be over by next turn.

The chaos made it easy for Toby and his mother to come and go. Peter's palace was overrun with middle-aged women and young men anyway, and everybody was distracted by the new governmental proposal. Toby was posing as Dickson Mu, a delegate from Eris. Cassandra wasn't acting at all like the Holy Mother was supposed to, so nobody suspected her.

Still . . . He tapped his glasses and said, "Call Evayne." The little dancing icon signified that she was being hailed—and this went on for a long time—and then a window opened in his interface, and she was there.

"How are you?" she said in a clipped and guarded tone.

"Always talking on the phone, but never getting together," he said. "When are we going to have dinner?"

"Very funny," she said flatly. "You know how delicate things are."

"Actually, Evie, I don't. You had some chores you were going to do. Did you get to them?"

"Where do you think I've been the past forty-five years?"

"Oh!" He'd last spoken to her two months ago, lockstep time. "You're not serious. You haven't been—" He peered at her in the little window. She didn't *seem* older.

Evayne grimaced. "Six years, Toby. For me, it's been six years since the last time I spoke to you. Seven since we woke Mom."

He sucked in his breath. "Does she know?" Evayne shook her head. "Tell her! Evie, she's not going to punish you forever! Six *years*!" His heart sank at the thought. This wasn't at all like the evidence of time he'd seen in the ruins just now. There were different kinds of time, and that which separated you from your loved ones was the slowest. "Where were you?" he ventured.

"Tau Ceti. Sirius. Points in between. Peter can tell you—he provided the ship. We were doing almost fifty percent light speed back and forth—a new record, I think."

"And . . . ?"

"Our clients and partners are winding down the Toby myth. The Emperor of Time is no more. It's already been a couple of generations, realtime, since I left Sirius. Any new immigrants into 360 are going to be several generations out of our official endorsement of the myth. Pilgrimages to Destrier are going to dry up soon, and since the keepers of Mom's tomb live in realtime anyway, they'll probably have turned it into a tourist trap and theme park by now. Except for the holdouts actually in the lockstep, you're safe now."

He snorted. "There're billions of those. But thank you. Thank you so much, Evayne. I really was serious about dinner."

She just stared at him. Under the weight of that gaze, Toby suddenly felt acutely self-conscious. His last words echoed in his ears and those platitudes sounded so glib that he instantly regretted them. In that second he went from not knowing that he was feeling any emotion at all to realizing he was being flooded with grief and longing. "I mean"—to his astonishment his voice cracked—"I never meant to leave you. I'm sorry I left, and I want to see you. To catch up . . . on all those lost years." Tears were blurring the inside of his glasses.

When he blinked himself into seeing again, he realized that Evie was wiping her eyes, too. Time was when she'd come to him, when she'd bawled in his arms, a tangle of limbs and hair butting his chin. It was so recent, those moments almost seeming more real than this one and that little girl more real than his hard-bitten older woman— who had already regained her own composure and said, "I know, Toby. Yes, I'd like to have dinner with you. We'll talk soon."

She cut the connection, but her words rang in his head, echoes of unstated regret distracting him enough that the aircar took over the flying. He didn't come to himself again until he felt it touching down and realized they'd arrived in a courtyard in central Calydon.

He queried the location of the Thisbe delegation and was told they were settling in to a redbrick hotel a couple of kilometers down the avenue. Too close to fly to, too far for a quick walk, which meant he would have to take a leisurely one instead. That was okay, because it gave him a chance to explore the crowds and architecture of the city as he strolled. There were hints of Consensus style to it all, but Barsoom had its own history and layers of culture. It was unbelievably rich, as was the diversity on the street. Toby found himself spinning around now and then to stare at a person—or thing—that had just passed by him while he'd been ogling something else. Great fun.

As his footsteps approached the Thisbeans' hotel, though, they slowed even further. Eventually he came to a stop just outside its main entrance.

He'd tried looking up the names of the delegation, but they weren't listed yet. And anyway, here he was.

He took a deep breath, stepped forward—

"Sir!"

All the air shot out of him. Toby turned. "What?"

Four of the Lockstep palace guard were standing there, accompanied by a small army of bots. The woman at the head of this squad saluted and said, "The Chairman requests your presence."

"The Chairman? He can—" Toby stopped himself. These people had no idea who he was, and nobody defied the Chairman. It might be fun to try, but the momentary courage that had led him to take that step into the entrance of the hotel was gone now anyway. He shrugged.

"Sure, whatever. Where are we going?"

To the other side of town, it turned out. Here was the palace proper—the Palace, with a capital *P* and emphasis and fanfares. The place was designed to impress by people who'd studied thousands of years' worth of such architecture. Toby suspected a few posthuman minds had added their insights into human herd behavior; even just stepping out of an aircar onto one of the upper residence levels, he felt himself shrink a bit with awe. It wasn't just the scale, the majestic sweep of the colonnades, or the beauty of the frescoes. The way all the lines of wall and pillar wove together, the whole building seemed poised to pounce on him.

Yet all he had to do was glance over and notice that one of the fabulous pieces of wall art depicted the Emperor of Time embarking on his mystical journey into the future . . . and he just had to laugh. He thanked his escort and hurried on to meet his brother.

"Sorry to tear you away from your ruins, but Evie's hardly been home a day and the delegates already want a speech from her. It's a good thing she's rested."

Peter stood with his arms crossed in the center of a domed chamber that rivaled the nave of any cathedral from ancient Earth. He was surrounded by the latest in virtualizing technology, so that as Toby came beside him, the walls appeared to fly away and the ceiling lifted off, and they seemed to be standing out in the open. There was even a breeze sliding slowly along the tiers of the city's biggest and oldest amphitheater. He and Peter stood at one end of it, on stage with one other person. It was Evayne.

"They've come to see both of us," said Peter. He was in full dress uniform. "Don't worry about them seeing or overhearing us," he added. "My stage projection's a puppet; I could moon the crowd and the projectors would compensate and make it look like I'd bowed."

"And I'm invisible and inaudible," said Toby.

"Yes—but you're here. Evayne asked me to call you in. She insisted, actually."

Invisible and inaudible—but not to Evayne and Peter. Toby thought he could accept that.

"Of course Mom wouldn't come."

"Of course not," agreed Peter breezily. "Oh, here we go. She's about to start."

Evayne's dais stood just off center in the giant oval of the outside theater. She walked alone to her spot, dressed in a fabulous gown of ivory white with gold hems. Her hair was drawn up and tangled with diamonds. As she walked, the most glorious fanfare Toby had ever heard rose in swells. It clutched at his heart though he didn't even recognize the instruments, let alone the style: the music, like so much else here, echoed out of the well of unguessable time that, somehow, his brother and sister had mastered.

There were tears in his eyes when the music ended. By that time, Evayne stood in her place, gazing up at the multitude that thronged the ancient amphitheater's seats.

She began:

"How could we have known, my family and I, when we began this, that time in a lockstep runs backward? To us founders, and to the smallest and original parts of the empire, our colony between the stars is only forty years old. As far as the youngest and largest parts of the lockstep are concerned, it is so old as to be one with the foundations of the universe. Immovable. Eternal.

"I remember the day Peter and I realized what was happening. Overnight, sixteen minor worlds, little orbs no bigger than Sedna, had been colonized by settlers from Alpha Centauri. All declared their intention to join the lockstep. They were excited to do so. They'd been hearing stories about us for generations! Together, their population exceeded that of all the worlds we already had. Peter and I panicked."

"Ha," said Peter. "Look at that little smile she's giving there. She's reassuring them that she's joking. But it's true. We freaked."

"This," she continued, "is why the Guides were created. They were to test immigrants, both individual people and entire worlds, to see if they would enrich the lockstep or might tear it apart. In retrospect, this was a good idea. Over the years we've excluded whole populations that would have obliterated our culture, enslaved or killed many of our people, or subjected us all to one of several dead-ending posthuman 'uplifts.'"

"Of course, she's not saying the obvious here," Peter pointed out.

The obvious was that the official state religion, Toby's cult, had also been engineered to stabilize incoming culture around conservative ideas. "Is she *going* to say it?" Toby asked.

Peter shook his head. "Maybe someday, but it's too touchy right now. Our own fault, of course."

"While centuries passed on the fast worlds, years went by for us," Evayne was saying. "*Only* years. How could we have imagined that there was such a thing as a 'lockstep civilization'? We'd been administering our little worlds for so short a time! This . . ." She paused and looked down, letting her shoulders drop. "This is where my brother Peter and I failed."

The amphitheater reverberated with sound—a roar of voices so broad that some might be cheering, some angry, it was impossible to tell. Peter laughed.

"To us, the lockstep was a tiny economic experiment we were making up as we went along! Our actions couldn't be so consequential that they would ring down the centuries. What we were building couldn't have a life of its own. It was just us back then, and we steered the ship because without us, it would have been rudderless. We failed to understand how time passes in a lockstep, and so we didn't notice when the ship became capable of steering itself.

"You no longer need us!" She raised her arms, appealing to the crowd, and again the sound swelled around her. When it died, she continued: "In the forty years of time that have passed in the lockstep, populations have moved in, but they've also moved out. Emigrants have taken our practices to other worlds and other locksteps, and honed and refined them over countless centuries. Our culture has touched those of other worlds again and again, like a hammer tapping a bell. Every thirty years another note, a reminder of who we are and how we live, resounding through the fast worlds. How could we have guessed that the echoes from the previous note would still be sounding when the next was rung? How could we know that its peal would grow and grow, amplified by time, until today the Guides have nothing to do—whole worlds of millions of people petition to join the lockstep, and they know more about how to live in 360 than we do!"

Again Peter laughed. "It's true. Kenani and the others were having a bit of a problem deciding how to tell us. But for a couple of years now, they haven't had much to do."

"The Guides, and our family's monopoly on the cicada beds, were necessary to stabilize our lockstep's culture and identity through its middle years," said Evayne. "But they're not necessary anymore. That is why you are here today. We began the lockstep and we have lived in it from the beginning, but you have lived with it longer! It's time you took the reins to lead us into the next era of lockstep time: the era of our full maturity as a civilization."

There was more—much more—but Evie was just embellishing and amplifying her themes. Toby and Peter watched, and listened to the changing murmur and roar of the crowd, and eventually, to thunderous applause, Evie finished and stalked majestically from the stage.

"She's gonna want a drink after that," said Peter.

Toby hardly knew what to say. "She . . . she really came around."

Peter shrugged. "She's had six years to accept the idea—and to preach the new way on the fast worlds." He tilted his head and tapped his nose mischievously. "Lockstep time, Toby. Get used to it."

He shook his head. "I'm . . . not sure I can."

Peter looked serious now. "I've been wondering about that. Actually, we all have. You scared Evie, dragging her so close to real-time on Thisbe. Didn't seem to scare *you,* though. And my people tell me you've developed a fascination with the fast worlds."

"Why wouldn't I? There's just so much out there!" Toby barked a laugh. "I mean, fourteen thousand years! Come on! I keep hearing about these amazing places, these incredible stories and histories. I want to see them all."

"Why don't you, then? Surely it's not *us* that's keeping you here?" Peter had crossed his arms again and now looked down his nose at Toby, becoming in that instant the elder friend rather than the little brother who'd shared Evie's speech.

Toby turned away. "I would," he admitted. "But you said it yourself: Lockstep time is tricky. If I step out of it for just a second . . ."

"You leave us all behind?" Peter shrugged. "You're right, you can't step in or out of lockstep time without damage. Still, if you want to see the universe . . . you *can* return. Just be willing to pay the price.

"Hell, maybe you *should* go. You could come back when you're older than me again and kick my ass!" He laughed richly and turned to go.

"I've got work," he said as he crossed the marble floor, but then he seemed to remember something and looked back. "Oh, by the way. Package for you. It's in my study."

With that he disappeared into a cloud of bots and human advisers who had converged on him from various directions. In a babel of conversation, he left the airy chamber.

Toby stared after him, mind blank; then he shook his head and put his glasses on. He needed the online maps to find his way around here.

Peter's study was two levels down and half a kilometer away, through a maze of corridors and chambers. There were guards and attendants everywhere, but they all smiled and waved Toby through. More than a few of them must have guessed who he was, but apparently Peter didn't employ fanatics. (Or maybe they just stopped being fanatics after knowing a real-life McGonigal for a while.)

He was distractedly focused on the map when he came around the last corner, and he'd passed so many people that at first he took no notice of two more. They were leaning on the gold wall next to the door to Peter's study, and it was finally their casual (and utterly out of place) stances that made Toby look up.

"Shy! Jay!"

Jaysir laughed. "You'd have walked right by us. What're yer watchin', Toby?"

"Just lost. But I guess this is the right place." He didn't know whether to shake hands or what, but Sheilif stepped into his hesitation and hugged him. Jay, as usual, just stood back grinning.

"When did you get in?"

"We hitched a ride with the Thisbe delegation," said Jay. "No, no, we didn't stow away! They gave us a cabin. Even a bed for Shadoweye."

Toby nodded but impatiently went on. "Did you find her? Is she here?"

Jaysir and Sheilif exchanged a glance. "We didn't exactly . . . find her," said Jay. "It's complicated. Why don't you take a look?" He nodded at Peter's study. Uncertain, Toby frowned at them and opened the door.

Like the room where he'd watched Evie's speech, the study was round, but much homier. It was lined in imported wood and paneled with bookcases. The carpet was deep green, featuring a compass rose in gold; north pointed to a single vast desk with an incongruous twentieth-century banker's lamp and blotter on it. Toby hadn't been here before, so it took him a moment to absorb the details—red leather armchairs, liquor cabinet—and then actually see what couldn't be a normal fixture of the place.

A small cicada bed, the kind used for babies or pets, stood next to a large Martian globe. A small shape was curled up inside it.

Toby took a hesitant step, then another, then one of those Martian bounds that could cover three meters. He flung open the bed's canopy and gathered Orpheus into his arms. Jay and Shy had followed him into the room, but Toby had all but forgotten them now.

"You—you're . . ." The denner was asleep, or unconscious, and his fur felt very, very cold. Toby fell into one of the armchairs, wrapping himself around his friend and trying to will his own body heat into him.

Thrum, thrum . . . There was the familiar vibration, coming from deep inside his own body. He hadn't felt it in a long time; he'd been using McGonigal beds to winter over since leaving Thisbe. He felt the strength of that signal building, though, like a call to Orpheus. *I am here, I am here,* it said.

Faintly, he felt an answering tremor through his fingers.

"He wouldn't wake up," someone said.

Toby closed his eyes. That hadn't been Shylif or Jay.

"We tried, but he wouldn't answer our call. Even after we healed his wounds, he dove deep, to places we couldn't follow. . . ."

Through tears, he looked up at Corva. She stood in a small doorway opposite the one he'd come in. Wrecks sat at her feet, his tail curled around his paws. "You disappeared," she went on. "I didn't know if your sister had killed you, or if you were on your way to Destrier like Halen said . . ."

Toby stood, shooting an accusing glance at Jaysir. "You said you didn't find her!"

The maker shrugged. "We didn't. She found us." Both he and Shylif were grinning shamelessly.

Toby went to her. He couldn't let go of Orpheus, whose purr was strengthening, but he lowered his face to Corva's. They stayed close in that way for long moments, then kissed. "What happened?"

Her mouth formed a rueful line. "I was *traded*. Me, in return for Thisbe being allowed to send a delegation to this conference thing." She wrapped her arms around him and put her head on his chest. He felt Wrecks doing a curling walk around his ankles.

"That's just so Peter," mused Toby; but he wasn't going to complain this time.

They stood that way for so long that Shylif eventually coughed discreetly, and Jaysir said, "We're . . . gonna be outside. If, you know, you need us."

Toby was intently examining Corva's face. Was she older? She seemed to guess what he was doing, because she said, "I've been back on lockstep time since you reset Thisbe's frequency. What time you and I have lost . . . well, we've lost the same amount, unless you've been down to realtime again . . . ?" He shook his head.

Orpheus purred in the warm space between her and Toby. She said, "What now? Are you the head the family? Are you really going to Destrier to wake your mother, like all the myths and stories say?"

He laughed. "She's wide awake and eating cupcakes about three rooms over." Corva blinked at him surprise. "Long story. But no, I'm not the head of the family. Never wanted to be. And I don't want to the Emperor of Time, either."

Corva gently disengaged herself. "But you are that," she said.

He gave a short laugh. "Huh?" Corva Keishion was the last person he would have expected to say such a thing.

She smiled at his discomfort. "No, really. You were supposed to make time come to an end, right? Well, you did—the old kind of time where the past pushes us into the future and farther and farther away from perfection. But remember, there's another kind of time, where the past doesn't push; one where the future invites us onward. Where it's not destiny that drives us but hope. Hope and surprise."

She stepped forward again. "You," she said teasingly, "were a surprise."

He drew her over to one of the armchairs and they sat together; it was a tight fit. "If you say so," he said. "I hope you're not too serious about it. Poor Evie's running around to all the fast worlds trying to squash the family myths. I wouldn't want to add one more for her to chase down."

It was on the fast worlds where the McGonigal stories had grown; it was ironic that it was in the lockstep that they would probably take the longest to die. They'd probably hang around for generations, long after the McGonigals were gone.

She saw his expression and said, "I really was just joking. Sorta. I don't know."

He nodded and sighed. "The only way I can live here is in disguise. Same with Mom. Neither of us is going to be able to have a normal life anywhere near Peter and Evayne. We can sneak around right now because of all the conference chaos, but that'll end. Then the cultists will start watching again."

"We can go away," she suggested.

"We?" He looked at her closely. "Do you really mean that?"

She shrugged awkwardly, not meeting his eyes.

"But what about your family? You worked so hard to return to them—"

"—And I didn't," she said, looking down. "I never did. I knew it the instant I saw their faces that first day. When we got to my house. It was too late. I mean, they're still my family and I love them all, and I love the Halen I grew up with . . . but the change between us . . . it's, well, permanent. It doesn't matter now if I go away for a while. Different is different.

"And that's made me wonder now, is there anywhere I can be at home? Anywhere that time's not come unslipped. Toby, I thought about it for a long time and I realized . . . I'd never find that kind of time in a place. The only way to live in time instead of moving through it is to be experience things with somebody else. To share the moments."

Toby nodded. She'd named the restlessness he'd been feeling for months now—that disconnect from his family, however much he loved them; the sense of skimming over the surface of the worlds he visited, however much he explored them.

Squeezing Orpheus a little tighter to him, he said, "I know you were joking about the Lord of Time stuff—sorta kinda. That's the thing, though; somehow, the whole weight of it's rubbed off on me, just a little. Everywhere I go, just when I start to relax I'll come across one of those statues, or a damned fresco of me, or somebody'll say my name like it's a prayer. I'm having a little trouble being *me* around here. I've been trying to escape it, but it's like a steady pressure in my skull . . .

"The only way for me to come back to myself is going to be if I leave, at least for a while, for places where nobody's ever heard of me. And there are such places. There're other stars and things beyond. I'd like to see them . . .

"But I don't want to do it alone.

"Corva, would you come with me to see the fast worlds, the Laser Wastes, the ancient suns and all those new Earths that they made while I wintered over?

"I promise we'll only be gone for a night."

"A night, or forever," she said and kissed him. "Yes, I'll come."

Orpheus opened one eye to observe this, then shifted into a more comfortable position and went back to sleep.